MORE PRAISE FOR TOM COOPER'S

THE MARAUDERS

"It's always the voice, the singular sound of a place like none other, that draws you into a regional mystery. In Tom Cooper's first novel, *The Marauders*, that beguiling music comes out of the Louisiana bayous."

—*New York Times Book Review*

"Self-assured and highly entertaining ... Cooper's writing is taut, his story is gripping, and the characters and their problems will stay with you long after you finish this book."

—*Library Journal*, starred review

"This is one hell of a debut novel. Cooper combines the rough-hewn but poetic style favored by writers like Charles Willeford with the kinds of miscreants so beloved by Elmore Leonard, all operating in the tumultuous modern-day disaster that is New Orleans. With crisp, noir-inspired writing and a firmly believable setting, Cooper has written an engaging homage to classic crime writing that still finds things to say about the desperate days we live through now. Somewhere Donald E. Westlake, John D. MacDonald, and Elmore Leonard are smiling down on this nasty, funny piece of work."

—*Kirkus Reviews*, starred review

"Cooper offers a believable portrait of a bayou town and a cast of deeply engaging characters wrestling inchoately with the likely extinction of the only life they know. There is real substance and humanity in this fine debut novel."

—*Booklist*, starred review

"Cooper's novel is a blast; descriptions of the natural beauty of the cypress swamps and waterways, along with the hardscrabble ways of its singular inhabitants, further elevate this story."

—*Publisher's Weekly*

"More fun than a book about the aftermath of an ecological disaster has any right to be."

—*Esquire*

"Wade into moral muck with the pill-popping, treasure-hunting, one-armed hero of this finger-lickin'-good Louisiana swamp noir."

—*O, The Oprah Magazine*

"A sometimes hilarious, sometimes heartbreaking 'swamp noir' gumbo with echoes of John Kennedy Toole, Larry Brown, and Daniel Woodrell . . . *The Marauders* is as grounded in the simple truth as it is awash in the outlandishly eccentric."

—Shelf Awareness

"I can't wait for Cooper's next book. Nor can my wife, and she and I seldom agree about novels. He's fun to read—he keeps your head up and your eyes big."

—*Garden and Gun*

"This is rare for me, very rare, that I was utterly unable, because of a novel, to get up from a chair and answer the phone when it rang or eat when I was hungry or go to bed when I was weary. Rare, but this book has left me hungry and sleepy and neglectful of somebody I hope will call back. That his book is smart and funny and dazzling in its prose is obvious. He also can tell a hell of a story. Tom Cooper is a newly minted American literary treasure."

—Robert Olen Butler

"The first great book of the 2015 beach season is already here. . . . Tom Cooper's debut novel, *The Marauders*, certainly should not be confined to beach season or to the implication that it's light or airless good fun, but it seems to be a book that should be savored on a deck overlooking the beach or pool with a cold beer nearby . . . an enjoyable and impossibly difficult to put down novel."

—*Free Lance-Star*

"The very best fiction transports us effortlessly to places we've never been and involves us deeply with characters we've never met; and though I've never lived in the Louisiana bayous, or shrimped all day with one arm in oil-polluted waters, or obsessed over a dead pirate's treasure while chewing up painkillers like candy, or been hunted by anyone as sadistic as the Toup brothers, Tom Cooper's brilliant, fast-paced first novel, *The Marauders*, took me there, set me right down in the miserable heat and the mud and the dread, and though it might sound strange to say, I will be forever grateful to him for that."

—Donald Ray Pollock, author of *Knockemstiff* and *The Devil All the Time*

"*The Marauders*, Tom Cooper's beautifully written chronicle of the misadventures of the denizens of a dying Louisiana fishing village, pleases in so many ways. It's funny, sad, and wise, sometimes in the same sentence. An outstanding debut."

—Richard Lange, author of *Angel Baby* and *This Wicked World*

"*The Marauders* is a novel so compelling, so unsettling, so scary and hilarious that you won't be able to put it down. You might as well pour yourself a drink and settle into your comfy chair. Set in Louisiana's Barataria swamp after the ecological disaster that was the BP oil spill, the novel chronicles the end of a way of life for Gulf shrimpers and explores a muddy world of greed, grit, and gumbo. Tom Cooper is an eloquent new voice in the extraordinary world of Southern fiction. And, trust me on this, the spectral and relentless Toup brothers will haunt your dreams."

—John Dufresne, bestselling author of *Louisiana Power & Light*

"Tom Cooper has written a first novel with sustained, top-drawer prose, and that is a beautiful and uncommon thing."
—Pete Dexter, National Book Award–winning author of *Paris Trout*

"Tom Cooper has Louisiana dead to rights. Every aspect. Jeanette, the sleepy bayou town ravaged by man and nature alike, is rendered in Technicolor detail. Its residents, lifers, and visitors alike leap from the pages. The story rolls like a tide, handling triumph and tragedy alike with a dark, mischievous humor that Cooper wields expertly.... There's more than a hint of the Southern gothic here, more than a little Flannery O'Connor.... It's easy to forget this is his first novel. Some books require boxes of tissues. This one requires, as Cooper writes, 'an ass-pocket whiskey bottle.' Get you a drink and get comfortable. You won't be moving until you hit the last page."
—*The Advocate*

"A debut novel that does nothing in half measures. It isn't afraid to take risks, dabble in darkness, and skirt the edge of ruin, and this is what makes it such an exciting read.... *The Marauders* takes readers on a rollicking adventure deep into the heart of Louisiana's marshes as well as some of the darkest corners of the human psyche.... The plot is brisk, the characters are captivating and the writing is lush and striking. Cooper's writing is the kind a reader can happily get lost in, and his depictions of the Deep South are so evocative that if he ever gets tired of fiction, he might give travel writing a try. But *The Marauders* is such an impressive offering from an audacious new voice in fiction that one can only hope it is but the first of many. As far as bibliophilic treasure hunts go, this one is literary gold."
—*BookPage*

"Cooper's intricate, accessible weaving of his characters with each other and his deep, delightfully eccentric descriptions of this area of Louisiana show that he's just beginning what will hopefully be a satisfying career as a novelist."
—*BookBrowse*

THE MARAUDERS

THE MARAUDERS

A NOVEL

TOM COOPER

B\D\W\Y
Broadway Books
New York

Copyright © 2015 by Tom Cooper

All rights reserved.
Published in the United States by Broadway Books, an imprint of the Crown Publishing Group, a division of Penguin Random House LLC, New York.
www.crownpublishing.com

Broadway Books and its logo, B \ D \ W \ Y, are trademarks of Penguin Random House LLC.

Originally published in hardcover in the United States by Crown Publishers, an imprint of the Crown Publishing Group, a division of Penguin Random House LLC, New York.

Library of Congress Cataloging-in-Publication Data is available upon request.

ISBN 978-0-8041-4058-4
eBook ISBN 978-0-8041-4057-7

Printed in the United States of America

Book design by Anna Thompson
Cover design by Michael Morris
Cover photographs: (swamp landscape) Panoramic Images/Getty Images;
(airboat) Courtesy of Owens Welding Inc.

10 9 8 7 6 5 4 3 2 1

First Paperback Edition

To my parents,
Lynn Elizabeth McIlvaine
and
in memory of Thomas Michael Cooper.

THE MARAUDERS

THE TOUP BROTHERS

They came like specters from the dark maw of the bayou, first ghostly light in the fog, then the rasp of a motor: an aluminum powerboat scudding across lacquer-black water. From a distance the figures looked conjoined, Siamese twins. As the boat drew closer the bodies split in two under the moth-flocked floodlights. One stood fore, the other aft: the twin brothers Reginald and Victor Toup. When they were kids even their mother had trouble telling them apart. That was long ago, half their lives, and now their mother was dead. Shot through the temple in New Orleans's Roosevelt Hotel before their father turned the gun on himself.

Tonight they motored under a three-quarter moon, thirty pounds of marijuana hidden under a tarp in the bait well. Reginald trolled the boat and Victor crouched on the prow, surveying the bayou through night-vision binoculars. They'd made this run so many times they could tell you things about the swamp that no map could. You rarely came across anyone out here. Not after dark, not this far, not outside shrimping season.

This of course was the point.

A flicker of motion ahead drew Victor's eye. On an islet a half mile distant a small light bobbed and shimmied like fox fire before sputtering out.

Victor held up his hand and Reginald cut the engine and lights. They were plunged into dark, moonlight banded across the water, the only sounds the insects and frogs singing in full chorus, the soft slap of waves against the hull.

"What?" Reginald asked.

Victor said nothing. He peered through the glass and waited. Reginald stepped behind him, black rubber hip boots creaking. Side by side, the brothers' resemblance was uncanny. The same side-parted black hair and hard-bitten faces, the same mineral-gray eyes full of cunning. The same way of leaning slightly into the night, torsos angled stiff, like bloodhounds scenting a rumor of prey. But there were differences, slight. Reginald had the beginnings of a gumbo paunch but Victor did not. Reginald had no tattoos, but Victor had them on his arms and on the side of his neck: the head of a gape-mouthed Great White shark, a mermaid and trident, a spiderweb in the crook of his right arm, a black widow spider in the middle.

Any other differences between the twins a man would have to delve deeper than the surface to discern.

For a time nothing moved. Stars were strewn horizon to horizon, bands so tangled and thick they looked like white paint flung on a black canvas. Ursa Minor and Cassiopeia and Orion like puzzles you had to make out.

Victor shifted on his boots and adjusted the focus of the binoculars. The light winked on again, skeltering among the trees.

"Thinks we left," Victor said.

"Who?" Reginald asked.

Victor didn't answer, only watched. Anchored a hundred yards from the islet was a ramshackle shrimp boat, on the islet shore a beached pirogue and a Coleman lantern dimly glowing. A man in hip boots waded in the bracken, sweeping a metal detector coil over the ground. In his other hand was something that looked half scoop, half shovel.

The man heard something in his headphones and halted. He passed the metal detector coil a few times over the same spot and then dug for a minute with the shovel-scoop. He stepped to the shore edge and shimmied the shovel in the water and hunkered down, sifting through the dirt like a gold panner.

Victor lowered the binoculars and shook his head.

"Tell me," Reginald said.

"A guy," Victor said. "Digging holes."

"Why?"

"Fuck should I know? Burying his wife."

Reginald took the binoculars from Victor and squinted through the glass. "Got a metal detector," he said.

"Know him?" Victor asked.

"I've seen him. I think."

"Metal detector," Victor said. He shot a scoffing breath through his nose. "I've seen it all."

"What's he, with the oil company?"

Victor didn't answer. He unshouldered his semiautomatic Bushmaster and got the man's face in the crosshairs of the reticle scope. He looked in his late forties, early fifties. Deeply pocketed eyes, shaggy hair winged out from beneath a yacht cap. And look, he was missing an arm, in its place a prosthesis.

"Missing an arm," Victor said.

"I know who that is," Reginald said.

Victor asked who.

"The redhead? Crazy big tits. Got stoned at our place a couple times. Renee?"

"Reagan," Victor said. "Oh, yeah."

"Reagan. That's her daddy."

Victor lifted the rifle again and squinted through the scope, his finger resting in the curve of the trigger.

"The hell you doing?" Reginald said. He'd always been the more diplomatic of the two, Victor the more hotheaded. Maybe it was because Victor was the firstborn, the alpha, a full hour longer in the world than Reginald. This was one of Reginald's theories, anyway.

"Too close for his own good," Victor told Reginald.

"We'll talk to him."

Victor could squeeze the trigger right now and the man's life would be over in an instant. He'd done it before. Out here. But he lowered the rifle and said, "Luckiest day in his life, son-bitch doesn't even know it."

LINDQUIST

His arm was missing. Lindquist was positive he'd left it in his pickup two hours before. He wasn't in the habit of misplacing his thirty-thousand-dollar myoelectric arm or of leaving his truck unlocked, catchwater bayou town where everybody knew everyone or not.

A few other pickups sat under the bug-flurried sodium vapors. Nothing else but cypress lisping in the night breeze, a bottlefly-green Buick bouncing on the blacktop past Sully's bar. But Lindquist kept looking wild-eyed around the oyster-shell parking lot as if his arm had wandered off on its own volition. As if he might find it standing next to the blue-lit tavern sign, thumbing a ride.

Lindquist went back into Sully's. Sully was wiping the bar with a hand towel and peered over the top of his wire-frame glasses. At one of the back tables three men were gathering cards and poker chips, and they looked up too.

Lindquist stood in the doorway, lips pressed in a thin pale line, some dark emotion building behind his face like a storm front. "Somebody took my arm," he said.

"Took?" Sully said.

"Stole," Lindquist said. "Somebody stole my fuckin' arm."

A stymied silence fell over the room, for a moment the only sound the jukebox: a Merle Haggard song, "I Wonder If They Ever Think of Me," playing faintly. The men glanced at one another and shook their heads. Finally one of them, Dixon, began to laugh. Then Prejean and LaGarde, the two other men at the table. Their teeth flashed white in their sun-ruddied faces and soon the narrow pine-planked room filled with their laughter.

"Screw you guys," Lindquist said.

The laughter stopped as quickly as a needle lifting off a record.

"You joking?" Dixon asked.

Lindquist joked a lot, so it was hard to tell.

"Probably left it at home," Sully said.

"Like hell," Lindquist said.

"Call Gwen," LaGarde said. "See if you left it at home."

Lindquist stared stiff-jawed at LaGarde. LaGarde put his hands on the tabletop and looked down. Gwen was gone, had been for months. Most likely she was at her parents' house in Houma, where she usually fled when she and Lindquist were arguing. She always returned after a few days, but not this time. The men didn't know the full story, but the gist was probably the same. A quarrel about money, about bills, about their daughter, about God knew what.

Sully stepped from behind the bar and the men got up from the table. They searched under stools and chairs, kicked open bathroom stalls. Then they went outside and canvassed the lot. Lindquist stooped and peered under the trucks. Dixon went to the edge of the lot and passed his boot back and forth through the sedge. Prejean did the same on the other side. LaGarde walked out to the blacktop and looked in both directions.

Afterward the men stood under the sodium lights, batting mosquitoes from their faces.

"Why didn't you just wear it?" Dixon asked Lindquist.

"You wear it in this heat," Lindquist said.

Twenty minutes later the sheriff arrived. Villanova. He picked up his khaki cowboy hat off the passenger seat, got out of the cruiser, sat the hat on top of his mastiff head.

The men stared, faces malefic in the red and blue bar-light.

Lindquist told Villanova about the poker game, about how his arm was missing when he returned to his truck. Villanova fished a small spiral notebook out of his shirt pocket and scribbled down the names of the men who'd left earlier. Lindquist insisted whoever took his arm had to be a stranger. A lowlife drifter so drug-addled and devoid of moral compass he'd steal a prosthetic arm from someone's truck.

"And you're sure you didn't leave it home," Villanova said.

Lindquist narrowed his eyes. "You leave your arms at home?"

Your thirty-thousand-dollar arm, he wanted to say. Without his wife's insurance from her job at the bank, Lindquist could have never afforded the prosthetic or the months of physical therapy after his accident. And even with Gwen's insurance, Lindquist had to pay fifteen grand out of pocket, money he put on a high-interest credit card he paid only the minimum on every month. A debt he'd take to his grave, but he couldn't exactly shrimp with a five-dollar hook arm from Kmart.

Villanova wrote something down. "You have the serial number?"

"The serial number?"

Villanova pinched the bridge of his nose. "The serial number for the arm, Lindquist."

Lindquist shook his head.

"Well, you can always call the doctor. Call wherever you got it. That might make sense."

The men scattered their separate ways, Dixon and Sully back into the bar, LaGarde and Prejean off to their trucks. Lindquist stood beside his truck door, jangling through a wad of keys. A full minute passed before he found the right one. Then for another half minute Lindquist jabbed the key around the lock, scraping metal. Finally he scrunched one eye closed and slipped the key inside.

Villanova watched from across the lot. "What you doing?" he asked.

"Driving home."

"Like hell. You're drunk."

Lindquist squinted at Villanova, head listing as if to music only he could hear. "Just a little," he said.

"It's late, Lindquist. Get in the car."

For a time the men were silent as Villanova drove along the trafficless two-way. They passed a palmetto grove, a field of saw grass. A nighthawk winged across the moon, its silhouette like an emblem on a coin.

"Knock knock," Lindquist said.

"Still at it with your jokes, Lindquist."

"Knock knock."

"Loses an arm and tells knock-knock jokes."

"Anita."

"Anita who?"

"Anita big ol' pair of titties in front of me."

Villanova shook his head. The police radio popped and hissed with static.

"So you all were playing poker," Villanova said.

"Yeah."

"For money?"

"What you think?"

"That's illegal."

Villanova kept both hands tight on the wheel, both eyes on the road.

"Knock knock."

"It's late, Lindquist."

Villanova didn't need to ask him for directions because he knew the way. He'd driven Lindquist home from the bar a few times because he was too wrecked to drive himself.

"You worried about the oil?" Villanova asked.

Lindquist said he was. Everybody in Jeanette was. Hell, folks were in a shithouse panic.

"Could be better than they're saying," Villanova said. "But I got a feeling it might be worse."

Soon Villanova bumped onto a gravel driveway that cut through wild privet to a brick ranch house with a gray-shake roof and satellite dish. A birdbath, its basin filled with scummy water and leaves, stood in a dead flowerbed.

Awkwardly, Lindquist reached his left arm across his lap and opened the door.

"You okay, Lindquist?" Villanova asked.

Lindquist stooped and looked into the car. "Yeah. You?"

"Yeah. Favor? No crusades just yet."

Lindquist nodded.

"Got your keys?"

"Yeah."

"Check for me."

Lindquist took his keys out of his jeans pocket, jangled them, gave Villanova a thumbs-up.

"Still know how to use them?"

"So long, Villanova," Lindquist said. He shut the door and stepped aside as Villanova turned the car around. He watched the taillights jitter like fireflies down the driveway, one pair and then two and then one again when he squinted an eye.

Lindquist opened the front door, flicked on the light, sniffed. A sweet-sour stink, of rancid bacon grease and chicken fat, wafted from the kitchen. And the den was littered with grease-mottled takeout bags, empty beer cans, month-old newspapers still in their cellophane bags. Lindquist wondered what his daughter, Reagan, would think if she dropped by for a visit, what his wife would think if she came back.

Like that was going to happen.

He moved to pick up one of the bags but his arm wasn't there. He went to the kitchen and got an Abita out of the refrigerator and then he sat at the cluttered dining room table. Bills, all months overdue. Mortgage, credit cards, diesel, insurance. And books stacked four and five high: *The Story of the American Merchant Marine. The Pirates Lafitte. The Journal of Jean Lafitte. The Pirate Lafitte and the Battle of New Orleans. Biogeochemistry of the Wetlands: Science and Applications.*

Among the books were time-yellowed maritime maps as stiff as parchment, marked with red felt-tip pen in Lindquist's hieroglyphic hand. A metal detector lay across the table with its circuitry box open and its wiring sticking out. Gwen used to bitch when he left these things on the table, but now he could keep them where he goddamn well pleased.

Lindquist leaned on one ass cheek and took out a Pez dispenser from his pants pocket and flicked the head. Donald Duck spat out an oblong white pill: Oxycontin, whittled by Lindquist with a pocketknife so it fit perfectly into the dispenser. With the bottom of his Abita bottle he pummeled the pill on the dining room table until it was crushed to dust. Then he plugged a nostril with his forefinger and leaned over and snorted the powder, tipping his head back and rubbing the dust off his upper lip.

Lindquist unfolded one of the maps over the table, a fraying map in hachured black and blue ink of the Barataria, its serpentine waterways and archipelagos of barrier islands. Over time Lindquist had made his own adjustments to the cartography, crossed out cheniers succumbed to time and tempest, drawn new islands and hummocks sprung up over-night. One was shaped like a tadpole, another like a paw track, another like an Egyptian udjat. Over some of the islands he'd drawn X's, over others question marks.

He uncapped a purple felt-tip pen with his teeth, studying the map, marking over one of the islands. He reached for his beer, but his right arm still wasn't there. He dropped the pen and clutched the bottle, thinking of the last thing Gwen had told him before she left.

You're in a bad place, she'd said. *You need help.*

Lindquist finished his beer, went to the refrigerator and got another, sat back down at the dining room table and opened his laptop. In Google he typed *Jean Lafitte* and pulled up more than a million results. Then he typed in *Lafitte* and *Barataria* and got nearly two hundred and fifty. He typed in the words *treasure* and *gold* and *pirate* and then he typed in other search terms until he stumbled upon a treasure-hunting board where men—only men—had posted their metal detecting stories. One of the posts showed pictures of brass mushroom buttons and musket balls and doubloons, another a War of 1812 artillery button, another yet an 1851 Officer's Eagle Sword belt plate.

He was still at the kitchen table drinking his beer and browsing through the treasure pictures when his e-mail pinged. He opened up the new message and read it.

TO : LINDQUIST007@gmail.com

FROM: Youredead98989898@gmail.com

WE KNOW WHO U R. WHERE U LIVE. U TRESSPASSING PRIVATE
PROPERTY. THIS IS UR ONLY WARNING.

Lindquist's heart kicked and his body went rigid. He sat for some time
at the dining room table wondering what to write. Then he typed one-
fingered. "WHOSE THIS?" He tapped the delete button several times.
Rewrote the original message. Hesitated. Hit send.

He waited, the only sounds the ticking house timbers as they sighed
out the heat of the day, the thumping of moths against the windowpane.
The faint white hum of the lightbulb filament in the ceiling fixture.

Lindquist's e-mail pinged again.

TO : LINDQUIST007@gmail.com

FROM: Youredead98989898@gmail.com

STAY AWAY FROM THE ISLANDS, FUCKFACE.

WES TRENCH

Midnight. Wes and his father followed the trail from their house toward the harbor. Even from a quarter mile distant, through the palmetto brakes and waist-tall swamp grass, they could hear singing voices carrying through the marsh, the faint quick-tempo strains of zydeco music: the blessing of the shrimping fleet. For the past five years Wes and his father had forgone the ritual, waiting until Father Neely was done blessing the boats until they journeyed to the docks. Wes's father was still angry at God about what happened to his mother. They both were.

One of many things they never spoke about.

It was dark except for the beams of their flashlights skeltering across the ground, the cherry of Wes's father's cigarette. His cotton-white hair, high and tight. Above them a cloud-dimmed quarter moon gleamed through a lacework of live oak branches. They followed a bend in the trail around a stand of sand pine and crossed a rough-board footbridge over a creek. A black snake sidewindered across the water and slipped inklike into the bracken.

Now Wes could hear the grumbling of boat engines, the wheezing stutter of an accordion. The clickety-clack of a washboard, a boat captain shouting orders at his crew. "Don't lay them nets there," said a man with a salt-cured voice. "Starboard, asshole, starboard."

One of Wes's earliest memories was of making this trip through these same woods. On an August night like this, breezeless and heavy with the scent of loam. His father was sprightlier then because this was before his chronic backaches, before the shrimping hauls got smaller and smaller, before all his hair turned white.

Wes's mother held his damp hand in hers as they followed his father in the dark. He could feel the cold metal kiss of her wedding ring.

"How many shrimp you gonna catch, Daddy?" Wes asked.

"Know Mount St. Helens?" his father said.

"Naw, sir."

"Mount Rushmore?"

"Naw, sir."

"You know Miss Hamby, your math teacher with the big ass?"

Wes's mother told him to hush.

He was happier then, Wes's father. Hopeful. They all were.

It was around this time, maybe a year or two later, when Wes came home from school and found a midnight-blue Schwinn waiting for him in the driveway. His father had hauled in a three-ton catch, ridiculously lucky, and bought the bike, new, on a whim.

And later that night while his mother washed the dishes Wes saw his father come up to her from behind and put his hands on her hips. She turned around and they kissed with their eyes closed, something he saw only once or twice before and once or twice after.

Wes didn't know this then, but he knew it now: whoever said that money didn't buy happiness was a damn fool. A damn fool who'd never been poor.

On the other side of the bridge Wes and his father followed the trail up a slippery rise. They stepped over a lichened footlog and saw the harbor lights glimmering through the pines. About thirty or forty people stood on the docks, their silhouettes against the amber lights of the pier. Ship captains and crewmen stood aboard skiffs and oyster luggers, filling bait wells with ice, untangling trawling nets. A few of the boats were already entering the bay, their Christmassy red and green pilot lights glinting on the horizon.

Wes's father flicked his cigarette into the bushes and they stepped onto the dock. In the harbor parking lot a few folding tables were set up with crockpots of gumbo, paper plates, plastic spoons. Transistor radios droned in competition, one playing a pop station out of New Orleans, another an AM talk show out of Baton Rouge. A big-bellied old woman was boiling crabs in a gas-lit kettle. A hunchbacked man fingered the mother-of-pearl buttons of his wheezing accordion. Another man scraped his vest frottoir with rusty spoons.

Wes had known these faces his whole life. They were captains and crewmen, crabbers and trappers. In May they shrimped for pinks and in August for whites. In the fall some of them went after alligators and oysters. And they were the sons and daughters of captains and crewmembers, still too young to help on the boats. The heavyset wives with harried faces and graying hair. The grandmothers and grandfathers with rueful eyes and worried toothless jaws.

"Hey, Bobby," a man said to Wes's father. He had on yellow waders and pulled a cigarette pack from his shirt pocket and tapped the bottom with his gnarled forefinger. He lipped the cigarette.

"Where the hell you been, Davey?" Wes's father said.

"Daytona," Davey said. "Workin' on one of those charter boats for a bunch of rich Florida fucks."

A few years ago Davey had worked for Wes's father, but he quit and joined the crew of a bigger boat when the hauls got smaller and smaller and when the price of shrimp went down. A bigger boat meant a bigger paycheck. Wes's father didn't begrudge him the fact. He knew how hard it was scraping by in the Barataria and probably would have done the same.

"You like it over there?" Wes's father asked.

"Yeah, it was paradise," Davey said. He lit his cigarette and scrunched one side of his face against the smoke. "Just about gave all this up," he said, gesturing across the bayou at the boats shambling out of the harbor, at the bent trees brooding over the water.

At the end of the dock a bare-chested little boy pissed gleefully into the bayou. When he finished he zipped up his camouflage shorts and hopped barefoot like a monkey back to his mother. Wes was about this boy's age when he started coming out here to the harbor. Young enough to remember the air of festivity that once presided over these first nights of the shrimping season. The fais-do-dos, the Cajun dances. Those were better times for everyone in the Barataria. Before the bayou started grubbing out smaller and smaller hauls of shrimp. Before the oil spill. Before Katrina.

Before Wes's mother died.

"Any word yet?" Wes's father asked.

"Couple of guys already radioed in," Davey said. "Shrimp look thin. Early yet, though."

"Oil?"

"Everywhere."

Davey looked at Wes. "How you doin', podnah? Thought you'd'a gone Ivy League on us by now."

Wes forced a grin and shook his head. College, he already knew, was pretty much out of the question.

"Boy, is that gray in your hair already?" Davey said.

"A bit, yes sir," Wes said. Just after his sixteenth birthday, the gray had begun to pepper the sides of his head. A little at first, but every time he got his hair cut there were several new grays and Wes guessed he'd be as white-haired as his father before he turned thirty.

"You two come on over to the house for supper when all this dies down, huh?" Davey said.

"We will, Davey," Wes's father said. "You say hello to Kelly and Renee now."

"Shuh, shuh."

Wes followed his father down the dock to their boat and hopped onto the deck and untied the ropes from the dock cleats. He heard someone step behind him and turned. It was Father Neely in his cassock and alb, the sweat on his forehead gleaming in the dock lights.

"How you, Father," Wes said. He stood and shook the man's hand. Soft and damp. Never a day of boat work in his life.

"Wesley," Father Neely said. "Good to see you, son." He glanced up at the boat, said hello to Wes's father, who was coiling up the mooring rope. He only held up his hand and turned his back. Then he climbed the metal ladder up to the wheelhouse. Through the window Wes saw the spark of his lighter, the guttering flame of the candle nub beside the wheel. Another spark when his father lit a cigarette.

"You guys missed the blessing," Father Neely said, tactful enough to not say *again*.

"Running late tonight," Wes said.

"Shuh, of course," Father Neely said. He glanced up at the wheelhouse and smoothed down his smoke-yellowed mustache with his thumb and forefinger. He looked back at Wes and dug in his robe pocket and fished out a St. Christopher medallion. Wes hesitated. He knew his father wouldn't want it but neither could he exactly turn it down. He took the medallion and pocketed it and thanked Father Neely.

"I'll pray for a prosperous season," Father Neely said.

Wes thanked him again and said that they needed all the praying they could get.

––– ––– –––

Their boat, the *Bayou Sweetheart,* was a thirty-three-year-old Lafitte skiff, one of the few of its kind in Jeanette that survived the hurricane. Weeks after the storm, when Wes and his father began picking through the ruins, they found the boat miraculously intact, sitting on top of the levee as if placed there by a benevolent giant's hand.

Like many other Baratarians, Wes and his family had chosen to ride the storm out. Or, really, Wes's father had chosen for them. When Wes's family woke on the morning of August 28 and turned on the television, the weatherman on WGNO news out of New Orleans was predicting a Category 5 hurricane. One-hundred-and-fifty-mile-per-hour wind gusts, fifteen-foot storm surges, levee breaks. A monster.

The first winds were just beginning, moaning in the eaves, and outside the sky had already blackened to charcoal, so dark the trees in the yard threw off a strange glow, as if lit from within.

"We should leave," Wes's mother said for the umpteenth time.

They stood before the old Zenith in the den. Still in their bedclothes, faces puffy with sleep.

"You know how many times they've said this and it turned out to be nothing?" Wes's father said. The worry wasn't yet showing in his eyes, but there was an edge in his voice.

Thunder shook the house and rattled the windowpanes. Their black Labrador, Max, scampered to the kitchen and hid under the table, where he watched them timorously, head on forepaws.

"We can stay in Baton Rouge," said Wes's mother. She meant her parents' place.

"Come on, Dad," Wes said, wondering how his father could be so blasé, wanting to take him by the shoulders and shake some sense into him.

But his father was watching the television, rubbing his unshaven chin, hardly listening. "Then you and Wes go ahead and pack. But you better get to it. Now. Before the roads get too choked up."

"You too. You're going."

Wes's father shook his head as if this were out of the question. "I gotta tie down the boat. Help other guys with theirs. I gotta board up these windows. There's a million things."

"Listen to the TV," said Wes's mother.

"They always say this stuff. It's their job."

All morning Wes figured his father would come to his senses and change his mind, but no. And by afternoon, when the first bands of the storm lashed the Barataria, it was already too late to leave. That night the hurricane hammered Jeanette like a djinn. Within hours, houses and mobile homes were smashed apart and swept away like dollhouses. Docks ripped from land and carried down streets turned into raging rivers. Boats snapped away from their moorings and were sucked into riptides.

By the time the storm had run its course, several people in Jeanette drowned in the flood.

Among them Wes's mother.

That was almost exactly five years ago, and the anniversary of his mother's death, August 29, was just half a month away. A day Wes was dreading. Half a decade ago: that meant he'd now lived almost one third of his life without her. He was amazed so much time had passed. Yet the pain was still there, the regrets and resentments between him and his father. There were little things about her he was forgetting, gestures and sayings he struggled to remember. But he recalled her voice distinctly, sometimes even heard it in his dreams. The sweet soothing lilt, a soft halcyon balm on his nerves. *Oh, it'll be fine, Wessy. Oh, Wessy, stop being such a worrywart.*

What a strange pair Wes's mother and father had been, she the quasi-Bohemian peacekeeper in Birkenstocks, he the hotheaded live wire. Wes often wondered whom he took after most. He preferred to think he was more like his mother in certain respects—the most important, like temperament. But he wasn't sure. As time passed he found himself growing angrier, more doubtful and worried, like his father. But his father's stubbornness and resourcefulness, those were good, and Wes felt those beating in his blood.

Sometimes Wes caught his father glancing at him strangely. He supposed it was because he looked a lot like his mother now that he was full grown. He was slightly short and narrow-shouldered, just like his mother, and his skin browned darkly in the sun instead of reddening to brick like his father's. And Wes had his mother's sharp widow's peak. Her wide-set green eyes, teal in the winter and pale mint in the summer, depending on the darkness of his tan, the color of shirt he wore. Girls in his high school were always telling him what pretty eyes he had. Wes's mother used to say he'd never have a problem with the ladies as long as he stayed a gentleman and kept his eyes in his head.

Recently a memory came back to Wes that he'd long forgotten. One of his friends, Tommy Orillon, offered him a stick of gum at a Fourth of July barbeque and Wes took it, not knowing it was blackberry-flavored. As soon as the taste flooded his mouth, Wes remembered the time his mother took him blackberry picking when he was eight or nine.

The day Wes remembered, a sunny Sunday morning in late June, he and his mother held their own tin pails and they were picking among the thorny bushes beside a still-water creek, making a kind of game out of who could gather the most. Wes picked his blackberries so quickly he ended up nicking his hand in dozens of places with the briars. The lashes began to sting only when the game was over, after they returned home. His mother cupped his hands in hers as he sat crying on the fuzzy cover of the bathroom toilet. "Poor Wessy," she said, gently daubing his fingers with a Mercurochrome-soaked cotton ball. "It's okay, it's okay," she said, stroking her fingers through his hair.

— — — — — — — —

Tonight Wes's father commandeered the wheel while Wes readied the booms. Under the cloud-shawled moon they yawed through the bayou, passing buoys hung with oil company signs.

DANGER, DO NOT ANCHOR. GAS LINE.

PROPERTY OF BP OIL.

CAUTION: PIPELINE.

Wes fiddled with his cell phone, checking Facebook, because soon they'd have no signal.

"Quit fooling with that phone," his father called down from the wheelhouse. "Like a baby on a titty. I swear."

Wes clenched his jaw and pocketed his cell phone. Starboard was a peninsula bowered with dwarf oak and scrub pine. Through the rushes Wes could see a small graveyard, bone-white mausoleums like crooked teeth, a brick fireplace like a basilisk in a clearing. An antebellum mansion belonging to the Robicheaux, a five-generation Creole family, once stood here. They'd evacuated before the storm and when they returned they found everything in ruins and went back to Texas. Last Wes heard, they were running a fried chicken stand in Galveston.

When the *Bayou Sweetheart* reached the pass, the water was scrummed with boats passing back and forth within feet of each other, jockeying for position. A festive glow suffused the water from their red and green running lights. Horns shrilled madly in the night. Men screamed threats and curses from pilothouses and decks.

A tire-bumpered oyster lugger passed their boat. A wizened deckhand, maybe thirty, maybe sixty, impossible to tell, shouted at Wes. "Hey," he said. "Hey, lookit."

When Wes turned, the man tossed something from a tin cup. Wes twisted away, but too late. A foul-smelling yolk splattered across his face. Wes wiped with his hand and looked at his fingers. Chum.

The man and his crewmen cackled. Wes gagged against the fishy reek and cleaned his face with the end of his shirt. The man on the oyster lugger shucked down his waders and mooned him. His ass was enormous and inflamed-looking, like an orangutan's.

Wes's father slowed the boat to quarter-speed and Wes lowered the booms and dipped the nets into the water. Other boats passed within yards, laboring crewmen hunched in shadowy cameo. Wes moved between starboard and port, checking the booms.

A familiar round-bottomed shrimper, sixty feet long and hung with a Confederate flag, glided alongside them. The captain shouted something from the wheelhouse and Wes looked up. It was Randy Preston, a man who years ago worked on his father's boat. He grinned down with his too-big dentures and Wes gestured up at his father, who got on his megaphone and leaned out the starboard window. "What you got so far, Randy?"

"Nothing worth a shit."

"That bad?"

"Wife's gonna divorce me."

"Could be a good thing," said Wes's father.

"No shit." His boat was moving out of earshot so Randy had to shout quickly. "Heard on the radio they were catching a lot five miles west. I'm gonna see what's going on over there. Get out of this mess."

"Let me know if it's any good," Wes's father said.

"Yeah, yeah," Randy said. He held his arm out his window and made a jerk-off motion with his hand. "Keep a firm grip on yourself, Wes."

Wes grinned and shot a bird at Randy. Randy leaned out of his window and shot one back. After a while his boat drifted away and was lost among the rest.

Wes hitched the starboard trawl to the winch. The motor smoked and strained and soon the swollen net emerged from the water like an amniotic sack, inside a squirming mass of fins and pincers and glinting black eyes. Then Wes went port and began winching up the other net.

His father put the boat in neutral and climbed down the wheelhouse ladder. With drip nets they dumped the haul into the sorting box and then they put on gloves and poked through the teeming pile. Hard-shell crabs snapping their pincers like castanets. Catfish and flounders and fingerling baitfish. Soft-shell crabs by the hundreds, so tiny and luminescently pale they looked like ghosts of themselves. A baby stingray whipping its barbed tail, a snapping turtle shooting its head back into its shell.

And then there were pinkie-sized shrimp, their brains and hearts beating like small black seeds beneath their rice paper skin.

"Worst I've ever seen," said Wes's father. His thousand-times-washed chest-stripe polo shirt, the same kind he always wore, was already stuck to his back with sweat.

Wes said nothing. He knew what was coming. His father was pissed and he was going to take it out on him. Wes was screwed if he said anything, screwed if he didn't.

"Gonna be out here for a fuckin' month."

Wes kept quiet, sorting through the fish and crabs and shrimp.

"This is it. This swamp is gonna fuck us. It's gonna fuck us like a thousand-dollar whore."

Wes flipped a baby catfish off the boat.

"Watch that sting-a-ree," his father said.

"I'm watchin' it."

"No you ain't. How many times I gotta tell you about those sting-a-rees? All I need, a trip to the hospital."

Wes lobbed a croaker back into the water.

"Jesus Christ," his father said. "End of the world out here."

It took them several minutes to toss the pile off the boat. Most of the fish and crabs swam back into the bayou's keep, but a few lay stunned on top of the water, finning in dazed circles.

His father climbed back up into the wheelhouse and again Wes lowered the nets. While the *Bayou Sweetheart* moved along the pandemonium of boats, he checked his watch. The hands told him that it was half past two. His eyes felt hot and grainy and he wanted nothing more than to have this whole ordeal behind him. He longed for a shower and the cool clean sheets of his bed. But he knew they'd be out here for several hours more at least. Maybe days.

If he and his father didn't kill one another first.

- - - - - - - -

When Wes and his father docked at Monsieur Montegut's two days later, it was an orange and foggy dawn. Three young deckhands in creaking rubber waders scrambled aboard the *Bayou Sweetheart* and scooped the shrimp into huge woven baskets. Whenever a shrimp fell onto the deck, seagulls swooped down and lit on the gunwales. One would snatch up the small pink morsel and wing away, a cawing mob chasing after.

The deckhands carried the baskets onto the dock and poured the shrimp into sorting vats. Then the shrimp were separated from the ice and dumped onto a rusty conveyor belt that rattled and groaned into the bargeboard tin-roofed shed, where the shrimp were loaded onto a scale.

The first weigh-ins of May and August were always the tensest, the bellwethers of the spring and fall seasons. Some years the bayou was such a miser that Mother Nature seemed to be telling the trawlers to give up. Other years, few and far between, seemed blessed, the Barataria giving up more shrimp than they dared hope for. Old-timers talked about the fabled hauls of the twenties and thirties, the apocryphal salad days. How the swamp hadn't been the same since the oil companies brought in their diggers and started chewing up the land. Nowadays, trawlers considered themselves lucky if they made enough to pay their bills and feed their families. And if they ended up with a little more on the side to squirrel away—lagniappe—that was nothing short of a miracle.

When the deckhands finished unloading their haul, Wes and his father stepped off the boat and walked down the splintery dock into the open-sided weighing shed. Monsieur Montegut stood rheumy-eyed and haggard behind the scale, a cigarette dangling from the crimp of his mouth. He shook their hands. Told them that if the price of shrimp went down any further he was going to sail out to one of the British Petroleum oil rigs and blow the fucking thing up himself.

"Well, let's see what you have here," Montegut said. "Sure you two got better things to do than socialize with my old ass."

First Monsieur Montegut weighed their total haul. Seven hundred and twenty-six pounds. Not nearly as much as Wes and his father had hoped for.

"These look a whole lot bigger than some I've been seeing," Montegut said. "You shoulda seen the last guy. *Lucky Sevens*? Not a one bigger than my pinkie. And I got the hands of a geisha girl."

Wes's father huffed a polite laugh through his nose.

There was still some hope, Wes knew. The total weight of their haul didn't matter as much as the size of the shrimp, how many it took to make a pound. If it took only thirty or thirty-five shrimp to make a pound, they were in business. If it took sixty or seventy, then the trawling expedition was a bust.

Wes's father lit a cigarette and watched as Montegut took a metal ice scoop and dug into the pile of shrimp. These he dumped on a smaller butcher scale. Montegut added four or five shrimp to the scale until the red needle quivered up to two pounds. Then he transferred the shrimp to a waist-high wooden table and began counting. His puffy lips moved and his stubby fingers flicked as he tallied.

Wes stood quietly beside his father. From the corner of his eye he could see his sagging shoulders, his lined face. Maybe it was his imagination, but his father's age in the last few years seemed to have come suddenly upon him. He climbed down the ladder slower and slower these days. His body was still wiry but the flesh under his arms was loose and flabby in a way that reminded Wes of a chicken's wattle. And he lumbered stiffly around the boat, clutching his coccyx and wincing.

There was a reason why you saw so many billboards for chiropractors and acupuncturists when you drove into the Barataria. Many guys, their backs were shot before they were even thirty. By forty, they were drinking whiskey every night to keep the pain at bay, scoring Oxycontins from their doctors and friends just to make it through another day of trawling. And by fifty, most of them were over the hill and ruined.

Wes's father was forty-eight.

After a few minutes, Montegut had counted out a hundred and five shrimp.

Wes's father flicked his cigarette onto the ground and heeled it out with his boot. "You mind counting again, Willy?"

Patiently, Montegut took another scoop of shrimp. Weighed. Counted. This time the number was one hundred and ten.

"Fuck," said Wes's father, palming the top of his head like he was polishing a bowling ball.

"How bout we stick with the other number?"

"Appreciate it, Willy."

"Hey, shit."

In the tawny morning light they walked out of the weighing shed and headed down a plank-board path toward Montegut's office. Wes's father's eyes were on the ground and his mouth was cinched. Wes knew that numbers were running wildly through his head. How many days were left in the season, how many hours they would have to spend on the boat for the next several weeks, how much a gallon of diesel cost, how many bills needed paying.

He was sure he'd hear plenty about it later.

They passed a ragtag collection of sheds and warehouses rotting from the salt and sun. A shrimp boat named the *Jean Lafitte* was moored in one of the slips. A one-armed man in camouflage cargo pants shouted at Montegut's sons as they unloaded the shrimp from his boat. "Look at that," he was saying. "Spillin' them shrimp all over the place. That's two pounds of shrimp right there."

Once they passed out of earshot, Montegut looked over his shoulder. "Son-bitch gets crazier by the year."

Montegut's office was the size of a storage closet, its metal desk littered with papers. Receipts, invoices, bills, time cards. On the wall hung a smoke-yellowed map of the Barataria waterway system. A tide chart, more recent, was tacked up next to it.

Montegut poured coffee from a pot into a Styrofoam cup and then he reached for the bottle of Jameson sitting on top of the filing cabinet. He poured a dollop of booze into the cup and took a swig. Then he slipped off his necklace and took one of the keys that hung from it and opened his desk drawer. From the drawer he took out a large metal box and opened it with another key. He reached inside and withdrew a thick sheaf of one-hundred-dollar bills and licked the ball of his thumb and counted them out. He handed the money to Wes's father, who looked at the bills woefully.

Montegut sat in his office chair and leaned back and tapped his finger, his wedding band thumping against the blotter. "Ask me, it's more the media's fault than anything," he said. "Acting like it's the end of the world. You know how they like to exaggerate. Wanna draw it out so they have a story to scream about every night."

Wes's father pocketed the bills and thanked Montegut. Back at the harbor, he let loose a stream of curses. Wes let out some of his own as he hosed down the deck. His stomach was sour from eating only protein bars and canned ravioli, his tongue charred from his father's burnt chicory coffee. Aside from thirty-minute catnaps in the cabin, he and his father had kept awake the full forty-eight hours straight. This wasn't unusual, not in the beginning of the shrimping season. You heard about crews staying out there for a week at a time. Some of the Vietnamese trawled for two weeks in a row. The spring after Katrina, Wes and his father had stayed out in the Barataria for four days running. But that was when there were two other men on the crew. When Wes's father was younger, stronger.

At the harbor, Wes's father dug into his pocket and took out some bills. He counted off a few and handed them to Wes. Four twenties. Eighty dollars for more than forty hours' work.

They stood facing one another. His father's eyes were crinkled against the morning sun, the whites webbed with scarlet. "What?" he asked.

"Eighty dollars," Wes said.

"That's right."

"Where's the rest?"

"There ain't no rest."

"Two days for eighty dollars."

"You think I feel good about it?"

"Crazy," Wes said.

"Hey, watch it."

Wes bit his bottom lip, picked at his eyebrow.

"There's a lot of things you're not figuring. The gas."

"Eighty dollars."

"Wes, how am I supposed to give you more when there's no more to give?"

Wes walked away from his father toward his truck.

"Where you going?"

Wes didn't answer.

"Listen," his father called to his back, "I want you back here by nightfall. And don't forget the ice."

Wes kept walking.

"Wes, you hear me? Don't forget the ice."

COSGROVE AND HANSON

A nurse called from a New Orleans hospice and told Cosgrove that his father was dead. Congestive heart failure, a peaceful passing in his sleep. Cosgrove hadn't spoken to the old man in half a decade, was surprised he lasted this long. He'd never taken care of someone's funeral and there was no living family he could call, so he was clueless about what to do next. Too embarrassed to ask the nurse, Cosgrove took the city bus to the public library where he sat at one of the carrels and searched *what to do when someone dies* on the computer.

Next morning Cosgrove set out from Austin to New Orleans in his seventeen-year-old Corolla, a rattletrap jalopy with a cracked windshield and a sugar-ant infestation in the glove compartment. The back bumper was held together with duct tape, and ten miles east of Houston on I-10 Cosgrove heard grinding like rocks in a blender as the car lurched and shimmied. He looked in the rearview mirror and saw the bumper rolling wildly in the road like a suicide by self-defenestration.

He drove on.

The day of his father's burial was gloomy and windswept, scrummed with clouds like an armada of dreadnoughts. Styrofoam cups rollicked over the cemetery lawn, and tattered stick-flags snapped over the veterans' graves. The wind kept blowing the purple drugstore chrysanthemums off the coffin, and Cosgrove gave chase among the mausoleums like a cat after a windup toy. Finally he picked up an egg-sized stone off the ground and weighed the flowers down.

When the minister asked for a eulogy, Cosgrove at first was speechless. During the sermon he'd kept waiting for a stranger to belatedly arrive. A lost cousin or forgotten acquaintance. But the folding chairs around the gravesite stayed empty.

Cosgrove got up from his chair and clenched his lips, looked down at his rented shoes. "He trusted in the Lord and kept his path straight," he said. Something he'd heard a televangelist say the night before on the motel television. As soon as the words left him, he realized how falsely they rang. About his father, about himself. In reality his father's path couldn't have been more crooked, his rambling around the country like one of those wandering dotted lines they showed on movie maps. A paper trail of bad checks and attorney bills and court summonses.

That night Cosgrove walked from his motel to a bar in the French Quarter and matched three Siberian businessmen shot after shot of Basil Hayden's Bourbon Whiskey. The last thing he remembered before his blackout was getting into an argument with one of the men about the World Cup, about which he knew nothing and didn't give a fuck. He had someone in a headlock, and someone else had him in a headlock, and they lurched around the bar like some tangled monstrosity, knocking over tables and chairs.

End of memory.

Next morning Cosgrove woke with a blinding hangover. In a jail cell. Curled fetally on the floor.

Six or seven other miscreants shared the cell, hard-eyed men who looked like they'd been courting trouble since the day they were born. A few paced like caged animals, clutching the bars and howling declarations of innocence. Others sat with their backs against the cinder block wall, eyes shut, heads bowed like penitents.

One bulge-eyed man kept raving about "the famous lawyer Jim Diamond Brousard." "You just call Jim Diamond Brousard," he said. "Tell him that Ricky Hallowell is in trouble."

Another man with a port-wine stain on his cheek had his pants pulled down around his ankles and was shitting without compunction in the corner toilet. He shot Cosgrove a beleaguered look and went about his business.

The police report read like a furloughed sailor's escapades, a story he and his roofing buddies back home would have laughed about. Public intoxication, disorderly conduct, pissing on a jukebox, resisting arrest. He doubted only one part, that he was crying about his father when they shoved him into the back of the police car.

No, that didn't sound like him at all.

- - - - - - - -

The judge must have hated him on sight because he sentenced Cosgrove to two hundred hours of community service, a punishment insanely disproportionate to the crime. Cosgrove stayed in New Orleans because there wasn't much waiting for him back in Austin save for a crappy roofing job, hell on earth during the summer. Some underwear and socks in an Econo Lodge drawer. His other sole possessions, a cache of childhood mementos and his birth certificate, were still in a safety deposit box in Miami, where he'd left them after a short, ill-fated stint—he'd gotten sun poisoning—as a barback in a South Beach hotel pool-bar.

He feared he was turning into a gypsy, like his father. Maybe in a new place he'd find a career, a woman, a life. He certainly hadn't in Austin.

And his fortieth birthday, four months away in January, loomed before him like a storm front. Maybe the best way to weather the sea change was in New Orleans.

Cosgrove rented one side of a sherbet-colored double shotgun in Mid-City and got a job at a neighborhood sports bar shucking oysters. And three days a week, on Mondays and Wednesdays and Fridays, he showed up at eight in the morning for community service. With a dozen other offenders, deadbeat fathers and druggies and drunks, he waited outside the station in his Day-Glo vest and ragged jeans until a deputy carted them in a windowless white van to their duty for the day. Sometimes they worked in groups of three or four, cleaning graffiti with wire brushes and sandblasters in Jackson Square. Other days they worked en masse, picking up condoms and carnival beads with pointed sticks from the squalid banks of the Mississippi.

A month into his sentence, Cosgrove was dropped off in front of a derelict two-story Victorian with faded purple shutters and lopsided porch columns. It was late August and hot, sparrows keening in the gray-green oaks, bougainvilleas in moribund bloom. A bantam-bodied man with a small pinched face and a black ponytail hanging out the back of his camouflage baseball cap got out of the van with him. They stood on the sidewalk regarding the house.

"Good God Almighty," the ponytailed man said. He had on a TOM PETTY AND THE HEARTBREAKERS T-shirt and frayed denim shorts two or three sizes too large, held up by a canvas belt with a gigantic gold and silver rodeo buckle engraved with the initials JHH.

The deputy, a gourd-shaped Dominican named Lemon, looked at the ponytailed man and then glanced down at his clipboard. "Hanson, is it?" he asked.

"John Henry Hanson," the ponytailed man said. "Yessir." He hung his thumbs from his canvas belt.

"What does it look like, Hanson?"

Hanson turned again and considered the sagging house. Paint was peeling off the clapboards in great leprous swatches and the front porch steps were spavined and weather-warped. Off to the side was a carport with a corrugated tin roof. No car, only buckets and paint cans and pallets of lumber, shovels and rakes and other gardening tools leaning against the walls.

"I'm no carpenter," Hanson said.

"Man of your mental caliber can manage a little sanding and painting, I'm sure," said Lemon. "You have any trouble with the hammer and nails, ask Cosgrove. He'll tell you which pound which."

Deputy Lemon got into the van and lurched away into the morning traffic. Hanson sidled up next to Cosgrove and watched the van turn down Magazine Street. Cosgrove, six foot two with a lumberjack beard, felt like a grizzly bear next to the little guy.

"Bet that son-bitch is on his way to fuck somebody's wife," Hanson said, gripping his belt buckle.

Up close the house looked even worse than from the street, beyond hope of repair. The front windows were cockeyed, many of the panes broken and covered with scraps of cardboard. Here and there the porch boards were missing, and from underneath the house the ammonia stink of animal piss wafted up as strong as poison.

Cosgrove and Hanson got to work with their scrapers. Lavender scabs of paint fell from the stanchions and motes of plaster swirled in the air. The only sounds for a while were the scratching of their tools, the rattle and groan of traffic on Napoleon. Ambulance and police sirens wailing in the distance.

When Hanson's rhythm slowed, Cosgrove, feeling watched, glanced over his shoulder. Sure enough, the man was looking at him askance.

Cosgrove asked him what he wanted.

"Not very friendly, are you?"

Other people, mostly women, had told him the same. "Why don't you talk?" they asked. "Why don't you listen?" Because he liked silence, he wanted to say. Because there was nothing he wanted to say and nothing he wanted to hear. At first they found his silence alluring, mistaking it for mystery, depth. But then they learned there was nothing behind it except indifference, maybe a low-grade depression.

"Just trying to work," Cosgrove said. Already his white V-neck T-shirt was stuck to his back with sweat.

"Work. Shit. We're a corporation now?"

Cosgrove hadn't wanted to seem unfriendly, just quiet. The less conversation, the better. Some guys never stopped once you let them get started. This guy already seemed one of them.

"Why you here?" he asked Hanson.

"Forged autographs."

"Who?"

"Presidents. They busted me for selling pictures with fake autographs on them in Jackson Square. Some tourist got his dick in a pretzel because I was selling signed photographs of George Washington. Went to the cops."

"There're no photos of George Washington."

"Bullshit. How'd they have painted those pictures?"

They got back to work. After a while Hanson asked Cosgrove how he ended up here.

"Public drunkenness," Cosgrove said.

Hanson shook his head and snorted incredulously. "In New Orleans?" he said. "That's like cops going out to the cemetery and arrestin' folks for being dead."

- - - - - - - -

The next few days of Cosgrove's community service were much the same. In the morning Deputy Lemon dropped them off and left them to their business. In the late afternoon he returned and surveyed their work like a plantation dandy, touring the house with his hands clasped behind his back. Whether Cosgrove and Hanson put in two minutes or two hours of work, his reaction was always the same. "All right, gentlemen," he said, "that'll do." Sometimes Lemon even gave them coupons. For laser tag, for free pancakes and car washes, for complimentary admission into a Bourbon Street strip club called Love Acts.

Lemon seemed to give even less of a shit than other cops in New Orleans, which Cosgrove had thought impossible.

One afternoon, about two weeks into his community service, Cosgrove finally caught glimpse of the widow. In a rose-colored terrycloth robe hanging askew from her bony shoulders she watched him querulously through the kitchen window, her snowy hair as bed-headed as a child's.

Cosgrove, digging up a dead rosebush, leaned against his shovel. Raised his hand, half smiled.

The window blind dropped as swiftly as a guillotine blade.

That afternoon as they took a break Hanson asked Cosgrove if he knew why they were fixing the old widow's place.

Cosgrove grunted, didn't give a shit.

"Lady's going to die any day now and she owes county taxes all the way back to 1982," Hanson said. He took off his cap, stroked his ponytail. "Soon as she kicks it, state's taking everything. Down to the lightbulbs and hinges and every aspect."

"So?"

"So? So, her family comes from French pirates. Lafitte. Exiles from the Caribbean. Been here all the way back. Practically invented crime in this city. Practically invented fuckin'."

Sitting on the porch step chewing on a tuna fish sandwich, Cosgrove wondered if there was a moment in the day when shit wasn't flying out of Hanson's mouth. He stuffed the remaining half of his sandwich back into the brown paper sack and asked Hanson how he knew all of this.

"Did a little snooping around," Hanson said. "Came out here on my day off with a tie on and knocked on some neighbors' doors. Told them I was from the Census Bureau. This old lady, turns out she's a real piece of shit. Always starting hell with the neighbors. Kicking them off her lawn during Mardi Gras. Every goddamn aspect."

Cosgrove wondered what kind of person would believe this man had anything to do with the Census Bureau. Someone blind and deaf, he suspected. Someone crazy. Someone brain-damaged.

But he was intrigued despite himself. "I don't see how it should make one bit of difference to us."

Hanson smiled, crooked but clean teeth. "You seem like a man who can keep a secret," he said.

"You know nothing about me."

"I know enough. You're not a rat. You've seen me fucking around here all day and haven't said anything to Lemon. That counts for something in my book. Money, I'm guessing you don't have much. Otherwise a lawyer with a state school diploma would've gotten you off."

"That's a whole lot of assuming."

"Am I wrong?"

"What're you on about?"

"Okay, what am I on about. The old lady, I bet she's got some treasure in that house."

GRIMES

Brady Grimes was here on behalf of the oil company. In their parlance, a liaison to minimize liability. Some such horseshit. Whatever designation they bestowed on him, he knew his purpose: to gather the signatures of as many fishermen and trawlers as he could. The public relations clusterfuck of the next several years was unavoidable, but the flood of compensation claims and lawsuits, the mob of lawyers and ambulance chasers, could be held at bay.

So, the oil company sent Grimes to shake trawlers' hands, to listen to their stories, to offer words of promise and consolation. But most importantly, to collect signatures. For a ten-grand settlement, a pittance compared with what British Petroleum might have to pay years down the line, the company would protect itself from further claims. Better to open the checkbook now and make amends before the true extent of the oil damage surfaced years ahead.

"Do what you do," Ingram, Grimes's boss, told him. "Show your all-American face. Smile your all-American smile. Commiserate. Apologize, promise, lie. Anything. As long as they take the money and sign on the dotted line."

At first Grimes protested. Why him? Why not someone who never stepped foot in southern Louisiana? After all, he was born in the Barataria, and as soon as he graduated high school he couldn't leave fast enough.

Ingram said this was precisely the point. "Those swamp people will notice a Yankee right away," he said. "And we want to send somebody who seems like they have a stake in the place."

"But I don't," Grimes said. "I hate it there."

"Seems, I said."

"What if they don't sign?"

"Grimes. Who am I talking to here? Of course they'll sign. They've got no money. They've got to eat, right? Do I like it any better than you do? No. But it's business. Trick is, you make it seem you're doing them a favor. 'Oh, this is terrible, a fucking tragedy, but let me help you out.' You offer them ten grand at first, enough to make a difference. If they put up a fight the first few weeks, up it to fifteen. No way they'll turn down fifteen. That's enough to pull the stakes, take the circus somewhere else. Up it to fifteen but only give them a day. After that, then the settlement goes back down to ten. Put on the pressure."

In the thrall of his deviousness, Ingram continued. "Tell them whatever huge payoffs and settlements they're waiting for? A mirage. Which is true. You know how many forms they'll have to fill out? How many of their forms will be quote-unquote lost? It'll drive them crazy. They'll never want to see another piece of paper as long as they live. Then there will be one appeal after another. As all that so-called settlement money gathers interest. A win-win situation."

A win-win situation; Grimes found that hard to believe. News of the oil spill, the Macondo blowout, grew grimmer by the day. *The end of the bayou as we know it,* people were saying. Rita, Gustav, Katrina, these seemed like the bell tolls of the apocalypse, but this was really it. The oil company officials said one thing, the news anchors another, and then marine biologists flown in from universities far and wide contradicted them all. No one was sure what to believe except that the numbers were startling. The amount of oil and poison in the water, the millions upon millions the shrimping and fishing industries lost. Grimes had even heard about a trawler taking his own life, some poor bastard so broke and broken he shot himself through the temple at a Fourth of July barbeque.

Ecologists worried about the crude washing into the marsh. One tropical storm, one unlucky shift in the winds, would bring in a black tide that laid waste to the ecosystem. Herons, terns, cormorants, laughing gulls, frogs, lizards, alligators, redfish, mullet, oysters, crawfish, deer, muskrat.

And, yes: shrimp.

Last spring, a few months ago, as the desperation and confusion grew, there was mention from oil company executives of top kills and junk shots, talk from congressmen of setting fire to the sea. "Setting the sea on fire!" Baratarians marveled. Why not just bomb the goddamn town and get it over with?

Columnists opined in editorials that it was time to wean off the oil tit. Coastal Louisianans wrote letters back, saying that a drilling moratorium would be the final deathblow to the community.

People pointed fingers at British Petroleum, at Halliburton, even at the oil rig workers, of whom eleven were dead and over a hundred injured. Baratarians were certain of only one thing: none of the talking heads on television were telling the truth. BP said most of the oil was out of the water, that the cleanup operation was a success, but most of it was still there, deep down and out of sight.

And Baratarians didn't need to hear the truth in order to know it. All they needed to do was look around. The truth was in the water and in the air and in the strange tides that washed ashore the dead birds and fishes, bone by blackened bone.

- - - - - - - -

The company put Grimes up in a cracker-box motel in Jeanette, Louisiana, and by the end of the first week Grimes lost track of the hours he spent in living rooms and kitchens, in bayou shacks and shanties, listening to fishermen rail about the oil spill. Some of the men were old, others young, but they all had in common a seemingly inexhaustible outrage. They hoisted themselves out of chairs and lifted their T-shirts, showing him the angry rashes on their chests and arms. They complained of mysterious afflictions of the eyes, ears, and throat they said they never had before the rig explosion or dispersants. They pounded tables with their fists and called him obscene names and made threats. A few even spat out curses in French.

They almost always ended up taking the money.

He spent countless hours poring over the settlement papers, painstakingly explaining every nuance of legalese while the men listened woodenly. Sometimes Grimes suspected the trawlers were acting thickheaded out of spite. A coon-ass wariness of outsiders. But Grimes wasn't an outsider. He was from the Barataria, couldn't recall a time when he didn't want to leave it. One of his trademark refrains, when people asked him about his past, was that he was born wanting to leave the swamp. That he wanted to leave it while still in the womb.

He thought he'd blend in easily once he was up in New York or Boston or Chicago. But as time passed and he entered his thirties it began to dawn on him that he'd always be an outsider. He was an outsider in the Barataria when he was growing up, so it had been foolish of him to think he'd belong someplace else simply by virtue of wanting to be there. Sometimes Grimes suspected that no matter how far he distanced himself, no matter how much time he spent away, there was a certain stink of the South that would never wash off him.

Up north people heard the bayou in his mouth, those telltale cadences. Untraceable to his ears, but there. And hearing his accent, people wanted to know about his past. Where was he from?

"Down South," he'd say. "Little place middle of nowhere. Long ago. Another life."

"Oh wow," they'd say, nodding, pretending to be more interested than they were, "no kidding."

Knew this guy was a coon-ass, Grimes was sure they were thinking. *Coon-ass:* one of those words like *nigger.* You could use it as a curse, a belittlement, an endearment, a self-deprecation, a damnation. It could be a complex muddle of all these things, depending on who said the word. Context was everything, context and intention.

"Living down there must've been paradise," they'd say, "all that seafood."

And Grimes, "Sure, oh yeah."

Grimes detested seafood. All of it. He'd inherited from some obscure tributary of his family's gene pool an aversion to the stuff. Shrimp, crab, redfish, it all tasted the same. Like rotting garbage marinated in sulfur water. But when Grimes was growing up, his family was so poor they often had to catch their meals, which meant seafood. He'd smother the shrimp and crawfish in ketchup and Zatarain's just to choke the garbage down.

And now here he was, years later, driving hour after hour through the Barataria in his rental car. Nothing changed; still hardly even a town. No superstores or megamalls, just a loose strew of markets and restaurants and go-go bars around the crossroads. The whitewashed spire of a Catholic church, the squat cinder block hulk of a correctional facility, a tin-roofed zydeco dancehall. Roadside stands run by trawlers and fishermen, Creoles and Cajuns and Isleños selling crawfish and satsumas, their craggy faces like sun-basking turtles.

Amazing the place was still standing. The clapboard houses on creosoted pilings, so jury-rigged they looked ready to topple into the oblivion of the swamp. Same with the makeshift piers, the mud boats and trawling skiffs. Now and then Grimes spotted signs for SWAMP TOURS, some enterprising local who'd slapped a magnetic sign on the side of his boat. Grimes went on these tours against his will during high school field trips. Twenty dollars a head, a guy would take you into the bayou. He'd point out the hummock where escaped slaves once hid from their owners. The man-made hill where a thirty-two-room antebellum mansion once stood before the hurricane of 1915. The place on the horizon where the treasure-laden ships of the pirate Jean Lafitte once sailed.

The state's dearth of infrastructure was awe-inspiring. Third World countries would deem the place an outpost of civilization. He passed through Lilliputian enclaves, most of them nameless, no more than a few clapboard houses and shanties scattered on pilings along the levees. He made countless wrong turns, followed single-lane roads until they turned to rutted dirt lanes that dead-ended in swamp.

"Recalculating," the GPS said. A scolding woman's voice.

He would tell the machine to shut the fuck up.

"Recalculating," the GPS would say again.

"Fuckin' murder you," Grimes said, lambasting the dashboard with his fist.

"Up ahead make next left," the GPS told him.

There was no left. No nothing. Only cattail and bladderwort and black puddles of mud as far as the eye could see. Trackless swamp.

Grimes executed a thirty-point turn like an old crone, engine straining and smoking, wheels spitting up gouts of slime.

How much longer would he be here? A month? A year? Maybe he'd died and gone to hell.

On the leather passenger seat of the Town Car was a printed-out list of names, fishermen and trawlers who'd filed complaints and claims with the oil company. So far he was halfway through the K's. For a spell this heartened him. This epic clusterfuck would soon be over. But then he gave the list a closer look, noticed all the surnames beginning with T's and S's. And the Z's. He'd never seen so many Z's in his life. An orgy of Z's. *Zatarain. Zimboni. Zane.*

Then the other names. *Trench* and *Toup. Lindquist* and *Larouche.* Names he knew, names that were carved on the tombstones in the picayune cemeteries dotted around Jeanette.

And among the names on the list was his own: *Grimes.* The only surname beginning with a G remaining. *Chris Grimes.*

His mother.

A visit he was dreading and putting off.

At night Grimes returned to his motel room on the verge of collapse. He poured three fingers of whiskey into a plastic motel cup, loosened the knot of his tie, and threw himself onto the bed. He flicked aim-lessly through the channels with the remote, the wash of pictures lulling him into a daze. President Obama delivering a sit-down news interview about the future drawdown of United States troops in Afghanistan. J. D. Salinger's toilet for sale on eBay. A possible peace talk between Israel and Palestine in September. The Barataria was so small and smothering, it was easy to forget there was a whole other world going on out there.

Sometimes Grimes came across local news channels covering the oil spill and stared in revulsion at the horrific video footage. Seafowl and porpoises and fish, all dead in lagoons of muck. And in New Orleans, at an oil company press conference at the civic center, a trawler had thrown a lemon meringue pie in a lawyer's face. The news showed someone's cell phone footage. An old man in overalls who resembled a disheveled Ichabod Crane bum-rushed the stage and slung the pie at the lawyer's head. The man's face was all meringue with a screaming mouth in the middle. Peo-ple clapped and hollered. The lawyer was wiping the goop from his face and flinging it off his fingers when a security officer Tasered the trawler. Then three more security guys dragged the man out of the building.

People were losing their bearings, for sure. He needed to be careful. Maybe he should buy a gun. A knife. Some mace, at least.

"This place is living hell," Grimes would tell his boss, Ingram, on his smartphone.

"You're the best guy we have."

"Bullshit."

"Sure you are."

"I'm not."

"Well."

"Jesus. Then put somebody else on the case."

"The case. You make it sound like a murder mystery."

"The job, whatever. Get someone else."

Ingram let out a long beleaguered breath that Grimes was supposed to hear. "Nobody else wants to go out there. Everybody's got families and shit."

"There's got to be someone lower on the totem pole. How about Franklin?"

"Franklin's wife has breast cancer."

"How about Snyder? Get him on a plane."

"He's in Pittsburgh."

"They have airports in Pittsburgh."

"It's his nephew's bar mitzvah."

"I'm beginning to hate these people."

"See? That's why you're there."

Grimes darkened many doors his first few weeks in the Barataria, and with each slight, with each obscenity and threat the trawlers hurled his way, his defiance and disdain grew. Before long he realized it wasn't only some allegiance to his company, some craven fear of losing his job, that kept him here. He was compelled by a resentful brinkmanship. Some sense that all of this was a game played against a group of people whom he'd never liked and who had never liked him. A long-belated comeuppance.

Ingram wanted him to collect signatures? Well, Grimes would gather more signatures than Ingram dared dream, so many signatures they'd erect his statue in the corporate headquarters' aviary. The trawlers and their families said they'd never sign? Well, Grimes would keep knocking on their doors and slick-talking on their porches until they relented, until they begged him to proffer his papers and pen.

Because Grimes was above all else a practical man. Numbers: life was a game of numbers. How much money you had in the bank, how much money you made, how many years you had left to live. Numbers murmured in his head throughout the day. Three more signatures today, three hundred signatures this month, two hundred thousand in the savings account, one hundred thousand in the stock portfolio. He did fifty push-ups in the morning, fifty sit-ups at night. He had three shots of bourbon on weekday nights, five on weekends. He ate red meat once a week, chicken five, pasta and carbs only on Sundays, a green or red apple every day.

So far in his life, the numbers were working in Grimes's favor.

Recounting Grimes's conquests someday in the not-too-distant future, Ingram would say, "This son of a bitch," and from the head of a baronial country-club table would raise his snifter of cognac in Grimes's honor. Beefy-faced businessmen with sharp grins and golf tans would follow suit as Grimes sat back trying to seem humble, inwardly basking in his glory. "Story?" Ingram would continue. "This son of a bitch? Right here? Goes down there, to whatever the fuck town, fucking town he was born and raised in. They spit on his face and shit on his shoes. But Grimes? 'Sign right here on the dotted line.' This guy right here. To his own mother. How's that for balls? Sign here on the dotted line. Saved my life going down there. They would've had my grandson's nuts in a Mason jar. Would've crucified me just for the fun of it."

LINDQUIST

A headache slamming in his temples, Lindquist woke wearing the same T-shirt and jeans he wore the day before. He went to the bathroom and stuck his head under the running faucet and raked his fingers through his hair, a deranged tangle because he'd cut it himself—left-handed, as if there were another option—in the mirror.

Then Lindquist rummaged in the attic for his old hook arm. It was a half hour before he found it in a cardboard box full of Christmas decorations. The thing was ugly and too small but he supposed it was better than walking around with his nub making everyone embarrassed and sick.

In the kitchen he filled a ten-gallon Igloo cooler with ice water and then went to the living room and picked among the pill bottles crowded on the television tray: Oxycontin, Xanax, Percoset. He unscrewed the plastic twist-tops with his teeth, shook six or seven pills out of each bottle, swept them one-handed into his zippered hip pack.

Outside Lindquist looked around the empty driveway and yard for his truck. It wasn't until he searched the garage and walked out to the street and glanced around that he remembered the night before. He couldn't find his truck because his truck wasn't there to find. Villanova had driven him home from the bar and his truck was still in Sully's lot.

Lindquist shook his head. Even this little movement lit white fire behind his eyes, stirred a green wave of nausea in his gut.

He went back inside and called the taxi service from the kitchen phone. Despite his daughter's insistence, he still didn't own a cell phone and didn't care to. Who would call him anyway? Bill collectors. His daughter, looking for money. Certainly not his wife.

He walked out to the access road and stood waiting in the chaffweed, insects chattering in the grass, swallows shrilling in the trees. Not yet nine and already the heat was like plaster of Paris settling in his lungs. It wouldn't be for another few months, late October, before the weather began to cool.

Soon a taxi pulled up, a root-beer-colored Buick with a hand-painted escutcheon on the side door. TAXI, it said.

Lindquist got in and the driver eyed him in the mirror.

"Sully's."

"Sully's?" A little shake of his head. "Sully's won't be open yet."

"My truck's there."

"Ten dollars," the driver said.

Lindquist waved the driver on.

They passed a marshy field thick with cattail in the middle of it a cabin raised on stilts, rusted generators and oil drums in the mucky yard. For three generations a family named Robicheaux had lived here, but they left for Florida once the oldest, Larry, sold his shrimping business after Katrina.

The driver was watching Lindquist in the rearview mirror. His face looked familiar. Those foxlike eyes, the bitter curl of his lip. As if he believed something owed him was looking increasingly unlikely he'd ever see. An aggrieved man-child.

Suddenly the name came back to him: Naquin. Jeremy Naquin, once a rising-star wide receiver from Lindquist's high school. That was then and this was now and here the motherfucker was. Driving a cab.

"Naquin?" Lindquist said.

The cabdriver's eyes seized on him in the rearview mirror.

"Gus Lindquist. Jeanette High."

The man's eyes grinned. "Shit, Lindquist. Thought that was you. How you been?"

He wigwagged his hand. Then he realized Naquin couldn't see this, so he said, "Eh."

"Story of my life," Naquin said. "Fair to middling. Ever write a book about myself, that's what I'm going to call it. *Fair to Fucking Middling.*"

One time in gym class, decades ago, Naquin had gripped Lindquist by the middle like a squealing pig and held him upside-down over a locker room toilet. He dunked his head over and over again as a dozen other boys egged him on. This was when Lindquist weighed all of a hundred and fifteen pounds with change in his pockets. Now, half his life past, Lindquist found himself strangely grudgeless. Here was Naquin now, gone to fat, driving a cab that smelled like foot rot and fried onions.

"Never see you around," Naquin said. "Thought you'd split."

"Don't get out much, me."

The car rattled over the potholed road. Next to Lindquist the ice chattered in the cooler.

"Hey, I'm just going to say it. Some fucking luck. Your arm."

"Yeah," Lindquist said.

"Know what I remember about you?"

Lindquist thought: *Dunking my head in a fucking toilet?* But he asked what.

"The pirate books. Always had your nose buried in them pirate books. Still into that shit?"

"Kinda."

"Ever find anything?"

Now all Lindquist could see of Naquin was his grin in the rearview mirror. "Not much, me."

"I might need to get me into that," Naquin said. "Metal detecting. Wife says I need a hobby besides shitting on her hopes and dreams."

Lindquist laughed a wry laugh through his nose and the two of them fell quiet for a minute.

"Hey," Lindquist said.

"Yeah?"

"Why don't blind men skydive?"

"The who the what?"

"Because it scares the shit out of the dog."

Naquin's eyes were puzzled in the mirror.

"Joke," Lindquist said.

"Oh, all right," Naquin said. He gave Lindquist a delayed smile. "Yeah, I'm gonna remember that one. People'll like that."

In Sully's oyster-shell lot Lindquist got out of the cab and pulled out a twenty. He held out the bill but Naquin waved the money away through the open driver's window.

"Shit, I feel kind of bad about everything, Lindquist," Naquin said.

Squinting in the sun, Lindquist shoved his hand in his pocket, unsure what to say. "People don't change," his wife often told him in their last days together. This, of course, after Lindquist promising he would.

Well, here was someone right here to disprove her theory.

"Hey," Naquin said, shaking his head as if jarring himself from a trance. "You ever find any treasure and need a guy to dig? Way it's looking, doesn't seem like I'm gonna win the lottery anytime soon."

Lindquist said sure thing. Naquin waved and then Lindquist. He watched the cab bounce away in the churning dust.

- - - - - - - -

Lindquist was an hour late when he got to the marina. One of the men, King, was already gone. Only Dixon, sitting shirtless on top of a blue plastic cooler, remained on the dock. His eyes were raw and bloodshot and he winced when he rose, rubbing his lower back with the heel of his hand. Not yet thirty, Lindquist thought, and the poor son of a bitch's body was already falling apart like a Taiwanese can opener. Before he knew it he'd be gobbling painkillers by the fistful, crushing them with a mortar and pestle and snorting the powder.

Like himself.

"Where's King?" Lindquist asked.

"Indiana," Dixon said.

Lindquist was expecting Dixon to say in his bed. In the hospital. At the bar. Not Indiana. Not somewhere half the fucking country away.

"Hell's he doing in Indiana?"

"He's through. Ain't coming back."

"Through?"

Dixon nodded, eyes ticking everywhere but the one place he wanted to look. Where Lindquist's prosthetic arm should have been.

"That's what he told you? I'm through? I'm through and I'm going to Indiana?"

"He said tell Lindquist I'm going to Indiana. I'm through."

"Well," Lindquist said with a weary sigh, "the day ain't getting any younger."

They hopped on the *Jean Lafitte,* a fifty-foot round-bottomed shrimper with avocado-green trim and a pirate flag hung from an outrigger. Before long they nudged into the bayou, the water shimmering like foil under the sun, the oak-studded cheniers and cypress cisterns sliding past.

After prepping the nets Dixon climbed up to the wheelhouse and stood behind Lindquist. He fished a toothpick from his jeans pocket. Leaning against the wheelhouse wall, he jabbed between his teeth.

"See the way the water's moving," Lindquist said. "Strong tide'll flush those shrimp out of the marsh real good."

Dixon was busy with his toothpick.

Lindquist took the Donald Duck Pez dispenser from his pocket and flicked the head. A pill popped out and he smashed it between his molars, jaw working in a slow bovine rhythm. Over the years he'd grown to like the bitter taste of the pills.

Dixon was watching him.

"You staring at my nub?" Lindquist asked.

"Naw."

"You can stare."

Dixon looked at the wheelhouse floor, the boards worn smooth and silvery, grime heeled so deeply into the grain of the wood that no amount of scrubbing would ever remove it.

"Looks like the end of a sausage, don't it?"

Dixon considered Lindquist's nub.

"Like an elephant's asshole," Lindquist said.

Dixon grinned uneasily. "Naw."

"What kind of son-bitch would steal an arm?" said Lindquist.

"What you gonna do?"

"Not much I can."

"You gonna get another, I mean."

"I got that old hook arm over there." Lindquist pointed his chin at the corner of the wheelhouse, where the battered old thing was propped next to a Louisville Slugger baseball bat. "Just hate wearing it."

They were quiet for a time, the only sounds the grumbling engine, the sloshing waves.

"Maybe it was a guy missin' an arm hisself," Dixon said.

Lindquist couldn't tell whether Dixon was joking. "Whoever's probably halfway to Missouri by now."

Dixon was sheepishly watching Lindquist. "Something I gotta tell you," he said.

"Yeah?"

He switched the toothpick in his mouth from one corner to the other. "This's tough."

"Well, hell. Just say it, Dixon."

"Today's probably my last."

"Last what."

"Shrimpin'."

Lindquist took off his yacht cap and raked his fingers through his thinning hair. He turned to the wheelhouse window and steered. The bayou was opening up now, small white-topped breakers buffeting the hull of the boat, a covey of pelicans flying in V-formation over the water. "Well, let's just see how it goes," Lindquist said.

Dixon pushed off the wheelhouse wall and took a step toward the ladder as if about to leave but then he stopped. "Well. No probably about it," he said. "Wife wants me to take that BP money. Puttin' up booms. They handing out cash left and right. Bills like they's coupons."

Lindquist waited.

"You think that's bad?" Dixon asked.

Yes, he wanted to say, but he told Dixon no.

"You're judging me."

"Shit, money's money. Especially when you got kids."

Lindquist meant what he said. His own daughter he rarely saw or spoke with though she lived only two miles away in the new trailer park on the edge of town. Once a month, twice if he was lucky, she dropped by the house to see how he was. That was the pretense at least. Lindquist often suspected that her mother dispatched her. *Go see if your father hasn't OD'd on those pills. Go see if your father's taking care of himself. Go say hello to your father, he's probably lonely.*

Other times Lindquist reckoned that Reagan only visited for the money. Not that he had any to spare, but he always forked some over anyway. Twenty here, fifty there. Lindquist knew damn well where the money was going. Drugs. Only marijuana, he hoped, but he knew there was probably some coke mixed in there too. Some pills, knowing Reagan. Meth: he prayed to Jesus not.

It wrenched Lindquist's heart to think how distant he'd become from his daughter. He tried not to think of how pretty she'd once been. How her once milk-smooth skin was already wrinkled with bitter lines around the eyes and mouth. She patched her face with makeup, but anybody could look and know she was in trouble.

"You should do it yourself," Dixon said now.

"Work for the oil company?"

Dixon nodded.

Lindquist scowled. "Don't care for that, me."

"Well, you don't have to marry 'em."

"Let's see what happens."

"Lindquist. Listen to what they're sayin' on the news. They were showing some restaurant in New York. The owner hung a sign on the door. Braggin' about how their shrimp are from China. 'No Gulf shrimp served here,' it said."

"Fuck New York."

"All you gotta do is put up some booms," Dixon said. "Shouldn't be too hard." He opened his mouth as if about to say more but then he stopped himself. *Even with one arm,* he was going to say.

"You think those booms're helping?"

"They say it stopped about eighty percent of the oil in Alabama."

"'Course they did," Lindquist said.

"What?" Dixon said.

"Don't be stupid, Dixon." He didn't mean it unkindly, and it didn't sound so the way it came out.

"I ain't bein' stupid. I'm bein' optimistic. There's a difference."

Dixon opened the wheelhouse window and flicked his mangled toothpick into the water. He dug into his pocket for a new one and stuck it in his mouth. Then he leaned back with his boot heel cocked against the wall.

Lindquist steered, craning his neck so he could see into the green-black water. Through the port window was a hawk, small as a drifting piece of ash, circling over a locust-bowered islet. Herons with stilt-like legs stalked in the marsh grass. Only a few other boats were out this far, oyster luggers and Lafitte skiffs.

On the radio, voices crackled back and forth, captains bitching about their paltry hauls.

"Didn't bring your metal detector today?" Dixon asked.

Lindquist always brought his metal detector when they went out trawling. There were inevitable dead hours in the bayou, when the tides slackened and the shrimp swam back in the marsh, when there wasn't much to do except play cards or whip up a meal or catch some sleep. Lindquist would anchor the *Jean Lafitte* and pirogue to one of the barrier islands, metal detecting any patch of land accessible by foot. He never found much and the men ribbed him about it, but he liked to imagine the day he brought something back to the boat. A piece of Spanish gold. A jeweled necklace or diamond ring. He liked to imagine the look on their faces when they saw the treasure gleaming in his palm, proof after all these years that there had been some truth to his craziness. Shit, they were liable to buy metal detectors of their own after that. There wouldn't be a patch of unturned land in all of southern Louisiana.

"Son-bitch is broken," Lindquist told Dixon.

"Jesus, Lindquist. You make a deal with the devil or something?"

"I've been looking all around to make a deal with him, me, but he's out of town."

Dixon grinned.

"Yeah, I'm liking how this tide looks," Lindquist said.

"Guess I better lower those booms," Dixon said.

"Hey, Dixon."

Dixon stopped and faced him.

"Let's just see how it goes, huh?"

Dixon gave a small doubtful shrug.

"I got a good feeling, me," Lindquist lied.

"That optimism?" Dixon asked.

"Go lower the booms, Dixon."

It was ten in the morning, the air sodden with heat, when they tied onto Monsieur Montegut's dock. Montegut's sons, four shirtless boys in jean shorts and work boots, hoisted the shrimp-heaped baskets onto their shoulders and hop-stepped over ropes onto the dock, where they dumped the shrimp into the sorting box. In their haste the kids let dozens of shrimp dribble from the baskets and they blanched as soon as they hit the deck.

The way Montegut's sons kept heedlessly working as if the loss meant nothing pissed Lindquist off. "Must be five bucks right there," he told the boys. "You gonna give me five bucks out your pocket?"

Montegut's squint-faced sons didn't say a word, only eyed him darkly.

Lindquist and Dixon stepped into the shed to watch the weigh-in. Monsieur Montegut dug his metal scoop into the glistening mound of shrimp and weighed out two pounds. Then he placed the shrimp on the counting table and began to pick through them.

Lindquist watched with his mouth open. He thought of his wife. For all he knew she was making more money today than he'd net in the next week. Meanwhile the divorce papers sat waiting on his kitchen table and she'd be asking for alimony as soon as he signed them. He thought of his daughter, smoking and snorting money he didn't have. Twenty-four years old. He was an old man when he was twenty-four. Nowadays kids that age were still sucking on the tit.

Dixon stood tensely beside him, worrying over his own troubles.

"Eighty-ninety," Montegut said finally.

"Well, hell," Lindquist said.

Montegut clenched his jaw but when he spoke his voice was measured and cordial. "We go through this every year, Lindquist. Every year you think I'm rippin' you off when you know the truth as well as I do."

Lindquist found himself staring at Montegut's teeth, fake and over-large and country-club white. The V of his chambray shirt was open and a gold chain with an OUR LADY OF GRACE medallion was nestled in the russet excelsior of his chest hair.

"Count 'em again," Lindquist said.

"I'll count 'em a thousand times if you want me to."

"Count 'em. Please."

Montegut started counting again. Lindquist's eyes shuttled back and forth, his mind working like a ticker.

The number the second time around was the same.

Lindquist and Dixon followed Montegut down the dock toward his office. Lindquist could hear the man's sons chuckling and shit-talking behind his back.

In the steam-bath heat of his office Montegut keyed open a desk drawer and hauled out a metal strongbox. He sat the strongbox on the blotter and keyed it open and took out a sheaf of bills. He licked the ball of his thumb and counted out six twenties and held them out to Lindquist.

Lindquist took the money and slipped it into his shirt pocket. For all his doubts about Montegut, for all his jealousy toward him, he knew the man wasn't a thief. Hell, with shrimp prices the way they were and all the stuff on the news, he was probably paying him more than he could afford.

"See you," Lindquist told Montegut, all the civility he could muster.

Montegut nodded at Lindquist, then at Dixon.

At the harbor they roped the *Jean Lafitte* back into its slip and climbed stiffly as zombies onto the dock. When they were in the gravel parking lot standing next to Dixon's truck, Lindquist fumbled in his pocket and took out the money. He counted out four twenties and gave them to Dixon. Then Dixon counted the money himself and looked at Lindquist. "Hell, Lindquist," he said.

"What?"

"I counted out the money he gave you."

"Yeah?"

"You gave me more than half."

"Yeah."

"I can't."

"One more day, Dixon. That's all I ask. Everybody's got bad days."

Dixon stared down at his boots, as if his resolve might vanish if he looked at Lindquist directly. "I can't, Lindquist," he said.

Lindquist was looking over Dixon's shoulder at the faraway treetops, green-gray and hazy in the heat. "Well, if you change your mind," he said.

Dixon nodded and climbed into his truck and started the engine. He lifted his fingers off the wheel in a little wave and jerked the truck into gear.

Watching the truck lurch away, Lindquist reached into his hip pocket and fished out the Pez dispenser. He thumbed the duck head and popped out a pill. He palmed it into his mouth and chewed until bitter dust coated his tongue.

That morning before returning home Lindquist went to Trader John's and tacked a handwritten help-wanted ad on the board next to the door. DECKHAND WANTED, ONE HUNDRED DOLLARS A DAY GARANTEED. NO DRUNKS. NO CRAZIES. Lindquist put his e-mail address and home number at the bottom, the times when he could be found at the harbor.

WES TRENCH

What did he want to do with his life? Wes's father would ask him. It wasn't really a question, Wes knew, but his father's roundabout way of pointing out that it was almost certain what he'd end up doing, whether he liked it or not: shrimping. Like his father, like his father's father, like six generations of Trenches before that. Wes's dad wasn't trying to be cruel, only realistic. And the reality was this: bayou boys almost always grew up to be bayou men.

Also a reality: Wes had missed so many school days helping his father this year, he'd have to repeat the eleventh grade. If he was lucky, he'd graduate by the time he was nineteen. He was almost eighteen already. Most of his friends, also the sons of trawlers, had already dropped out of school to work full-time on their fathers' boats. "Too fool for school" was their motto.

Only one, Jason Talbot, had received an LSU scholarship for football.

Wes wasn't an athlete and he wasn't a good student. His highest grades were in English because Mr. Banksey, the biggest bleeding heart among the teachers in school, let his students write short stories for their final papers. Who couldn't tell a story, Wes figured, so he did.

"You have a fine imagination and the heart of a poet," Mr. Banksey had written at the end of the paper, awarding Wes an A, his first since middle school. Wes was proud. For a day or two. But then the old stubborn pragmaticism he inherited from his father jabbered in his ear like a devil on his shoulder. He figured that he couldn't exactly write *Mr. Banksey says I have a fine imagination and the heart of a poet* on a job application.

In an ideal world, Wes thought, he'd have more time to figure out what he wanted to do with his life. But seventeen in the Barataria was different from seventeen in other places. Guys in Jeanette, many were engaged by the time they were seventeen, some already fathers. Two of the thirteen girls in Wes's homeroom class were pregnant and showing, their bellies so big and swollen they had to sit in special chairs at a foldout card table to the side of the room. The biology teacher, Mr. Hargis, joked that he'd give the girls extra credit if they gave birth in his class. Instructional experience for everyone, he said.

But Wes actually wanted to be a shrimper, with his own boat and business. His father had built his own boat by the time he was eighteen and had a three-man crew before he was twenty. Wes's plan, which he told his father about, was to start a new kind of shrimping business once he finished building his boat. He'd hire a few of his high school buddies as deckhands and they'd sell shrimp right off the dock, skip the middlemen and warehouses and wholesalers. They'd offer only the biggest, freshest shrimp, just hours—minutes—out of the water, shrimp so big his customers would have no trouble cleaning them, not like the puny shrimp they sold in the supermarkets. With Facebook and Twitter, he could start a kind of bacon-of-the-month club, the kind he saw advertised in the back of hunting magazines, except with shrimp. And instead of every month, it would be every day. *The freshest shrimp in the world, harbor slip 89, six sharp,* he'd message his subscribers. On weekends he might even let tourists, day-trippers from New Orleans, on the boat. For fifty dollars a head they'd get a tour of Barataria Bay and could catch shrimp themselves, or at least witness up close all the work that went into it. Wes would let them carry aboard their own coolers so they could fill them chock-full instead of paying by the pound.

Wes's father seemed to like the idea, which surprised him. Except for the internet part. He hated computers and cell phones. "You sure all that's legal?" he asked Wes.

"Pretty sure," Wes said.

His father shook his head, gave him a rare compliment. "Got to admit, you got a head on you, kid."

A few times a year Wes and his friends went to the French Quarter, where they met boys and girls from all over the country, boys and girls who, even when two or three years older, seemed much younger. Soft-hearted and unscathed by the world. They'd never lose an eye to a bait hook like Monty Blevins from shop class. Never know someone who cut off three of his own fingers for insurance money like Peter Arcinaux's father. Never see their mothers drowned in the floodwaters of a hurricane.

In five or ten years, these kids would be doctors and lawyers and college professors and Wes would still be trawling in the Barataria. One far-flung day in the future they'd find themselves sitting in the elegant light of a Manhattan restaurant, no way of knowing they were dining on shrimp that Wes had caught himself. Shrimp hoisted out of the bayou and trucked up the Eastern seaboard all the way from Jeanette. By then, Wes would likely have a wife and children. And, a thought he found depressing but couldn't help thinking: maybe he'd already be hunchbacked and bitter and brokenhearted like his father.

He hoped not. He hoped he was happy shrimping, and he hoped the bay was clean by then, because he loved life on the water.

— — — — — — — — —

In retrospect, maybe the story he'd written for Mr. Banksey was more a memoir. Except that wasn't exactly right either, because wasn't a memoir supposed to be pure truth? In the story, or whatever Wes had written for Mr. Banksey, truth and fact bled together, a muddle of confabulation.

Everything Wes wrote in the story about the hours before the storm was picture-perfect true. Wes's father boarding up the downstairs windows. The vans and trucks loaded with suitcases and children lurching past their house. The way the tree shadows in the yard grew tensely still and the way the air outside tightened like a held breath.

And Wes's mother, begging his father to leave.

The storm would peter out and turn away at the last minute, Wes's father insisted. Just like the rest of them.

"You've gone *braque*," Wes's mother said.

Anger brought out my mother's French, Wes had written in his story.

In the margin, Mr. Banksey wrote, *Good stuff.*

When the storm hit, it didn't sound like a freight train, the way Wes often heard it described in other hurricane stories. It sounded like nothing he'd ever heard. *A kraken's roar,* was what he wrote. A cannonade of debris hammered the house while a deluge slashed down from the sky, rain filling the street and yard, rising so deep it topped the rosebushes and hydrangeas. Soon the water lapped up the porch steps and seeped under the front door. At first it was only an inch or two, but within an hour a foot of muddy swirling water filled the the bottom story and Wes and his parents were sloshing through the house. Somewhere a levee had broken and Jeanette was swallowed in a rolling storm surge.

When the power blacked out Wes and his parents went upstairs with flashlights and gallon water jugs. They sat on pillows on the floor and played Scrabble by lantern light while Max, head on forepaws, cowered under the bed.

They played Scrabble: Wes would later marvel at this.

At one point during the game Wes's mother used the word STUBBORN.

Wes's father told her that she had quite a wit. He was trying to act calm, but Wes could tell from the hard set of his shoulders that he was scared.

A few minutes after, his mother spelled DUMB with her tiles.

"Okay," his father said. "I get it."

Sometime after midnight the wind wrenched a piece of plywood from one of the downstairs windows and the glass shattered, wave after wave of water surging into the house.

That was when they stopped playing Scrabble and started praying.

Dawn found them on the roof of the house. All Baratarians kept axes in their attics in fear of storms like this, and Wes's father busted a hole through the ceiling so they could climb through. Max paced back and forth along the roof peak, whimpering and wagging his tail and staring down into the tumultuous water. The hurricane had turned the streets into swift canals full of spinning debris. Scraps of lumber and rags of plastic, trash can lids and window shutters. Cars and trucks were completely underwater, but the sky was oddly tranquil, gray like an old nickel.

Before the storm, Wes's father had roped his pirogue to the front-yard oak tree. The only smart thing he did. The little boat jounced in the water, but it was intact and afloat. Wes's father got a hundred feet of nylon anchoring rope out of the attic and tossed the line like a lasso, trying to snag the pirogue. He missed the first time and the second. On Wes's father's third toss Max scrambled down the roof, tail wagging, and launched into the water.

Instantly the wild current sucked him away and under.

Wes would never know if what happened next was an accident, or if his mother meant to go after the dog. She went skidding down the slope of the roof on her behind and caught herself on the gutter with her tennis shoes. The pipe gave, twisting away from the house with a great metallic shriek, and then she went tumbling into the water.

"Oh shit," she said while airborne. Those were Wes's mother's last words. The ones he heard.

Wes and his father watched the raging water, bodies poised as if they were about to fling themselves into the flood. Then Wes's eyes met his father's. Pure animal panic. An awful look Wes knew right away he'd never forget.

For a second, ten or twelve yards away, Wes's mother's head popped up like a bobber. That was what Wes would always remember the clearest. Her crazed and twisted face, the terrified look in her eyes. Her open mouth making no sound. Then the water sucking her back under.

His father screamed Wes's mother's name. "Sandy," he shouted again and again, as if this would bring her back.

From this point onward in his story for Mr. Banksey's class, everything Wes wrote was pure fiction.

For instance: weeks later, when he and his father were living in Baton Rouge, they were eating dinner in a fried chicken restaurant and Wes's father, drunk on whiskey, asked, "Do you blame me?"

In the story, Wes said, *Of course not*.

In the story, Wes and his father said they were lucky to have each other.

In real life, Wes had said, "Yes."

That was five years ago and, even half a decade on, nothing felt healed. No, the wound of his mother's death still felt as big as the hurricane itself.

- - - - - - - -

The next evening when Wes showed up on time at the marina, his father was nowhere to be found. It was twilight, quiet save for the gibbering of frogs and insects. At the end of the dock the *Bayou Sweetheart* was unlit in her slip. Wes got out of his truck and paced in the bleached-shell parking lot. Another trawler got out of his truck and waved at Wes before trudging down the dock to his boat.

As he paced, Wes had a nagging sense that he was forgetting something. He chalked it up to the perpetual unease that he felt around his father these days. Lately they argued about everything. About how much money should be spent on a lightbulb, about how to set the house thermostat, about what kind of gas Wes put in his truck.

His father gave him the most hell about two things: Wes's boat and the BP settlement money.

Wes started building the boat in the backyard when he turned fifteen, just as Wes's father and grandfather had done when they were the same age. Now the keel of the boat, reared on cinder blocks under a gunny-roped tarp in the backyard, sat untouched for months. Wes's father used to poke fun at his shoddy craftsmanship and welding, eyeing the ragged seaming, running the flat of his hand along the hull like a cattle baron. "See this?" he'd say. "This wood, you'll have to throw it out, this whole section. And this metal, look. See how it's bent? No way a boat's going to float if it's built like this. It'll fall apart like a Polish submarine. One mistake leads to another. Listen to me."

Wes would stand back, burning with the impulse to tell his father that he never asked for his advice. That the boat was a work in progress. That he'd prove his father wrong and the boat would turn out to be the most beautiful he'd ever seen, whether it took three months or three years.

But Wes hadn't touched the boat in months and now it languished in the backyard under a moldering vinyl tarp. Like a dead elephant. Wes's father stopped mentioning the boat, which was somehow worse than the shit-talking. Maybe his father was right. Maybe he'd given up without knowing it. Scared to move forward, scared that the more he built the more he'd prove his father right. The first Trench in generations not to build his own craft.

"You seem glad," Wes said one day, surprised he'd said it, let alone thought it.

They were lugging their toolboxes home from the harbor when they passed the boat in the backyard. The evening sky was plum and scarlet above the treetops, a muggy spring night.

"Glad about what?" his father asked.

"That I stopped building the boat."

They walked on a moment before his father said, "Why'd I be glad?"

"Because you were right," Wes said. "That I wouldn't finish."

His father cut him a look. "I don't think about the boat."

"Because you never took it seriously."

"If you don't take it serious, how you expect me to?"

"What's that mean?"

"Forget it."

They stopped and faced one another.

"Where's your time go? Your money?" his father said. "I'll tell you. Screwing around."

"I'm working all the time. For you."

"Yeah, okay."

"If I had more time, the boat would have been finished a long time ago."

"With what?" his father asked. "Popsicle sticks?"

"You want me to steal the wood?" Wes asked. "Go in the shipyard and steal the parts?"

"Why you getting so nasty? You brought it up."

"Loan me the money."

"Crazy talk."

"Loan me the money and I'll have this boat done in three months. You'll see."

"What money, Wes? I don't have a nickel to piss on."

"Well, neither do I. When I do, I'm going to finish the boat."

Wes's father only looked at him rankly and shook his head.

And then the other night at dinner, when Wes mentioned the BP money. He and his father were eating supper when a news story about the oil spill came on the television. The pretty reporter woman was talking about the settlement checks the trawlers and fishermen were getting for their cleanup work and business losses in the spring.

"That guy come by to talk about the settlement again?" Wes asked.

"Comes nearly every day, little dapper dickhead," his father said.

Wes looked at his father and waited.

"Why?" his father asked.

"Why not just take the money?" Wes said. "It's free."

"Free? Is that how you look at it?"

Wes shrugged.

"Somebody burns down your house and offers you five dollars. That's free?"

Wes kept quiet, already regretting mentioning the subject.

"Let's get this straight. It's not free. Not when they destroy the place you've lived all your life. That's about as far from free as you can get."

All of these things were on Wes's mind when his father drove his truck into the gravel lot at half past nine. Wes was sitting on the dock with his feet dangling over the side and rose as his father hobbled across the lot and down the dock. His white hair was mashed on one side, like he'd slept on it, and his cranberry polo shirt with the white chest-stripe looked rumpled. He passed Wes without a look or word.

He spoke only once they were aboard the *Bayou Sweetheart* and he had the engine running. "Your friend came over," he said.

Wes looked at him quizzically.

"The oil guy. Guy you want me to go to prom with."

Was said nothing. It was going to be one of those nights.

"Guy wouldn't let me go. Real slickster. On and on and on. Try to be polite, people'll fuck you ten ways to the altar."

Wes stooped to untie a mooring rope from a dock cleat.

"What's that?" his father said from the wheelhouse.

"I didn't say anything."

"All right then. It's already late."

Wes checked the nets and trawls as his father piloted across the languorous purple bayou. Wes couldn't see any oil in the water, not yet. A good sign.

Once they reached the pass Wes lowered the trawls and Wes's father steered the boat against the current. Twenty minutes later he shifted the boat into idle and Wes lifted the swollen nets. The haul looked considerable, much better than the night before. His father climbed down from the wheelhouse and put on gloves and helped Wes load the catch onto the sorting table.

As they picked through the shrimp, a realization struck Wes like lightning. The ice. "Remember the ice," his father had said.

He picked through the teeming haul, dread clenching his gut. He braced himself for the inevitable moment, wondered what he could do. He decided he'd play dumb. Pretend that it was his father who was supposed to bring the ice.

When the time came to ice down the shrimp, Wes's father looked around the deck. He put both hands on his hips and glanced about with his mouth open.

"Where's the ice?" Wes's father said.

"Huh?"

"The ice. Where is it?"

"I don't know."

"You don't know."

Wes shook his head.

"What's the last thing I said yesterday?"

Silence.

"I said get the ice."

Wes picked at his eyebrow.

"Get the fucking ice. Nineteen thousand times. Might as well been in your ear with a megaphone."

"Yeah."

"Huh?"

"All right."

"All right?" His father's eyes seared on him. "What fuckin' planet are you on? All right?"

"I'm sorry, okay?" Wes said.

"Are you on drugs?"

"No sir."

"I hope you're on drugs. I hope to sweet Jesus you're on drugs. I hope you're sky high on some fucked up thing right now."

"All right," Wes said.

"All right. All right. All right. Because if you're not, we got a problem. We gotta go to the doctor. Fuckin' tonight. Get your brain fuckin' scanned. Because there's a fuckin' problem."

"We're wasting time."

"Wastin' time, he says. I'm wasting time. I hope you're on drugs, man. I pray to God."

Wes's father stepped up to him and slapped him on the back of the head. Wes whirled around in disbelief. His father hadn't hit him since he was a little kid, when he draped him over his knees and spanked him for using a dirty word in first grade.

"You just hit me," Wes said.

"Lucky I don't kick your ass in the water."

Wes glared. "You never made a mistake? Never?" As soon as the words left his mouth he regretted saying them because his father no doubt knew what he meant.

His father's face twisted and he gritted his teeth. He shook his head hard and quickly, as if to fling out what he just heard. "I hope to sweet holy shit you're sky high on drugs. Because we can fix that. We can take you somewhere and fix that. If you're not, I don't know what we're gonna do."

They stood there facing one another on the swaying boat, the chortling engine the only sound. Half a mile away were the pilot lights of two or three other boats.

Wes's father hissed through his teeth and climbed the wheelhouse ladder.

When they returned to the harbor, Wes couldn't get off the *Bayou Sweetheart* fast enough. He jumped on the dock and went toward his truck, his father following close behind.

"Where's the heart?" Wes's father said to his back.

Wes looked over his shoulder at his father like he was crazy but kept moving.

"Where's the heart, Wes? For the transplant? The heart transplant. Say what? You forgot it? Well, the little girl who needed the heart is dead now. Boy, you really fucked up this time."

Wes turned. Surprised, his father stopped dead in his tracks.

"I quit," Wes said.

"Quit?"

"Yeah. I'm through."

"You quit? Bullshit. You're fired. You get fired when you fuck up. You don't quit."

"I'm fired. Yeah. Whatever. I'm not doing this anymore."

"You won't be forgetting the ice for me anymore?"

Wes turned again and stalked toward his truck.

"Where you goin' to work?" Wes's father said to his back.

Wes said nothing.

"I don't think I saw any help-wanted ads that said they were looking for guys who forget ice."

Wes took the key ring from his pocket and unlocked his truck door. He could hear his father a few yards away from him, his steps slowing. Tentative, almost apologetic.

"Come on, we're wasting time," his father said, his voice softer now. "Let's get the ice and get back out there."

"I can't," Wes said, unable to look at his father.

"This is crazy. You're the one who forgot the ice and you're angry at me?"

Wes sat behind the wheel with the door still open and started the engine.

"Okay," his father said. "We'll see. I give you two days. Shit, a day. Bring the ice. You know what, forget it. I'll get the ice. Because you probably won't remember."

Wes closed his door.

His father stood there staring. "Good luck," he yelled. "You'll need it."

COSGROVE AND HANSON

Cosgrove was sitting on the backyard stoop of the widow's house during his lunch break when he sensed someone behind him. He turned and saw the widow glowering through the cracked door. Cosgrove had seen plenty of spiteful old women in his time, but this lady's eyes were radioactive with scorn. He felt reproached for an offense he never committed. An offense that had never even occurred to him. All the offenses ever committed by man.

"Afternoon," Cosgrove said. He stood and backed off the porch into the grass. He was supposed to keep his distance, one of Deputy Lemon's rules.

"Go to hell," the old woman said.

Cosgrove, speechless, looked down at the unbitten green apple in his palm.

"Who are you?" the woman asked.

"Community Service. Fixing your place up."

"Your name."

"Nate Cosgrove."

"I never authorized this."

"No need. The city did."

The woman's baleful gaze remained locked on his face. She seemed to

regard him as beneath her, a petty criminal. Cosgrove, for whatever reason, wanted to explain that he was a high school graduate. That he took
three semesters of community college before his mother got sick. If life
had gone a certain way, which it had not, he could have been a doctor or
a lawyer or a college professor. He could have been anyone he wanted, or
so he consoled himself.

One thing he was surer of every day: all you needed in life was a good
start.

"I don't like the looks of you," said the old woman, the bitter wrinkles
around her mouth tightening.

"Well, I'm sorry."

"Are you mouthing off?"

It was still spring but the weather was already hot. A pendant of
sweat hung from Cosgrove's brow and dripped into his eye. He blinked
against the sting of salt.

"Don't you wink at me," the woman said.

"I didn't," Cosgrove said.

The woman turned and slammed the door. Cosgrove heard the clock-
ing of the deadbolt, the rattle of the burglar chain. *You're a rapist,* the old
woman was trying to say with the sound. He cursed the lady and chucked
the apple into the blighted privet bushes and went back to painting the
backyard picket fence.

Twenty minutes later the old woman emerged again from the house.
Cosgrove ceased painting, the brush dripping butterscotch splats in the
grass. He watched the woman cross the lawn with exaggerated caution,
her steps slow and measured, as if she'd fall apart if she moved any faster.

When the woman finally reached Cosgrove, she fished in her robe
pocket. By the time Cosgrove realized what she had taken out, it was too
late to duck aside. She pressed the button of the little spray canister and
a lethal mist clouded around his eyes.

Pepper spray.

The pain was instant and surreal. Cosgrove wailed and collapsed to
his knees. The world was obliterated in an excruciating white haze. He

clenched his eyes and rubbed the lids, but the pain only spread like fire into his hands. He crawled blindly toward the house until his head knocked against something hard. He reached out. One of the crepe myrtles. He wrapped his arms around the trunk like a deckhand clinging to the mast of a tempest-tossed ship.

Cosgrove saw a figure approaching through the hot stinging fog. He cringed and blocked his face with his arm to fend off another attack from the old woman.

"What in blue fuck?" It was Hanson.

"Bitch pepper-sprayed me," Cosgrove sobbed, rubbing his eyes with the heels of his hands.

"Well, quit touchin' your face. Shit."

For a few minutes they sat in silence, Hanson lotus-style in the grass, Cosgrove slumped against the tree with tears and snot running down his face. In slow increments his vision began to return. The leaves of grass. The house with its scabrous clapboards and ugly purple shutters. Hanson's pensive face. The sunlight glinting off his belt buckle.

"Kill that bitch," Cosgrove said.

"You gonna tell Lemon?" Hanson asked.

"What you think?"

"Tell Lemon. See what happens. Crazy old bitch, she'll accuse you of rape. God knows what aspects. And guess who they'll believe first."

"Why you give a shit?" Cosgrove asked.

Hanson's eyes were grave with some secret knowledge. "I think you might not be seein' at an opportunity right in your face."

— — — — — — — —

Hanson's reasoning: The whole goddamn city was crooked anyway. Once the old lady died—this piece-of-shit old lady who, by the way, had pepper-sprayed Cosgrove for no reason—the junk would end up in a dump. Provided the city officials didn't hawk the stuff themselves and line their pockets with lagniappe, more than they were already stealing. Besides, what good was a bunch of old vinyl records going to do the woman? Antique rugs, silver candlestick holders, antebellum salt and pepper shakers? A 182-year-old obstetrics book?

Maybe Hanson was right. What had he done to deserve two hundred hours of community service during the ass-end of summer? How much would he have made shucking oysters all that time? And what had he done to deserve getting pepper-sprayed in the face?

A few days after the old woman pepper-sprayed Cosgrove, Hanson came up to him as he was finishing the last coat of paint on the backyard fence and asked him to check something out. Hanson's eyes were wide, almost gleeful, and Cosgrove was curious despite himself. He put his paintbrush down on the lid in the grass and followed Hanson to one of the living room windows. Through it he could see Ms. Prejean, slumped on the living room sofa in her terrycloth bathrobe. Her eyes were shut, her underjaw unhinged.

"Now get a load of this," Hanson said, grinning at Cosgrove. He slammed his palm on the glass, waited, slammed again. The woman remained inert as stone. "Lady must be on a thousand pain pills," said Hanson.

"Don't fuck with her," Cosgrove said.

"Go on to the front door and wait a sec."

"What's this about?"

"Jesus, man, trust me for once."

Pretending he was more put-upon than he was, Cosgrove went around the house to the front door and waited. Soon he heard someone on the other side unlocking the bolt and rattling the burglar chain. Expecting another attack from the old woman, he retreated a step and blocked his face with his forearm, but it was only Hanson, grinning.

"Come on. Check this shit out."

Cosgrove stood there.

"Dead to the world, man. I'm telling you."

Inside, the derelict Victorian was just as neglected as outside. Dim and dusty, redolent of old smells leeched into the blue rose wallpaper: cabbage and smoke, pesticide and moldering wood. Mouse leavings were scattered like jimmies along the baseboards. And there in the den was old Ms. Prejean snoring softly on the sofa, a television tray across her knees, its top scattered with pill bottles and wadded tissues like soiled corsages. A thread of drool gleamed on her white-whiskered chin.

"How'd you get in here?" Cosgrove whispered.

"Kitchen window. Above the sink. No latch. Opened it and slipped right through."

Now Hanson approached the old woman and stooped, raising his hands before her face. He clapped, a single sharp smack that echoed thinly through the house, but the woman didn't stir.

Cosgrove told Hanson they should get the fuck out.

Hanson picked one of the pill bottles off the tray and inspected the label. He shook out a pill, palmed it into his mouth, swallowed it dry. Then he put the bottle back in its place. "Come on, all it'll take is a second," he told Cosgrove. "You want to see this, trust me."

Upstairs, several rooms branched off from a dark hall, one of them a small office with a fixed ladder leading up to the attic. Hanson climbed the rungs and Cosgrove followed. Once Hanson was stooped in the crawlspace, Cosgrove poked his head up. Faint light fell through the small leaded-glass window, but it was bright enough to see the bounty spread before him.

There were antique porcelain dolls and mirrors, colored glass plates and perfume bottles, vintage quilts and cobalt crockery, Victorian chairs and curio cabinets. There were stained-glass lamps and old brass instruments in leather trunks with ornate hinges. Never mind the cardboard boxes stacked four and five tall, full of God knew what. The bounty seemed endless. You could have furnished three houses with what was up there. A sheik's palace.

In the next few days of their community service Cosgrove and Hanson carried antique end tables and Tiffany lamps and boxes of baronet china right out the front door. Like professional movers. Nothing out of the ordinary here, folks.

A buddy of Hanson's, a one-eyed waffle house cook named Greenfoot, came by each day with his flatbed truck and they filled the back. Greenfoot took the loot to a pawnshop in Mid-City and returned an hour or so later with fistfuls of cash. A hundred, sometimes two or three.

Twenty percent for Greenfoot, the rest for Cosgrove and Hanson.

Lagniappe.

One afternoon Greenfoot returned from the pawnshop with far more money than they expected. Five hundred. For the first time in years Cosgrove had a nest egg, two thousand dollars, squirreled away in his bank account. Not much compared with most guys his age, but a small fortune considering the pittance he'd arrived with in New Orleans. Cosgrove found himself in a near-exultant mood. And he felt healthier than he had in years. The work around the widow's house had hardened the soft places on his body, tightened his gut.

Maybe he'd made the right decision, staying in New Orleans.

"Got something else for you guys," Greenfoot told them with a sly one-sided grin.

Cosgrove and Hanson followed Greenfoot into the tin-roofed carport and Greenfoot took a ziplock bag from his pocket. Inside was a nugget of weed the size of a golf ball, pale green and shot through with tiny orange and purple hairs. The smell even through the sealed ziplock bag was overpowering, buzz-inducing.

"Smells like a mermaid's pussy," Hanson said, thumbs hooked on his canvas belt.

"Indeed," said Greenfoot.

They sat on the concrete in the shade, and Greenfoot took out a green glass pipe and packed a nugget of weed into the bowl.

"Lemon," Cosgrove said.

"You and Lemon," said Hanson. "What're you guys, fucking?"

Greenfoot held out the pipe to Cosgrove but Cosgrove shook his head. Greenfoot shrugged and gave the pipe to Hanson.

"Where's it from?" Cosgrove asked, expecting Greenfoot to say California. Afghanistan. Mars.

"Where'd I buy it?"

"Grown."

"Barataria," said Greenfoot, his bloodshot eye fixed on Cosgrove. The glass eye, lighter brown, was always aimed in the same direction, slightly upward.

Hanson was blowing out a cloud of pungent smoke. He shook his head slowly back and forth, his ponytail swinging rhythmically. Every time Cosgrove thought Hanson was finished exhaling, smoke kept billowing out like some kind of Cheech and Chong gag.

"The what?" Cosgrove asked. He'd never heard of the Barataria.

"The swamp. Barataria Bay. Can't be more than fifty miles from here. Homegrown shit, son."

The cicadas shrilled in the oak trees and cars rattled down Napoleon.

Greenfoot sucked in smoke, held it, exhaled.

"Shit is loud," said Hanson. He stared glassy-eyed and grinning at a rake propped in the corner of the carport. "Brain's screaming at me. Freestylin'."

"People grow weed in the swamp?" Cosgrove said.

"Indeed. Weed's a weed, son," said Greenfoot, professorial. "It'll grow anywhere. Just got to know what you're doing."

"Give me that pipe," Cosgrove said.

He took the pipe from Greenfoot and lit it. Drew in smoke, held it in his lungs, hacked it out.

"There you go, son," said Greenfoot.

"I got the lungs of an elephant," Hanson said. "I know every fuckin' aspect of the universe."

Soon Cosgrove's head felt like a helium balloon drifting into the ether.

"Look at this motherfucker," Hanson said, pointing his chin at Cosgrove. "He looks like a werewolf. Anybody ever tell you that? That fuckin' beard growing into your eyes. A werewolf. Fuckin' Sasquatch."

Hanson and Greenfoot laughed. Then Cosgrove laughed with them.

By God, he hadn't felt this good in years. Maybe what women often told him was right, that he suffered from minor depression, should be on some kind of medication. He sat in a mellow trance, a wrecked grin on his face. Was this what people meant by *peace*?

"Best pot I ever smoked is Cali Gold," Cosgrove heard Hanson saying.

"Sensi," said Greenfoot.

"White Owl," Hanson said.

"Lemon," Cosgrove said.

"Lemon," Hanson cackled. "Who the fuck is named Lemon?"

"Lemon and lime, partners in crime," said Greenfoot.

"Remember that Lemon-lime guy?" Hanson said. "The black Lemon-lime guy? In the commercials?"

"Fuck you talking about?" Greenfoot said.

"I feel like I've been staring at this rake for a thousand years," Hanson said.

They cackled together for about half a minute. Then they passed the smoke around again.

"Lemon-lime guy scared the fuck out of me when I was a kid," Hanson said, indignant. "The 7-Up guy, man."

"I need more of this shit," said Cosgrove.

"The black Lemon-lime guy with the deep aspect to his voice."

"It's the best," Greenfoot said.

"Dreadlocks growing out my ass," Hanson said.

"The Barataria?" Cosgrove said.

"Two brothers got an island of the shit," Greenfoot said. "That's what they say on the boards. I belong to a forum. Ganjadude-dot-com. Had a boat? Go looking for it myself."

"I need more," Cosgrove said.

"Alaskan Thunderfuck," Hanson said.

"Stuff's a cross between Southern Puke and A Thousand Starfishes," Greenfoot said. "Comes from a granddaddy plant thirty years old. Sticky as hell. They only use the top leaves. According to Ganjadude dot com."

"Ganjadude dot com," said Hanson. "Call me that from now on."

"Know anybody with a boat?" Cosgrove asked.

"Those guys, shit," Greenfoot said. "What I heard, they'll cut your arms off. Crazy shit."

"I'm gonna shit on Lemon's shoes," Hanson said.

"But a whole island," Cosgrove said.

"Ever been out in the Barataria?" Greenfoot said. "You'll never find that place. Might as well be Ponce de León looking for the Fountain of Youth."

GRIMES

Lindquist: Grimes suspected the man a retard, at very least a mental case. Grimes knew from anecdote and hearsay that half the Barataria considered Lindquist harmless. A village idiot. The other half thought there was something seriously wrong with the guy, digging up dead people's jewelry, brain-fried on pills.

Twice Grimes had visited Lindquist's house meaning to get his signature and twice he'd left empty-handed. The man would not stop talking. Talking and joking and babbling about pirate treasure. It was obvious to Grimes that he was in a bad way, that his wife was gone—the metal detector parts and maritime maps all around, the dust along the baseboards and ceiling fan blades, the scummy plates and glasses stacked on top of the end tables and television.

Now Grimes was at Lindquist's a third time, sitting at the paper-strewn dining room table while Lindquist told one of his dumb jokes. Something about a triple-dicked Weimaraner. Grimes wasn't listening. He was thinking of his mother. That morning in the parking lot of the Magnolia Café he'd glimpsed her through a window sitting alone in her booth. He turned quickly around and got back in his car, drove away with his heart slamming and his palms sweating.

"And then?" said Lindquist. "And then, the Weimaraner says to the nun, 'Dog's got to bury his bone.'" He slapped his knee and leaned over the table and exploded in shrill laughter.

Grimes smiled stiffly at Lindquist, teeth clenched like he was biting through rope.

"You hear the one about the fat lady in the Thanksgiving parade, Mr. Grimes?" Lindquist asked.

"Mr. Lindquist," Grimes said. "I've got an appointment coming up soon."

Lindquist made an exaggerated O with his mouth. The salt-and-pepper hair poking from under his yacht cap in greasy wings. He wore the same tent-like T-shirt and baggy camouflage pants as when Grimes saw him last. Maybe the man never changed his clothes, which wouldn't surprise Grimes, given the state of the house.

"Come back later then," Lindquist said. "I'll be around same time tomorrow."

"If you sign now, I won't have to bother you again."

"Oh, it's no bother. You okay."

Grimes straightened and took a breath. "My bosses?" He leaned forward, palms on the table. "Between us? They're kind of assholes."

Lindquist nodded. "Oh, yes sir. I know how that is, me." Then, pouching out his lips, "But I wouldn't want to rush into anything."

"Mr. Lindquist. Friend to friend? Look at that number in the third paragraph."

"Come back later. After I talk to my lawyer."

"You've got a lawyer?"

"Well, I gotta find one."

Grimes took a deep breath. "Mind if I ask you a personal question, Mr. Lindquist?"

Lindquist flicked his hand: go right ahead.

"Where's your arm?"

Grimes asked because he already knew the answer. A few days ago, at Magnolia Café, he'd overheard about Lindquist's stolen arm. Two oil rig workers were joking about it at the counter. "Thing's probably getting more pussy than Lindquist ever did," one of them said.

Lindquist shook his head somberly. "Stolen," he said.

"You're kidding."

Lindquist shook his head again.

"I have a sister. Regina. Without a leg. Lost it in a water-skiing accident on Lake Heron. If some guy stole her leg? I don't know what I'd do. Probably kill the guy."

Grimes had no siblings. Sometimes he wondered if he would have turned out any differently if he had a brother or sister.

"What happened?" Lindquist asked.

"Right into a buoy. Bam. Good-bye leg. Spring break."

"Well, hell. She live around here? One leg don't bother me."

Grimes couldn't tell if Lindquist was joking. "We'd like to replace that arm," he said. "The company and me."

"That arm, I don't know. Irreplaceable."

"We'll buy you a better one."

"Thirty-thousand-dollar arm."

A thirty-thousand-dollar arm. Grimes had never heard of such a thing. On top of everything else, Lindquist was an extortionist. "I'll see what I can arrange," Grimes said.

"It was the only one I was ever comfortable with. Others made me itch or feel funny."

"If you sign this, we'll get you a new one. A better one."

"I want one exactly like the old."

"Of course," said Grimes, thinking, *Kill this motherfucker.*

The Toup house was within shouting distance of the harbor, a mint-green prefab sitting on two-story stilts far back on a pine-crowded tract of land. White shutters and trim, a front yard full of gargantuan banana trees, a wrought iron bench before an adobe hearth. One of the brothers, huge-shouldered in a Guy Harvey T-shirt, stood on the welcome mat as Grimes mounted the stairs. He visored his eyes against the ten o'clock sun and listened with a put-on expression while Grimes stated his business.

Grimes was surprised when the man gestured him into the house. He expected more resistance given the rumors about the brothers he'd heard.

In the den the other brother sat in a leather armchair eating a bowl of cornflakes. He scowled at Grimes, a fat drop of milk hanging from his bottom lip, then looked at his brother for an explanation.

The first twin told the other that Grimes was from the oil company, that he'd come to offer a settlement.

They sat at the dining room table and Grimes rolled up his shirt-sleeves three times apiece like a stumping politician. He snapped open his satchel and withdrew an inch-thick sheaf of papers.

The surly brother's eyes flared in disbelief. "Great goddamn," he said. "Paperwork up the ass. Get rid of some and then a motherfucker drops off twice as much five minutes later."

Grimes did not take kindly to being called a motherfucker, especially by a tattooed coon-ass. But he knew saying anything wouldn't work in his favor. Swampfucks, thinking they were tough. He'd like to see them in New York. In Boston or Chicago. They wouldn't survive a day without getting fucked a thousand different ways.

"Well, sit," the surly brother told Grimes.

The first twin began to thumb through the papers. He'd finish one page and then hand it to his brother and then move on to the next.

"Kill you guys to write plain English?" said the brother with the tattoos. A spiderweb. A trident. A Great White shark.

"Hey, I don't write them," said Grimes. "I were the one to write it, I'd say this is a good deal. Sign here. Short and sweet."

The brothers kept reading, the only sounds the ticking of the kitchen wall clock, the sigh of the air-conditioning. Grimes looked around. The house was clean and well lit and airy, solidly middle-class. The furniture was heavy and dark, cherrywood and African mahogany, not the cheap pressed-wood stuff Grimes saw in living rooms and kitchens throughout the Barataria. Hell, there were even African violets on the windowsill, a ficus tree in the corner.

Grimes watched the brothers. Uncanny, the resemblance. "I've got a twin brother," he said.

"Yeah?" said the first twin.

"Pretty much the end of the story," he said.

"We some kind of soul mates 'cause you got a twin?" said the second.

Grimes cleared his throat. Stood and hitched his pants. "Use your pisser?" he asked.

"Shit?" said the tattooed brother.

Grimes shook his head.

"Down the hall. Second on the right. Don't even think about taking a shit."

In the hallway bathroom Grimes cursed the brother while he pissed. Midstream he took the toothbrush from the porcelain holder next to the sink and whizzed on the bristles and then stuck the toothbrush back in its hole.

On the way back to the den Grimes passed an open bedroom door and glimpsed something that made him pause. A prosthetic arm sticking hand-up out of a widemouthed vase or umbrella stand in the corner.

I'll be damned, Grimes thought.

When Grimes returned, the tattooed brother was standing at the table and the paperwork was ripped to shreds, confetti strewn on the floor. The other brother, looking uneasy and embarrassed, was in the kitchen taking plates out of a dishwasher.

"That the kind of money you're offering everyone?" the tattooed brother asked.

Grimes took his satchel and shouldered it. "Appreciate your time," he said.

"Get the fuck out of here," the tattooed brother said.

Grimes descended the steps swiftly, a chill at the base of his neck like it was in the crosshairs of a rifle scope.

- - - - - - - -

The next day at dusk Grimes found Lindquist at the harbor and told him he had some important news to share.

Lindquist hobbled down the gangplank onto the rickety pier. Eyebrow cocked, he flicked the head of his Pez dispenser and popped a pill in his mouth and mashed it between his molars.

"Your arm," said Grimes.

Lindquist's bloodshot eyes bulged. "You find it?"

"Not sure if I'm at liberty to disclose. It's a sensitive issue."

Lindquist stepped beseechingly toward Grimes. "Mister," he said, "you know how screwed I am without that arm?"

Grimes was quiet.

"I mean, look at this damn thing," Lindquist said, jigging his hook arm.

They stood in the sweltering twilight next to Lindquist's boat. Even the *Jean Lafitte* looked crazy to Grimes, its pureed pea green, its varnished wood warped and flaking.

"Let's just say I'm pretty sure I found your arm," Grimes told Lindquist. "But I have to be discreet."

"We ain't friends?"

This took Grimes aback. He'd been called all manner of things over the past several weeks, but friend was far away from any of them. "Sure we are," said Grimes.

"Tell me," Lindquist said.

Far out in the bay the red and green pilot lights of shrimp boats and oyster luggers glimmered. Most of them by now were working on behalf of the oil company as "Vessels of Opportunity."

"I don't want to start any trouble. For you, for me."

"There won't be no trouble."

Mosquitoes hummed around them.

"Well, if we're friends," Grimes said, swatting, "let's do each other both a favor."

Lindquist pondered this. Then he said, "You mean those papers?"

Grimes nodded.

"Well, hell. Mister, I'll sign those papers. Give me them. Sign those papers in my blood, me."

"Promise you won't say how you learned," said Grimes.

"Swear on my life."

"Might lead to a lot of trouble."

"Swear to God." Lindquist placed his hand flat on an invisible Bible.

"Well," Grimes said, "let's get this done."

They walked the wobbly gangplank onto the *Jean Lafitte*. Grimes fished the papers out of his satchel and sat them on a wooden cutting board and handed his Mont Blanc pen to Lindquist. Lindquist signed quickly and gave the pen back.

"Those Toup twins," Grimes said.

Lindquist looked stunned. Disbelieving.

"I saw it in their house," Grimes said. "Sticking out of a vase. A spittoon or something. Like it was some kind of sick joke."

Lindquist, already scheming, shunted his eyes back and forth.

"You promised," Grimes said. "You didn't hear it from me."

THE TOUP BROTHERS

It was dusk, bats flitting like flecks of ash above the massed trees, when through the front window the Toup twins saw Lindquist coming up the porch steps. Clutching single-handed onto the rail, he hoisted himself slowly, in place of his missing prosthetic an ill-fitting hook arm too small for his body. By the time Lindquist reached the raised porch Reginald and Victor were already waiting outside.

"I'm gonna ask you fellas right out," Lindquist said. His face was red and shiny with sweat and his breathing was rough. "You seen my arm?"

The brothers glanced at each other.

"Matter of fact I have," said Victor.

Lindquist waited, mouth slack, eyes darting. He wore an oversized white T-shirt, a captain's cap, camouflage cargo pants.

"I saw it drinking at Sully's," Victor said. "Grabbing ass. Dancing around. Raising hell."

The brothers laughed the same neighing horsey laughter.

Blood shot into Lindquist's face. "I'll call Villanova if I have to," he said.

The brothers stopped laughing.

"You threatening us?" Reginald said.

"I just want my arm. Give me my arm."

Victor crossed his arms over his chest. "You still going in the bayou?"

"That's government water."

"Ours."

"I ain't poaching. If that's what you think."

"What're you doing out there?" Reginald asked.

Lindquist kept quiet, the muscles in his face twitching.

"What're you doing out there, Lindquist?" Reginald asked again.

"Treasure hunting."

The brothers neighed.

"Holy shit," Victor said. "You got any idea how crazy you are?"

"Ain't none your business."

"Every bit my business," said Victor.

"Well, hell. I find anything, I'll give you some."

"There isn't shit out there," Reginald said.

"That's a thirty-thousand-dollar arm," said Lindquist.

"Thirty thousand dollars, my ass," Victor said. "What's it, Gucci?"

"Screw you guys," Lindquist said. He turned and began to waddle down the steps like a geriatric, again clutching the rail one-handed.

"Got any jokes for us, Lindquist?" Victor said to his back. "Tell us a joke."

- - - - - - - - -

Yes, Reginald and Victor had taken the arm. At first they considered keeping the arm as leverage, possibly returning it if Lindquist forswore searching further in the Barataria. But then that nosy prick from the oil company saw the prosthetic. The look on his face when he returned from the bathroom to the den, no doubt about it. And a few hours later when Lindquist showed up demanding his arm and making threats about Villanova, they knew what had to be done. That night when they boated into the Barataria, Victor tossed the prosthetic into the bay where no one would ever find it.

Next morning there was a knock on the door and Reginald looked out the peephole and saw Sheriff Villanova standing on the porch with his hat in his hands, his gourd-shaped face flushed from the heat.

"Got a minute?" he asked when Reginald answered the door. Reginald knew from the grave steadiness of his eyes that he'd come about Lindquist. Reginald always suspected that Villanova knew exactly what he and his brother were up to in the Barataria, just as he suspected Villanova didn't much care as long as it wasn't meth or gun-related. As long as it didn't get him into any trouble. Surprising, how a few thousand dollars dropped in the proverbial coffer could loosen a man's mores. Especially if the man had a nasty video poker habit and a mistress in New Orleans.

Reginald led the sheriff inside to the dining room table, where Victor was playing a game on his cell phone. "Heya, Sheriff," he said, putting down his cell phone and standing. He shook Villanova's hand and sat back with his arms folded across his chest.

"Coffee?" Reginald said.

Villanova shook his head and sat, leaned back with his hat balanced on his knee and his legs in chocolate ostrich-skinned boots crossed. With his thumb and forefinger he stroked his pencil mustache. "You two know I been okay to you."

"Sure," said Reginald, sitting.

"And you been okay to me."

"Hope."

"So, let's have right out with this."

The twin brothers waited.

"Lindquist," Villanova said.

"Yeah?" said Reginald.

"Know him?"

"Sure," Victor said.

"Somebody's messing with him," Villanova said.

"Us, you think?" said Reginald.

Villanova hesitated a judicious beat, peered about. Through the pristine windows was the shimmering jade of morning, the stout pines and oaks. The house was barren and tidy, African violets on the shelves and sills.

"No, I don't," Villanova said, "but he thinks."

"Guy's a basket case," Victor said.

"You know who he is," Villanova said.

"Yeah," Victor said. "One-armed asshole. With the metal detector."

"You guys steal his arm?" Villanova asked.

Victor brayed laughter.

"I don't even know what to say," Reginald said.

Villanova looked down at the table with his eyebrows raised. "It's crazy, I know. But he thinks you two had something to do with it."

"Guy's a pill head," Victor said.

"How you know that?" Villanova asked.

"Everybody knows," said Victor.

"Stole his arm?" Reginald said incredulously.

"Yeah," Victor said. "Why'd we want to mess with a cripple?"

"Maybe he was metal detecting in the wrong place."

"That's what he does," Victor said. "Digs holes in all the wrong places."

Villanova mulled this over.

"He's pissed off lots of people with that metal detector," Reginald said. "Especially after the storm."

Villanova shunted his eyes back and forth between the brothers. "Maybe you're right," he allowed, "but I doubt they'd steal the guy's arm."

"We didn't either," Reginald said.

"Figured as much," Villanova said, and stood. One-handed, he jammed his hat down on his head. "Favor, though? Best don't even look at him the wrong way. Guy's a little unhinged."

LINDQUIST

Shrimping with one arm was harder than Lindquist recalled.

When Dixon didn't show up that afternoon Lindquist sailed alone on the *Jean Lafitte* into the Barataria. Every hour proved a greater farce than the last. Lindquist would lower the booms, scramble up the wheelhouse ladder, steer the boat, scramble down the ladder, lift the booms. Then he'd haul the catch from the nets to the sorting box.

Sorting: that was the hardest part of all. Picking one-handed through the teeming hill of sea life, blinking the sting of sweat from his eyes. The catfish with their whipping whisker-barbs, the sting-a-rees with their switching razor-tails. Within minutes his fingers were raw and bloody and his hand felt like a block of wood. All for a measly twenty or thirty pounds of shrimp, hardly enough to pay for the diesel. Hardly enough left over for a pack of gum.

Then he'd do it all over again like a Keystone Cop. Down with the booms, up the ladder, down the ladder, up with the booms.

Every so often he looked at the sky imploringly, half hoping that lightning would strike him dead and put him out of his misery. If he stopped to think how tired he was he'd probably collapse. The endless sweatbox nights and afternoons. His shirt was glued with sweat to his back, and his legs and arm ached and his eyes stung with salt and fatigue.

Worse, this hellish heat would not abate until October at the earliest. If he was lucky.

Pills: he lost count of how many pills he took. They seemed to work less and less these days. It took two to feel only half as good as he used to feel after taking one.

His second day alone in the Barataria he was sorting through his first haul when a giant blue crab seized the forefinger of his hand. Even through the glove he felt the angry bite of its claw. He flapped his hand and it clung onto his finger and he flapped his hand more and still it clung on. He chopped his arm down and slammed the crab against the gunwale and then he jackknifed his arm. The crab went flipping wildly into the water.

A tranquil rage possessed Lindquist. There was something liberating, almost soothing, about surrendering to the fact you were fucked.

Carrying a purple velvet Crown Royal bag full of trinket jewelry, Lindquist entered Trader John's general store. He kept a dwindling cache in case of emergencies when he needed money for pills, for diesel, for bills. The original owner of the shop, John Theriot, was long dead, the place now run by his wife. Lindquist nodded hello at the old woman and started for the counter but saw a young couple browsing the jewelry display. He stuffed the bag into his camouflage cargo pants and beelined to the back of the store, where he stopped in front of the used tools hanging from the pegboard wall. He stood in the same spot with his hands clasped behind his back, gazing up at a sod cutter as if it were a Picasso.

When the couple left and Lindquist heard the little bell chime above the door, he came up to the counter. He removed the bag from his pocket and untied the cinch strings and spilled a cache of jewelry on the counter. "Wanting to sell all this," Lindquist said. "One price for all."

Watches, necklaces, rings, most of it cheap gold-plated stuff, fair trinkets you won for tossing a Ping-Pong ball into a goldfish bowl. But amid the junk were a few pieces that looked worthwhile, perhaps even valuable.

Mrs. Theriot's narrow nose flared as she studied the jewelry. Lindquist knew that the woman disliked him, considered him no more principled than a looter. The bones of her face were hard and dour, out of keeping with her too-bright button-down pineapple shirt. While she picked among the rings and necklaces he studied the 2010–2011 New Orleans Saints schedule hung on the wall behind the counter. The season opener, against the Vikings, was coming up in early September.

"Where'd you find all this?" Mrs. Theriot finally asked.

Lindquist grinned a coy grin. "Oh, I can't tell you that now."

"This might be somebody's, I mean."

His grin quickly fell. "You saying I stole it?"

"Nobody's saying that."

"Never stolen a thing in my life, me. I ain't no thief."

"Nobody's saying you're a thief either."

Now Lindquist's face was flushed and his mouth was twitching.

"Lots of stuff went missing after the storm," said Mrs. Theriot. "Lots of stuff folks are still looking for."

Lindquist sighed through his nose and glanced at the floor. He leaned in closer and drummed his fingers on the glass, hatching some scheme in his head. "Tell you what. They come in and recognize it before it's sold, they can have it."

The woman shook her head. "Not sure if that's a good idea either."

"How come?"

"Well, people are going to line up straight to Mississippi claiming things are theirs that aren't."

"Hell, I'm not saying put a sign up saying free jewelry."

The woman waited.

Lindquist said, "If somebody looks at the stuff funny, then you know something's up and maybe he's telling the truth."

Mrs. Theriot picked through the pile on the counter. "Most of it's worthless," she said.

Lindquist pointed. "Look at that watch. Somebody's gonna want that watch. And that ring. Look. Solid gold. Diamond's not big, but it's real. Solid gold around it."

"I'll give you one hundred dollars for all of it right now."

Lindquist looked quickly away and then quickly back, a kind of vaude-ville double-take. "One hundred dollars," he said. "Come on now."

"One hundred dollars."

"Well, hell. That watch right there alone is worth a hundred."

"I'll be lucky to sell it for half that. People aren't buying a lot of jew-elry these days. They're not buying a whole lot of anything."

"Everybody needs a watch."

"If I make more than a hundred dollars," Mrs. Theriot said, "we split the profit fifty-fifty. This stuff, we'd be lucky, though."

Next morning a kid was sitting atop his cooler on the deck in front of the *Jean Lafitte*. Black-haired with gray already peppering the sides, pale green eyes lighter than his dark skin. He asked Lindquist if he was the captain looking for deckhands.

Lindquist asked Wes how old he was and Wes said seventeen, eighteen very soon.

"Look a little small," Lindquist said. "Can you work a winch?"

"Yessir. I can work everything on a shrimp boat."

"You only seventeen but you got all that gray in your hair?"

Wes shrugged. "Yessir."

Lindquist studied Wes. "I seen you around."

"Lived here my whole life so I guess you probably have."

"Yeah, I seen you," Lindquist said. He nodded vaguely as if trying to recollect where. Something clicked behind his eyes. "Monsieur's several days back."

"I was there. Yessir."

"Trench's kid, ain't you?"

Wes nodded.

"What's wrong with his boat?"

"Nothing."

"How come you two not working together is what I mean."

Wes plunged hands in his pockets and kept silent.

"Oh boy, it's like that now, huh?"

Wes shrugged.

"He gonna be pissed?"

"At me maybe. Not you."

"I don't need any more motherfuckers pissed at me. I got enough of those to last a lifetime."

"I guarantee, sir."

"You on drugs?"

"No sir," he said.

"Blaze?" Lindquist asked.

"Do what?"

"Do you blaze?"

"I don't know what you mean."

"Smoke reefer."

"No, none of that."

"You crazy?"

"No sir."

"Can you work a wench?"

"Yeah. Yes sir."

"You good at lifting trawls?"

"Yessir."

"You ever been to Sing Sing?"

"Where, sir?"

"Congratufuckinglations," Lindquist said. "You're hired."

WES TRENCH

The late afternoon was warm and cloudless, the sun a fat shivering coin of pewter, cicadas shrieking in the live oaks. Wes watched the bayou slide past, its sluggish currents pulsing with life. Who knew what gargantuan oddity lurked beneath. Wes imagined a catfish the size of a sofa, a turtle the size of a dune buggy. That was one of the things he still loved about the bayou. Its mystery.

They passed a chenier, above its tree line a circling coterie of buzzards. A carrion stench hung in the air. Something dead, a deer or a possum, was in the woods. Even after they passed the island the gray aftertaste lingered in Wes's mouth like poison.

"Let one go?" Lindquist called down from the wheelhouse.

Wes looked up, visoring his eyes with his hand. "Say what now?"

"You let one rip?"

"We just passed something."

"You passed something?"

"Something's dead in those woods."

"You uptight."

Wes didn't know what to say. "I don't think so," he said.

"You uptight. All that gray on your head. You uptight."

Wes went back to untangling the nets. They were the sorriest he'd ever seen, full of holes and clumsy patches. He supposed his nets would be in crappy shape too if he were missing an arm.

After a minute something struck Wes on the back of the head. Hard, like a rock. He grabbed his skull and whirled around and glared.

Lindquist grinned down from the wheelhouse.

"You throw something?" Wes asked.

Lindquist was laughing. "On the deck," he said. "By your foot."

Wes looked down at the tinfoiled roll of mints and picked them up.

"Suck a few of those," Lindquist said. "Get that nastiness out of your head."

Wes opened the roll with his thumbnail and popped a mint into his mouth. He was about to toss the mints back up when Lindquist said, "Keep them. I got plenty, me."

Wes lowered the nets and let the water pass. Twenty minutes later he winched up the trawls and heaped the hauls on the sorting table. Then Lindquist came down the wheelhouse ladder and they put on gloves and together picked through the squirming heap of sea life.

"Look at these pissant shrimp," Lindquist said.

Lindquist looked at Wes as though expecting him to argue otherwise. He grabbed a baby gaspergou and underhanded it off the boat. It flipped its tail and smacked the water.

"Knock knock," Lindquist said.

"This a joke?" Wes asked.

"Yeah, a knock-knock."

"Who's there?"

"Little Boy Blue."

"Little Boy Blue Who?"

"Michael Jackson."

Wes whistled a small laugh through his nose to make Lindquist think he was amused.

At sunup the shrimp were unloaded and weighed at Monsieur Montegut's and then Lindquist piloted the boat back to the marina. In the parking lot Lindquist counted out Wes's share and handed it to him.

Wes thanked Lindquist and put the money in his pocket without counting it.

"You don't wanna count it?" Lindquist said.

"I trust you."

"You'll be here sundown?"

"If you want me," Wes said.

"Well, hell. Why wouldn't I? You a good worker."

COSGROVE AND HANSON

If Lemon ever suspected any devilment on their part, he didn't show it. "Looking good, gentlemen," he'd say, inspecting their work, or lack thereof, at the end of the day. "Looking real, real good, real good," he drawled through his smirk. Somehow you knew he was fucking with you, knew he didn't care if you were fucking with him. He grinned and thwacked their backs with his beefy hand. He seemed high or drunk or both. Cosgrove wouldn't have been surprised. His front teeth looked purple, wine-stained, and Cosgrove could have sworn he caught some astringent medicinal odor, maybe spermicide or sex lubricant, wafting off him.

Hanson's last day of community service was in late August. Cosgrove's own was just a week or so off. For old times' sake, Hanson wanted to loot the widow's attic one last time.

"I think we've already pressed our luck," Cosgrove said.

"Pressed? Like she pressed that button and blasted that shit in your face?"

That's all the convincing it took. Just like old times, Hanson snuck through the kitchen window and let Cosgrove through the front door. While they were climbing the stairs they heard the old woman's voice, frail and just-woken, from the living room.

"Turkey's in the oven," she said.

Cosgrove stopped on the stairs. Then Hanson stopped. Cosgrove looked over his shoulder: what the fuck?

"Boys?" the old widow said. "Turkey's almost done."

"No sweat," Hanson called back.

"The fuck you doing?" Cosgrove whispered.

"Lady doesn't know her ass from a hand grenade."

"You boys put on the game if you want."

"Yeah, good game. Watching it."

From a far-flung room of the house a grandfather clock chimed one.

"Turkey good?" asked the woman.

"Turkey's delicious, ma'am."

"You boys go upstairs and play until dinner's done."

"Let's get out of here," Cosgrove said to Hanson.

"A minute," Hanson said.

They ascended the pull-down stairs into the sweltering attic and started rummaging through cardboard boxes. At first Cosgrove didn't find much. Photographs and daguerreotypes. Bronzed baby shoes. Corsages stuck inside scrapbooks. Then he came across an old brass-hinged leather portmanteau. Inside he found old letters written in calligraphy on parchment: some in French, others in Spanish, only a few in English. At the bottom of the trunk were more recent envelopes, return and forwarding addresses typewritten, ten- and fifteen-cent stamps, postmarks from the United States: Louisiana and Mississippi and Texas.

Cosgrove quickly perused the letters. Several were from the seventies and eighties, from doctors and professors with Creole-sounding names who claimed to be members of "The Lafitte Study Group." After 1994, they started referring to themselves as part of "The Lafitte Society." The letters were common in theme: addressed to Esther Prejean, wanting to know about her mother's side of the family, the Boudreaux. Was Esther's maiden name Boudreaux, and did she have any relation to Marie Boudreaux, née Butte, née Breaux, who received settlement checks from the Lafitte estate in Galveston? If so, she might be a living part of the fabled Lafitte lineage, a sixth- or seventh-generation member of the famous privateer's genealogy and an invaluable part of their historical research.

So on and so forth.

As far as Cosgrove could tell, the letters went unanswered. The widow, it seemed, had no interest in entertaining genealogical queries. Maybe she didn't know the answers. Or maybe she wanted to keep certain mysteries to herself. Whatever the reason for her silence, it would remain unknown, the woman was so far gone now. So far gone she didn't notice strangers ransacking her attic for days on end.

"You find anything?" Hanson asked.

"You were right," Cosgrove said, wiping his dusty hands on his ragged jeans. "The old lady, coming from pirates."

Hanson grinned a monkey grin. "Told you, motherfucker."

Cosgrove grunted.

"Find anything good?"

"Just letters."

Hanson stood, ducking so he wouldn't hit his head on the low slope of the ceiling. It was sweltering in the attic and his face was ruddy, his shirt stuck with sweat to his torso. "Maybe you'll believe me next time," he said. Then he jerked his head. "About having a heat stroke. Let's get out of this dump."

Before Lemon picked them up that afternoon they were lounging in the shade of the front porch taking turns sipping from Hanson's plastic hip flask of tequila.

"You feel bad at all?" Hanson asked. "All the stealing we done?"

Cosgrove shrugged. "A little."

"Bitch pepper-sprayed you."

"Yeah, I keep reminding myself."

They were silent for a minute.

"What you gonna do now?" Cosgrove asked.

"Fuck knows," Hanson said. "You?"

"Oysters. Same shit."

Hanson reached into his shirt pocket and pulled out a joint and handed it to Cosgrove. "Goin' away present," he said. "Shit you liked so much."

Cosgrove took the joint. "Sure appreciate it."

"Maybe I'll see you."

"Yeah, maybe."

- - - - - - - - -

In early September Cosgrove completed his community service sentence and soon afterward was laid off from Captain Larry's Oyster House. Tourists were no longer buying Gulf Coast seafood. The restaurant, a neighborhood tradition for forty-five years, would close its doors in a week.

Cosgrove was perusing the job section in the *Times-Picayune* when he came across an oil-spill-related help-wanted ad. No references or background check required, immediate hire for American citizens of age. With one condition: "Must love birds!" the ad said.

Did Cosgrove love birds? Hell yes for fifteen dollars an hour.

He signed up in front of the public library on Tulane and that afternoon was bussed with thirty-odd volunteers to Jeanette, a bayou town forty-five minutes outside of New Orleans. An encampment had been built within shouting distance of the bayou: Quonset huts and double-wide trailers, port-a-potties and a low-slung mess hall, an impromptu barracks with rows of cots inside.

Cosgrove stepped off the bus and wandered the encampment, a black duffel bag containing almost everything he owned in the world hung over his shoulder. Volunteers in plainclothes milled about, some of them wizened vagabonds like himself, others moneyed-looking boys and girls—even their suntans looked rich, their teeth—here no doubt to fulfill another good deed they could tick off in their college application letters.

Television reporters stood here and there in front of cameras, imparting grave news about the oil spill. A young platinum-haired journalist in a blue silk blouse stopped Cosgrove and asked him what he thought about the catastrophe.

Cosgrove stood before the camera like a spooked animal.

"Think the situation's getting better?" the woman asked.

"I don't know," he said. "I just got here."

"Is it as bad as you thought it would be?" the woman asked in a stiff clip.

Cosgrove shifted his weight from one foot to the other. "Well," he said, crossing his arms. "It's pretty bad."

The woman waited, the microphone in Cosgrove's face like a rattlesnake.

"God-awful," Cosgrove said.

"Well, good luck to you," the woman told him. "We thank you for the important work you're doing."

Cosgrove nodded.

The woman turned away, searching for the next person to accost. As Cosgrove walked off, the woman's words lingered with him. No one had ever told him that his work was important or thanked him for any job he did. The approbation, though misdirected, filled him with a warm buzz.

— — — — — — — —

There was a certain satisfaction in the work, Cosgrove had to admit. Five days a week at eight in the morning he reported for duty in a hangar-like cleaning facility, where large plastic tubs like baby baths were rowed side by side along narrow tables. In each of the tubs was an oil-covered bird: a pelican or egret or heron. Volunteers in smocks and gloves sprayed down the birds and swabbed the black gunk from their wings. They shampooed them with dish detergent and rinsed their feathers with a nozzled hose and then they passed the bird on to the next tub, where the process was repeated. At the final cleaning station they were rinsed and toweled dry and then they were carried outside to the aviary, where they remained under observation until deemed healthy enough for release. Finally, if they were lucky, they were flown to Florida and set free in Tampa Bay.

The first bird Cosgrove cleaned, a pelican, keened like a tortured child and wriggled from his grasp. Two other cleaners, crew-cut lesbians in overalls and brogans, came over and helped him pin down the bird.

Its eyes were swollen with clotted oil, its feathers ragged with grease.

Anger knotted in Cosgrove's throat. The bird would live only a day or two longer if it was lucky. Or cursed.

Cosgrove rested a hand on the nape of the bird's neck and dunked it baptismally under the water. Then he sprayed its feathers, and its wings began showing through the clots of oil.

"There you go," said one of the women, "you're a natural."

Cosgrove, surprised to find himself blushing, thanked the pair.

- - - - - - - -

Cosgrove was into his second week at the sanctuary when he heard someone coughing at a table behind him. The cough sounded like "Cos-grove! Cos-grove!" Cosgrove, cleaning the oil off a spoonbill's wing, turned and spotted Hanson staring craftily across the room. Hanson put down the nozzle of his hose and wiped his hands on the front of his baggy jean shorts and ambled over, a rooster fish swagger out of proportion to his size. His gigantic rodeo belt buckle caught the light.

"You believe in fate, Cosgrove?" Hanson asked.

"Unfuckingbelievable."

"Thought you'd never see me again."

"What're you, stalking me?" Cosgrove joked.

They fist-bumped. Cosgrove saw that the right side of Hanson's face was blotched with a fading green-and-purple bruise. He asked Hanson what happened.

"At the bar some dude catches me lookin' wrong at his lady," Hanson said, hanging one thumb over his canvas belt. "Hell, I didn't know she had a man. Wouldn't've made the gesture I did. Tried apologizing, but the guy told me to get down on my hands and knees and beg. Some shit-for-brains Jackson, Mississippi, son-bitch. I told him, 'Bitch, John Henry Hanson never got on his knees for no-goddamn-body.' Then I says something about his mother and he punched me good."

Cosgrove whistled through his teeth.

"Oh, I got in some good licks. Don't you fuckin' doubt it." He nodded, eyes bulging. Then, as if Cosgrove had asked, "Saw an ad in the paper. Cleaning birds for fifteen an hour. No drug tests or other aspects. Fuck yeah."

For a few minutes they only worked, Hanson pinning the spoonbill down, Cosgrove washing the oil from its neck feathers with the hose. After a while Cosgrove lifted the bird and brought it to the next station. Then he dumped the gunky water from the tub and filled it with fresh water from the hose. Finally he went to the neighboring station and took a pelican from the rubber-aproned man working there.

Hanson held the pelican down as Cosgrove sprayed.

"Got any of that shit?" Cosgrove whispered.

Hanson had to tip his head back to look him in the eyes. "Wish. You?"

Cosgrove shook his head.

"Kind of bird is this?" Hanson asked.

Cosgrove looked at Hanson for a second before answering. "A pelican, man."

"Pelican my ass," Hanson said. He looked over at one of the volunteer veterinarians three tubs down. "Hey, doc. Kind of bird is this?"

"Pelican," the doctor said.

"Looks like a piece-of-shit bird to me."

"What's your name?"

"John Henry Hanson, sir."

"Do your work, Hanson," the doctor said.

Hanson lowered his voice. "Everybody's making such a big deal about these birds," he said. "They cure cancer? They good at blowjobs?"

"It's ecology," Cosgrove said.

"You're a man of few words, Sasquatch. Anybody ever tell you that?"

Cosgrove grunted and for a while they worked in silence.

"Hey, remember that island Greenfoot was talking about?" Hanson said. "Right around the bend, ain't it?"

GRIMES

The problem with these coon-ass swamp people, Grimes thought: they were too dumb to see an opportunity when you dropped it right in their laps. Year after year they tried to eke out a livelihood in the bayou—doggedly, stubbornly, willfully blind to reality—and every year it was more like squeezing blood out of stone.

Bob Trench. This man was particularly stubborn. Worse, perhaps, than the Lindquist lunatic.

Today, his third visit to Bob Trench's house, Grimes knocked on the front door and when there was no answer he went through the side yard toward the back. Enormous brown grasshoppers took wing, clattering like broken party favors. Trench stood in the backyard under a trawling net stretched like a gigantic spiderweb between two persimmon trees. Untangling a knot, he looked up at Grimes. His thick fingers, working with insectoid agility, didn't slow. "Jesus," he said.

"Afternoon, Mr. Trench," said Grimes.

Grimes put his hands on his hips and surveyed the yard. Mown grass, a trimmed chinaberry tree, a Weber grill with a wrought-iron table and some chairs around it. And on the far side of the yard, just before the lawn ceded to brush, was a boat-shaped hulk under a rain-puddled tarp.

"Beautiful place you got," said Grimes, nodding in appreciation.

Trench said nothing. Cicadas droned in the far-off pines.

"Real beautiful yard. Hope I have a place like this someday. Peaceful."

"This is trespassing. And harassment."

Ignoring the remark, Grimes said, "Place looks older than the rest around here. Solid." He stepped out of the sun into the persimmon shade. Just a fraction cooler. His white fitted shirt was sopping and stuck to his back and he could smell the onion ripeness of his underarms. He knew all too goddamn well the heat would last well into September, maybe mid-October.

"Only had a foot of water," Trench said without looking up.

"Yeah?" Grimes said, not caring, but trying to seem like he did. Numbers were running through his head, how many people had signed, how many people still needed to. He could visit ten more houses today if he worked quickly enough.

"When I was standing on the roof," said Trench.

Grimes laughed an exaggerated openmouthed laugh. Maybe he was making a little leeway with the bastard. Finally.

Trench's mouth kept tight as he moved onto another knot. "Twelve foot of water," he said. "Had to rebuild it."

Grimes raised his eyebrows.

"You ever hear of the Road Home program?"

"No," Grimes said.

"One of those government programs meant to help people after the storm," Trench said. "Complete bullshit. Sent me a letter saying may we please offer you zero-point-zero-zero. May we please offer you nothing. A form note. Because I had insurance. Which covered a third of my losses."

"Guess I'd be pissed too," said Grimes, swatting away a horsefly. He wondered if telling Trench that he was Chris Grimes's son would soften the man's attitude. Probably. And probably this was a card best played later.

"Guess?" said Trench. He patted the front pocket of his orange polo shirt and fished out a cigarette. One of those svelte women's cigarettes, a Virginia Slim. He lit it and kept it smoldering between his clenched lips, squinting against the smoke, which was the same shade of white as his hair.

"Add insult to injury?" Trench went on. "I had a deckhand. A drunk. Worthless as tits on a tomato. Kept him on because he had a wife and kid. Had a boat before the storm. Piece-of-shit boat. Couldn't've been worth more than a few grand. No insurance. Motherfucker never paid a bill on time in his life. Well, government pays him seventy thousand dollars for the thing. He buys a thirty-thousand-dollar boat, pockets the rest. Spent the rest in Harrah's casino in New Orleans. Then, big surprise, he cracks the goddamn boat all to hell a month later. Fuckin' drunk."

Grimes was taken aback by Trench's gregariousness. He was beginning to suspect that Trench might harangue anyone within earshot. The Antichrist.

"Don't take this the wrong way, Mr. Trench," Grimes said, "but why are you telling me all this?"

"Leave if you want," Trench said from one side of his mouth. The cigarette, long-ashed, still burned in the other. The ash dropped and flecked the front of his orange polo shirt and he flicked the smudge away.

"No, it's interesting. But why? If you dislike me so much?"

Trench sidestepped to another knot. "I don't dislike you."

"No?"

"I hate you." Trench didn't look up.

Blood batting in his face, ears burning, Grimes said, "I understand you're angry, Mr. Trench."

Trench kept working, breathing roughly through his nose.

"I'm only trying to help."

Silence.

"You think there's some wild conspiracy against you?"

"Go away."

"I'm not from the government."

"You are the government."

"I'm with the oil company."

"No fuckin' difference."

"I'm not a political man, Mr. Trench."

"The second you started working for that company you got political. Bobby Jindal, Haley Barbour, fuckin' Riley. One great big orgy. And you're in the middle."

Grimes sighed and shook his head. Trench's cheeks and ears, he saw, were an unhealthy shade of red. If the man wasn't careful he'd have a heart attack before he knew it. Would serve the bastard right. He imagined Trench collapsing to his knees, writhing on his back in the dirt, an upside-down bug. "Ready to sign?" Grimes would say, hovering above him with the Mont Blanc pen and papers like the Grim Reaper.

"I'm just going to flat-out ask," said Grimes. "What will it take?"

"For what?"

"To sign."

"Nothing."

Grimes pinched the bridge of his nose and breathed deeply, as if patience was something he could draw from the air. "I don't understand, Mr. Trench."

"That's fine. You don't have to."

"But I want to."

"Where those folks going?" He pointed his chin to the side of the yard. As if there were someone there to see.

Grimes glanced. "Your neighbors?"

"Folks in my yard."

"Folks in your yard?" Grimes looked again, shook his head in bafflement.

"My folks, buried in the ground."

Now Grimes saw. Beyond a stand of oaks at the edge of the yard was a scattering of lichen-spotted tombstones, one much newer than the rest and glaring like a bright tooth in the sun.

"They can be reburied," Grimes said.

Trench's jaw dropped with parodic incredulity. "Dig them up?" he asked.

Grimes knew he had to proceed cautiously. "It's done much more often than you would think."

Trench looked down at the ground, scratched the side of his nose with his forefinger.

"These are licensed people. Consummate professionals. Your folks"—in Grimes's ears the word came out with all the mellifluousness of a turd plopping into a tin bucket, so Lord only knew how Trench heard it—"they'd be treated with the greatest care and delicacy."

"Guess it wouldn't matter either way to them."

After a moment Grimes allowed that maybe it didn't.

"I'll never sign," said Trench. He took a final suck on his cigarette and spat it in the grass, heeling it out with his boot.

"I get that a lot."

"Listen to me," Trench said, pointing. "You can set me on fire and ask to piss out the flames and I'll never sign."

"One more question," Grimes said.

Trench folded his arms over his chest and glared at the ground.

"Why here?" Grimes asked. "What's so special?"

Trench said nothing. And his silence so infuriated Grimes that he spewed the venom that had been building up for weeks. "This is the middle of nowhere," he said, "the end of the world."

Trench smirked sardonically. "Is it, now?"

It was dark when Grimes returned to his motel room. He poured three fingers of bourbon into a plastic motel cup and sat on the edge of the creaking bed. He wrestled off his shoes and loosened the knot of his tie and called Ingram on his cell phone.

"I made a mistake," he said.

"What now, Grimes?"

"I lost my temper."

"What happened?"

"I couldn't help it."

On Ingram's end of the line, a lighter snapped. Ingram was trying to kick his cigarette habit, but it seemed he smoked every time he was on the phone with Grimes.

Ingram asked what happened.

"I told this Trench guy that this place was a shithole."

"No, Grimes. No."

"I didn't use those exact words. I said something like this is the end of the world."

Ingram breathed slowly through his teeth. "And what did he say?"

"He didn't say anything. But he didn't seem to like it."

"Grimes. You just pissed away weeks of work. Months. Because you couldn't keep your mouth shut. How many times do we have to go through this?"

"It hasn't happened in a while."

"It shouldn't happen ever."

"You don't understand. This guy. This guy, he's like Bartleby the fucking Scrivener."

"I'm hanging up, Grimes."

"The story. By Melville. The one about the file clerk? His boss keeps asking him to do the simplest things, the simplest most basic fucking common-sense things you can imagine, and the guy, no matter what, keeps on saying I'd rather not. You want some lemonade? I'd rather not. You want a raise? I'd rather not. You want a blowjob? I'd rather not. That's this guy. Bob Trench."

"Level with me, Grimes."

"What?"

"Are you drinking again?"

"No," Grimes lied. "Why?"

THE TOUP BROTHERS

It was half past one when the black Suburban shuddered up the twin-rutted drive to Lindquist's house, the only light from the moth-haloed porch globe throwing the long shadow of the birdbath, like a fedora'd man's silhouette, across the yard.

The Toup brothers knew that Lindquist was now on his boat in the Barataria. That his wife had moved out months ago. That his kid, Reagan the redhead with the big tits, was grown up and living on her own. Small town like this, all you had to do was ask around. Sometimes you didn't even have to do that much. They also knew that someone who spent so many nights metal detecting in the bayou had to be convinced he was chasing after something worthwhile.

Victor and Reginald stepped around the house, peering through the windows one by one. The night was silent save for the calling of crickets and frogs, their footfalls in the dead leaves and nettles. The stealthy rustling of an animal, possum or raccoon, creeping farther into the woods.

The front door lock was cheap and flimsy and it took Victor all of five seconds to jimmy it open with a snake-rake pick. They stepped inside and Victor fumbled for the wall switch and flicked it on.

Goodwill sofa. Green shag carpet from the seventies. Wood-paneled walls.

"Looks like a place you die in," Victor said.

The stench of garbage wafted from the back of the house. The brothers turned to one another with wrinkled faces. They went past the littered dining room table to the kitchen, where they found three black trash bags heaped beside the back door. One of the bags was split and a tar-black puddle of slime had seeped onto the olive-green linoleum.

"Fuckin' slob," Victor said, holding the back of his hand against his nose.

The brothers walked again into the living room and went down the end of the hall to the master bedroom. Victor flicked on the light and went to a chest of drawers and riffled through socks and underwear and T-shirts. Reginald sat on the edge of the unmade bed and sorted through the junk in a nightstand drawer. A half-furled tube of ointment. A green pocket-sized Bible. A pair of drugstore reading glasses. Empty prescription bottles.

The brothers searched through another bedroom and then they returned to the kitchen, where they opened the cupboards and looked through coffee cans and cereal boxes.

Victor stood for a moment with his hands on his hips, staring up at the water-stained ceiling. He went to the refrigerator and opened it and peered inside at the barren shelves. A festering onion speckled with blue-gray mold. A six-pack of Abita beer. A bottle of Texas Pete hot sauce.

The brothers were back in the living room when Reginald called Victor over to the dining room table. They stood for a moment studying the array of old maps. Victor picked one of them up, a map of the Barataria waterways and islands, the complex maze of canals and cheniers. They owned such maps themselves. On this one Lindquist had marked with purple pen his meandering progress through the bayou, a stuttering line like a stitch. The path stopped at the small pear-shaped chenier where they'd seen him the other night. A scant half mile away was the dewdrop shape of their island.

"Look at this," Victor said, pointing.

Reginald looked and huffed air through his nose.

"Goddamn if this guy ain't crazy," Victor said.

LINDQUIST

Lindquist was asleep on the couch when someone knocked on the front door and woke him. He sat upright and rubbed his stinging eyes and blinked down at his watch. Three o'clock in the afternoon. The night before he'd returned home and discovered his bedroom drawers opened and mussed, cans and boxes toppled over in the kitchen cabinets. At first he figured either Gwen or Reagan must have let herself in, but then he remembered they didn't have the new keys. No, he must have fucked things up himself while somnambulating in a fog of beer and pills.

There was knocking again, this time more insistent. He rose from the couch and shuffled toward the door—quietly, in case it was a creditor. He held his breath and squinted through the peephole. On the doorstep stood his daughter, wearing a purple blouse printed with little cream-colored flowers, and a white chiffon scarf wrapped loosely around her neck. Her hair was done up with bobby pins and she looked bright-eyed and rested. A welcome change.

"I hear you in there, Daddy," Reagan said through the door.

"Yeah, yeah," Lindquist said. "Hold on."

He turned around and glanced quickly about. The remnants of a ground-up pill on the coffee table, an incriminating streak of pharmaceutical dust. He went over and swept the powder onto the floor and heeled it into the carpet.

Lindquist smoothed the back of his hair and opened the door. Reagan stepped in and pecked him on the cheek and looked around the room. "Jesus, Daddy," she said. "You been partying?"

"Me, naw," he said. "Nothing like that now."

She went to the couch and sat with her red leather purse in her lap. Lindquist sat in the faded plaid recliner across from her.

"Wasn't expecting company," he said.

"You look thinner."

"I lost an arm."

"Daddy. That's not funny."

Lindquist shrugged. "Hey, were you in here last night?" he asked. Lightly, because he didn't want to sound accusatory.

"Here, the house?"

"Yeah, I came home this morning and a bunch of my papers were messed up. Stuff in my bedroom."

"I don't even have a key anymore. Remember? Mom changed the lock after you guys had that fight two or three years ago."

Lindquist made an O with his mouth. Yes, the famous Fourth of July fight where he'd gotten drunk and high on pills at a party thrown by one of Gwen's coworker friends. He'd told nasty Polish jokes and set off cherry bombs in his prosthesis and ended up accidentally burning some lawn furniture. Gwen threw him out of the house for that fiasco and he had to stay at the Econo Lodge in Houma for a week.

"Maybe it was Bosco," Reagan said.

"Oh, baby. That cat's been dead two years."

Now it was Reagan's turn to look surprised.

Finally Lindquist saw why his daughter was wearing the scarf. The raspberry medallion of a hickey showed over the edge of the fabric. He thought about asking Reagan if her boyfriend was a lamprey. If she was attacked by a plunger. But some jokes were verboten, a courtesy he tendered exclusively to his daughter.

He picked a nub of fabric off the tattered arm of the recliner and rolled it into a pill between his thumb and forefinger and flicked it booger-like across the room. It pinged off his daughter's ear—Lindquist could see the little gnat-sized thing in the sunlight—and landed somewhere in the carpet.

"Nice hickey," Lindquist said. He couldn't help himself.

Reagan ignored the comment. "Why you wearing that nasty old thing?" she asked.

"I like this shirt, me."

"The hook arm."

"You don't like it?"

"Where's your other?"

"I kinda like this old hook arm, me. Wait until the first guy screws with me. Wham! Right in his face with this thing. Word'll be all over town. Don't screw with Lindquist. He'll mess you up with his hook arm."

His daughter was watching him. Waiting.

"It was stolen," Lindquist said.

Reagan's jaw dropped and her bottom teeth showed, the same expression his wife got when she was distressed. Getting more like her mother every day, his girl.

"Oh God, Daddy," she said. "Why didn't you tell me?"

"What good would it do? You gonna get a search team together?"

"I would've come over. To cook. To whatever."

"To cook?" Lindquist asked.

"Why you gotta say it like that?"

"I'm just playing."

"You're playing rough today." She filched a box of cigarettes from her purse and shook one out and lit it. She inhaled and blew out smoke and leaned forward to tap the ash of the cigarette in the beanbag ashtray on the coffee table.

Lindquist glanced at his watch. Five hours from now he'd have to be back in the bayou if he wanted to get any decent shrimping done. The prospect of nearly killing himself out there with the mosquitoes, all for forty or fifty dollars, made him nauseous.

"What kind of sick dickhead would steal an arm?" Reagan asked.

Lindquist shrugged. "How's your mother?"

Reagan turned her face and looked at him sideways.

"I can't ask?"

"I'm not gonna be a go-between."

They were quiet for a while, Reagan surveying the cluttered room, the dining room table strewn with tide charts and boating maps and pirate books.

"Still at it with the metal detecting?" Reagan said.

"You think it's weird?"

"A little."

"Well, hell. You used to think it was cool."

"Yeah. When I was little."

Lindquist slapped his thigh and got up. "Almost forgot," he said. "Got you something."

"What?"

"A surprise."

"I didn't come for anything," Reagan said to Lindquist's back as he went down the hall.

In the bedroom he opened the bureau drawer and rummaged among the loose change and receipts and Mardi Gras trinkets. He picked out a heart locket hung on a wisp-thin gold-plated chain and blew off the lint and dust. He glimpsed his daughter in the bureau mirror. She was standing at the dining room table and she picked up one of his pill bottles and opened it. She shook out a couple pills and slipped them in her purse and set the pill bottle back in its place.

In the den Lindquist held out the necklace to his daughter. Her smile faltered. She was expecting more, something else. Money, no doubt.

"Found that metal detecting."

She dangled the necklace from her fingers so it caught the light. "It's pretty," she said.

"Tell your mother. Tell her I'm finding treasure."

"You're something else," Reagan said. She hugged him and Lindquist hugged her back, his hook arm angled awkwardly.

There was something about her posture, an expectant air, that told him she was waiting for something. Lindquist dug into his pocket and took out a twenty-dollar bill and handed it to her.

"You sure?"

He reached out and held her fingers and closed them around the bill. "Only money," he said.

WES TRENCH

After Lindquist left him at the harbor, Wes opened all the windows of his rickety Toyota truck and made a makeshift bed in the truck cab. A dusty-smelling moving blanket for a mattress, an old T-shirt for a pillow, a beach towel for a top sheet. He was filthy and hot and exhausted but had trouble falling asleep because it was the fifth anniversary of his mother's death. Somewhere, right now, his father was no doubt grief-stricken over the fact. Like him. Well, he'd have to suffer on his own. They both had to suffer on their own now. Wes thought of his mother's voice, tried to fill his head with its sweet soft cadence—*it's okay, Wessy*—and he wept himself to sleep. Every so often the calls of trawlers woke him, their raucous voices carrying across the bayou, but he turned on his side and sunk back under.

Come sundown he was startled awake when someone rapped his knuckles on the window glass. Lindquist. Only faint orange light remained above the treetops, like the torn edge of pumpkin-colored construction paper, birds flitting through the gloaming.

Wes opened the rear cab door and slid out.

Holding a metal detector in his good hand, Lindquist winced at the sight of Wes. "Christ, kid. You die?"

"Sorry."

"Well, hell. Change your clothes at least. Closet's in the cabin. Grab any old thing. Just so I don't have to smell you."

Wes went aboard and Lindquist followed. From the cabin closet Wes dug out an old pair of jean shorts, so big around the waist that he had to belt them tight with a length of nylon rope. Then Wes found an old T-shirt that said THE BAHAMAS on the front and put it on.

When Wes climbed onto the deck in his new clothes, Lindquist was peering down from the wheelhouse as he coasted through the twilit bayou.

"I wanna tell you something," Lindquist said.

"What's that."

"You look like an asshole."

"They're your clothes," Wes said.

"You're wearing them wrong."

After a while they were out in the bay and Wes put the starboard net in the water and let out one hundred feet of cable and locked down the winch. He did the same with the port side and then he waited with his arms crossed over the gunwale. A chemical stink hung in the air, like he imagined napalm might smell in those Vietnam movies his Dad liked to watch. His Dad: he tried to push him out of his head. He spat into the water and looked out over the dark and muggy bay. From a distance came a whining grumble, which grew louder until a two-prop plane passed about five hundred feet overhead, its roar so loud Wes covered his ears.

Soon Lindquist slowed the boat to quarter speed and Wes hoisted up the nets, watching the cables and grates as they swung aboard. He dumped the haul on the deck and took the wooden paddle from its peg on the wall and began to poke through the pile of wriggling sea life.

Lindquist idled the *Jean Lafitte* and climbed down the wheelhouse ladder and squatted on the deck, sorting through the fingerling fish and puny shrimp with the hook of his prosthetic arm. Several of the fish were dead. So were a few blue crabs.

Lindquist picked one up, turned it over and looked at its gills, which were supposed to be pinkish white but were dirty gray. "Ever wonder why we're doing this?" he asked.

"Sometimes," Wes said. His eyes were watery and stinging from the chemical fumes. He wiped his cheek with the back of his hand.

"No matter how hard you work, comes to nothing."

"My dad says that a lot."

"Your old man's right."

They were quiet for a time. Lindquist tossed a croaker back into the water, Wes a baby redfish cankered with lesions the size of hot pepper flakes.

"You smell that?" Lindquist asked.

Wes nodded, made a face.

"Suppose this stuff is poisoned?"

"They say it's okay on the news. The Environmental whatever."

"EPA?"

"Yessir."

"You believe them?"

"I don't know."

"I've seen shrimp with no eyes, me," Lindquist said.

"I saw a three-eyed redfish one time."

"Saw a three-tittied mermaid, me."

They chuckled.

"Just you and your pop?" Lindquist asked.

"Yessir."

"Ma split?"

"She's gone."

"Indiana?"

"What?"

"She go to Indiana?"

"No, she's passed."

Lindquist's eyes fell somberly on Wes. "Well, hell," he said. "Sorry to hear that, kid." Then, just a few seconds later, "Knock knock."

At first Wes thought he misheard Lindquist. Surely he wasn't telling a joke now.

"Knock knock."

"Who's there?" Wes asked grudgingly.

"Asshole."

Wes waited. "Good one."

"No, you gotta say 'Asshole who.'"

"Asshole who?"

"Asshole wearing my clothes fell asleep in the back of his truck."

Wes shook his head.

At dawn they dropped off their haul and Lindquist paid Wes in the harbor parking lot. Already the air was beginning to burn and simmer, steam rising in a thick fog off the bayou. They were walking to their trucks in the marina when Lindquist asked, "You gonna sleep in your truck again?"

"I guess so," Wes said.

Lindquist grunted and walked over to Wes. He rooted in one of the sagged-down pockets of his cargo pants and took out a key ring and tossed it to him. Wes caught it one-handed against his chest and Lindquist told him to take the small silver key on the end.

Wes asked if he was sure.

Lindquist nodded and said, "Just don't burn the fuckin' boat down, all right?"

- - - - - - - -

For the next several days in early September, after he and Lindquist returned at sunup from shrimping, Wes stayed behind on the *Jean Lafitte*. He hosed the bycatch slime from the deck and bathed in the boat's tiny standing shower and then he lay down in the single bed with the lumpy mattress and pillow. The cabin was small and wood-paneled, on the walls an antique brass barometer, a rusted Louisiana license plate, a sun-faded poster from the 1970s of Farrah Fawcett in a red swimsuit. The shelves were crammed with treasure books and magazines and Wes flipped through them when he was trying to get to sleep. He came across a bunch of stuff about Civil War sites and shipwrecks, about pirate treasure in Louisiana and Alabama and Florida. The pages of these were always dog-eared and finger-smudged. Wes had to admit the pictures and stories were interesting, if far-fetched and crazy.

Then there were a few books about the pirate Jean Lafitte. Wes read one of them straight through. He already knew some of the background from school. Louisiana was once the back of beyond, the book said, passed back and forth between France and Spain like a bastard child. Then Thomas Jefferson bought the territory from Napoleon for less than three cents an acre. But Louisiana stayed an outpost. A backwater way station along the route of westward expansion. Especially the Barataria, its labyrinthine expanse of waterways and barrier islands an ideal haven for runaway slaves and refugees.

And pirates, according to the book, which was why Jean Lafitte chose the Barataria as his base of operation. Here Lafitte and his privateers staged raids on cargo ships, ferried the booty via pirogue to New Orleans. The French and Spanish in the city didn't care where their goods came from as long as they got them. The whores got their perfumes and silks, the Creoles their spices and tobacco, the bourgeoisie their booze and slaves.

For some time Lafitte's enterprise and infamy only grew. Gunners and shipbuilders and carpenters—outcasts from all over the globe—joined Jean Lafitte's crew. They reared families, grew crops, built stockades and brothels. The Barataria became a home away from home for pirates and outlaws and bastards. And Lafitte himself was rumored to have sired a bastard child or two. The author's word: *sired*. Wes didn't know what it meant and didn't have a dictionary but figured it must have meant fathered.

When Governor Claiborne issued a reward for Lafitte's capture, the pirate did what a pirate does. He hid his riches far and wide across the bayou. His fellow brigands, knowing their heyday was over, probably did the same.

There weren't many passages about lost gold in the book, but they were all highlighted. Maybe Lindquist was onto something after all, Wes thought. He didn't see the harm in Lindquist's treasure hunting. And he didn't think it was crazy. If he never found anything, so what? He wasn't hurting anybody.

And who didn't like a treasure hunt? Wes suspected everybody was chasing after treasure in a way. A lottery ticket, a baseball card, a long-lost photo of a high school sweetheart.

A boat.

- - - - - - - - -

Wes and Lindquist kept shrimping, one dismal outing after the next. They left at dusk and returned at dawn, dragging themselves off the boat like mannequins. Montegut's payout was always far less than they hoped. Almost insulting. Every day restaurants were canceling their shipments and ordering freeze-dried shrimp imported from China, Montegut explained. Even bragging about the fact on their signs and menus.

Wes had trouble sleeping at night because he kept worrying about his father. He knew the longer he stayed from home the harder it would be to come back. If he ever did come back. Probably he would. Maybe his father had been trying to reach him, but Wes hadn't paid his cell phone bill. What was the point? It wasn't like he had a social life. And girls, girls were as unreachable as gods. He'd only kissed and felt up one girl, Lucy Arcinaux, a pretty *jolie* blonde from high school he'd dated a month. But Lucy was like any sixteen-year-old girl and when she learned how much time Wes spent on his father's boat, how little time he had for socializing, she dumped him. Part of Wes was still angry at his father for this.

Day after day Wes and Lindquist saw fewer and fewer trawlers out in the Barataria. Sometimes there looked to be more planes and helicopters in the sky than boats in the water. One minute Lindquist was bitching about BP, how he'd like to blow up all those rigs out there with dynamite. The next he was telling jokes about French hookers, homosexual penguins, and Polish priests with peg legs. To Wes the jokes sounded no different than his angry cursing. Like both were dredged up from the same deep-down bitter place.

Wes spent what little money he made on canned goods and toiletries and other sundries. The rest he squirreled away for his boat. He knew it wouldn't add up to much, but what he couldn't afford with his savings he could beg and scrounge and borrow. One thing about growing up in the swamp, it taught you to be resourceful. There used to be a time in the Barataria, not long ago, when people eked out their livelihoods solely from the bayou. They shrimped and crabbed. They poached alligators for their hides and trapped muskrats and nutria for their skins. This was in the time of his grandparents and great-grandparents, before everyone sold their land for pennies an acre to the oil companies in the twenties and thirties, before BP gouged away at the marsh with their canals and pipelines. The few octogenarians still alive in Jeanette spoke of that era with melancholy nostalgia. They spoke of how different the Barataria was back then, an untrammeled wilderness untouched by man and time. How different the water and air had been, how much sweeter the seafood. Even the sunlight looked different.

But a strain of that old Baratarian resourcefulness remained in the people of Jeanette. It remained in Wes and it would probably remain in his daughters and sons if he had them. After that, who knew. In other places, even as nearby as New Orleans, Wes was always shocked to discover how clueless kids his age were. They couldn't change the oil and tires of their cars, let alone build something like a boat from scratch.

- - - - - - - -

One night Lindquist carried his metal detector onto the *Jean Lafitte* and at two in the morning when the shrimping was nil he oared his pirogue to one of the cheniers dotting the bayou. Wes went with him and they banked on the shore of an islet the size of a kiddie pool. Lindquist swung the coil over the mucky ground while Wes followed behind with the lantern and shovel-scoop.

After a while Lindquist leaned on the metal detector and rubbed the shoulder of his hook arm. His mouth was twisted and his face was red and he seemed to be in some kind of pain. He caught Wes staring.

"You lookin' at my hook?" Lindquist said.

"Naw." Wes looked away, his face burning.

"Don't bullshit a bullshitter."

"How'd you lose it?" Wes asked, a nervous blurt.

"'Nam."

"A mine? Or was it shot off?"

"A tiger came out of the jungle and ripped it off."

Wes looked at Lindquist with shock.

"Just ran out of the jungle and knocked me down and ripped it clean out of the socket. Simple as that. Motherfucker was a professional. Then he took off. With my arm hanging out of his mouth. Like a cigar."

Wes stared gape-mouthed at Lindquist.

Lindquist snorted. "Kid," he said.

"What?"

"I wasn't in any war, me."

Wes kept quiet.

"I wasn't in 'Nam. You think I'm old enough to have been in 'Nam?"

"Then what was it?"

Lindquist looked Wes in the face. "An accident with the winch. That's all. An accident. I wasn't saving any babies or taking a bullet for any-body." Now he glanced away, his face going stiff. His voice was hard and matter-of-fact. "I was fucked up. Drunk and on a bunch of pills. I don't even remember what I was doing. So fucked up, who knows. A cross-word puzzle. Whatever. One minute my arm was there and one minute it wasn't and it was a horror show. I still have nightmares about it when I don't take my pills. So I always take them."

Surprised by Lindquist's honesty and unsure what to say, Wes looked at the ground and dragged the toe of his boot through the mud. "Well, hell," Lindquist said, "enough of that." He took the Donald Duck Pez dis-penser from his cargo pants and flicked a pill into his mouth. The night was so quiet Wes could hear Lindquist's teeth crunching up the pill.

COSGROVE AND HANSON

Tired of the rough living in the barracks, Cosgrove and Hanson rented side-by-side hundred-dollar-a-week rooms in a shit-hole Jeanette motel with a NO PROSTITUTION sign in the parking lot and a stray cat infestation in the courtyard. A nefarious aura presided over the place. How the doors were never open, how the windows were always curtained, how the occupants, almost all solitary middle-aged men, entered and exited their rooms with illicit stealth. Cosgrove's neighbor was a young prickish-looking businessman who drove a Lincoln Town Car and left browning apple cores in the gravel. He never spoke with Cosgrove and Hanson, never even looked their way more than a split-second glance, as if deeming them not worth the trouble. At least he was quiet. Other tenants, Cosgrove couldn't say the same. Sounds of revelry often woke him in the middle of the night. A woman's pillow-muffled moan, a man's baboonish grunt, an ass-pocket whiskey bottle shattering on the macadam.

Both their rooms had airport-blue carpet and equestrian-themed oil paintings and tube-model televisions from the eighties. The cinder block walls were painted shiny beige with hardened drips like veins. Lime and rust stained the bathtubs and toilets. Every so often they found a pubic hair in one of the nubby bleach-smelling towels.

Complimentary pubic hairs, was Hanson's joke.

Hanson started letting the feral cats into his room six or seven at a time. Many of the cats were six-toed. Hemingway cats, according to Hanson. He was full of trivia such as this. The man couldn't name the vice president of the United States, couldn't point out the continents on a map, but he knew everything there was to know about insects and Vikings and the Kennedy assassination. An encyclopedic repository of bullshit, Hanson was.

Hanson fed the cats nubs of beef jerky from a ziplock bag he kept on the nightstand. He pinched the morsels between thumb and forefinger, waiting for the cats to stand on their hind legs like circus seals. He whiled away hours in this fashion, perched on the edge of the bed with a beer in one hand and the beef jerky in the other.

Several times Cosgrove reminded Hanson that cats weren't dogs.

"Bet you fifty dollars that I'll have one of these sons-a-bitches walking across the room in a week," he said. "Strutting."

Within a week Hanson's legs were riddled with angry red bumps. There wasn't a moment in the day when he wasn't scratching himself like a leper. The housekeeper, a round-faced Vietnamese woman always shouting foreign curses into her Bluetooth headset, must have ratted Hanson out to the manager because a handwritten warning was slipped in an envelope under his door. The motel was not an animal shelter, the letter said. The letter also told Hanson to stop filling his Igloo cooler with the motel ice.

"These fleas been here since this shit-hole was built," Hanson told Cosgrove, incensed. "Probably the only thing holding this place together. Rip open the walls and it's a bunch of fleas holding hands."

"You're thinking of termites," Cosgrove said. He stroked his beard and flipped through television channels. NASCAR. College football highlights. News footage of a polar bear mauling a zookeeper in Milwaukee.

Hanson wouldn't stop talking, especially when he was drunk and high. Tonight he'd made a gravity bong with a plastic two-liter bottle of Big Shot pineapple soda and smoked what he called "middies" at the bathroom sink. Hanson told Cosgrove he never had a wife or kids. Didn't want them, had no use. He'd passed through all the contiguous United States save for the Dakotas, which he thought the government should bomb for reasons he never elaborated upon. He'd followed Bob Dylan and Tom Petty for three months on their joint 1987 tour. AC/DC for two months on their 1988 Blow Up Your Video tour. His father, a hotdog vender, was struck dead by a cement truck when Hanson was just a boy. A year later his mother remarried a macaw breeder who wanted Hanson out of the house the minute he turned eighteen. Hanson dropped out of high school and enlisted in the army on his birthday. A few weeks later he was on a Greyhound bus headed to Fort Bragg but was discharged soon after when the infirmary doctor discovered his heart murmur during a routine checkup.

Also, Hanson had served a year at the Texas State Penitentiary in Huntsville. "No cops like Texas cops," Hanson told Cosgrove. "You think the cops in Louisiana are crooked? Make Lemon look like a saint. I was roofin' out in Austin and got mixed up with the wrong people. Full of the wrong people, fuckin' Texas. Most of 'em construction. Fuck's this shit you got on? *Cosby Show*? Change the channel."

From the dinky Formica table Cosgrove thumbed the clicker. It was past midnight and he was on his ninth beer and his head was spinning. The walls kept coming at him, like the room was collapsing in on itself. He told Hanson he needed sleep.

"Tell you what?" Hanson said. "If I could live this bullshit life over?"

Cosgrove got up from his chair. "I'm going," he said.

On his bed, eyes closed, Hanson kept talking. Cosgrove stepped out of the room and shut the door quietly behind him.

– – – – – – – –

The marijuana growers, they learned after some reconnaissance, were twin brothers. Reggie and Victor Toup. At first people in Jeanette were loath to divulge any more information. One guy said they'd better keep their noses up their own asses if they knew what was best for them.

Another guy asked them if they were with the government. Yet another asked what butt-fuck place they were from, said they'd end up in the hospital shitting out their kidneys if they weren't careful.

As a last resort Cosgrove and Hanson plied the men with alcohol. Soon they learned that the twins' father and mother died in the 1980s. Some bizarre love triangle that ended in gunfire at New Orleans's Roosevelt Hotel. The twins' mother, fed up with her husband's philandering, sought solace in her own lover's arms. A Greek restaurateur, husband of twenty-five years, father of three college-aged girls. One day the twins' father followed the couple to the Roosevelt, knocked on the door of their honeymoon suite when he knew he'd find them in flagrante. When the Greek answered the door the twins' father barged into the room and shot him in the stomach with a Colt .45. The Greek toppled to the floor and crawled on his hands and knees to where his suit lay on the carpet and fumbled out his own gun, a Smith & Wesson Model 13. The Greek shot the twins' father in the kneecap and the father went down and fired again, this time striking the Greek in the shoulder. Then more bullets were fired and by the end of the pandemonium the twins' father shot his wife in the face. On purpose, by accident, no one would ever know. And by the time the cops arrived ten minutes later the three of them were dead. A bloodbath. All you had to do was go to a New Orleans public library and look the story up in the *Times-Picayune* microfiche.

Afterward the twins went to live with their grandmother, already so old and addle-brained that the teenage boys pretty much ruled the roost. By thirteen the boys were taking midnight joyrides in her Cadillac. By fourteen they were stealing liquor and cigarettes from the general store, selling the stuff at markup prices on the playground. Within two or three years they were high school dropouts, the Barataria's biggest growers of marijuana.

- - - - - - - - -

They left Hanson's truck in the harbor parking lot and crossed the road to the twins' house. It was half past midnight and the mud-and-fish stench of the bayou was thick in the air. Every so often the wind switched directions and a chemical stink, of petroleum or oil, swept over them.

The house was just where they'd heard. A tidy, mint-green place on pilings across the street from the wharf, a light on in one of the windows. The kitchen: they could see the dark-wood cabinetry, the hanging ceiling light of varicolored glass.

"Wouldn't mind living in a place like this," Hanson said.

Cosgrove grunted, scratched his beard. He was wondering how Hanson had talked him into this madness. He wanted money and he wanted more of the marijuana, but many people wanted those things and didn't go breaking into houses.

They climbed the stairs and Hanson knocked on the door. No answer. Then Hanson went down the stairs and found a tomato-sized rock in the yard and came back up, hurled it through one of the sidelight windows.

The alarm shrilled.

Hanson reached carefully through the broken glass and unlocked the door and went inside. Cosgrove followed. Hanson picked up the rock from the foyer floor and stepped back and hurled it at the alarm code box. The rock smashed the plastic and pieces flew but still the alarm shrieked deafeningly.

Cosgrove saw Hanson's mouth working crazily but he couldn't hear a word.

Hanson picked up the rock again. Hurled it.

The alarm screamed on.

"Holy shit," Cosgrove said, but he couldn't hear himself.

Hanson held up three fingers: three minutes.

Hanson went into the kitchen and flung open cabinets. In the bedroom down the hall, Cosgrove eviscerated drawers, flinging socks and underwear and T-shirts. He went into another bedroom and did the same. Nothing. In the hallway bathroom he looked through the medicine cabinet and saw only the usual sundries: toothpaste, dental floss, aspirin.

Cosgrove and Hanson met in the foyer. Hanson was shouting soundlessly, pantomiming wildly. Cosgrove screamed back and shook his head.

They went out of the house and thudded down the stairs. Then they sprinted through the yard and across the street.

In the truck they could still hear the house alarm.

They sat catching their breath, Cosgrove glaring at Hanson.

"Fuck you want from me?" he said.

"Unbelievable," Cosgrove said.

Hanson reached into his pocket and gave Cosgrove a paper towel with numbers written on it in ballpoint pen.

"Coordinates," Hanson said, stroking his ponytail, still breathing roughly. "Off a GPS on the kitchen counter. Somewhere in the bay."

GRIMES

Grimes was not, as townsfolk first assumed, a wayward stranger who'd taken a wrong turn off the highway. Actually? His face was familiar, the eyes and mouth. Maybe he was a relative of someone they once knew. And after word spread through town that he was here for business, an oil man, the looks from people in Jeanette grew sharp and threatening. In the café, in the general store, in Sully's bar.

Even the kids around the Barataria, switch-skinny children with old-soul eyes, sensed something about him. Something off. Loitering in the convenience store parking lot, playing videogames in trawlers' living rooms, hacky-sacking in the motel roundabout, they beheld him with frank apprehension. Like he was some kind of bogeyman in white button-down shirt and tie.

His whole life, people treated him this way. With suspicion. Even when he was a kid. Especially when he was a kid. Grimes's classmates said he was spooky, said he stared like a serial killer. They called him Jeffrey Dahmer, Charles Manson, Crazy Eyes.

In football during gym class the boys hit him harder than anyone else, power-driving him so hard into the dirt that once he was knocked cold. And in his gym locker they left obscene pictures, of humongous dicks, cut out from pornographic magazines.

One time in the cafeteria line a group of kids behind Grimes broke out in jackal-like laughter. He started toward his table with his face burning, clutching his tray, and the laughter grew. When he sat down at the table with the other outcasts—the Dungeons & Dragons freaks, the deformed goths—he reached and felt his back.

Sure enough: a purple Post-it that said MARSHMALLOW FAGGOT in big block letters.

Whatever that meant.

There was just something about him that people never liked.

"People hate me here," Grimes said to Ingram one night on the phone.

"They'd hate Mother Teresa. People shoot the messenger."

Grimes lay in bed with a motel cup of scotch balanced one-handed on his chest. His pillow was thin and smelled dank. Tomorrow he would talk to the maid about the pillows. If there was a maid. Maybe go to the department store and buy his own pillow. If there was a department store within fifty square miles of this godforsaken shit-hole.

"I don't feel right. I've been having these nosebleeds."

"Allergies."

"Something in the air, I think."

"Don't say that. Don't say that to anyone. Ever."

"Feels like I'm dying."

"Last time I went to Louisiana I couldn't shit right for a month. Something in the water. Don't drink the water. You drinking the water?"

Grimes felt sick and exhausted and missed the cool gray days of the city, the polychrome electric nights. The glowing signs of Chinese and French and Spanish. He missed the shark-like limousines and the kamikaze taxis and the restaurants and bars open all night, the smoked glass and submarine lighting. The panoply of strange faces, never the same. He missed the noise. God he missed the noise, the deep drone of the city, the crying sirens, the lunatics proselytizing on street corners, the bass and treble of traffic. Most of all he missed anonymity. In a city you could be anyone. In a city your past didn't have to matter. You could have any past you liked as long as you could imagine it and tell someone with a straight face. Sometimes you could even manage to deceive yourself.

"You been back to Tench's?" Ingram asked. "Is that the guy?"

"Trench," Grimes said. "No."

"Go."

"I know."

"Tomorrow."

Grimes was silent.

"Let's make a deal."

"I'm listening."

"How about a paid vacation when you get back? Two weeks. November, December, whenever you want."

"How about that promotion?"

"We can talk. If everything goes right."

Thoughtfully Grimes sipped his scotch.

Next day Grimes went to Trench's house but he wasn't there so he went to the harbor. It was late afternoon, the smothering heat almost unbreathable. Grimes found Trench blasting fish guts off the deck of his boat with a spray hose. The runoff piddled into the water where frenzied baitfish pecked at the gore.

Four signatures so far today, Grimes thought. If he was lucky, Trench would make five. Maybe he'd have time left over to get six or seven. "Seven signatures today," he'd tell Ingram on the phone.

"Where's the kid?" Grimes said. Because he had to say something. A half-eaten Granny Smith apple in his hand, he stood on the rickety dock, the wood so weather-worn it looked like bleached bone. Sunstruck water flickered through the cracks in the wood.

Trench didn't answer. He tucked the spray nozzle into the armpit of his lemon-colored polo shirt and rummaged in his front jeans pocket and pulled out a cigarette. A Virginia Slim. As usual.

Trench lit the cigarette and impaled Grimes with his eyes.

"I'm just a middleman, Mr. Trench." *Five,* Grimes thought. "You know Chris Grimes?"

Trench thumbed the side of his nose, blew smoke.

"That's my mother," said Grimes. He smiled and took a bite from the apple.

Trench absorbed this. "Good lady. Great lady. But the apple fell far from the tree. Apple rolled down the gutter and right the shit out of town."

"I'm trying to be civil, Mr. Trench."

Trench hissed through his teeth.

"I'm trying to help." Grimes looked around for a trash can to put his apple in but didn't see one so plopped the core in the water.

"Help? A hundred thousand in fishing gear just sitting there. You paying for this?"

"You'll be using that gear again. Before you know it."

"Fuck my ass I will. Mississippi icehouses ain't even buying."

"You're upset, Mr. Trench. I would be too."

"Upset? Is that what I am?"

Now Trench was hosing off a contraption that looked half giant monocle and half sieve. "Yeah, how about this? Paying for this too? Forty grand, this fucking thing."

Grimes wiped his sopping brow with the back of his hand.

"Helps save turtles we never used to catch anyway. The government planted them. Call it Black Sunday round here. Some guy got it on video-tape. On his phone or what-the-fuck-ever. Helicopters dropping shit on a Sunday. Monday, people are catching a fuck-ton of turtles. Turtles we'd never seen before. You got a turtle? I got twenty. You got a turtle? I got thirty. Before that? Not one. Day my hair went fucking gray."

Grimes stood speechless in the smiting sun. He wondered if there wasn't a soul in the Barataria who wasn't cracked.

God, to be done with this man once and for all.

"You're wondering why I'm telling you all this," Trench said. He went to the gunwale and leaned over the water and spat out the nub of his cigarette. Then he went back to spraying the turtle sorter. "I'm sick of getting fucked. So I ain't signing."

"Mr. Trench," said Grimes.

"Mr. Trench, Mr. Trench. I asked you a million times to leave me alone. You're stalking me."

Grimes shaped his eyes sincerely. "You know, Mr. Trench, sometimes people want to help. Help. Even people who work for companies. It's been known to happen."

His face kneading, Trench hesitated, let this soak in. Then he threw up his hands. "All right," he said, "I'll look at your papers. For a minute. That's it. Show me the number."

Incredulous, Grimes didn't move.

"What you waiting for? Better come before I change my crazy-ass mind."

Grimes stepped onto the gangplank and when he was halfway to the boat Trench pointed the spray nozzle and blasted him with water so cold that Grimes felt his heart clench. He shrieked and turned and tottered and almost toppled into the water. Then he jumped back onto the dock.

Trench kept spraying.

"Fuckin' coon-ass," Grimes said.

"Oh, the truth comes out," Trench said, laughing now. "Mr. Coon-ass. Mr. Coon-ass."

Grimes turned away, making himself stroll as still the water hammered at his back. "Big mistake," he said.

Trench was still cackling and spraying.

THE TOUP BROTHERS

Their house was ravaged, broken glass in the foyer and drawers eviscerated in the rooms, boxes and cans tossed about the kitchen floor. Reginald went quickly through the house as if the culprit might be hiding somewhere. Victor squatted and studied the shoeprints on the foyer floor, cursing under his breath. Two different pairs skewed back and forth, one big and the other small. When Reginald returned to the foyer Victor showed him the tracks.

"Lindquist," Victor said.

"Could've been anyone," said Reginald.

"Bullshit," Victor said, his face red and clenching like a fist. "Lindquist."

"Somebody older and maybe a kid looks like," Reginald said.

"I've seen a kid with Lindquist."

"He's regular-sized."

"Who else would it be?"

"Anybody."

"Bullshit."

"Better not leap to any wild conclusions," Reginald said.

"Somebody's gonna get killed."

"No they aren't either."

"Somebody's gonna get hurt," Victor said.

- - - - - - - -

For a few days Lindquist gave the twins' island wide berth, but then one night without the kid he ventured southeast toward their part of the bayou. The brothers followed his avocado-green shrimp boat from a distance, their lights off and their motor at half speed.

When Lindquist anchored, the brothers anchored too. Reginald watched through the binoculars as Lindquist lowered the pirogue from the shrimp boat and oared toward the little chenier, an isolated figure in the dim orange glow of his Coleman lantern. After a while he shored his boat and hauled out his machine and began to swing the metal-detector coil back and forth along the tideline. Every now and then he set the machine on the ground and dug a hole with the shovel-scoop. Prodded through the overturned dirt with the tip of his boot.

Reginald saw that Lindquist wore camouflage cargo pants, army surplus. A hooked prosthetic arm. And he kept taking something out of his pocket and fiddling with it, popping peppermints or gum into his mouth.

The guy was persistent, Reginald had to give him that. And thorough. A warning or two wasn't going to ward him off. Maybe not even a gunshot. Something more persuasive was required.

Not murder, not yet. That was an absolute last resort. Besides, the swamp already held too many of their secrets. If one was discovered, others were likely to follow. One mistake begot another, one suspicion led to the next. While the swamp had always proved their greatest alibi and accomplice, it would hold only so many bodies before they started washing up bone by bone.

The present body count was up to three, all belonging to overambitious and undertalented loudmouths who'd tried to poach on their marijuana trade. None of them heeded the Toup brothers' warnings and ended up dead, secreted in the farthest reaches of the bayou, sunk into the mud and murk with stones in their pockets, one with his throat slit ear to ear, two with bullets through their hearts.

- - - - - - - -

Lonny Brewbaker, a redoubtable ne'er-do-well, owed the Toup brothers five hundred dollars for drugs. Money they'd likely never see, but they let him accrue the debt nonetheless, knowing that sooner or later he'd have to make good with a favor instead. One night Victor called Brewbaker to collect this due, said he needed the biggest live alligator he could find, never mind for what.

Brewbaker told Victor to give him a day.

Next night the Toup brothers went to Brewbaker's, a rust-ruined doublewide with a briar-choked yard and a Scotch-plaid sofa on the porch. Victor pounded on the door and Reginald stood behind him as June bugs thumped against the bug zapper.

A bent-backed man with sunken cheeks answered the door. He had on Bermuda shorts and a New Orleans Saints Drew Brees jersey and fluorescent orange Crocs. He jutted his chin in greeting and hobbled down the steps.

The twins followed Brewbaker to the backyard. Under an enormous oak tree was a chain-link cage, inside it a crouching alligator six or seven feet long. Brewbaker took the flashlight out of his pocket and shined it into the fencing. The alligator's eyes caught the light and flared like rubies. Its snout was muzzled with duct tape.

"Look at the size of this thing," Reginald said.

"Fuck you pull this off?" Victor asked Brewbaker.

"Shit," Brewbaker said. He set the flashlight on the ground, angling the beam so it shined into the cage.

"This might be extreme," Reginald said.

Hands on hips, Brewbaker hesitated. Maybe hoping the brothers would call off whatever crazy scheme they had planned.

"Extreme, shit," Victor said.

"Let's just get this fuckin' thing in the truck," Reginald said.

Brewbaker unlatched the gate and swung it open and stepped inside. The alligator hissed and backed up in the corner. Reginald and Victor stepped into the cage with Brewbaker and the men moved toward the alligator in a wide-kneed crouch like Sumo wrestlers. Brewbaker lunged and got the alligator into a headlock and then Victor closed in, wrapping his arms around the tail. Reginald joined the fray, bear-hugging the middle.

"Hold on," Brewbaker said. "Holy shit, hold on."

They sidestepped out of the cage, slip-sliding in mud, clinging onto the alligator, its three hundred pounds of thrashing muscle. They went through the side yard toward Brewbaker's truck.

Twenty minutes later, the alligator in the cab, they sat inside Brewbaker's truck, reeking of mud and reptile piss. Their clothes and faces were filthy, and in the dim glow of the dome light the whites of their eyes looked crazed.

Brewbaker laughed, then the twins.

"Now what?" Brewbaker said.

"Drive," Victor said. "We'll tell you."

At Lindquist's house Reginald and Brewbaker waited in the truck while Victor stepped onto the porch and pressed the doorbell. He glanced at his watch, then over his shoulder. After a minute he took out his snake-rake pick and jimmied the lock and stepped inside and turned on a light. Then Victor came back outside and gave them a thumbs-up.

The men hauled the alligator into the house and down the hall into the master bedroom, where they pinned it to the floor. Brewbaker gripped the alligator's neck while Victor took out a pocketknife and sliced off the duct tape. Then the men leapt away from the alligator as if from a bomb, scrambling out of the room, Victor switching off the light and slamming the door.

In the hallway the three of them listened. Soon came the *thunk, thunk, thunk* of the alligator's tail against the walls. The scrabbling of its claws.

Brewbaker grinned and shook his head. Then the twins grinned and soon they were all laughing.

Brewbaker said, "We even?"

LINDQUIST

Again Lindquist visited Trader John's with his purple velvet Crown Royal bag full of cheap jewelry, the dregs of his emergency cache. He was bleary-eyed and stubble-faced, his fatigues dirt-caked at the knees. He saw three other men at the counter, local trawlers he recognized, and his eyes bugged. Then he noticed the men's eyes on the bag in his hand and figured his jig was up. Reluctantly he went to the counter.

"How you, fellas," he said.

"There he is," said one of the men. "Blackbeard the pirate." This was Michael Franklin, a little pigeon-chested guy who always reminded Lindquist of a lawn jockey.

Lindquist shifted his weight and breathed an uneasy half-laugh through his teeth. For a moment the only sound was the bubbling bait wells, the electric hum of the drink coolers. The other two men, Jarred and Ricky, watched Lindquist, eyes simmering with menace.

"What you got today, Lindquist?" Mrs. Theriot asked.

Lindquist put the bag on the counter, kept his hand protectively on top.

"Sell any of that stuff?" he asked.

"About that," the old woman said. "Somebody came in claiming the watch. Garret? The pastor?"

Lindquist watched her, chewing air. Was there one person on earth not trying to fuck the next sideways?

"Would've called you," the woman said, crossing her arms over her chest, her billowy pineapple shirt, "but didn't have any number. And I figured you'd make the same decision I did. A pastor, probably honest."

"Well, hell. He have any proof?"

She gave Lindquist a look: proof?

"A receipt?" asked Lindquist. "Anything?"

"What, you got to carry around a license for a watch now?" Jarred said. "Greencard if it's foreign?"

"He didn't have any receipt," Mrs. Theriot told Lindquist. "He pretty much just looked at the thing and made this face and went, 'Hey, that's my watch.' His face, I just knew."

Lindquist's eyes roved the merchandise in the glass case. "How about that ring?" he said.

"You know Tracy Bascombe?"

Lindquist pulled at his chin.

"Tracy Bascombe, George's kid?"

Lindquist waited.

"Married that Marshall boy still in Afghanistan? Organized all that sandbagging stuff?"

"Million rings in the world look like that," Lindquist said.

"That's true. But before she even touched the ring she told me to check if there was one of those little inscriptions written inside. You know how people do with the dates and all? No way she could have seen it from where she was."

Lindquist looked away and stared at the hotdog rotisserie. Behind the grease-scummed glass the desiccated sausages turned lazily on their spits.

"Where you finding this shit, Lindquist?" Michael asked. "You breaking into people's houses?"

Lindquist ignored him. "Did anything sell?" he asked. "Any damned thing that wasn't claimed?"

"That pocket watch," Mrs. Theriot said.

"How much."

"Five dollars."

"Five dollars?"

"I'm going to tell you something, Lindquist," Jarred said.

Lindquist's eyes settled hard on Jarred.

"People don't care none for you digging up their shit and trying to sell it."

"Listen. That's bull. I'm just looking for stuff. What I find it's on land that don't belong to nobody. Nobody that ain't a corporation."

All eyes were on him.

Lindquist's face twisted. "And it just so happens to be theirs? Well, hell. Then there's got to be a statute of limitations."

"A what," Jarred said.

Lindquist hesitated. Said, "Look, pretty much everything belonged to someone else at some point, didn't it?"

The men traded glances.

"You want to show us what you got today, Lindquist?" Mrs. Theriot asked.

"Got to admit, I'm curious," Michael said. He looked at the others.

"I'm curious," Ricky said.

"Damn right you're curious," Jarred said.

Lindquist upturned the bag and spread the loot deftly, like a flimflam artist performing a shell trick. Then he looked up with a tight poker face. Or what he thought was one.

"Look at all that," Michael said. "Gotta take me up this metal detecting shit. "

This time Lindquist's pile was even bigger than before. Most of the pieces were crudded with dirt, but a few gave off a newish gleam.

"Goddamn," Michael said, "my class ring."

He reached into the pile and snatched the ring away before Lindquist could make a move.

"Bull," Lindquist said, grabbing air.

Michael took a step back with the ring clutched in his fist. "I'm telling you. Popped my cherry wearing this ring."

Jarred reached into the pile and plucked something out and Lindquist whirled. Jarred drew back and turned and held the jewelry piece to the light. "I can't believe it," he said. "My grandmother's locket."

"Bull," Lindquist said.

"Everybody hold on," Mrs. Theriot said.

Then Ricky snatched something out of the pile, a gold necklace with a dewdrop pearl pendant, and scuttled sideways. "I swear on Holy Christ this is my wife's. Where'd you find this, Lindquist?"

Jaw agape, Lindquist looked around at the men. Before anyone could take more he scooped up the remaining trinkets and shoved them back into the bag.

"I want proof," Lindquist said.

"I'll prove it," Jarred said. "With my boot to the back of your fuckin' head."

"Hey," Mrs. Theriot said. "None of that in my place now."

Lindquist glimpsed something in the glass display that made him pause and furrow his brow. A thin gold necklace with a heart pendant. "Where'd you get that?" he asked Mrs. Theriot. "The one with the heart?"

"Why?" Jarred said. "You gonna say that's yours now? That you lost your little heart necklace?"

The men chuckled.

"If you're gonna keep that stuff you stole from me, I want compensation," Lindquist said.

"Compensation? Matlock all of a fuckin' sudden."

"A finder's fee," Lindquist said.

"You ain't getting goose shit."

"Screw ya'll," Lindquist said.

"Lindquist," Mrs. Theriot said, but Lindquist had already turned and was stalking toward the door.

Once outside he jeered through the glass and shot out his middle finger. He let loose a wild spate of obscenities and saw the men laughing through the glass, the old woman chiding them with a wigwagging finger.

In a pill-and-beer stupor Lindquist got home late from Sully's bar, stumbling out of his clothes in the hallway, tossing them willy-nilly about. In the dark room on the way to the bed, he tripped over something large and heavy and went flying face-first into the carpet. For a moment he lay stunned and spread-eagled on the floor, wondering if he'd had a stroke. Yes, he was fucked up on pills. Yes, he'd had a little too much to drink. But Lindquist prided himself as a man who knew where his own goddamn furniture was.

He was struggling from the floor when he heard a gurgling sound, phlegmy and reptilian, in the room. Lindquist's heart gave a single hard knock and then quickened. He scrabbled to his feet and turned and saw a hunched kayak-like shape, low to the floor, stepping tentatively toward him.

He told himself he had to be dreaming. There could be no other explanation. But he leapt onto the bed and switched on the lamp and shrieked like a castrato when he saw what he saw.

An alligator. Six feet, maybe seven.

A fucking alligator in his bedroom.

Lindquist cringed against the headboard. The alligator also retreated, crouching near the door with its leathery tail lashing and its snaggled teeth bared.

To make sure he wasn't dreaming, Lindquist pinched his cheek, hard, but felt only a phantom twinge of pain, dulled from the booze and pills. Otherwise nothing changed. Mud and shit and piss were still smeared on the carpet and the walls. One of the decorative tables was still knocked over and Gwen's porcelain penguins and pigs were scattered across the floor.

"Get," Lindquist said. He flapped his hand in an inane shooing gesture. "I said get now."

The alligator hissed through its candy-corn teeth.

Lindquist opened a nightstand drawer and took out the first thing his fingers clasped. His wife's dildo, a hideous purple thing with a bulbous end like a plum. He tossed the phallus at the alligator and it bounced off its head and landed nearby in the carpet.

The alligator scrabbled into the corner and turned to watch Lindquist with ravenous yellow-gold eyes.

"Good God," Lindquist said. He snatched up the night-table phone and dialed with shaking fingers.

"Is this an emergency?" the operator asked.

"Yes, yes," Lindquist said.

"What's the emergency?"

"An alligator," Lindquist said, breath shaking into the phone. "Alligator in my bedroom."

WES TRENCH

Lindquist, Wes noticed, had been acting strange all night. Spooked and jittery. One thing, he wasn't telling any of his corny jokes. And the deeper into the Barataria he piloted the *Jean Lafitte,* the more anxious-seeming he grew, throwing wild glances right and left out the wheelhouse windows, a kind of restless apprehension twitching in his face.

Around midnight Wes finally asked what the matter was and Lindquist told him that somebody put an alligator in his bedroom.

"Say what?" said Wes, figuring it another of Lindquist's jokes.

"An alligator, in my bedroom," said Lindquist, his face tight and serious.

Wes was speechless.

"Six or seven feet, this thing. Might as well have been twenty. Nearly scared me to death."

"You call the cops?"

"Yeah. Two deputies came and shot it in the head and dragged it out."

They were taking a break from trawling and were down in the boat's galley, two redfish fillets sputtering in a frying pan on the gas stove. A downpour crackled on the deck above them and thrashed against the little galley window. The distant lights of the nearest boat were a wavery blur. Every so often a prong of brilliant purple lightning speared soundlessly down far out in the Gulf. Lindquist rose from the table and went to the stove and turned over the filets with a fork. The smell of garlic and onion and cayenne was making Wes's mouth water. For the past few days, he'd had only canned Vienna sausages and crackers to eat.

Lindquist set plates down on the galley table, one for Wes and one for himself. Pan-seared redfish with a side of dirty rice: Zatarain's, right out of the box. Wes began scarfing down his food, though it was a bit heavy on the cayenne pepper. His eyes watered and he coughed. Lindquist laughed and asked Wes if the food was spicy enough.

After a while Lindquist said, "I think it was them twins, me. The Toup brothers."

"Why'd they put an alligator in your room?"

"They're crazy's why."

They kept quiet for a while, Lindquist chewing his food groggily, a slow bovine grinding of his jaws. Every so often his eyes would shut for several seconds and his grip around his fork would loosen like a baby's. Then he'd open his eyes and settle them hazily on his plate.

Wes assumed it was the pills. Lindquist was always taking out that Pez dispenser and swallowing one or two of whatever was inside.

"They think I'm after their reefer," Lindquist said.

Wes said nothing because he couldn't tell if Lindquist was joking.

"I told them I had no interest. That I was just metal detecting. They took my arm anyway. The good one I had."

"You know that? For sure?"

Lindquist nodded. "Got no proof, but I'm sure. Somebody told me. Then I told Villanova about it. Course he did nothing."

Wes let out a loose and breathy whistle of surprise. "Maybe I'd stay away from wherever they want you to stay away from."

"I can't. I won't."

The rain pinged like BB's on the galley window glass.

Lindquist clicked down his fork. "I've been searching the Barataria my whole life. They got no right to tell me I can't. And ain't like I can stop. Not now. Not after this long."

Wes asked him what he'd do with real money if he ever found some.

"Stop trawlin', that's for sure. Move away. Far away. Whole damn place is falling apart. And buy myself a new arm. One that does all kinds of fancy shit."

Then Lindquist asked Wes the same question. Wes told him he didn't want to leave the Barataria if he could help it, but with all the oil and the damage to the marsh, it was hard to predict. When he finally finished building his shrimp boat, if he did, he'd start his own business, a kind of shrimp-of-the-day club. "Eliminate the middle man," he said. "Like they did in the old days."

"Well, hell," Lindquist said and shook his head.

Wes asked him what.

"You're a damn genius, kid."

"Naw," Wes chuckled.

"A damn genius."

Lindquist said he wished his daughter were as frugal and ambitious. When she earned a buck, an hour later she lost two. The goddamnest thing. Wes had no idea what to say and didn't want to insult Lindquist's daughter so he kept quiet.

"What you gonna name it?" Lindquist asked. His voice was spitty and slurred.

The rain had slowed and now there was only bayou darkness beyond the water-webbed window. Wes turned away from the window and looked at Lindquist.

"Name it?" Wes said.

"The boat, kid."

"I don't know yet."

"None?"

"I was gonna name it after my mama, but I had second thoughts. My mama's not a boat, you know?"

Lindquist nodded sleepily.

Wes shrugged and set down his fork. "So, I guess I'll wait to name it. Don't want to jinx it."

Lindquist said nothing but he studied Wes in a way that seemed like he decided something about him right then, though Wes couldn't tell good or bad.

- - - - - - - -

An hour or so later after the rain they had the trawls lowered in the water when Wes noticed the boat veering off course. They were headed straight to one of the small barrier islands in the mouth of the bay. Wes looked up and saw Lindquist hunched over the boat wheel, head canted to the side, eyes shut. Dead asleep.

"Mr. Lindquist," Wes shouted.

Nothing.

Wes cupped his hands around his mouth. "Mr. Lindquist."

Lindquist didn't stir.

They were about three hundred yards from colliding with the island. Pretty soon the hull would scrape the bayou bottom and the *Jean Lafitte* would be shipwrecked.

Wes scrambled up the ladder two rungs at a time and once in the wheelhouse shook Lindquist's shoulder. His eyes snapped open and he peered about groggily.

"We're headed toward an island," Wes told him.

Lindquist's eyes went deranged and he grabbed the wheel and turned it sharply to the right. When the boat was back on track he slapped his cheek. Then he looked at Wes. His face was red with embarrassment. "What?" he said.

"You fell asleep."

"Yeah. So?"

"Wanna go lay down?"

Lindquist paused. "What you mean?"

"Let me take care of it."

Lindquist looked at Wes darkly. "You saying I'm screwed up?"

"I'm asking if you're okay."

"Okay?"

Wes was quiet.

"Are you okay?" Lindquist said in a girlish voice. "Are you okay?" he said again, taunting. His eyes scalded Wes. "I got plenty of that bull from my wife."

Wes stayed silent.

"*You okay?* She'd ask every five seconds. Giving me that look. Like you're giving me now."

"I'll say it. You take a lot of those pills, Mr. Lindquist."

"Yeah? So?"

"One friend to another, just thought I'd say it."

"We're not friends. I'm your boss, me. You're my employee. That's the situation."

Wes swallowed, his face burning hot. "All right," he said. "But we're friendly."

"Not right now we're not."

Wes climbed back down to the deck and busied himself with the nets. In his head he replayed his conversation with Lindquist over and over again while he muttered curses under his breath. Just another two or three hours, he thought. Then he'd be away from this guy, maybe for good. But what then? Back to work for his father? That would be trading one kind of hell for another.

Before long Lindquist called down from the wheelhouse window. His voice was completely changed, even friendly. "Hey, Wes," he said, as if nothing had happened.

Wes looked up.

"Knock knock," Lindquist said.

Wes shook his head and hissed spitefully through his teeth.

"Knock knock," Lindquist said, louder.

Wes waved Lindquist off and turned his back.

"Well, hell," Lindquist said. "Fine, if that's the way you wanna be."

They didn't speak again until they'd taken their shrimp to Monsieur Montegut's and were back in the marina parking lot. As they stood near their trucks in the tangerine light of dawn, Lindquist gave Wes half the money, not the usual third.

"You made a mistake," Wes said.

Lindquist squinted against the sun, crow's feet wrinkling the corners of his eyes. "Severance pay," he said.

"Look, if this is about the pills, Mr. Lindquist, I'm sorry. It's none of my business."

"You're right. It's not." Then, maybe because he regretted being so harsh, Lindquist's voice softened. "It's not about the pills, kid."

Wes kept silent.

"I can't do this anymore," Lindquist said.

"Do what?"

"Shrimping. I'm done, me. Probably gonna put up booms for those folks. Clean oil. Nurse baby pelicans. Who the hell knows."

"I won't mention the pills again, Mr. Lindquist. Just let me work."

"Kid. It's got nothing to do with the pills. Look at the water. Watch the news. We're going out there and working to lose money. We were doing anything else, they'd lock us in a loony bin for acting this way."

Wes nodded. "This is a lot of money," he said.

Lindquist swatted his hook.

"Well, thanks," Wes said. He dug into his pocket and held out Lindquist's boat keys.

"You can stay another few nights if you want. Until things sort out."

"I'll be all right."

"You goin' home?"

"Probably," Wes lied.

"Talk to your pop. Don't be a moron."

"All right, Mr. Lindquist."

Lindquist turned and walked toward his truck, held up his hand. "Take care, kid."

"Take care, Mr. Lindquist," Wes said back.

COSGROVE AND HANSON

They needed a boat if they were going to find the twins' island. Provided it existed. They needed a boat but Hanson had no money and Cosgrove refused to squander any of his meager savings on a pipe dream. Hanson told Cosgrove he had something he took from the widow's house he never told him about.

A ring.

"A ring?" Cosgrove said. "We agreed. Just stuff in the attic."

"It was in the attic."

Cosgrove stared at Hanson. A hard look of recrimination.

"Hey, Sasquatch, I'm telling you now, ain't I?"

They took the diamond ring to a pawnshop just off the highway. Trader John's.

"Like to see how much this's worth," Hanson told the old woman in the Hawaiian shirt standing behind the counter. He reached into his pocket and chinked the ring down on the hand-smeared glass. The woman picked the ring up and turned it around in her gnarled fingers, forehead seaming as she squinted through a jeweler's loupe.

Cosgrove glanced at the merchandise behind the counter, sun-faded bric-a-brac hung from the walls: banjos, taxidermied animal heads, medical apparatus among Saints paraphernalia and anti-Obama bumper stickers. Whole damn parish had its life on consignment. Pretty soon people would be hawking their body parts for beer and cigarette money. Kidneys and corneas on layaway at Trader John's.

"Where you find this?" the woman asked.

Without pause Hanson told the woman that the ring had once belonged to his fiancée. Penelope. Dead.

The clerk let the loupe drop, and the glass swung from the chain around her neck. She shot back her wobbly chin and clucked her tongue.

"Car wreck," Hanson said, adjusting his rodeo belt buckle. "That wasn't bad enough, there was a guy with her. Young dude."

A plump cat, marmalade-orange, leapt onto the counter and strolled up to Hanson, staring with intense yellow-green eyes. "Dude had his pants down," he said, stroking the cat's head. "Down to his ankles. Both of 'em got themselves in such a frenzy she drove 'em both right off a bridge into the river."

Cosgrove wondered if Hanson had made up all this soap opera bullshit in advance. He hoped to God so. He hated to ponder the kind of warped mind that could conjure this craziness on the spot.

Hanson went on. Surreally. "Wearing this very ring I bought for her. I didn't know whether to cry or dig her up and kill her again."

Hanson made a show of musing on this. The old woman's face remained as inert as wood. Maybe she'd heard it all during her seventy-five or eighty years on earth. "Know what," the woman said. "All this sounds mighty silly to me."

Hanson huffed out an indignant breath and raised his eyebrows. He took off his camouflage cap, smoothed back his black ponytail, put the cap back on. "Well, I don't know what to tell you. I guess my life is silly then."

The old woman offered nine hundred dollars for the ring. Fifteen hundred, Hanson said. Nine hundred, countered the woman. Twelve, Hanson said. Nine, said the woman. Ten, Hanson said.

Nine, said the woman.

- - - - - - - - -

Their next day off Hanson called a number from an ad in the paper and twenty minutes later they were on their way in Hanson's Dodge to the other side of Jeanette. When they showed up to the brick ranch house, a stout bald man with a jazz patch and a wad of tobacco bulging his cheek limped out. He shook their hands, his fingers the roughest Cosgrove ever felt in his life, like tree bark.

The man led them to the backyard, where a T-shaped pier jutted out into a pea-soup-green lagoon. Cosgrove and Hanson looked over the aluminum powerboat, ten feet long and outfitted with an old lawnmower engine. The man stood with hands tucked in his pockets and his thumbs hooked in his belt loops, spitting tobacco juice in the water. Minnows rose up to the surface and nibbled at the bubbles with tiny kissing mouths.

"So where do we take it?" Hanson asked the man.

"Take it?"

"Where do we park it?" Hanson kept edging closer to the man. The man kept edging uneasily back, every so often glancing at Hanson's shirt, which said METALLICA, KILL 'EM ALL on the front, above a drawing of a bloody hammer and gore-splattered tile.

It took a second for the man to figure out what Hanson meant. "You don't have a slip?"

"No."

The man scratched his chin and considered this. "Well, I guess you can rent a slip pretty cheap at the marina. If you don't have your own pier."

"How do we get it there?" Hanson asked.

The man looked at Hanson as if he were joking. "You drive it."

"Can we tow it, I mean?"

"You got a trailer?"

Hanson shook his head.

"Then you got to drive it."

"You got one for sale?"

"Naw. Naw, I don't have no trailer."

The three men stood in silence, gazing at the boat as if it would solve these dilemmas.

"Just askin'," the man said, "you got a license, right?"

"Driver's?"

"Boating."

"Sure."

The man looked at Cosgrove. Cosgrove shrugged. He imagined the man telling his buddies about them later. *You never believe these dipshits came here the other day never been on a boat in their lives.*

"Hell, none of my business," the man said.

"It's a fuckin' boat," Hanson said to Cosgrove. "How many aspects is there?"

- - - - - - - - -

Mid-September Cosgrove and Hanson fell into a regular pattern of reconnaissance. Every night after their shift at the bird sanctuary they piloted into the Barataria and explored the archipelago of islands, wandered shorelines by the feeble light of their lanterns like revenants of an apocalypse. The islets and cheniers were innumerable, most of them hardly more than patches of marshy weed. The coordinates Hanson took from the GPS led only to an island with a skeletal willow tree, its branches filled with sleeping white egrets. No marijuana. But they used the island as a reference point. If the twins' island was anyplace, it was probably around here.

Sometimes they saw solitary boat lights shining far out on the horizon. Otherwise the bay was eerily bereft of human life. Maybe nobody else was stupid enough to come near this place. Every day the signs posted around the beach were direr in their warnings. AVOID WATER. AVOID DEAD ANIMALS. DON'T SWIM. DON'T BREATHE.

GET THE FUCK OUT, the signs would probably read in a week or two.

As far as Cosgrove and Hanson could tell, nobody was around to enforce the rules.

Cosgrove wondered why he was such a willing accomplice to Hanson's dumbfuckery. Why he deferred to the whims of this latter-day village idiot. But there really wasn't any mystery to his acquiescence. He was desperate. Desperate and, yes, curious. Curious to see what would become of all of this. Curious to see if there was any truth to Hanson's bullshit. He figured all it would cost him was a week or two more of his life. A week or two: he had that. Time was all he had.

Besides, Cosgrove had nowhere to go, no other prospects on the horizon. He was stuck in the ass crack of Louisiana making fifteen dollars an hour as part of an oil cleanup crew. And this was probably as good as things were going to get for him. Of course he knew that searching for an island of marijuana was crazy. But he also knew that every so often fools stumbled upon fortune, whether by fate or fluke.

GRIMES

Grimes parked on the side of the rutted dirt road and got out of his car. For a while he stared at the yard—if that's what you could call it—crunching on a Granny Smith apple and debating whether to brave the jungle-thick wilderness before him. Then he did. He tossed the apple and cut through the tall briars and weeds, arms working like he was swimming against a current, grasshoppers pinwheeling through the air with a papery rattling of wings.

By the time he reached the porch of the dilapidated bungalow he was red-faced and gasping, his clothes dusty and stuck with cockleburs.

A hollow-templed old man sat on a cane rocker in the porch shade. "Fixin' to get killed today," he grumbled under his breath.

"Sir?" Grimes said, though he'd heard.

"Dis private property you're on."

"Don't mean to inconvenience you, sir," Grimes said, still struggling for breath. The number 4 burned in his head like a neon sign. Four signatures so far today. Four months left in the year, four decades on earth, four decades to go.

Grimes stood in the sun just beyond the shadow of the house and shaded his face with his hand. When the man said nothing, he looked left, where there was a wire chicken coop at the edge of the yard. Yard birds jibber-jabbed and strutted around the meal bin. Then he looked right, where a pirogue was propped upright against a tin-roofed toolshed. The door of the shed was open wide, and muskrats and nutria skins hung from the exposed ceiling beams.

"I'm looking for Donald Baker," Grimes said finally. "Mr. Baker filed a claim with us. Know him?"

"I might."

"You him?"

"What's your business?"

"British Petroleum."

"You have one heartbeat to turn around and get your ass off my property," the man said.

"Sir? I've come to give you your settlement."

The man settled back in his chair. "Settlement for what?"

"For your troubles. If you're Mr. Baker. Who filed the claim. You him?"

"You came here to give me money is what you're saying."

"I have the check right here."

"I don't keep no bank account."

"I'm sure you can still cash it. With your ID. With identification."

"Don't have none that either."

"Are you Donald Baker?"

"I might or might not be."

Grimes put his hands on his hips and looked down at his muddy shoes. "I can tell maybe it's the wrong time."

"It'll never be the right one."

At a loss for what else to say, Grimes half-heartedly raised his hand and turned, waded back through the weeds toward his car. When he glanced over his shoulder, the old man was still staring, his face hard as stone.

- - - - - - - - -

Next day Grimes returned and slogged through the tall grass and brambles of the old man's yard. Not a cloud in the sky and the sun was glaring over everything like molten pewter. By the time Grimes reached the hardpacked clearing around the house, he was already sopping with sweat.

The old man watched him from his porch chair. "You got cash?" he asked.

"Cashier's check," Grimes said.

"You're telling me all I have to do is sign a paper and you give me the money."

"That's exactly what I'm telling you."

"I'm Donald Baker," the man said.

"Well, then, Mr. Baker," Grimes said. "Now we're getting somewhere."

The old man rose from the cane chair, waved him inside.

Grimes stepped into the cabin and glanced about, taking in the hanging swatches of flypaper, the swaybacked sofa upholstered with stitched-together nutria skins, the holes in the walls patched over with flattened sardine tins and scraps of cardboard. Five hours of daylight left, Grimes thought. If he got this visit over with quickly, he could visit ten or twelve other houses.

"You thirsty?" the old man asked.

"I'm okay."

"Let's get you some water."

"I'm fine."

"I bet you parched."

At the kitchen table Grimes sat straight-backed and tight-shouldered with his leather satchel in front of him. He snapped it open and withdrew a manila folder and from this pulled a sheaf of Xeroxed papers. The old man went to a tin bucket on the counter and ladled some water into a porcelain mug with a cracked-off handle. He walked over to the table and placed the mug in front of Grimes.

Grimes stared down, hands in his lap. The mug had a lip-smudge on the rim.

The old man pulled back his chair and sat across from him. "Have you a drink," he said.

Hesitantly Grimes brought the mug to his lips and took the daintiest sip. Grimaced. Swallowed. Then he sat the cup back down and pushed the paperwork across the table.

The man stroked his chin, made a show of studying the paperwork. Grimes doubted the coon-ass understood a word. "And you ain't from the government," he said.

Grimes shook his head.

"A thousand dollars for nothing."

"Well, your community has suffered. We want to make good on the promises we made. To rebuild the community."

"Gotta piss," said the old man, rising with surprising quickness, his knee bones popping.

After the old man thumped down the hall, Grimes sat brooding about his mother. Every day he dreaded more the prospect of his visit. He pictured her face, her lips rumpled, her wet eyes tight and scolding. "You've been in town how long?" she'd ask. Then would come the moment he dreaded most of all, the moment he reached into his satchel and drew out the papers. She would harrumph and look them over and tell him how disappointed she was. Like a year ago, the last time they spoke on the phone.

Grimes decided he would see her today. Definitely today.

No, not today. Tomorrow.

Today.

Grimes's mind was still seesawing when the old man barged back into the kitchen, peacock feathers in his hair like a half-assed Indian headdress. Muttering gibberish, eyes rolling like a gutted sow's, he clutched a glass brimming with amber liquid that looked like apple juice.

Grimes half stood, mouth agape, not knowing what to think. "Mr. Baker," he said.

"*Putain!*" the old man said. "*Nique ta mere!*"

"Mr. Baker," Grimes said. His eyes ticked between the man's face and the glass.

The old man jerked his arm and doused Grimes with what was in the glass. Piss. Grimes knew right away from the smell. He let out a strangled sound of shock and jerked upright. His chair tipped back and smacked the floor.

"What's this?" he said, glowering. "This fuckin' piss?"

"*Nique ta mère!*"

"Goddamn lunatic."

"*Ta gueule!*"

Grimes shouldered his satchel and, still facing the man, scuttled backward like a crab out of the kitchen. He wiped furiously at his face with his shirtsleeve. In the den he turned around and flung the door open, cursing as he vaulted down the porch steps two at a time.

THE TOUP BROTHERS

Working the motorboat's tiller, Victor picked up speed where the canal opened into the bayou proper. Before long they passed an enormous dead willow, its branches full of slumbering egrets. Hundreds glowing like white ornaments in the dark. This was the place where people usually turned back, the point of no return. They'd have no reason to venture this far unless they were looking for trouble. Or trying to escape it.

Tonight the twins were out to check on their island. On the floor of the boat were gunnysacks full of tools and traps.

"You remember 'Spy vs. Spy'?" Victor asked Reginald, shouting above the motor.

Neither of them had said a word in twenty minutes.

"Yeah," Reginald said. They'd collected *Mad* magazines when they were boys and they'd especially liked "Spy vs. Spy."

"I loved those books," Victor said. "Bet they're somewhere in the attic. I should find them."

"They'd probably suck now."

"I bet some of those booby traps would work. Medieval shit."

For a while only the sound of the motor, the soft roar of wind in their ears.

"You feel sorry for this guy?" Reginald asked.

"Fuck him."

"It's obvious something's wrong."

"Fuck him."

"You blunted the teeth on those traps?"

"You asked me a million times."

"Did you blunt the teeth?"

"Yes, Mother Teresa."

"All of them?"

"Yes."

"I don't want another body out here."

"Well, I blunted them."

They banked on the island and hopped from the boat, sweeping their flashlight beams. In the underbrush they stepped over the waist-tall barrier of fencing and slogged through the night-damp vines and brush, careful to avoid the traps they'd already set. In the middle of the island their crop, raised on wooden platforms and ceiled with camouflage shade cloth, was untouched. Thriving, rankly fecund. In their separate pots the plants sagged under the weight of their heavy buds and filled the night air with their skunkiness. Soon they'd be ready to harvest.

"See," Reginald said. "Worried for no reason."

"Fuck him," Victor said.

They went back to the boat and hauled out the gunnysacks and began laying their traps. Victor set a bear trap with filed-down metal teeth on the ground. He prized open the jaws, raked leaves over the trap with his boot. Then he stepped backward and crouched on his heels and began to place another.

Meanwhile Reginald dug into the dirt with a garden trowel. He gouged a divot a foot deep, stabbed a shish-kebab skewer point-side up into the hole, covered over the trap with sleech.

The brothers worked this way for the better part of an hour until they'd set all the traps. Then they met at the boat, their faces sweaty and shining in the dark.

"Probably enough," said Reginald.

"Fuck him," said Victor.

LINDQUIST

Like a child counting down the days till Christmas, Lindquist waited a few days, all the time he could stand, before he resumed searching in the bayou. Any longer and he would have been too torqued up to function, like those tin windup toys his grandparents used to keep in their playroom for the kids. He remembered turning the toy's butterfly key until it would go no farther, the tin dinosaur sputtering and jerking in fits as if it were possessed. Lindquist felt a clenching nerve in the very center of him, the tightening of an enormous screw. He worried he'd snap like one of those cheap tin toys, running amok in a grocery store with his limbs crazily aflail, knocking bottles and cans and boxes off the shelves until the clerk drew a gun from beneath the counter and took him down.

Lindquist left the harbor at half past twelve. A horror movie fog rose off the water and the air stank of oil. From the wheelhouse window Lindquist could see scores of floating dead fish, bellies flashing white in the boat's perimeter of light.

He took out his Pez dispenser and flicked the plastic duck head and popped a pill in his mouth. Then another. A one-two punch of Oxycontin and Percoset. He chewed the pills into a fine powder and swallowed the narcotic dust. His body filled slowly with a warm pink euphoria.

Before long he passed the salt dome with the wooden cross wreathed in plastic flowers. Then the islet with the enormous dead willow tree. To-night its skeletal branches were empty. Sometimes the egrets were there, sometimes they weren't. A mystery.

It was almost two when he reached the spit of land covered with marsh grass and cypress stumps and salt-stunted tupelo. He anchored his boat and got into his pirogue, lowered it into the bay, oared toward the island. He saw flickering movement in the corner of his eye and twisted around, but it was only his own shadow jerking along the illuminated water.

Before long he nosed the pirogue onto the thin ribbon of bracken that made up the shore, and got out of the boat and wallowed wide-legged over to a cypress stump. He set the lantern down and went back to the boat and retrieved the metal detector and shovel-scoop. He leaned the tool against the stump and switched on the metal detector and began to sweep the coil. Salamanders like squiggles of ink slithered away across the slimy leaves.

The metal detector blipped faintly. He put the machine aside and started spiritlessly but quickly digging. Like an automaton. Slime filled the hole like blood in a wound. Lindquist kept gouging away. A hook-armed silhouette, the only light for miles his lantern on the trampoline-sized hump of sediment.

After a half minute the shovel-scoop blade tinked against something small. Lindquist stooped and rooted through the mud and his fingers seized on something coin-shaped, heavy for its size. He stood and stuck the tool into the ground, and then he went to the lantern and crouched to inspect the coin-shaped piece of metal.

A washer, he thought. *A lug nut.*

His heart quickened.

He spat on the object and rubbed the mud off on his pant leg and then looked again.

It was a coin.

It was.

And no ordinary coin. Embossed on one side was the bewigged profile of some royal personage. On the other side was a seal or coat of arms.

Lindquist leapt upright and looked absurdly around. No one. The plashing of tiny waves. The moon a milky blot behind a cloud.

He held the coin up to his eyes and stared. Kept staring, still not quite believing what he saw.

"Well, hell," he said, a low whisper to himself. Then his voice raised in insane glee. "That's right," he said, "that's goddamn right."

– – – – – – – –

The gold coin was the size of a half dollar, its weight satisfyingly heavy in Lindquist's palm. He spent hours fondling the doubloon, worrying it between his fingers, flipping it across his knuckles like a street-corner magician. Mealtimes he placed the coin on the table and studied heads and tails. Printed on one side: CAROL.IIII.D.G.HISP.ET IND.R.1798. On the other: IN.UTROQ.FELIX.AUSPICE.DEO.FM.

Within a day Lindquist knew by heart every surface intricacy of the coin. The tiny chips along its edge. The palimpsest of scratches fine as spider silk along its face. He could spot the doubloon in a lineup of a hundred similar coins if he had to. With his eyes closed. By touch, by weight.

Lindquist knew the coin would fetch hundreds, maybe thousands, at a collectors' auction. But he wouldn't part with it, not this one.

Here was proof he was right. Right for the first time in his life.

Others? He'd part with other coins no problem. Why, there might be hundreds, thousands, in the Barataria. And he thought of this possibility hundreds, thousands, of times a day.

If he found other coins—he would, he knew it—he'd pay off his debts first thing. He wasn't a ne'er-do-well. He was simply a man who'd fallen on hard times. Like most folks in the Barataria. The way these creditors had treated him: like he was an animal. Pretty soon they'd bust down the door with a medicine ball and drag him away in chains.

What was it the diesel guy at the wharf told him? "You're not a check bouncer, Lindquist," he said. "You're a dribbler. A Harlem Globetrotter."

Then the man dropped Lindquist's check on the pine-plank floor of his office. He stared down at the check. Kept staring. Lindquist asked what the hell he was doing. The man said waiting for the check to bounce back up and knock out one of his teeth.

The diesel guy: Lindquist would pay him off first thing. *Here's a little something for you,* he'd say, handing the man an extra twenty. *Man of my word, me.*

The diesel guy would never make fun of him again.

And he would give some of the money to that Trench kid, for his boat. Good kid, Wes. If only his daughter were half as good. A horrible thought, he knew, but true. Maybe all Reagan needed was an opportunity, another chance. A lot like him, with Gwen. Well, he'd give his daughter another chance. With a little money she could go back to school—to University of New Orleans, to Nicholls State—and straighten herself out. "You're still young, you still have a shot," he'd tell his daughter. He pictured the two of them sitting at a window booth in Magnolia Café, a sunny afternoon, and he'd unpocket the check and push it across the table.

And Gwen. Of course Gwen. Hopefully she'd give him another chance too. With some money in the bank, things might be a little different this time around. Funny, the power of money. People said it couldn't buy love, but it could keep people together, which was pretty much the same, wasn't it?

He imagined Gwen and himself on a far-flung vacation in the near future. A Caribbean dusk, a beach with sand like confectioners' sugar. Spindly palm trees, their wind-bent silhouettes against the tropical gloaming. What would he be doing? Metal detecting along the tide line, the quicksilver surf warming his toes. And nearby in her umbrellaed lounge chair Gwen would be sipping a coconut cocktail. He'd look over and she'd smile and then he'd smile. She'd lift her drink in a little toast, the light of love and admiration in her eyes once more.

The bank. Lindquist's wife had told him not to come here, but the bank held two hundred and thirty dollars of his money. His only money. Well, if his only money was in this place, didn't that make the place partly his too? In his reasoning: yes.

When he walked into the bank ten minutes before closing on Friday afternoon, his wife's coworkers looked up cold-eyed from their desks and carrels. At her teller window Gwen was counting out bills for an old Vietnamese woman in a foam neck brace. When she glanced up at the door and saw Lindquist her expression soured.

Lindquist walked to the customer service table and picked out a deposit slip and stub pencil. Then he sat on a vinyl-cushioned chair under a plastic ficus tree and balanced the deposit slip on his knee and started filling it out. Four dollars and thirty cents. He'd never usually bother with such a small amount but he wanted to show Gwen the coin. He wanted to show Gwen he'd been right all along.

When his wife finished with the Vietnamese woman, Lindquist got up and zigzagged through the maze of velvet ropes and went to her window.

"Hey, Gwen," he said. He put the deposit slip and the money on the counter.

Gwen looked down and saw how much money was there and spitefully shook her head.

"How you doing?" he asked his wife.

The other tellers were watching in a way they thought discreet.

"Not too good," Gwen said, glassy-voiced. The neck of her purple sateen blouse was open and Lindquist could see the livid red of her chest.

"Why not?"

"I think you know, Gus."

"Well, hell. I'm just making a deposit. Ain't here to cause any trouble."

She took the money and deposit slip and clacked away at her computer.

"I like that color on you," Lindquist said. "That fingernail polish. That's a good color. Real flattering."

Gwen printed out the deposit receipt and handed it to Lindquist.

"Have a good day," she said.

Lindquist stood there with the slip in his hand, grinning like a dog. "I got a joke for you," he said.

"Please, Gus."

"You're in a bad mood. Maybe this joke'll help."

"It won't." Gwen sounded immensely tired.

"You haven't heard it yet."

"There's people waiting. This is my job."

Lindquist glanced over his shoulder. No one.

"Knock knock," Lindquist said.

Gwen said nothing.

"Knock knock," Lindquist said again, louder.

"Who's there?" Gwen asked in a small drowning voice.

"Dewey," Lindquist said, resting his forearm on the counter, leaning his face closer to the glass. Then he said, "You're supposed to ask 'Dewey who.'"

"Dewey who?" Gwen asked quietly.

"Dewey have to use this condom?" Lindquist said. He threw his head back and cackled, his Adam's apple jerking up and down like a grease-slicked ball bearing.

Gwen's face was red and twitching.

"Didn't like that one?" he asked.

Behind Lindquist a man cleared his throat. Lindquist turned and saw one of the managers, that guy with Bela Lugosi hair staring like some sheriff in a standoff, his arms crossed psychotically over his chest.

"Excuse you," Lindquist said. He turned back around and grinned at his wife. He saw that the orange-haired teller next to her was watching.

"How you doin', Marcy," Lindquist said.

"Good, Gus."

"Glad to hear it. Your hair looks nice today. That's a good look on you."

"Thanks, Gus," Marcy said.

"Well, hell. Don't thank me for telling the truth. Telling the truth is easy."

"Please, Gus," Gwen said.

"Please what?"

"Please leave."

"That's kind of rude. I'm a friendly customer."

"Have a little dignity is all."

"Sure, I'll have some," Lindquist said, looking around as if for an hors d'oeuvres tray. "Where is it?"

By now the room was silent, only the sound of the air-conditioning, of people shuffling papers and scratching their pens.

"Knock knock," Lindquist said.

Gwen stared at the counter.

"Knock knock," Lindquist said again.

Silence.

"Okay, fine," Lindquist said. He looked at Marcy. "Hey, Marcy, knock knock."

"Who's there?" Marcy said.

"Little Boy Blue," Lindquist said.

"No," Gwen said. "Don't ask him. Marcy, don't do it."

"Marcy, ask who's at the door," Lindquist said.

"I'm not sure if I should, Gus."

"Where's people's sense of humor?"

No one said a word.

The desperado cleared his throat again.

"Okay, I'll quit bothering you," said Lindquist. "One little thing first, though." He grinned and reached into his pocket and set the doubloon on the counter.

Gwen glanced down at the coin but her face showed no change in expression. "You're going to get me fired," she said.

"But look. That's a doubloon. A real doubloon. I found it, me. That's the real deal there."

Gwen's eyes were wet and now Lindquist saw the tear on her cheek. She knuckled it away.

Lindquist slipped the coin back in his pocket. "All right, okay," he said. "I'll leave."

About three in the morning Lindquist heard a heavy thump on the boat deck, scuttling footfalls. Adrenaline shot through him. He looked through the wheelhouse windows. No one. The bay in hushed slumber, dark as dark could be, the diminutive sound of waves against the hull. He wondered if back at the wharf a dog had snuck onto the boat. Maybe some other animal.

These possibilities were careening through his head when Lindquist heard someone clamber swiftly up the ladder. He looked frantically about for something he could use as a weapon. Only a Louisville Slugger propped in the far corner, too far to fetch because the person was already halfway up to the wheelhouse.

At last a head popped up from the floor like some fiendish jack in the box. One of the Toup brothers.

"Evening, Lindquist," he said. He came into the wheelhouse and stepped close enough forward that Lindquist could see his third eyebrow, fainter, between the two.

"You're crazy," Lindquist said.

This one was Victor. He knew because of the tattoos on his arms.

Victor's eyes seared with contempt. "You know what I can do to you?"

Now ten or twelve yards away a light came on in the bay. Lindquist glanced. A small listing motorboat, the other brother, Reginald, standing like a sentry, a vale of dark beyond.

Victor went to the metal detector hanging from its peg and took it from the wall. He wrapped both hands around the handle like he was holding a golf club and slammed the coil against the floor over and over. Lindquist watched disbelievingly. The coil twisted away from the machine and dangled askew from its wiring and then Victor flipped the metal detector around and began smashing the other end. The control box exploded apart, shards of broken plastic and red and green wiring. One of the screws struck Lindquist on the cheek, raising blood.

Victor tossed the ruined machine to the floor and glared at Lindquist. A giant-shouldered troglodyte, a menagerie of tattoos on his arms. "We told you," he said.

"You gonna pay me for that," Lindquist said, childlike. He saw the handgun handle poking from the waistband of Victor's black jeans, an insignia that said SIG SAUER.

"Pay you? I just busted the fuck out of it."

"I don't even smoke it, me."

"Smoke? What the hell you talking now?"

"Reefer."

Victor bared his teeth. "You have no idea how close to fucked you are."

"What I do to you? Why you bothering me?"

"Don't think I don't know what you did to my house, you fuck." This time the *fuck* came out with such venomous force that spittle flecked Lindquist's face. He recoiled.

"Your house?"

"I'll bust your fuckin' head, Lindquist."

"Stealing my arm wasn't enough?" Lindquist said. "How about the alligator in my house?"

Victor glared, rough breaths scraping quickly out his nose.

"I'm seeing Villanova," said Lindquist.

"Go to Villanova. I'll deny everything. 'Hell you talking about, metal detector?' Everybody knows you're a crazy pill-popper. Even your own daughter says."

Lindquist blinked, mouth twisting mutely.

"Look at you. Fuckin' retard."

Victor stared another moment and then started down the ladder, his eyes staying on Lindquist until his head ducked out of sight. Then Victor jumped back onto the motorboat and it rocked under his weight. Reginald started the motor. The brothers crouched, Victor staring up at the wheelhouse. Lindquist watched the boat cut away, its light shrinking to a wavery dot before fading altogether.

Lindquist stared at the broken machinery on the floor. He cursed softly and reached to pick up the machine but then he sat back down.

An irreparable ruin.

Lindquist's throat narrowed and grew hot. He didn't want to cry but he did.

- - - - - - - -

Lindquist leaned against the counter, forearms on the glass, his voice lowered to a conspiratorial whisper though there was no one else in Trader John's to hear. He asked the owner, Mrs. Theriot, to keep secret what he was about to say.

"What's with the funny voice?" Mrs. Theriot asked.

"I need you to keep quiet about this."

"Get off the glass."

It was early morning and sun shined brightly through the shopwindows. Lindquist hadn't slept in a day and his head hummed with exhaustion. The follicles of his scalp hurt, his eyelids. He'd been rationing his pills because only a dozen were left. Earlier he'd ransacked his house looking for something he could pawn, but everything of worth was already hocked. The flat-screen television, the stereo, the microwave, the blender, all of them sold. For pills. Ostensibly the appliances had been collateral, but Lindquist never returned with the money so Theriot ended up selling the merchandise.

Now Lindquist eyed the metal detector, a waterproof Fisher, hanging from the wall behind the counter.

"I got something, me. Need you to keep it out of sight for two weeks."

"A week."

"Ten days?"

"A week. Always been, always will be a week."

Lindquist hesitated, looked around uneasily. Then he unpocketed the coin and chinked it down on the glass.

Theriot raised her hoary eyebrows and picked up the coin. She tapped it on her teeth. Then she studied one side and then the other through her jeweler's loupe.

"My," Mrs. Theriot said. "Where'd you find this?"

"Serious," said Lindquist. "Don't show anyone. Please."

Mrs. Theriot looked at Lindquist speculatively. "Look at you. When's the last time you slept?"

"Give me ten days?"

"A week."

Lindquist pointed with his chin. "That metal detector up there."

WES TRENCH

Wes looked around the parish for work, walking the docks and talking to ship captains and deckhands. Nobody was hiring and everybody was hurting. The captains, comrades in penury, were contrite when turning him down. "You might want to try Captain John over there in the Grand Pass," they'd say. Or, "You try Harry Bogardus's boat yet? The *Mustang Sally*? Piece of shit, can't miss it."

The sweltering days slid into mid-September and the heat was nigh apocalyptic. Halloween still seemed very far away. Nights Wes slept in the public park in the cab of his truck. His eighteenth birthday fell on a Monday and it didn't seem much different from any other day. He bought himself a Twinkie and went to the movie theater to see some movie about Wall Street with Michael Douglas.

Wes knew he should give up, go home with his head hung low and beg his father's forgiveness. It had been more than a month. More than anything else except maybe his bed, he missed building his boat. He'd wanted to finish it in time for the next shrimping season, but no way was that going to happen now. Maybe it would never happen. Maybe he should leave the Barataria like everybody else. Give up.

- - - - - - - -

One night a loud rapping on the cab window woke Wes and he jerked upright, striking his head on the ceiling. He clutched his skull and when his eyes adjusted he saw it was Lindquist.

Wes told him hey, raked his fingers through his bed-headed hair, opened the gate and slid out of the truck.

"Well hell, kid," Lindquist said, squinting at him. "Livin' like a vagrant."

Head still foggy with sleep, Wes shrugged and glanced at his watch. 3:25 a.m.

"Why don't you just go home?" Lindquist asked him. "Bury the hatchet?"

Wes shook his head.

"That bad, huh?" Lindquist asked.

"I guess so."

Lindquist sat beside him on the gate and they were quiet for a while.

"What're you doin' out here?" Wes asked.

He lifted up his metal detector and rattled it. "Detecting. Thought I'd take a break from the bay."

Wes nodded.

"You look like crap warmed over."

Wes considered this. "I guess I feel better than I look."

"Let's hope. Because you look dead."

Wes chuckled.

"Meet me in the marina tonight," Lindquist said. "Sundown."

"You shrimping again?"

Lindquist shook his head. "Harder metal detecting and digging with one arm than you'd think."

Then he told Wes that they'd be out there for at least a couple of days, to think it through. Wes said he didn't need to and was up for it. Any work would do.

It was harder work than he imagined, just as Lindquist warned him. The bugs, the heat, the methane-smelling muck. By the end of the first day his fingers were blistered and his hands were crabbed from so much shoveling.

And by their second day out Wes no longer knew where they were in the Barataria, they'd drifted so far. He was used to sticking to one part of the swamp, and these islands looked unfamiliar. Five or six hours' sleep a night, bloody hands, an aching back, and neither Wes nor Lindquist had a thing to show for it. But Lindquist's enthusiasm burned unabated, as if he were driven by a force stronger than faith.

On the eve of their fourth day out Lindquist was metal detecting in the canebrake fringed along a little island's shore when his machine blipped. It was early evening, the last light leeching from the sky, tatters of purple and pink and orange above swag-bellied clouds. Gnats swarmed around their heads, thick as wreaths of smoke.

Lindquist passed the metal detector coil over the same spot three or four times. Finally he pointed to a place on the ground just above the tideline. He unpocketed his flashlight and flicked the beam over the sand. Fish bones and shell and silica. "Right here," he said. "There's something."

Wes didn't move. Sweat was running down his face, into his eyes. Where this man got his energy was beyond him. He was a freak of nature.

"What you waiting for?" Lindquist asked.

I want to go home, Wes wanted to say. But he began slowly and spiritlessly digging, flinging clods of dirt over his shoulder. Lindquist stepped sideways to dodge the blitzkrieg and passed the coil of the machine over the turned dirt. For a while Wes only dug and soon it was full dark, the sough of soft warm wind in his ears, the cane whispering on the shore.

Soon Lindquist picked something off the ground and made a noise that was part moan, part exclamation. He was clutching something small in his hand and ran to the water and washed it off. Then he turned, almost tripping as he ran out of the water, his face crazed in the dark.

"I told you," he shouted. "Look at this."

In the palm of Lindquist's grimy hand was a silver money clip embossed with an Aztec calendar. Wes took the clip and brought it to his face for a closer look and saw a tiny stamped inscription on the back: MADE IN TAIWAN.

- - - - - - - -

Wes remembered one of his high school friends, how he used to act like Lindquist was acting now: manic. The friend, Preston Teague, caused such a commotion in class—jabbering and fidgeting and chuckling—that their homeroom teacher, Mrs. Brown, would make him spend the remainder of the period in the hallway. He'd sit on the linoleum with his back against the lockers, muttering to himself, thumbing the buttons of his cell phone, tapping his sneaker on the floor.

Then the next day Preston would seem like another person, trudging sullenly into homeroom under the weight of his backpack. He'd stare wall-eyed at his desk, doodling boobs and butts and funny faces on a sheet of loose-leaf in his Trapper Keeper.

Yes, Lindquist reminded Wes of Preston. That strange energy, that ferrety way of jerking his head left and right. Like he wanted to go in every direction at once.

Lindquist slept only an hour or so at a time, catnaps. Then, inexplicably refreshed, he'd wake and stay up for another eight. Wes worried Lindquist might give himself a heart attack. And all those pills he took. He didn't know how old Lindquist was and knew better than to ask, but whatever age, all those pills seemed dangerous.

One night they'd just finished metal detecting their last chenier of the day and were sitting on the foredeck of the *Jean Lafitte*. It was three hours until dawn, the moon such a thin wan sliver that Wes had never seen so many stars at one time. They were sprent in milky festoons all the way to the edge of the earth. Even Lindquist, usually indifferent to such spectacles, beheld the sky with wonderment, his head tipped back as far as it would go, his mouth open so wide Wes could see his uvula.

Wes told Lindquist that maybe they should go to shore for a day or two. Come back out to the Barataria refreshed.

Lindquist flicked a dismissive look at Wes, said nothing. He turned his attention back to the map spread across his lap. Every so often he would put down his flashlight and squiggle down a mark with a green felt-tipped pen.

The boat jostled in the slight chop, a misty spume feathering Wes's arms and face.

"One more day," Lindquist said, as if just having finally heard Wes. "One more and we'll take a break."

"Mr. Lindquist. I don't feel right. I'm getting boat-sick."

"Been out here just three days."

"It's been a week."

"Bull."

"A week and a day, maybe."

Lindquist looked shocked. "You sure about that?"

Wes nodded.

"Well hell, so what? Those Vietnamese stay out here two weeks at a time."

"I don't know if I can, is what I'm saying."

"You never know you can until you do."

Wes shook his head.

"You hungry? I'll cook you something."

"Naw, it's not that."

"Let me cook you something. I got some onions and garlic in the galley. I can whip up some red fish. I'll take it easy with the cayenne and hot sauce this time."

"I'm not hungry."

"Knock knock," Lindquist said.

Wes picked at his eyebrow, nausea roiling in his gut. Lindquist was grinning and staring at him. Wes knew Lindquist wouldn't give up until he played along. "Who's there?" he said, barely able to get the words out, he was so tired.

"Little old lady," Lindquist said.

"Little old lady who," Wes said miserably.

"Shit, you're a good yodeler."

"That's stupid."

"But you're smiling."

"Because it's stupid."

"But it works. You're smiling."

"Mr. Lindquist, I gotta get off this boat."

"Why?"

"Because."

"Because ain't a reason."

"Because we've been out here for a week."

Lindquist's face changed, his lips slackening into a loose O. As if he were trying to solve an algebra problem. "You swear not to say a word of this to anyone?" he asked.

Wes nodded, not caring.

"Gold. I already found some. A doubloon."

Wes could barely find the words. "Well, whatever you're looking for, it'll be out here tomorrow," he said. "And the day after that. We can cover more ground after we rest."

"But someone might get to it before we do."

"Mr. Lindquist, no disrespect?" Wes said. "Nobody's out here."

"The twins are."

"I haven't seen them."

"That's because we headed away from their island. Now we're headed back. We skipped ahead a dozen islands. Now I got to backtrack."

An owl hooted on a neighboring island. Another hooted back.

"I can't do it," said Wes.

"What if we find more?" Lindquist asked.

Wes picked at a bug bite on his knee.

"If we find more, you'll be getting some."

"I need to go now. I'm sick. I need to be on land for a while. Please take me back."

Lindquist scratched the back of his neck, peered irritably about. "Well, you go home then."

"You'll take me?"

Lindquist flicked his hook arm dismissively. "Go by yourself."

Wes didn't get it, felt stupid. "You want me to swim?"

"Of course not. Take the boat."

"Leave you here?"

Lindquist nodded.

"I can't do that," Wes said. "No way I'm doing that."

"Then you have to stay."

"The hell," Wes said.

"Take the boat. Leave the pirogue. They won't see me this way."

Wes brooded, clenched his jaw.

"Come back for me in a day. I'll stick due east. Won't be but a few islands away."

Lindquist got up and went into the cabin and returned with a backpack hung from his shoulders. In his good hand he held his metal detector and he tossed it into the pirogue and climbed in.

"Please don't do this, Mr. Lindquist."

But Lindquist dropped the little boat into the water. "A day or two," he shouted up to Wes, oaring one-armed.

"Mr. Lindquist. Don't do this."

Lindquist's voice was already small. "It's an adventure."

Then Wes was alone in the bayou darkness, silent except the smacking of waves against the boat. He looked north, where the harbor lights of Jeanette glimmered so far and faint on the horizon they might as well have been a mirage.

He started the motor.

COSGROVE AND HANSON

A week into their searching, late September, Hanson was batting his way through the bracken, Cosgrove slogging close, when nearby in the woods an owl let loose a piercing call. Startled, Hanson tripped over a cypress root and toppled forward. He rolled on his back in the mud like a pig in a sty, cursing and trying to rise.

Cosgrove swung one leg and then the other over the root, holding the lantern over Hanson.

Eyes gleaming white, Hanson glared up at him, his face so slathered in muck he looked like something discharged from an elephant's rectum.

"Fuck you doing with that light?" Hanson said. "Can't see shit."

Cosgrove fought a twitching grin.

Hanson held up a muddy hand. "Help me here," he said.

"Hell no," Cosgrove said.

"You laughin'?"

Cosgrove felt a slow spreading grin.

"Fuckin' lift me up."

Cosgrove grimaced and took Hanson's hand and pulled him up and then they returned to the boat and started toward the next chenier.

A petro-stink hung thickly in the air, a smell like hot tar in summer. Cosgrove saw spangles of crude in the water, the flotillas of diarrheic froth. He worried about the fumes he was breathing, all those ominous-sounding toxins he heard about in the news. Benzene, arsenic, Corexit. Dolphins, he'd heard, were coughing and bleeding out their assholes. Not good.

"Feel like shit warmed over," Cosgrove said, shouting over the motor. He felt a headache coming on.

"You'll feel plenty right once we find what we're going to find, Sasquatch." A crooked-toothed grin, very white, on his muddy face.

How many times had Hanson said this in the last few weeks? Countless. But now, this time, ten yards away from the island, they exchanged a glance. Hanson sniffed, then Cosgrove.

An evocative scent. Green and resinous, unmistakably familiar.

They said nothing, as if superstitious that one word would jinx the possibility.

They banked on the tideline and Hanson leapt from the boat. Cosgrove followed. A few yards inland the island was corseted by a barrier of waist-tall wire fencing, a vermin blockade. They stomped a section flat and then they crossed it and began wallowing through the buggy bracken.

"Wait a second," Cosgrove told Hanson.

Hanson halted, threw an impatient look over his shoulder.

"If somebody set up that fence, they probably set other stuff."

Hanson gaped at the dirt as if the thought hadn't occurred to him.

Cosgrove looked about and went to a sapling cypress and snapped off a stick from one of the low limbs. Then he moved slowly deeper into the underbrush, stabbing the ground like a blind man with a cane.

Salamanders like squiggles of ink slithered away across the slimy leaves.

When something seized the stick with a loud metallic snap, Cosgrove leapt back. In the moonlight he saw the dull glint of metal. A trap, its jagged jaws locked around the end of the wood.

"Well son of a bitch," Hanson said.

Cosgrove's heart whomped in his ears, a sound like a cotton-wrapped hammer striking tin. He crept along, Hanson following close behind.

As they drew closer to the center of the island the familiar smell grew stronger.

"It can't be," Cosgrove said.

"Would be the perfect place," Hanson said.

"I'll saw off both of my feet," Cosgrove said.

Once in the clearing Hanson let out a high-decibel sound of jubilation. A tent-revival cry. In awe they stood side by side and swept their flashlights. Before them was nothing less than a miracle of ingenuity. Posts stood up from the mire and on them were raised wooden platforms teeming with marijuana plants, a kind of elevated hydroponic garden. Canopied two feet above the plants were sections of camouflage shade cloth strewn here and there with clumps of leaves. The marijuana plants sprouted from two-gallon containers filled with some kind of pale fertilizer that looked like aquarium gravel. Among the containers was a network of snaking tubes running out of rain-harnessing buckets.

Impossible to tell how much marijuana there was because it was so dark. Certainly enough weed to get the whole state of Louisiana high for weeks on end. Cosgrove vacillated wildly from doubting what he saw to believing it. He wondered if there was some herbal equivalent of fool's gold. The raised garden had to be as big as a tennis court. The smell was thick and dizzying.

"Look at this Willy Wonka shit," Hanson said. He flung himself giggling into the plants, hugging a great thatch of them to his chest and burying his face in the leaves.

"Careful," Cosgrove said. A strange mixture of jubilation and dread swept through him. How could they be this lucky? Nobody was this fucking lucky.

Hanson tore at the leaves, stuffing wads into the pockets of his jean shorts. His hands were shaking and his face was sweaty and wild.

"Hanson," Cosgrove said, a heaviness in his gut like a premonition. "Place is rigged. Gotta be."

"Best goddamn day of my life," Hanson said in a voice tremulous with joy.

Cosgrove waited and took a breath and then stepped into the plants. He pulled a handful of leaves, then another. Soon, his fingers were sticky and his head was spinning and he pulled at the plants with abandon.

‑‑‑‑‑‑‑‑‑

The next night they boated again to the island, Cosgrove manning the engine, Hanson smoking a fifteen-gram blunt the size of a banana. Ordinarily Cosgrove would have scoffed at such waste, but they already had more marijuana than they knew what to do with.

As they yawed toward the island of marijuana Hanson offered Cosgrove the blunt.

Cosgrove waved it away. "One of us gotta stay sober," he said.

"That's your problem," Hanson said. "Too goddamn sober."

Cosgrove pshawed. He marveled at Hanson's state, his eyes scarlet-webbed, his mouth slack and spittled. An overgrown idiot child at the tail end of a three-day party. If the coast guard or game warden stopped them, he'd shoot Hanson on sight for looking the way he did.

They ventured farther into the swamp, the reedy banks receding, the water whitecapping. Soon they passed barrier islands studded with dead cypress and water tupelo, shorelines corseted with crude-blackened boom.

Behind them the lights of Jeanette diminished, an orange glow understaining the sky. And ahead on the horizon were towering oil rigs, their hazard lights blinking far out in the Gulf.

"A spaceship," Hanson said, pointing.

"Have another toke," Cosgrove said.

"Shit's so wet it won't stay lit."

They passed an occasional oyster lugger or Boston Whaler sailing under an orange triangular flag: VESSELS OF OPPORTUNITY, private boats hired by BP to patrol the waters for oil and fallen boom. The boats slalomed through the water with no seeming coordination, paths crisscrossing, booms almost colliding. Rumor was, BP paid them a thousand dollars a day. Sign the check-in sheet in the morning, sign out at night. Simple as that. No supervision.

A shrimp boat grumbled near, a flat-capped captain in the wheelhouse, two young deckhands staring at Cosgrove and Hanson, their faces ghoulish in the red and green glow of the pilot lights. One of them had a cigarette hanging from his lopsided grin, the other a plaid rip-sleeved shirt unbuttoned all the way down.

"Heya, fellas," Hanson called.

"Heya, ace-hole," said the one with the cigarette.

The two men cackled and rumbled away into the night.

On the island of marijuana they stuffed garbage bags with fistfuls of sticky leaves. Every time Cosgrove heard a snapping in the wood, a rustling in the bracken, he froze and listened.

Within an hour they had trash bags full of the stuff, the smell of the plants so potent that even triple-bagged their scent was unmistakable. Resin stuck to their fingers like pinesap and their hands reeked even after scouring them with mud and swamp water.

When they returned to the motel they stacked the bags in Hanson's bathroom, shut the door, shoved a motel towel in the bottom crack, sprayed the room with evergreen air freshener. But still the stink of the marijuana was smothering, a hallucinogenic miasma fogging the room. Cosgrove felt high off the fumes alone. Anyone passing their door would have caught a whiff and known right away. The maid, the manager. Cosgrove imagined looking out the window and finding squad cars surrounding the lot.

They stuffed the bags back into Hanson's flatbed and drove down the access road. Four in the morning, a scimitar moon. In a glade a half mile away from the motel they came across a windowless scrap-wood toolshed. Ivy-covered, it stood behind thick-trunked oaks, almost invisible from the road.

Hanson parked on the road's shoulder and they carried the bags through the weeds and to the shed. Hanson set his Coleman lantern down on the floor of hard-packed dirt. Tacked to the walls were *Penthouse* centerfolds from years long gone. And the shed was full of cobwebs and dead wasps' nests, but it was dry and shady, as good a place as any they were going to find for drying and curing the marijuana.

They left the bags there and the next afternoon returned by foot and began to hang the branches from the ceiling rafters with packing cord. Scheming all the while how much money they would make and all the improbable ways they might spend it.

GRIMES

One of the first men in the Barataria to sign the settlement, Trench's neighbor George, told Grimes the news: Trench had suffered a heart attack while trawling and was now in stable condition at Mercy General. Grimes drove straightaway to the hospital and at the reception desk signed under the name "Peter Lorre" in the visitors' ledger.

Trench's room was half dark, the curtains open but a sheer window-hanging drawn against the overcast day. Half propped in bed, Trench was in a sea-foam-green crepe gown, plastic tubes snaking out of his nose and arms. The bed next to Trench's was empty. A small television mounted in the corner of the ceiling played soundlessly. One of those angry-judge shows.

Grimes was standing in the doorway when Trench's eyes settled on him. They reminded Grimes of a wounded animal's. Bleary and ill-omened, the defiance snuffed out.

Grimes unshouldered his satchel and held it by the handle, stepped into the room. When he drew closer to Trench he noticed the waxy color of his face, his hair as white as the pillow of the hospital bed.

"Came as soon as I heard, Mr. Trench," Grimes said.

In the hall a young black nurse wearing scrubs passed and Grimes smiled at her. She smiled back and then was gone.

"Got insurance, I hope?" Grimes asked Trench.

Trench blinked at the ceiling.

"No insurance? That's terrible."

Silence. A murmuring television from one or two rooms down the hall. From another room someone sneezing. Someone else, a young-sounding woman, saying, "Bless you, Mr. Lafourche."

Grimes studied one of the blipping monitors and pointed. "What's that thing?" he asked. "This jumpy line? Your heart?"

Trench's rasping breath.

"I hope you had insurance."

Finally Trench looked at Grimes. "Just give me the papers," he said.

Grimes widened his eyes theatrically. "You sure?"

After a pause Grimes took the papers from his case and lay them on Trench's chest. Then he handed Trench the orange Mont Blanc pen. Trench signed the paper quickly, a squiggled slash.

Grimes took the paper and studied it at arm's length. *Six,* he thought. Six signatures so far today. Then he tucked the contract in his satchel and took his pen.

"You tough?" Grimes asked Trench.

Silence.

"You tough?"

Trench kept tight-mouthed.

"Fuck you, Trench," said Grimes. He turned and sauntered out of the hospital room.

LINDQUIST

Lindquist remembered observing his father's tics when he was a kid, compulsive habits he never considered strange until he noticed his friends' fathers didn't touch doorknobs and toilet handles over and over, didn't look out the front door peephole twenty or thirty times a day. He supposed he inherited obsession from his father, the same way you're born with a sunken chest or harelip. It was in his blood.

"What if you're wrong?" Gwen used to ask him about the treasure. Her way of telling him that he was wasting his time. That he was losing his mind. Near the end, she wasn't even this polite, telling him his treasure hunting was sad and pathetic. "Thirty years and you still don't think you're wrong?" she said.

No, he wasn't wrong. Lindquist knew it in his blood. He knew it with providential certainty, the same way a dowser knew there was water in the ground, the same way a diviner knew a ghost was in the room. And as long as he kept searching, as long as he kept digging holes in the ground, he'd never be wrong.

- - - - - - - -

Lindquist hadn't seen anyone in this part of the bayou for how long? Days. And now here was a boat, its small light moving slowly toward him and he toward it. In the haze of evening heat it glimmered on the horizon like a dim and dying star. As it neared, Lindquist could tell the light belonged to a small boat. A trawling skiff. He knew this not by sight—the boat was still too far away to tell—but by the tinny insect-like whine of its motor.

The twins? His heart pumped hard and he felt an electric surge of adrenaline through his limbs. If it was the twins, he was probably as good as dead.

It wasn't the twins, but there were two men on the boat. One short and with a ponytail and filthy camouflage cap, the other tall and stoop-shouldered with a bearded face as grave as an undertaker's. They lifted their chins at Lindquist and Lindquist waved.

"What's up, fellas," Lindquist called from his little pirogue.

"What's up," the smaller man, a bantamweight, said. He wore a sleeveless T-shirt that said TOM PETTY AND THE HEARTBREAKERS on the front.

"Fishin'?" Lindquist said.

"Naw," the bantam said.

Lindquist could see now that there was a big black Hefty bag full of something on the boat. Trappers, Lindquist thought. Not that he gave a fuck.

"Was gonna say, wouldn't eat the fish out here."

"We ain't fishin'," the little man said. "You?"

"No. Just out here."

"Yeah. Same here. Enjoying the sights."

"Don't see too many folks out here," Lindquist said.

"Naw," said the small guy. He looked over Lindquist's boat. "Damn, this is quite a ways to row out."

Lindquist allowed that maybe it was. He looked at the other man, who still hadn't said a word. "How you doing," he said.

"All right," he said.

"You a trawler?" asked the little guy.

"Sometimes. You guys?"

"We're from Missouri," the bantam said. "Environmental work. Different aspects."

"You guys wanna hear a joke?"

The two men exchanged a weary look. The small one shrugged.

"Ever hear about the gay guy on the patch?"

The men waited.

"He's down to four butts a day," Lindquist said.

"Ha," the small one said. "All right."

"Well," Lindquist said.

"Well," said the small one.

"We better get going," the tall one said.

"You fellas wanna hear another?"

"We better get going," the tall one said.

The bantam waved and started his engine and began to pilot away. Lindquist waved back. They watched one another as they drew apart and went their separate ways.

Two or three days? Lindquist would've guessed it had been that long since the kid left him. Maybe a little longer. It was true that he lost track of time easily when he was treasure hunting. But it couldn't have been much longer than a few days because he still had a few bottled waters and protein bars left in the backpack.

It was four in the morning, Lindquist in the dim light of his lantern digging on the chenier, when the shovel blade struck something hard. A rock, he thought. Then he tapped the edge of the shovel against whatever it was and heard a hollow wooden knock. He hunkered down and swept aside grungy leaves and mud. Then he plunged his hand into the ground and ran his fingers along what felt like an old plank of wood, soft and splintered with rot.

A box, a very old wooden box.

Lindquist rose and picked up the shovel and shoved the blade under the box. He stepped on top of the blade and began prying it from the ground. At last something gave and Lindquist went toppling backward, ass in the muck.

He crawled quickly on his hands and knees to the hole. Inside it was an old dirt-stained wooden strongbox. He leapt to his feet and picked up the shovel and stabbed it into the wood, which cracked easily.

He was hallucinating, had to be. He'd been out in the Barataria for so long with so little sleep and food that he was simply seeing what he wanted to see. A fever dream. He'd run out of pills several hours ago and kept meaning to boat back to the harbor and return home for more. *One more hour,* he kept telling himself. *One more hole.*

Isn't this what happened to men who wandered the desert for days on end? They began seeing dreams and visions. They began seeing the very things they most desired to see.

In the dim lantern light he saw a glimmering in the wood and dirt. He knelt and reached and picked up a coin. He held it up to his face in the light. Gold. He plunged his hand within the box and rooted around. He felt coin upon coin inside. No guessing how many there were. Hundreds, surely. He scooped up a handful and held them to his face and he kissed them. The slime dirtied his lips. He didn't care. Exalted, he looked up at the sky.

The moment was so perfect that every accident, every misfortune, every heartbreak leading up to this seemed like blessed luck.

"Thank you, thank you," he said. He emptied pockets of his cargo pants and began filling them with the coins. "Thank you," he said.

THE TOUP BROTHERS

Next time they checked the island, the Toup brothers discovered their crop ravaged, whole swathes gouged out of what was once a garden as big as a tennis court. A blizzard of dead stems and leaves littered the ground, and plant pots were knocked off the platforms into the dirt. Impossible to tell in the dark the extent of the damage. Here and there in the mud was a discarded candy bar wrapper, a potato chip bag, a crushed beer can.

Victor paced, frenzied disbelief in his eyes as he looked over the plants. He cupped his hand over his mouth and spat curses and paced some more. "Good God," he said in a voiced strangled with anger.

Meanwhile Reginald surveyed the ruin from the edge of the clearing, his shoulders sagged with weariness. A dread of what would happen now.

"Look at this shit," Victor cried, looking at Reginald in a way somehow accusatory, as if he expected Reginald to argue otherwise. As if he almost suspected him complicit in the theft. "Looks like somebody took a weed whacker to it."

A night breeze, hot and tar-smelling, gently shook the leaves around them.

Reginald glanced around as if the marauder were hiding somewhere in the dark. His brother cursed and clenched his fists and kneeled in the dirt among the paw prints and bird tracks. He skimmed his flashlight beam over the ground and studied the boot marks in the mud. Two different pairs crisscrossed back and forth, one big and the other small. They tracked away toward the shore, where there was a large drag from a skiff boat in the mud.

"I'm gonna kill him," Victor said.

Reginald said nothing. Holding his lantern aloft, he squatted on his heels and picked up from the ground a joint stub as thick around as a 54-ring-gauge cigar.

"Lindquist, I told you," said Victor. "You wouldn't listen and here we are."

"All right, goddamn it."

"Right here. See."

"What you want? I see."

Victor's face was twisted with rage in the lantern light. "I want you to stop being such a pussy is what I want."

Reginald swatted his hand. He dropped the joint stub into the dirt and Victor came over and kicked it.

"Flagrant," he said.

WES TRENCH

Though just a mile down the road, home had never seemed so far away. Every part of Wes's body ached for his bed, but he couldn't stand the thought of facing his father. Instead he slept in the harbor parking lot in the cab of his truck, a moldy-smelling packing blanket for bedding, a balled-up T-shirt for a pillow. Even with the windows open the humidity was smothering, like a sweaty rag shoved in his throat. It was a few weeks into football season and still there wasn't the slightest hint of fall. There probably wouldn't be for a few more months. Sometimes he woke in the middle of the night gasping and sometimes the voices of captains and crewmen woke him. Dark forms, faceless and eerie, flickered by his truck windows, their shadows thrown by the tangerine glow of the parking lot lights.

Half delirious with exhaustion, Wes stopped by an old high school friend's house, Grant Robicheaux's, and Grant and his family acted genuinely glad to see him. And, thankfully, they knew better than to ask him about his home life.

They fed him a dinner of crawfish gumbo and homemade cornbread, his first real meal in a while that wasn't out of a can, and they made a bed for him on the sunroom sofa in the back of the house. By nine he was in a deep and dreamless sleep. But at midnight Grant's three basset hounds padded into the sunroom with their scrabbling paws and kept licking his face. In the morning his arms and legs were riddled with inflamed-looking flea bites and Wes wanted to cry, he felt so tired.

At breakfast Wes thanked Grant and his family for their hospitality and told them he'd better get home.

That morning Wes drove his truck to the harbor and climbed aboard his father's boat. He was dizzy-headed and could hardly keep his eyes open. He knew his father would find him when he came at sundown and he didn't care. Whatever wrath and humiliation he had in store for him, Wes was ready to face it.

Within minutes he fell asleep on the cabin cot.

When Wes woke it was full dark and he climbed onto the dock and waited. Half past nine. Usually his father would have been here by now. Most of the other slips were already empty.

Wes sat lotus-style on the worn wooden dock and watched the dirt road leading to the harbor. Stars and crickets, fish splashing in the bayou. After a few minutes headlights flickered through the trees and a truck came crunching into the gravel lot. Wes rose, braced himself. When he saw it wasn't his father's truck, the knot in his stomach loosened. The primer-spotted Ford stopped under one of the parking lot lights and Randy Preston, an old family friend, stepped out. He trudged toward the dock, lugging an Igloo cooler and smoking a cigarette.

"How you been, Wes," Randy said as he stepped up to him. His huge dentures glowed in the dark.

"Good. You."

"Good. Waitin' for your pop?"

"Yeah."

"He all right?"

"He's good."

"Good," Randy said and kept walking toward his boat. "Keep a firm grip on yourself, Wes."

"I will," Wes said, and flipped him a bird. "You too."

"Every night," Randy said, shooting a bird over his shoulder but not turning back.

Wes waited until ten and then he got back into his truck and drove to the house. The lights were off and the curtains of the front windows were open. Two newspapers, *Times-Picayune,* were still in their plastic bags in the driveway. Wes got out of his truck and picked them up and let himself into the house.

A rotting smell hit him immediately. He flipped on the light and went into the kitchen, where the stink was strongest. In the garbage bin on top of coffee grinds and newspapers were yellow curdles of chicken fat. Wes took the plastic bag out of the bin and knotted it and went to the backyard and threw it in the trash can. He glimpsed the heap of his boat, a forlorn sight under its moldy tarp.

He went back inside and checked the answering machine. The small illuminated screen said that there were twelve messages. Wes picked up the phone and scrolled through them. All unlisted numbers from the past three days, which probably meant creditors or some other bad news.

A drop of sweat ran down Wes's cheek and he rubbed it away. Then he realized. The house was much hotter than his father liked to keep it, as if the air-conditioning hadn't been turned on in a while.

He checked his father's bedroom. The bed was unmade, but that wasn't unusual. The bathroom was empty and so were the other bedrooms and bathrooms and the garage. Wes went back to the master bedroom and checked the closet. All his father's clothes were there, his luggage.

The rotting meat. The missed calls. The boat still in the harbor.

Wes's heart kicked like a frog leg.

He took out his cell phone and flipped it open and then remembered it was no longer working. He hadn't paid the bill. Like an asshole.

Wes got back into his truck and drove to the neighbor's house. Maybe Chuck knew something. He and his father were friendly.

Chuck, portly and pink-faced, answered the door. For a confused moment he stared at Wes, his white eyebrows moving up and down. Then, "You don't know, do you?"

Wes stood there.

"Oh, son. I'm sorry."

Full of dread and guilt, Wes rode the elevator to the third floor of the hospital where his father's room was.

One of the doctors had come out to the lobby to tell Wes the story: his father, after two days' working alone without rest, suffered a heart attack in the Barataria. In the wheelhouse he collapsed to his knees and crawled across the floor to the cabinet where he kept the emergency flares. He took one out and pulled himself up by the wheelhouse crankshaft and fired through the window. Another shrimper saw the flare and piloted to the *Bayou Sweetheart,* where he found Wes's father collapsed on the wheelhouse floor.

"Lucky man," the doctor told Wes.

Now Wes stepped out of the elevator and walked slowly down the hall. He kept his eyes carefully in front of him, trying not to look into any of the hospital rooms with the open doors. He felt the sickly, ill-omened stares of the patients from their beds.

When he entered the room his father lifted his head off the pillow and looked at the door. Then he laid his head back but his drug-clouded eyes stayed on him. Wes saw that there were tubes in his nose and on his arms and that his face was drawn and haggard.

He stepped to the bed, wondering if he should kiss him on the cheek like he used to when he was a kid. But he only rested his hand briefly on his father's shoulder. Beneath the overstarched hospital gown his body felt thin and frail, on the verge of breaking.

Wes took a chair from the corner of the room and drew it near the bed and sat.

"What're they saying?" Wes asked, picking at his eyebrow.

"I got three hours to live," his father said.

They were quiet for a time.

"I feel bad," Wes said.

"Don't."

"My phone was off."

"I know."

"I didn't pay my bill."

"Smooth move."

The television was on, a show about a pretty blond detective woman with a foul mouth and a fedora. They watched the television for a while as if deeply engrossed.

"I took the money," his father said, eyes still on the television.

Wes nodded though his father couldn't have seen him the way his face was turned.

"The guy came in here yesterday and I just signed right there on the dotted line."

"Well," Wes said.

"I don't even want to see this bill," his father said. "Soon as I see it, I'll have another heart attack. Then they'll bill me again."

"Want anything?" Wes asked. "There's a vending machine in the hall."

"Naw. I'm all right."

They stared at the television. A commercial for something called a discreet pocket catheter. Xylophone music, a middle-aged man playing Frisbee in the park with a trio of young women in halter tops.

"You can leave if you want," his father said. "You probably got things to do."

"I'm watching this."

"This? The commercial?"

"The show."

"You waitin' for the show to come back on?"

"Yeah."

"You like that show?"

"I don't know."

"What is it? Just some gal in a funny hat solving mysteries?"

"I don't know. I've never seen it before."

"She's pretty good-lookin'."

"Yeah." Wes rubbed his sweating palms up and down the thighs of his jeans.

When the show came back on they watched it for a while.

"Huh?" Wes's father said.

Wes picked at his eyebrow. "I didn't say anything."

"Making a lot of noise over there."

"I didn't say anything."

"About to have a fit in that chair."

"I'm just sitting here."

"Well, I guess you probably can leave. I'm getting tired anyway. Don't want to keep you."

"I'm all right."

"I'll probably take a nap anyway. These drugs they got me on."

Wes got up and went to the door.

"Hey," his father said.

Wes turned.

"I know I can be difficult to deal with."

"It's all right."

"Bring me back something to eat next time? If you don't have nothin' planned?"

"I'm coming tomorrow. That's my plan."

"A sandwich from Sully's or something. Hospital food's like poison. Probably is. So they can keep me here and bill me more."

"I'll bring you something from Sully's," Wes said.

"Hey, Wes."

Wes waited.

"I'm trying. You know?"

Wes nodded. "See you tomorrow," he said.

COSGROVE AND HANSON

There was so much marijuana hanging in the abandoned shed that even Hanson in his addled state admitted something had to be done. They'd never smoke or sell this much. Not in a million years. He called his old buddy Greenfoot who called another acquaintance and within minutes the phone in Hanson's motel room rang. It was half past ten Friday morning, the first of October, and from the nook table Cosgrove listened to Hanson answering the guy's questions.

"Maybe fifty," Hanson said. "Give or take five or ten."

He paced as far as the cord of the old-fashioned Bakelite telephone would allow and after a minute sat on the edge of the bed and winked at Cosgrove.

"Yeah," Hanson said. "Pounds."

The man on the other end of the line must have laughed because Hanson laughed too. "Yes sir," he said, "I'm telling you, every aspect."

Cosgrove and Hanson hauled the bags out of the shed to the shoulder of the road and stacked them in the bed of Hanson's truck. By the time all of the bags were in the back, they were heaped nearly a foot over the top.

Above the heat-hazed treeline hung a trace-paper ghost of moon.

"Craziest goddamn thing ever," Cosgrove told Hanson. He wiped his sopping forehead with the back of his hand.

"Got a better idea?"

"Yeah. A U-Haul."

"You ever driven a U-Haul in New Orleans?"

"I'll drive. I can drive a U-Haul."

"It's like Uzbekistan, man. Every aspect. And the kamikaze drivers. Mad Max Beyond the Fuckin' Thunderdome."

Hanson put his hands on his hips and studied the heap of bags. He climbed into the truck bed and sat on the pile, trying to squash it down.

"I'll drive the U-Haul," Cosgrove said.

"I'm not going off some bridge in a U-Haul full of marijuana."

"You got a tarp at least?"

"A tarp?" Hanson said, straightening his rodeo buckle. "Come on."

"A tarp's a normal thing. People have tarps."

"What would I be doing with a tarp?"

"Let's get a tarp at least," Cosgrove said. "Cover this shit up."

"These bags weigh plenty. They ain't going nowhere."

"This beats every goddamn bit of stupidity I've ever seen," Cosgrove said.

"You're like a fuckin' eighty-year-old granny, man. My tag's up to date. Brake lights're fine. Aspects check out."

Cosgrove let out a contemptuous breath.

Hanson drove past corroded mobile homes reared on girders, forlorn storefronts with out-of-business and for-rent signs hung in the dirty windows. Soon the only evidence of civilization was the road itself, the occasional passing car, a weather-faded billboard. JESUS IS LORD STUMP REMOVAL, said one. JIMMY DIAMOND BROUSARD, THE LORD'S LAWYER, said another.

They passed bogs of cattails and purple-blooming hyacinths, groves of sand pine, bright wildflowers among which tiny burnt-orange butter-flies flitted up like blizzards of confetti. On the road's shoulder a phalanx of vultures hop-skipped around something black and rubbery. Cosgrove saw white fangs gleaming among the scrapple of entrails. An alligator.

Cosgrove glanced at the speedometer. "Slow down," he told Hanson.

"Going fifty."

"Limit's forty-five."

"I just saw fifty."

They approached another traffic sign. "Forty-five, look," Cosgrove said. "Wake the fuck up."

Hanson eased up on the gas. It took them thirty minutes to reach the highway, Cosgrove turning his head every half minute to check the bags, Hanson hunched over the wheel like an octogenarian. Billboards for chiropractors and ambulance-chasing lawyers turned to advertisements for strip clubs and oyster bars. Soon they passed the Louis Armstrong airport, a plane flying so low over the highway that Cosgrove saw the silhouettes of the heads in the windows.

In Metairie the traffic thickened, jalopies lumbering, pickups weaving with suicidal speed in and out of lanes. A few police cars trundled serenely along, the cops oblivious or indifferent. Maybe they were drunk and stoned themselves. Enjoying below-the-dash blowjobs.

Cosgrove turned again and checked the bags. Still there, still secure. Still enough to land him in prison for a long time.

Hanson grinned his crooked grin at Cosgrove. "Easy Street."

"Just watch the road," Cosgrove said.

"Best fuckin' driver you ever seen," Hanson said. "Cool as an Eskimo's tits."

New Orleans reared into view, the crumbling brick factories, the gray and black skyscrapers wreathed in clouds of septic smog, the behemoth of the Superdome. Clustered under the highway were derelict tenements, many of them burnt down or gutted, most spray-painted with the National Guard's cruciform symbols. The ominous shorthand of numbers and abbreviations.

For what had to be the hundredth time Cosgrove looked around at the truck bed. A bag leapfrogged as the Dodge bucked up and down the potholed highway. Now, with terrifying inexorability, it slid toward the pickup gate.

Cosgrove watched. "There's a bag," he said, horror-struck. "Sliding."

Hanson, hand on top of his camouflage cap, glanced wide-eyed at the rearview mirror.

A large white delivery van now rode behind them, its bumper nearly touching theirs.

"Who's this cocksucker?" Hanson said.

"Watch that pothole coming up."

"Whole fuckin' city's a pothole."

Hanson crashed over the crater and the truck went airborne. Cosgrove watched as the bag leapt like a skydiver out of the truck bed. The truck slammed back down and bucked on its shocks. Behind them the delivery van whipped out of its lane and the driver punched the horn. The bag tumbled crazily about the macadam and other cars veered out of the way, an angry chorus of horns.

An eighties-era brown Tercel rolled over the bag and it burst open in an explosion of bright-green leaves.

"Bag," Cosgrove managed finally.

Hanson looked at Cosgrove.

"A bag flew out," Cosgrove said.

Hanson glanced at the rearview mirror with his mouth agape. "Should we go back?" he said.

"Go, goddamn it, go."

They sat silently, tensely, waiting for the sound of sirens.

After a while Hanson let out a little laugh. "Somebody's gonna have one fuck of a party tonight," he said.

Still no sirens.

This was New Orleans, after all.

- - - - - - - -

On Royal Street, Hanson parked in front of a pastel purple Creole town house: rococo ironwork galleries, tall shuttered windows, an enormous mint-green door with a gargoyle-headed brass knocker. Drunken tourists staggered along the sidewalk. A trio of frat boys wearing Florida

Seminoles T-shirts. An older man with an Asian girl in a Catholic school uniform. A grizzled construction worker wearing a joke-shop cap with foam titties on the front. All of them carried beer bottles or to-go cups.

When Cosgrove got out of the truck he was ready to kneel and kiss the ground. He might have if it weren't so filthy: dirty Mardi Gras beads and petrified dog turds and cigarette ends.

A warm breeze carried the smells of garbage and piss, of seafood and chicory-spiced coffee, of horseshit and rotten fruit.

The fetid spice box of New Orleans.

Hanson stepped to the town house door and rang the bell. A moment later a shirtless young man stepped out onto the upper balcony and peered down. He was crunching on a lollypop and flicked the stem into the street before ducking out of view.

Cosgrove and Hanson waited next to the truck. Down the street a horse-drawn carriage trundled toward them, the horse's hooves clopping on the cobbles. A skinny black man with a top hat shading his eyes gently worked the strop. Six or seven tourists sat on the benches of the bouncing carriage. They gawked at Cosgrove and Hanson as if they were part of the scenery.

A Japanese man lifted his cell phone and snapped a picture. Cosgrove stared him down.

When the kid came down he introduced himself as Benji. He saw the truck and the massive heap of bags and started to laugh. "You guys drove from the bayou like this?" he asked. He looked one way down the street and then the other.

"Just like this," Hanson said proudly, thumbs hooked over his canvas belt.

"God this shit smells," the kid said, and laughed again.

Cosgrove hadn't expected someone this young. He was no more than twenty-five, maybe closer to twenty. A boy. Good-looking in an American way, with sandy hair shagged over his eyes and suburban teeth. If Cosgrove passed him in the street, he'd figure him a trust fund kid, a Tulane student.

"Dude," the kid said, still marveling at the truck. "I'm gonna put this in my fuckin' memoir."

Benji and Hanson carried the bags into the town house while Cosgrove stood guard beside the truck. When they had all the bags in the town house they went together inside.

It was a high-ceilinged place that smelled of candle wax and book dust. Antique cherrywood furniture, objets d'art. A tall window gazed out onto a brick-walled garden presided over by a giant black olive tree, dozens of Tinkertoy birds chittering in the branches.

And, amid all of this, Cosgrove and Hanson's trash bags of marijuana heaped in the middle of the harlequin floor.

The kid reached into his pocket and drew out a Swiss Army knife and cut open a bag and pulled out a handful of leaves. He brought them to his face and sniffed. He twirled a sprig between his fingers and studied it.

"A lot of these pistils, still green," he said.

"Yeah?"

"Pulled early."

"I smoked the stuff," Hanson said. "Prime shit. Every aspect."

"No doubt, dude. Still wet though. Needs to be cured."

Hanson stayed quiet. Beside him Cosgrove stood with his arms crossed. There was something about the kid he didn't like. His ironic smirk. Of course Cosgrove was jealous. You would figure their positions reversed, a kid this age doing the grunt work instead of the other way around.

"Yeah, gonna have to cure this stuff," the kid said. "Can't sell it this way."

Hanson took off his cap, stroked back his ponytail, pulled the cap back on.

"You fertilize?" Benji asked.

"Yeah," Hanson said, sounding like a school kid guessing at the right answer.

The kid reached into his pocket and brought out another Dum Dum sucker. He unwrapped the lollypop and stuck it in his mouth, cheek bulging. "How often you fertilize?"

Hanson swallowed, mused. A vague wigwag of his hand. "Every other week."

"You shouldn't overfertilize."

Hanson shrugged.

"How often you water?"

"About the same amount."

"Tell me again. How long you been doing this?"

"Couple'a years."

For a moment Benji only stared at Hanson, switching the sucker from one side of his mouth to the other, the hard candy clacking against his teeth. "Where'd you steal this shit?" he asked.

Cosgrove glanced at the door, wondered how long it would take to run out.

"Nobody ever said that now," Hanson said.

"I'm saying it."

"Does it matter?"

"If somebody machine-guns my place tonight? Yeah."

"Nobody's gonna do that now."

"No?"

"No."

"Nobody followed you."

"I'm just gonna tell you the aspects straight. We found this place out in Barataria Bay."

The kid waited.

"There's an island out there full of this shit. So much, whoever grows it won't notice anything. That's how much."

"Out in Barataria Bay."

"Way out there. Middle of nowhere."

From outside came the sound of little twittering birds.

"And nobody knows about this," the kid said.

"You ask the people who called you. I'm a careful motherfucker."

"You drove from the bayou with all this in the back of your truck. And you're a careful motherfucker."

Hanson clutched one-handed onto his belt buckle. "I know what I'm doing."

The kid considered this, then looked at Cosgrove. "What's your story?"

"Just standing here," Cosgrove said.

"That's not a story."

"Look, man, I don't want any trouble."

"Neither do I. That's why I'm asking."

"He's telling you like it is," Cosgrove said.

"And I'm just supposed to believe you."

"Kid," Cosgrove said. "Stop talking to me like I'm your dog."

Benji threw up his hands. "I'm asking what I gotta ask," he said. "Put yourself in my shoes."

Benji and Cosgrove stared at one another. Then the kid sighed and shook his head and squatted. He ripped open another bag and brought a fistful of the bright green leaves to his face and inhaled deeply. He picked off some drier leaves and rolled them into a nugget between his thumb and forefinger and then he went to the mantel where he opened a wooden box and took out a small one-hitter of varicolored glass. He stuffed the nugget in the bowl and lit it and held the smoke. He waited a beat, exhaled, looked at Hanson and then at Cosgrove.

"This belong to the twins?"

"Twins?" Hanson said.

"I've smoked this before. Real mellow high. Loud but mellow."

"Maybe it's from the same seed."

"Five or six people in the country with this strain. If even that. Rest is mixed up with Green Crack and Agent Orange."

"Don't know anything about that."

"Shit's fertilized just the same. Same color. Same hairs. Same everything."

"We don't know any twins," Cosgrove said.

"Let's not shit each other," Benji said.

Cosgrove and Hanson were silent.

"Two of the biggest assholes I've ever met. Rob them blind if I could."

"Yeah, we don't know any twins," Hanson said.

"You sure?"

"Let's leave," Cosgrove told Hanson.

"Twenty cash," Benji said.

"Twenty?" Hanson said. "That's robbery. Should get a Lear jet for this shit."

The kid stood. "Maybe. Probably. But where else you gonna sell all this?"

"Thirty."

"Take the bags. Put them back in your truck."

"Twenty-eight."

"Take the bags."

"Twenty-seven and that's it."

"Take the bags. Go ahead. No hard feelings."

Several minutes later Cosgrove and Hanson were out on Royal Street, ten grand in hundred-dollar bills apiece stuffed in their pockets. Hanson wore a grin of dopey triumph. They hurried down the sidewalk, as if afraid that Benji might chase after them and renege on the deal.

A crowd of Friday revelers was already gathering. Two lumberjack-looking men passed, holding hands. A pretty black girl with a big afro pedaled a pedicab. A middle-aged woman wearing a leotard and what looked like a merkin made of neon feathers sauntered by.

From a few streets away came the brassy flourish of jazz horns. Farther off, the metronomic throb of 4/4 drums and bass.

"Raped," Cosgrove told Hanson. "We just got raped in there."

"Stuff wasn't even ours," Hanson said.

"Worst negotiator in the world."

"Hell, you were the one almost got into a fight with the guy."

Cosgrove was silent.

"What were we supposed to do? Sell it ourselves?"

Cosgrove knew that Hanson had a point. And he felt as if a weight had been lifted. Even his breathing felt lighter, unburdened. There were lots of things you could do with ten thousand dollars. People started over their whole lives with less.

They walked to Bourbon Street, into the pandemonium of a late-summer Friday night. Everyone was drunk. Canadian tourists, transsexuals, newlyweds, college kids, hucksters, erotic puppeteers, rednecks, cover band musicians. A cheesy stink hung in the air. Zydeco and funk and rap spilled out of barroom doorways, mad cries and laughter piercing through the music's roar. Fake cobwebs and giant cardboard pumpkins and skulls—early Halloween decorations—hung in strip club windows.

Cosgrove and Hanson bought hard liquor shots with beer chasers and wandered up and down the Bourbon Street strip. Inebriated college girls were slumped on curbs, vomiting between their splayed knees. A walrus-sized man wearing countless beaded necklaces lay comatose on the sidewalk. Drunkards stepped over him and on top of him. One kid stuck a smoking cigarette between the man's lips.

Hanson wandered into a souvenir shop and bought a black sateen jacket with a massive green appliqué marijuana leaf emblazoned on the back. He shrugged into it, strutted proudly. On the way out of the store a baseball cap, black with a fleur-de-lis and 2010 across the front, caught his eye. It said LE BON TEMPS ROULE in silver-stitched cursive across the bill. Hanson bought this too and chucked his filthy old camouflage cap in a trash can. In his new jacket and cap he sauntered pompously as a rooster, thumbs hooked on his belt. Walking beside him, Cosgrove noticed tourists smirking at the spectacle of Hanson. The nudging, the whispers: look at this guy. Something like pity and protectiveness sparked in Cosgrove's chest. *Did you motherfuckers just make twenty grand?* he wanted to say.

At the Old Absinthe House they drank two shots of tequila apiece and when they were back on Bourbon Street Hanson went again into the tourist shop. He tried buying another black sateen jacket before the Indian clerk pointed out that he was already wearing an identical one. Bewildered, Hanson thanked the man. Then he angrily told him that he wanted to buy another jacket, was about to, anyway, before his smart-ass remark. He'd take his business somewhere else. Where a man might buy two identical jackets, twenty identical jackets, if he so pleased.

Sometime after two at Lafitte's Blacksmith Shop Bar they fell into conversation with two fortyish women in halter tops. One wore a straw cowboy hat with puka shells on the band. The other wore a fedora cocked at such a rakish angle she had to be a tourist. On her forearm was a tattoo, the beatific face of her dead toddler son, the dates of the boy's birth and death above, SEE YOU IN HEAVEN, RUSTY below. Less than three years on earth. Hanson and Cosgrove knew better than to ask.

The women were hell-bent on merrymaking, both of them laughing so wildly at Hanson's jokes that Cosgrove suspected they were in some kind of contest or freshly escaped from a facility. Hanson moved two stools down so the women could sit between them. The one with the cowboy hat settled next to Cosgrove and he noticed the tan line on her ring finger. Like he gave a fuck.

The women said they were in town for a morticians' convention and weren't looking for trouble, only fun. Hanson told them they just won the lottery. Fun was his middle name. He bought everyone drinks.

Cosgrove told the women that he was the world's first African American astronaut.

"Sasquatch made a joke," slurred Hanson.

They all laughed for a long time at this.

At one point the cowgirl, Dixie, whispered to Cosgrove, "Got any other friends here tonight? I don't think Mary Ann's really into your friend."

Cosgrove stroked his beard. "Well, we're kind of a package deal," he said.

The woman considered this.

"Don't take this the wrong way?" Cosgrove whispered. "But the little fella? Hanson? Egyptian. Very well endowed. A camel. And oral sex, he's kind of famous. A wizard."

Jesus, he was beginning to sound like Hanson.

The cowgirl, to Cosgrove's relief, guffawed at this. She and Mary Ann excused themselves and when they returned from the restroom they seemed enervated, perhaps drugged. Mary Ann's face was flushed, her hat skewed more rakishly than before. "You guys have cocktails back at your place?" Dixie asked.

Cosgrove and Hanson brought the women back to the JW Marriott on Canal Street, where they had adjoining rooms on the twenty-first floor. Hanson took Mary Ann into his room, Cosgrove the cowgirl into his. When the woman got naked she seemed embarrassed of her C-section scar, but he told her he didn't mind and really didn't. Plus, she had tan lines and big puffy areola, which he especially liked. She asked him to turn off the light and close the drapes and when he did she thanked him and told him he was a gentleman. It had been a long time since a woman called him that.

Just before dawn, when the woman lay naked and asleep in his bed, Cosgrove went in his robe to the picture window and looked out at the city. Even from this high above the street he could hear the rat-a-tat of a second line, the blare of taxi horns. He watched the bustling expanse of Canal Street, its panoply of taxis and shuttles, of fast food restaurants and tourist junk shops. He saw the red-lit signs of the hotels nearby, the Roosevelt, the Astor. All the way to the right was green and yellow neon cursive that said Dickie Brennan's Palace Café.

Standing there taking in the Gothic neon panorama of New Orleans, Cosgrove for the first time since he could remember felt something like hope.

- - - - - - - -

Next morning they drove back to the Barataria and spent the day sleeping off their hangovers. In the evening Hanson went to check on Cosgrove and they lay silent in the separate twin beds watching television. They were both gray-faced and yellow-eyed and looked freshly dug from a graveyard.

"How much work we miss?" Cosgrove asked.

"What they gonna do?" Hanson said. "Fire us?"

Cosgrove grunted. Then, "What you got left?"

"Eight grand."

He cut Hanson a look. "You're kidding."

"Closer to seven five."

"Two and a half grand you spent," Cosgrove said, convinced they were the dumbest fucks in the world.

"Easy spending money. All those drinks and tips. The strippers and drugs. The hotel rooms."

Cosgrove closed his eyes and rubbed the stinging lids.

"How much you got?" Hanson asked him.

"Between the hotel room and drinks and shit? Spent a grand, about."

Hanson chuckled hoarsely, coughed. "We sure know how to party. Must've bought shots for fifty bitches."

They were quiet for a time.

"Hey, let me float something out."

"No."

"One more time."

"Hell no."

"We grab as much as we can."

Cosgrove lay with his eyes shut and pretended to ignore Hanson.

"Going one more time," Hanson said. "Choice is yours."

WES TRENCH

It was dawn when Wes parked in the harbor lot and got out of his truck carrying a paper sack from the mini-mart. A few bottled waters, protein bars, a big bag of smoked jerky. Stuff for Lindquist, in case he'd run out. It had been stupid of him, so stupid, to leave him in the Barataria. But Lindquist had been out of his mind and deaf to reason, on some kind of vision quest. Still, how foolish to leave him out here. He should have forced him at knifepoint, called the cops. Or stayed with him, seasickness be damned.

Something, anything.

Wes piloted the *Jean Lafitte* toward the island with the dead willow and when he reached it brassy fog was still rising off the bayou. The egrets were already roused from the branches and mobbed the shore, some standing one-legged and preening, others beaking the mud. Wes steered the boat closer to the island and cut the motor and scanned the bank.

No Lindquist, no boat.

He picked up the binoculars from the dash and glassed across the gray and green trees.

No Lindquist, no boat.

He opened the wheelhouse window and cupped his hands around his mouth and shouted for Lindquist. His voice petered out flatly, sucked into the immensity of the bayou. Then there was only the sound of purling water.

Sticking east, Lindquist had said, so Wes headed east and circled the next islet. He slowed the boat and opened the wheelhouse window and shouted hoarse-throated.

No Lindquist, no boat.

By the time Wes reached the third island the bayou was fogless. Farther out the water looked strange, darker, but it was hard to tell because the windows were so dirty, the glass scummed over with salt rime and grease. Wes would never hear the end of his father's bitching if he left a boat so filthy. He rubbed a patch in the glass with his palm but it did little good so he threw open the portside window. Yes, the water was darker, braided with ochre and red. And around the chenier was a black apron of crude.

"Mr. Lindquist," Wes called.

His mind raced. Maybe Lindquist had pirogued back to Jeanette and was safe at home. If he knew where he lived he'd check. If he knew his number he'd call.

Wes told himself he was worried for no reason. The bayou was enormous, yes, but Lindquist was resourceful. And a man, even a one-armed man in his shoddy condition, could easily row back to Jeanette. Even a one-armed man with a head full of pills. Men twice as old as Lindquist had done the same in the old days. All the time.

Wes opened the window and shouted again. A covey of plovers burst out of the brush and winged away, their high calls somehow peevish, as if censuring yet another disturbance from man.

– – – – – – – –

The G-Spot resembled a low-slung bingo hall, a dour-faced cinder-block building with a pink neon sign on the roof like a carnation in a widow's hat. Even with the truck windows rolled up Wes could hear the mortar fire of music in the bar. Inside, the thumping bass was nearly deafening, so loud Wes had to shout at the man behind the register, a shave-headed black Goliath, six foot and a half easy, whose muscled arms dangled in a way that seemed a threat.

"Twenty-one and over," the man said.

"Yessir," Wes said. "Don't need to go in. Just need to talk to somebody."

"Sure you do," the man said. "Get out."

"Lady named Reagan, sir. Lindquist."

The guy paused and stared at his face. "What're you, a stalker?"

Wes shifted nervously on his feet. His mouth was chalky. "No sir. It's about her father."

The man cleared his throat loudly and went out from behind the register and punched through the flapping double-doors. In the instant before the doors swung shut Wes glimpsed inside the bar proper. In the bathyspheric light a young blond woman in a skimpy bikini circled a pole, a dozen men huddled like vultures around the stage.

Wes waited, bass music thumping in his sternum. A peeling SACK IRAQ sticker was stuck on the face of the register.

Soon a long-necked redhead barged into the anteroom. She had on a string bikini and all the pretty chubby parts of her were bubbling out. It took every bit of Wes's willpower to keep his eyes on her face. He explained why he was there as Reagan's face knotted with worry.

"I'm sure he's at home," he told her. "I just want to make sure."

"I don't get it. Why take his boat?"

Behind the register the black guy was pretending not to listen, scratching with a ballpoint pen at a sudoku puzzle.

"I was sick and had to go back," Wes explained. "But he wouldn't. I must've asked him a thousand times. Really, ma'am, I did."

Reagan was waiting, arms crossed over her chest, so Wes felt obligated to say more.

"We were out for a week," he said. "But he wouldn't turn back. Refused. I told him I'd take the pirogue. He made me take his boat."

"How long ago was this?" She kneaded her bottom lip like a pill of dough between her fingers.

"Two days."

"Two days in the bayou on that teeny-ass pirogue."

"He had stuff. Supplies." The more Wes spoke, the more aware he was of how ridiculous he sounded. "I just wanted his address and number if that's okay."

Reagan asked the black guy for paper and a pen. Then she scratched down her father's address and number on the back of a receipt. She gave Wes the scrap of paper and then took it back and wrote down another number. Hers.

The black guy shook his head.

"Fuck off, Antoine."

"Your life," said the man. He went back to frowning at his puzzle.

"What's your name again, baby?" Reagan asked.

He hadn't told her. Every part of him felt like it was blushing. "Wes."

"All right, Wes," Reagan said, sighing out a long breath, patting her forehead.

"I'm sure he's fine," he said, but even to him it sounded a lie.

GRIMES

There she was again. Grimes's mother in the café window, sitting alone in a booth. He wondered if he should get back in his car and drive away like last time. No: he could put this off no longer. And he was still buzzed from his visit with Trench. He got out of his rented Lincoln Town Car and stood in the steaming heat of the parking lot. He took a breath, tightened his gut, walked into Magnolia Café. It was eight o' clock in the morning and there was no one else in the restaurant except the young gum-chewing waitress fiddling with her cell phone behind the counter. An old man on a corner stool drinking coffee, hunched over his paper.

Grimes wished them good morning.

Nothing. Not even a grunt.

Grimes had on his mirrored aviator sunglasses but his mother recognized him at once. The small muscles around her mouth twitched as he approached. She stood and Grimes pecked her on the cheek. She hugged him and he hugged her back and they held one another for a good five seconds. Then he sat across from her in the booth. "Take off those glasses," she said. "Let me see you."

Grimes took off and folded his sunglasses, setting them on the chrome napkin holder. His eyes pinched against the glare of sun. When they adjusted to the light he saw his mother up close for the first time in years.

Her face burled and beaten in the light. Her graying eyebrows. Her tea-stained teeth. But her eyes were lively and shiny and she seemed glad to see him. Nervous, as she always was around him, but glad.

"Oh, Brady," she said, reaching across the table over her plate of scrambled eggs and wheat toast and clasping his hands in hers. "It's been too long."

Grimes said it had been. "How are you?" he asked.

She didn't answer because the waitress was walking their way with a coffeepot and mug. She set the mug in front of Grimes and poured. Grimes's mother looked up and smiled. "How you doin', Grace? Okay?"

"Okay, Mrs. Grimes," the girl said softly. She didn't look at Grimes.

Grimes's mother waited until the girl was out of earshot before she spoke again. "Notice that?"

Grimes asked what.

"Usually sweet as can be. Can't get her to stop talking. Today?"

She was wearing an LSU baseball cap and now she removed it and set it beside her. Her hair was thinner, Grimes noticed. Grayer. Of course it was.

"What?" Grimes's mother said. "You come here to show me that paperwork?" She grinned as if she were joking.

"You think that's why I'm here? I wanted to see you."

Her mother scoffed him with her eyes.

"I was going to visit you sooner," he said.

"How long you been here?"

"A month about."

"Longer than that from what I've heard."

"I lose track of time," Grimes said, feeling guilty.

His mother said nothing, eyeing his face intently. Maybe trying to unravel the mystery of how they were flesh and blood.

"I don't know how things got this bad," Grimes said.

His mother sipped her coffee. She put her hands on the table and looked at them. Grimes looked at them too. The crescents of blackened grime under the nails. She could never get rid of that dirt. His father when he was alive could never get rid of it either. No matter how hard and how much he scrubbed with the Lava soap.

"One day passes and then the next," said Grimes. He hadn't meant to say what he was about to. There was a measured quality to what he spoke. As if he'd written the words beforehand and recited them in front of a mirror. "Before you know it, it's a month. Then a season. Then it turns into this thing, you know? This awkward thing. You don't want to call because it's been so long. Too many things to catch up on. Those little day-to-day things make up a life. You don't realize it, but they do."

"I know," his mother said.

"Well, there it is."

Grimes's mother sniffed, the wrinkles around her eyes deepening. She said, "Maybe we should talk at the house."

- - - - - - - -

The smell. That's what hit Grimes first. The smell of old books and aged wood and hickory smoke, of moldering cardboard boxes in the attic and of pine-scented floor wax, of his long-dead father's cigar smoke settled in the couch cushions and drapes. The nostalgic bouquet stirred in Grimes a muddle of feelings. Mostly a realization of how old he'd become, of how much time had passed, of how little had changed.

The house, Grimes's childhood home, was a sturdy ranch of blond brick that had fared well in Katrina. Only the charcoal roof shingles were new, some of the south-facing windows. Grimes toured the rooms of the house. His father's old study, with its bookcases full of *Farmer's Almanacs* and Civil War books and John D. MacDonald paperbacks. The den, with the ancient wooden-framed tube television and the floral-print sofa and velour La-Z-Boy where his father had watched his Saints and LSU football. The kitchen, with the parquet floor and olive-green Formica cabinets. And of course his bedroom, where everything sat exactly where he'd left it. The Masters of the Universe and Star Wars figurines on the shelves, the boxes upon boxes of comic books in the closet, the Kiss posters.

Kiss, how on earth had he loved that band so much? Now he couldn't stand to listen to them.

"Nothing changed," Grimes told his mother when he was back sitting at the kitchen table.

She was at the stove with a wooden spoon, stirring a pot of her red gravy, Grimes's favorite. When he was growing up, Monday had been red-beans-and-rice day, Sunday red-gravy.

The smell of sautéing garlic and onion and green bell pepper filled the room.

"Why would I change it?" Grimes's mother said. "Not expecting royalty anytime soon." She used to say *rug rats,* but she stopped four or five years back when it got awkward. When it became clear that Grimes was, and wanted to remain, a bachelor.

"There's this place Century Village I've been looking into," Grimes said.

His mother knocked the wooden spoon loudly on the rim of the pot, startling him. "Century Village? What, you have to be a century old to live there?"

"It's a nice retirement place in Boca, Ma."

"Boca Raton," she said, pronouncing it "Ray Tawn." She turned back to the stove, stirred. "A bunch of old New Yorkers. Then me. Some crazy coon-ass lady. Can you imagine?"

"Let me get somebody to clean my old room out at least. Maybe you can sell some of that stuff. Let one of your friends rent a room."

"Always had to have the toys first when they came out. The comic books and baseball cards."

Grimes sipped from his bottle of Abita. "Easy with that Zatarain's, Ma."

After a time Grimes's mother clanked the cover over the pot and got her own beer from the refrigerator. Then she sat across from Grimes at the time-scarred maple table. How long had it been since they sat together here? He couldn't even remember. Time was getting away from them both.

"Let's see one of those forms," his mother said with a heavy sigh. When he hesitated, she wagged her fingers. "Come on, let's see what trouble you're getting into."

He took his satchel hanging by its strap from the back of his chair and rummaged inside. He handed one of the contracts to his mother. Frowning, she flipped through the papers. "Everyone on earth selling their souls down the river," she said.

"Always so dramatic," Grimes said.

"Of course people'll sign anything if they're desperate. Lots of desperate people out there."

"They had a choice. I didn't hold a gun to their heads."

Her eyes settled on the table. She wouldn't look at him now. Couldn't look at him. "I just find it weird, is all."

Grimes felt his face and neck burning. "Well, I miss you. I really do."

"Of course I miss you. Very much. I'm your mother."

"Let's go to Commander's Palace. A day trip to New Orleans."

"Let me ask you a question," said Grimes's mother.

Grimes gestured quickly with his hand: go ahead, let's get this over with.

"What's in it for you?" she asked.

He shrugged. "It's a job." He took a quick swallow of beer, then another, so he wouldn't have to say more. But she was still watching, waiting. "It's a job. What do you want me to say?"

"They could have sent you anywhere."

"Ma? They made me come here."

"You could have refused."

"They made me come here. Made. I'm up for a promotion."

They fell silent, sipping their beers.

After a moment, "You know I never judged you for what you did."

"Sometimes it felt that way."

"But this?"

Grimes wondered what to say next. He closed his eyes and rubbed the lids with his thumb and forefinger and then he opened them and leaned with his arms folded over the table. "Did you ever stop to think that maybe all the things you believe aren't true?"

Grimes's mother was unnervingly silent. She gazed at his face now and an odd feeling swept through him. That his whole past was staring at him through his mother. His grandparents, their parents, their parents before them. Everyone, a legion.

"Maybe not everybody's out there to get you. You know?"

His mother got up to check the pot of red sauce. She returned to the table with another beer for Grimes and sat again. Now her face was sagged with some troubled emotion, her eyes downcast and watery. She said she had something to tell him. Now was probably as good a time as any.

He asked what.

She looked up finally. "I'm sick, Brady."

"What? Sick sick?"

She nodded slowly, looking Grimes straight in the face, wanting to make sure he understood.

"What? Tell me." *You're scaring me,* he wanted to say.

She told him. She went to the doctor a few weeks ago because her face was painful and swollen. Sinusitis, was the doctor's initial diagnosis. He'd seen the same illness in many of his patients, especially those who worked on the water and who'd been exposed to all the oil and dispersants. Then Grimes's mother told the doctor about her migraines. As a precaution the doctor ran a battery of head X-rays and discovered the tumors.

Grimes realized he'd been clutching his cold beer bottle all this time without drinking. He set the bottle on the table, his knuckles aching, his fingers chilly and pruned. "We'll get you a doctor. I'll get you the best doctor money can buy."

"Brady."

Grimes felt dizzy-headed, like he needed air. "Ma, I'll pay for it. Don't worry about money."

"They can't get to it. It's in the membranes. Leptomeningeal carcinomatosis. Doesn't sound like anything, does it? It sounds like Dr. Seuss." She smiled stiffly, but then the expression quickly vanished.

He shook his head. "This was one doctor, right? We'll get you another."

"Brady. It was Oschner. New Orleans."

He was still shaking his head, clutching his throat. "We'll take you to Tulane, Ma."

"Honey," she said. She reached across the table and Grimes took her hand in his. His fingers were still chilly from holding the beer bottle so hers felt warm. Knuckly and work-roughened.

Absurdly, he wanted to flee. His mother's sad slack face in the orange light of the kitchen, it was almost too much to bear. He wanted to flee, wanted to run away until this feeling of panic and doom like a gargoyle squatting on his shoulders lifted away.

Against his will he found himself thinking about all that oil, all those chemicals. Those couldn't be the cause, could they? Surely not so soon.

His mother tightened her grip. Then she let go and patted his forearm. "It's fine," she said. "I'm more worried about you."

Grimes didn't trust himself to speak. His throat felt salty and hot and he sniffed. He reached for his mother's arm but by then she'd already turned away and was rising from the table. She went back to stirring the red gravy, one of the very few things left on earth he allowed himself to feel nostalgia about.

After this, what would there be?

Before calling Ingram on his smartphone Grimes downed three quick fingers of bourbon. Then he sat on the edge of the bed in his trousers and starched white shirt and delivered the news to his boss. His mother had cancer. Inoperable.

"That's awful," said Ingram.

Grimes heard the snick of his cigarette lighter on the other end of the line.

"I don't know how much longer she has," Grimes said.

"I'm sorry, Grimes."

"They say it might be all the chemicals in the bay."

An edge came into Ingram's smoke-thickened voice. "No, that can't be right."

"Well, the doctors."

"The doctors are full of shit. There's no way. Listen to me. No way."

A long silence. Grimes couldn't even hear Ingram's breathing. He said, "Ingram? You there?"

"I'm here."

"I think I want to go home. Take my mother. See what they can do."

"Go home? Now? After all you've accomplished? Your numbers are through the roof, Grimes. You're like fuckin' Colonel Kurtz over there."

Grimes was silent.

"Get it? Kurtz? You and your book references?"

"I get it, Ingram."

Ingram blew out a long breath. "You can't go home yet. We need you, buddy."

In the corner of his vision Grimes saw a tiny flick of motion. He looked. A gray-green gecko scuttled across the wall, its pistachio-sized organs dark under its opaque skin. The lizard slithered up to the ceiling and stopped still in the corner, its black-seed eyes watching Grimes.

"Well, did you get her signature?" Ingram asked.

"Whose?"

"Your mother's?"

- - - - - - - -

On his way to the airport in his rental car Grimes passed the place where Donald Baker's house once stood. The house had been right goddamn there, Grimes was sure. He wasn't losing his mind. He had a pretty good memory despite the booze. He wasn't superstitious and he didn't believe in voodoo, but his mind kept returning to the old man. How he screamed garbled French curses as Grimes fled the house. How his luck had turned rotten ever since.

Grimes turned around, drove for a minute down the dirt road, turned around again. He remembered this willow the way you remembered a pretty face you saw in a crowd the day before. You never saw willows like that anymore, not that tall, not that wide around. A family of ten could picnic under the gangly shade of that willow.

He remembered this field of Louisiana iris, this grove of wind-sculpted pines standing in the fork in the dirt road. He hung a right and shuddered along. He passed the clearing again. Where there was once a roof peak the sky glowed softly purple between the trees, clouds like garlands of ochre smoke.

He pulled over on the side of the road and got out of the car and stood with his hands on his hips, wondering if he had the right place. He did. He wasn't losing his mind. The first time he'd come here by accident, the second by memory. This was the third time and he knew. That tupelo. He remembered that tupelo. He'd leaned against it after running out of the old man's house, shocked and gasping as he wiped the piss from his face.

Now he held down the top of the sagging barbed wire fence with the heel of his hand and swung one leg over and then the other. He began to wallow through the weeds. Insects burst in flight before him, landing on brittle stalks that sagged sideways under their weight.

Once in the clearing Grimes looked around. Nothing but chunky charcoal-gray dirt. He knelt and picked up a handful and let it hiss through his fingers. Here and there were scraps of metal, shards of glass, knots of shriveled and blistered plastic.

The frogs and crickets were piping up, and a bat helixed through the twilight and flitted off.

The house was right goddamn here. He knew it was. He wasn't losing his mind.

WES TRENCH

The first thing Wes noticed at Lindquist's house was the newspapers, several cellophane-wrapped *Times-Picayunes* scattered around the bird-bath in the khaki grass. Then the dead potted flowers on the porch, the wad of envelopes in the mailbox. Overdue bills, their telltale pastel blue and pink. *Attention, notice, urgent.* He'd seen plenty of the same envelopes at his own place, always knew he was in store for a miserable night of his father's bitching if he found them in the mailbox. As if his father believed wishful thinking would keep the creditors at bay. As if he har-bored the delirious hope that somebody would make a mistake or show some mercy.

Wes knocked on the front door and rang the bell. Waited. Knocked and rang again.

No answer.

It was late in the day, the evening sun throwing the long shadows of the pines and magnolias across the yard. Night bugs were beginning to whine and whir in the woods.

He went through the side yard to the back where a sliding glass door looked into the kitchen. He rapped on the glass so hard his knuckles smarted. Waited. Then he tried the door but it was locked. He shaded his eyes and peered inside. Dirty dishes in the sink, a KFC chicken bucket on the counter. And beyond the kitchen doorway a darkly carpeted room with a dining room table strewn with papers and books. Wes saw what looked to be a metal detector snapped in half, the mangled innards of its circuitry box spilling out.

It was three days since he'd abandoned Lindquist in the Barataria.

That evening Wes went to the sheriff's office and showed Villanova the place on the Barataria map where he'd left Lindquist. Wes told Villanova how he was treasure hunting with Lindquist in the bayou, how they'd stayed out for several days straight until he got sick and begged to go home. When he got to the part about leaving Lindquist in the Barataria with only a pirogue, he was embarrassed by how ridiculous it all sounded and looked down at the floor, scuffing the linoleum with his shoe.

Villanova contemplated the map. "That whole area right there," he said.

"Yessir."

"Big area."

"There's an island with a dead willow. Lots of white birds."

"That narrows it down to about ten thousand places."

The sheriff had a good-old-boy look about him, his beefy face, his pencil-thin mustache the kind guys wore in black and white movies from the 1930s. The ones Wes's mother used to love. "Born in the wrong era," she would joke. "Your dad's."

Villanova must have sensed Wes's worry because he said, "Son, that man's more stubborn than all my ex-wives combined."

Wes didn't know if he was supposed to laugh so he didn't.

"This won't be the first time," the sheriff said. "Don't know how many times his wife used to call because he went AWOL." Villanova marked the place Wes showed him with a red felt-tip. Then, "Maybe you can go out with the deputy, show him now. If you can?"

"Yessir."

Wes waited, picked at his eyebrow. "Something you might should know," he said.

Villanova asked what.

"Those twins, the Toups. Mr. Lindquist said they'd been bothering him."

Villanova sat back, his chair squeaking. He sucked in a deep tired breath and let it out slowly as he spoke. "Lots of people bother Lindquist and Lindquist bothers lots of people."

"Well, I figured you know."

A pause. "Lindquist's got problems, son. And that's all I'm at liberty to say." Then, "Relax. He'll turn up. Probably on his way back now."

- - - - - - - - -

Wes went into the Barataria with one of the deputies, Melloncamp, on the sheriff's motorboat. It was a humid night, the only wind their movement. A mile behind them the lights of Jeanette glimmered like an altar of votaries.

"Smell that oil?" the deputy shouted to Wes.

Wes looked at him. Face as round as a pie tin, a red copstache and shock of hair.

"All my dad talks about," Wes shouted back. The wind tore at his ears and whipped his hair. The sweat on his forehead was beginning to dry and his skin felt stiff.

"Those commercials," the deputy said. "You seen them? BP oil, some actor playing a trawler. Guy looking like Sam Shepard or somebody saying yeah, oh yeah, come in, the water's fine. Meanwhile birds and fish dying all over." The deputy tutted. "Ask me, somebody should be drawn and quartered."

"Dad says that all the time too," Wes said. "Only with a lot more cuss words."

The man smiled. A stubby row of hayseed teeth. "I worry that some son of a bitch will do just that. Some vigilante."

When they reached the island with the willow, Melloncamp cut the motor. The sudden silence rang in Wes's head. Astern, a fish shot out of the bayou, its fat body rolling in the moonlight. The white of its belly, the silver of its scales. Then it smacked back in the water and a cascade of wavelets slapped the sides of the boat.

"You sure it was here?"

Wes nodded.

The deputy got out his bullhorn and flipped the button and hello'd into it a few times.

"He ever find anything out here?" Melloncamp asked.

Wes wondered what he should say. "I'm not sure."

The deputy shrugged like he didn't care either way and called again into the bullhorn. He scratched his chin with his thumbnail. "Lindquist, always with that metal detector."

"Yeah."

"Always felt a little sorry for him growing up. Kids always pickin' on him. Making fun because he acted funny. Then they'd dog him into lots of crazy stuff. Do this, do that. Like he was some kind of performing monkey. He thought they were laughing with him, you know. But they were laughing at him."

They watched the island in silence until Melloncamp began to chuckle. "One time? This math teacher, Ms. Hooven? Lindquist put a condom full of tapioca pudding in her desk drawer. Oh boy, the look on her face. I'll never forget. Like somebody threw a brick at her head."

They laughed together about this for a little while.

Melloncamp sniffed. "Another time, I don't know where we were going. A field trip, I think. But I saw Lindquist eat a ladybug on the school bus."

"Say what?"

"Everybody dogging him. Lindquist was all like, don't think I will? Then he palms it and swallows it. A live ladybug. Like it's nothing. A piece of candy."

"Holy mackerel."

"Wait a second though. There's more. Now I remember. We were on one of those swamp tours, one of those boats. You won't believe this, but a little later Lindquist burps and the ladybug comes flying right out of his mouth."

They laughed together again.

"I never saw it, but another kid did. Swore by it."

Silence.

"He'll be back. Shit, guy lost an arm. Tough son of a bitch."

THE TOUP BROTHERS

The Toup brothers trudged up the shoreline of the island and advanced into the brush. Within a minute they saw light through the trees and they heard rustling, tentative and human.

When they came into the clearing they saw a short man with his back turned to them. About five feet nothing, baseball-capped and pony tailed. He was wearing headphones, pulling up marijuana plants and stuffing them into a black garbage bag. Victor moved stealthily through the brush toward the man, making no sound as he stepped over the soft dead leaves and nettles. When he drew closer he heard a familiar song coming out of the headphones. "Don't Do Me Like That" by Tom Petty.

Victor pulled the Sig Sauer from his waistband. "Hey," he said.

"Nothing stupid," said Reginald.

The small man went obliviously about his business.

"Hey," Victor said, louder.

No response.

Victor moved closer and kicked the man in the ass. Hard. He flew forward, howling like an animal, and landed face-first in the dirt.

"Cosgrove," the man said, an enraged wail. He snatched off his headphones. "Fuckin' kill you."

"Who's Cosgrove?" Victor said.

The man's posture stiffened and he scrabbled up and turned around. He stared wild-eyed at the twins. "How ya doing?" he asked. A jerky nervous smile. He was wearing a Tom Petty DAMN THE TORPEDOES T-shirt and jean shorts, and bits of chaff stuck to his chin and forehead. His baseball cap had a fleur-de-lis and LE BON TEMPS ROULE on the front.

Victor had the gun pointed at the jockey-bodied man.

"Why you pointin' that gun?"

"You been picking this crop?"

The man looked around. "Didn't know it was anybody's."

"What's your name?"

The man seemed reluctant to answer but then saw something in Victor's face that made him. "John Henry Hanson."

"Just growing in the wild, you thought?"

Hanson said nothing.

"Who's Cosgrove?"

"Guy usually with me."

"He here now?"

Hanson's jaw worked as if grinding a sunflower seed.

"Is he here now? You have exactly one second."

"Yeah, he's here," Hanson said, quieter now.

"Where?" Victor asked.

The man pointed his chin vaguely. "Probably the boat."

"What a colossal dumbfuck."

Reginald stooped under the low-hanging boughs and went through the underbrush looking for the man called Cosgrove.

Pointing his Sig Sauer in the man's face, Victor told him to get on his knees. He did, lacing his hands behind his head, his face muscles jerking with panic.

"Look, man," he said. "I'm sure sorry about all this. Take whatever I picked. It's yours. I don't need it."

"You're saying I can have it?"

"Yeah. Yes sir."

"That's real generous."

Silence.

"Mine, you say?"

"Yes sir."

"So why'd you take it in the first place?"

Hanson slowly shook his head.

Victor stepped forward and pressed the barrel of the gun into the flesh of Hanson's forehead. "So you're in charge now. Telling me what's what. Take what's mine, you're telling me. Like it's a favor."

"We'll leave. Right now. Never come back."

"That won't work."

Hanson gaped up at him, swiping his tongue over his parched lips. "Sure it will." A high pleading note had entered his voice.

"No, it won't."

"Why not?"

Victor stayed quiet.

"Why not? We're no narcs."

Victor stared without blinking at Hanson. At a loss for what else to say, Hanson looked at the ground, eyes ticking back and forth as he plumbed the depths of his brain searching for the right thing to say, the magic word that didn't exist. Around them insects hummed and scratched. Then there was the sound of approaching footsteps, the dragging of shoes across sleech and dead leaves. Reginald emerged from the brush with the other man, a broad-shouldered guy with a beard and the beginnings of a gut. Cosgrove.

"Found this rougarou," Reginald told his brother.

Cosgrove shot Hanson a weary, I-told-you-so look. Reginald had the barrel of his Bearcat Ruger revolver held to the back of the man's head and told him to kneel. He hesitated.

"On your knees," said Victor.

Cosgrove winced and got down on his knees next to Hanson.

"What's your name?" Victor asked the new man.

"Baker."

"What Baker?"

"Larry Baker."

"You sure?"

Silence. The hoot of a night owl from a nearby chenier. The wind sighing through the marijuana plants.

"We're already off to a bad start," Victor said.

"Why's that?"

"Because your name ain't that."

Cosgrove was quiet.

"What's your real name?"

"Nate Cosgrove."

"If I check your wallet, that's what it'll say?"

"Go ahead. Check."

"How about you?" Victor asked Hanson.

"I don't have my wallet. Check if you want. Go ahead and check, mister. I swear to God."

"Names're probably besides the point now," Victor said.

Hanson's lips twitched over his crooked teeth. He rolled a frightened glance at Cosgrove, who was making an effort it seemed to stare straight ahead without looking at the twins' faces.

"Neither of you are too bright, are you?" Reginald asked.

"I guess not," Cosgrove said.

"That's the first true thing you said all night," Victor said.

"I just don't know what to do with you two," Reginald said.

"Let us go," Cosgrove said.

"Let you go," Victor said tonelessly.

"We'll give all your money back."

Silence.

"With interest," Cosgrove said.

"What's in it for me?"

"You get your money back."

"So I just accept the money and let you go? For my troubles?"

"Yeah."

"Why?"

"We'll give whatever you want," Cosgrove said. "For your troubles."

"Whatever I want."

"Whatever you want," Hanson agreed.

"Your lives?"

Hanson's head drooped as if his neck had turned to rubber.

"Whatever I want. Right?"

"Fuck," Hanson said.

"I don't care how much money," Cosgrove said. "We've got thirteen, fourteen thousand back in the motel. Cash. I can get it right now. Right this second. Thirteen, fourteen easy."

Hanson glanced at Cosgrove, shook his head. His chin quivered. "These guys are fuckin' with us."

"Shut up," Cosgrove said.

"They're fuckin' with us."

"Shut the fuck up," Cosgrove said.

"Fourteen thousand?" Victor asked.

"Cash," Cosgrove said. "Right now."

"Fourteen thousand is nowhere near the number you gotta be. Not even in the same universe."

"You're marijuana growers," Hanson said. "You're fuckin' with us. Right? What's this, *Scarface*?"

"You'll never be found," Victor said. "That's the thing. Never."

"You're fuckin' with us."

"Blah, blah, blah," Victor said. He raised his gun and without hesitation shot Hanson in the face.

COSGROVE

Hanson's head exploded like a melon, the dark mist of blood hanging in the air even as the last echoes rippled across the swamp. For a moment the body remained propped on its knees before thumping backward in the dirt. The insects and brush animals ceased their thousand small stirrings, as if afraid a similar fate might befall them. Then there was only the ringing quiet of night.

The brothers looked down at Hanson's body through the gun smoke. The one without the tattoos glared at his brother. Clearly shooting someone had not been part of his plan. The brother with the tattoos dragged his fingers through his hair, thinking what to do with him now. Not whether to kill him: that was already decided. But what to do with the mess of Hanson, the mess of him.

Cosgrove shot to his feet and in the same motion launched into the brush. A gunshot rang behind him and a flak-burst of broken leaves stung his cheek. He ducked and tottered forward, clung onto a vine, righted himself. Another gunshot cracked and this time the bullet sang so close overhead that Cosgrove felt his hair curling like a spider in flame.

He batted both-handed through the gnarled growth and glimpsed the dimly speckled sky. He wondered if it was the last thing he'd see before ultimate darkness. A bullet through his brain. The executioner's hood lowered once and for all.

Cosgrove felt the third bullet before he heard it. His body shoved forward and there was the ugly roar of the gunshot in his ears. Pain like fire in his shoulder. He grabbed at the burning place and held his hand up to his face and saw that his fingers were slicked darkly with blood.

But he couldn't stop.

He staggered through the mire, his boots huge with mud, his vision swimming with white light. He shook the dizziness away until the jungle around him lurched back into focus, the wizard beards of moss, the tangled serpents of ivy.

He heard heavy footfalls following him. Snapping branches and crackling brush. Now one brother cursing at the other. Fuckface this, fuckface that.

Cosgrove's boot caught on something and he tripped forward. He fell on his hands and knees, noxious mud splattering his face. Behind him the sound of running stopped and one brother told the other to shut up. Cosgrove scrabbled on all fours to the nearest tree and hunkered down with his back against the trunk. His boots were sopping with muck and he could feel warm slime seeping into his underwear.

Several yards away, a flashlight shined through the trees. "You hit him?" said one of the twins.

"Yeah."

"Where?"

"The head."

"You sure?"

Silence. Then Cosgrove heard the rumble of an airplane flying high overhead. What he would have given to be in that plane right now, on his way to another place, on his way to a life besides his own.

The first twin said, "Well, he sure as shit didn't fly away."

"The fuck you hit him."

"He's dead around here someplace. How much you wanna bet?"

"How does he just disappear?"

"I hit him, I'm telling you."

"What the fuck, just shooting the guy like that?"

"I don't want to hear it."

"Bullshit. You'll hear it for the rest of your life."

To Cosgrove it seemed an eternity before the brothers retreated, their quarreling voices diminishing and merging with the susurrus of the night. Cosgrove could no longer see the flashlight but kept still. After a while he leaned into a patch of moonlight and examined his shoulder. In the dull blue light the gash looked black, but the blood was already congealing. A deep nick, nothing that would kill him.

He took off his filthy white T-shirt and cinched a tourniquet around his shoulder, drawing the knot with his teeth. He spat out the taste of blood and swamp water. Then he sat still, listening. The faraway caw of some bird. The hysterical prattling of insects.

Hanson was dead, he thought. Hanson was dead. He sat there for a long time with his head reeling, not believing it. He tried to remember who Hanson had in the way of friends and family. A macaw breeder, Hanson had told him. That was all Cosgrove could recall. Had he known Hanson's life would end like this, he would have paid more attention. Strange, how after a few months he knew so little about him, except this, the most important detail: the end. Now there were probably people out there who'd go to their graves never knowing what happened to him. And if Cosgrove didn't make it out of this alive, the same might be said for him.

It was a while before Cosgrove heard the brothers speaking again. Still far away, so distant that he couldn't make out what they were saying. "Lee's Quest," it sounded like. But the voices were rough, threatening. Then Cosgrove heard a quick volley of gunshots.

He sat still and listened. When he heard rustling in the wood, he stared into darkness, waiting for one of the brothers to emerge from the brush. *There you are, motherfucker,* the twin would say. He'd take a swift step forward, gun aimed, and then Cosgrove's world would end before he even heard the sound.

What then? Nothing. A body in the swamp, just like Hanson. A secret known only by scavenging reptiles and birds. Not a soul left on earth to remember him.

Cosgrove felt like crying, but his eyes stayed dry, grainy with exhaustion. The end of his life and he couldn't even muster tears.

Was this it: the end of his life? Would a stranger deem it even worthy of being called a life? He had no other life to compare it with, only lives shown in movies and television shows, lives recounted in bars by sentimental drunkards probably lying as much to themselves as to him. What floated up in memory now seemed random, flotsam and jetsam stirred up from the depths of his brain. He recalled a hand job from a wall-eyed girl with braces—he didn't even remember her name—in his beater Tercel after the high school prom. Recalled his father in the backyard one Fourth of July, lighting skyrockets from a bottle of Pabst beer. Recalled falling from a friend's tree house when he was nine or ten, walking half a mile home afterward, sobbing, with two broken ribs.

THE TOUP BROTHERS

Just before dawn the Toup brothers were scouting the far end of the island for Cosgrove when they saw a pirogue moving swiftly toward the neighboring island. A lantern glowed aboard it and a hunched figure was rowing violently. Victor looked through the reticle scope of his rifle and saw that it was Lindquist. He must have heard the gunfire and now he was fleeing, a hundred yards away from this island and about ten away from the neighboring.

"Lindquist," said Victor.

"This is what I'm saying," Reginald said. "One thing leads to another."

"Kill his ass," Victor said. He had the rifle aimed and was peering through the scope.

"No." Reginald seized the barrel of the rifle and jerked it upward.

Victor tore the rifle away from his brother and fixed his aim, his finger tense on the trigger. "He saw us. Shit, asshole's probably got a cell phone."

"You don't know that."

"Either do you."

"Wouldn't work this far out anyway," Reginald said. Then, "Villanova. He'll know right away it's us if something happens."

"Not if they don't find him he won't."

"Lindquist!" Reginald shouted.

"What're you doing? He's just gonna stop?"

"Lindquist!"

"He's a fucking dog?" Victor said. "He's just gonna come?" He fired three times in quick succession. The boat capsized and the lantern sputtered. He fired two more shots but from this distance it was hard to tell what he was hitting. If he was hitting anything at all.

He watched through the glass and waited. Nothing but the overturned skiff, the disturbance of waves. Then he saw Lindquist climbing onto the shore of the neighboring chenier, launching into the dark vines and branches. He fired three more times.

"Motherfucker," Victor said.

"Did you hit him?"

Victor gritted his teeth, said nothing.

Reginald asked again and this time when his brother didn't answer, he said, "Biggest clusterfuck I've ever seen."

LINDQUIST

He heard one of the twins call his name. Then one of them fired a few quick shots. A few more when he was capsized and thrashing in the water. His boots hit the bayou bottom and he half slogged, half flailed to the chenier. Once he climbed ashore one of the brothers shot again and he plowed into the bulrushes.

A hundred yards or so into the woods, he grabbed at his pockets. Most of the gold, if not all, was still there.

In a blind panic he staggered onward.

Soon daylight broke and the wildnerness gathered shape around him. The moss-hung oaks as big around as water towers. Cypresses as tall as obelisks.

Just beyond a deadfall of pine Lindquist came upon an old gray-faced bobcat. It scrabbled up a laurel tree and stared at him with enraged yellow eyes. Lindquist saw that the animal was missing one of its ears. Only a tattered nub remained. He felt a pang of kinship, but the animal didn't seem to feel similarly.

Muskrat and opossum and nutria: Lindquist lost count of how many of these he saw. He would hear rustling in the bracken and pause. The animals halted too, studying Lindquist with a distinct air of peevishness. Maybe they'd never seen a man before. Maybe some animalistic sixth sense picked up a whiff of doom.

The mantric drone of insects. Anoles with red flags flaring from their necks. Horseflies the size of plums. Beetles like potatoes with wings.

At noon he was passing through a glade of eelgrass when a shadow flitted across his face. He looked up. A buzzard hovered above him, huge and ragged, its face like a wad of spat-out gum.

When he looked up again a second bird had joined the first. A minute later, a third. They wheeled above him like a sinister mobile.

"Pieces'a shit," Lindquist said. He dropped to his knees and rooted one-handed in the mud and found a fist-sized stone. He stood and hurled it. It wobbled pathetically in the air, shooting five or six feet wide of the birds, and then it plopped down in the mud. Lindquist went after the rock and threw it again. This time a stitch of pain seared along his side and he groaned, grabbing at his lower back.

"Pieces'a shit," Lindquist said, glowering at the sky.

He gave up and moved on. Soon the buzzards gave up too, maybe figuring him not worth the trouble.

The swamp was a hellish obstacle course. There was no such thing as walking straight in the swamp. There were quagmires of mud, impassable brambles, murky lagoons, sloughs deeper than he was tall. Lindquist figured that for every three miles he wandered and zigzagged, he made it one mile north toward land.

One wrong move and Lindquist knew he was fucked. He imagined stumbling into a pit of quicksand. A vine dangling just beyond his grasp. His hook arm flailing uselessly as he sank deeper and deeper. The gold falling piece by precious piece out of his pockets, irretrievably lost in the mud.

WES TRENCH

Wes's father was released from Mercy General on a sunny Tuesday morning. The hospital had a strict policy: outgoing patients, no matter their condition, had to be wheelchaired out of the building. No exceptions, even for the mule-headed likes of Bob Trench. In the same cranberry polo shirt and faded jeans he was wearing when he was admitted—laundered, courtesy of the hospital—his father slouched in the chair as Wes shoved him through the automatic glass doors. As soon as they were out in the sun, he leapt to his feet like a pardoned prisoner and patted his pockets for cigarettes that weren't there.

"Feelin' okay?" Wes asked his father once they were in the truck and rolling out of the lot.

"Like a hundred bucks," Wes's father said.

One arm curled around the wheel, the other dangling out the open window in the sun, Wes kept his eyes on the road. He knew that one concerned look, one split-second glance of worry or doubt, would be enough to set his father off. He'd take it as an insult, a lack of faith in his powers of recuperation.

It was a warm breezy day, the sky that deep cerulean it wore this time of year after a good rain. The road, rutted and tar-patched, took them past a small cemetery, ten or twelve lichened tombstones leaning in a clearing dotted with wildflowers. In the corner of his eye Wes noticed his father fidgeting. He fiddled with the air vents, opened and shut the glove compartment, eyed the floor mat. He was looking for something to criticize, one stupid little thing he could bitch about to break the silence. *Look at this dashboard, look at these fucking windows.* But the windows were scrubbed spotless and the trash picked off the floorboards. If anything, his father could only point out the truck's myriad tiny creakings as they moved along, but those were no fault of Wes's. The Toyota, a hand-me-down from his father, had a hundred and seventy-five thousand miles on it. And the road was as bumpy as a spoon vest.

"Fuckin' penal colony in there," said Wes's father, as if continuing a conversation that was already underway.

Wes grunted.

"Say what?"

"I bet."

Ahead was a tin-roofed mini-mart of weather-slumped scrap wood. They were close enough now that Wes could read the metal A-frame sign in the crushed-shell lot. MILK. BRED. CIGS. ICE COLD BEER. GEAUX TIGERS. WHO DAT.

"Pull up," said Wes's father.

"Cigarettes?"

"Pull up. Gotta grab something."

Wes waited in the idling truck, watched two blackbirds chase one another around a dusty mulberry bush. A stub-tailed tabby, pregnant from the looks of her swag belly, crept up to observe the fray and after a moment it lunged at the bush. In unison the birds winged and swerved away, as if tied together with invisible string.

Wes's father climbed back in, tearing the cellophane wrapper off a pack of Virginia Slims cigarettes.

"Don't smoke in here," Wes said.

Wes's father lit a cigarette with a cheap plastic lighter that said FLICK THIS BIC in festive party-time lettering over an American flag.

Wes snapped a look at his father.

"One isn't going to kill me."

"How 'bout the one after that?"

"Aw, shut up. Let me feel good for a second."

Wes leaned his head out the window and breathed the clean outdoors air and didn't say another word.

The doctors ordered Wes's father off his boat for a month but his first day out of the hospital he kept himself busy around the house. He picked weeds in the front and backyard, cleaned scrap lumber out of the garage. His father didn't know he was watching, and through the kitchen window Wes saw him leaning his back against one of the backyard persimmon trees and resting an apprehensive hand over his chest. The same way you might touch a sick puppy to check its breathing.

That night they were at the dining room table eating a takeout casserole when Wes's father asked, "What's your problem?"

Surprised, Wes looked up. They'd been silent for several minutes, ESPN murmuring on the television.

Wes asked him what he meant. He had his forkful of casserole halted between his plate and lips. He'd been thinking of Lindquist. Imagining him dead and floating in the swamp.

"The sour look," his father said.

"Nothing," Wes said. He noticed his father's face was pink and splotchy, the tip of his nose red.

"All right. Suit yourself."

The clatter and scrape of their cutlery.

"Know what I wanna do?" his father asked.

Wes grunted.

"Wanna go after that oil guy. Grimes. Break his fuckin' kneecaps with a crowbar."

Wes couldn't tell if he was serious. "Yeah, you're not doing that."

"Sure makes me feel better picturing it."

"Picture it all you want."

Before long, his father asked again what the matter was.

Wes set down his fork and shook his head. He had no appetite though his stomach was growling and empty. "I shouldn't have left him there," he said.

His father only chewed for a moment, his brow scrunched. "I still don't understand what happened," he said.

"He went crazy. Hard to describe."

"He didn't go crazy, Wes." It was odd hearing his father say his name since he seldom did anymore. "He's already been there. For a long time."

"No he isn't," he said. He was about to say *wasn't*. Verbs were tricky in a situation like this. He remembered those months after his mother drowned, how they had so much trouble with the tenses.

Present, past. Was, is. None seemed right.

"At least not in the way people think."

Silence. Wes picked up his fork but only kept it clutched in his fist.

"Some guys, you got to let them make their own mistakes," his father said. "Because they're going to make them no matter what."

"If he doesn't turn up," Wes said.

"Should've, would've, could've. The signs on the road leading to living hell, trust me."

Wes knew what his father meant. Exactly. But he wasn't going to get into that discussion.

Apples and oranges.

- - - - - - - -

Apples and oranges, yes, but Wes couldn't help but remember how he felt after his mother drowned in the storm, the horrible black feeling that roosted in his chest. But that was later, not right after she died.

Right after, those first months after the storm, Wes and his father were never alone with their feelings long enough for them to take root. Too many things to do, too many distractions. Because their house was in ruins they lived for half a year in Baton Rouge with a cousin of his father's, where they slept on inflatable beds in a converted game room with a ping-pong table and Journey pinball machine. The cousin, "Uncle Eddie," was a car salesman, volunteer fireman, and part-time dog breeder—Labradors—and Uncle Eddie had a wife and three middle-school-aged kids, so people were always coming and going. And Wes's father was always on the move, shuttling every day between Baton Rouge and the Barataria in his truck, picking his way through the wreckage.

Besides, they still had hope then, Wes and his father. Irrational hope, insane hope, but hope. They never exactly expressed this hope to one another, didn't need to. It was there, the way they hung MISSING PERSON flyers on telephone polls and in store windows, the way they watched the local evening news with religious devotion, the way they constantly called the shelters and hospitals and police stations. Maybe the flood carried her far out into the bayou, spat her out on an islet where she awaited rescue. Delirious, on the brink of death, but alive. Maybe in all the pandemonium she'd somehow—the *somehow* part was hazy to Wes—ended up in Houston, bussed there with countless other evacuees from southern Louisiana. Maybe she was comatose in some hospital in a neighboring parish. Maybe she'd been knocked so hard over the head she couldn't remember her name.

Maybe, maybe, maybe.

This was the extent of their denial.

It was only after they moved back to Jeanette when they got the call one gray Friday afternoon in February. Wes was on the living room couch, penciling out a linear equation in a marble composition tablet. Homework. From the kitchen he heard his father say "Dental records" in a flat voice. Wes went and stood in the doorway, leaned his shoulder against the jamb and listened. His father's back was turned and his hand clutched the telephone cord like he was strangling it. Wes could hear the tiny bug voice buzzing out of the receiver.

Before long his father thanked the person on the phone and hung up and stood motionlessly, his hand on the wall as if for support. His shoulders jerked a few times like he had the hiccups. Wes could hear his breathing, loud and rapid.

"Dad," Wes said.

His father didn't answer. He stiffened his shoulders and started punching the wall, punching over and over until there was blood and busted plaster. Wes watched helplessly. He heard tiny cracking sounds, the crunching of his father's bones. When his father finally stopped there was a hole in the wall as big as a grapefruit and his hand was busted and pulpy, dangling limp at his side. The knuckles bled bright coins of blood on the linoleum.

"Your mother," he said in a choked voice. That was all.

Right then a feeling opened wide in the center of Wes, a feeling so monstrous and large he was sure it would swallow him alive. Sadness and anger and terror and regret all mixed together. His mother was dead and he'd never see her again. Never tell her he loved her. She would never see him win a track and field trophy or graduate high school or build his own boat. All of that was wiped out in one fell swoop, a history that could have been but would never be because they were at the wrong place at the wrong time.

Because his father had said, "We're staying."

- - - - - - - -

After that Wes's father got lost in his anger. He turned the way he still was today. Anything would set him off. An inopportune phone call, a slow traffic signal, a stale loaf of bread. The world was in collusion against him. With the slightest provocation, his face would turn an inflamed pink and his expression would bunch. Bottles were broken. Dishes and coffee mugs. A saltshaker was called a cocksucker, a broken tape measurer an asshole motherfucker.

His father had always been surly—Wes's mother, affectionately, used to call him the Grump—but now his fury was resolute and never-ending. Nothing and no one was spared.

Not even Wes.

He never called Wes names, never placed a hand on him, but he screamed at Wes for little meaningless mistakes. For not minding his tone of voice, for not turning out a light. Wes weathered these tempests the same way he used to weather rainy days when he was a little boy. He went to his room and shut the door and lay in bed with his headphones blaring, waiting for the tempest to end.

Why her? he'd think.

He tried to quash these bad thoughts down, but they sprang up over and over again, like a game of Whac-A-Mole.

He wondered how different life would be had his mother lived. Had his father died instead. He felt guilty and horrible for these feelings but he couldn't lie to himself. He loved his father but didn't like him very much.

His father never apologized for his outbursts, but sometimes Wes would find a little gift, a peace offering, waiting for him on the dining room table. A takeout dinner, a comic book, a candy bar. "Got this at the store," his father would say. "Had a special."

And, yes, sometimes Wes found himself feeling sorry for his father. Rarely, but sometimes. Especially late at night, when his father's screaming startled him awake. His heart still drumming, Wes would lie in bed listening to his father as he choked and groaned and jabbered in the middle of his nightmare. Then after a while the house would fall silent and Wes would drift back asleep.

Wes used to wonder back then why his father didn't leave the Barataria when he seemed to hate it so much. He suspected his father was punishing himself. It was only years later that he realized he didn't leave because all that remained of his mother was here, in the Barataria. He couldn't turn his back on history, on the past.

And it was only later still, after Lindquist disappeared, when Wes realized what it was like to carry such regret around, such anger, like a millstone around the neck.

The entire world hinged on a decision.

A word.

COSGROVE

Around noon Cosgrove heard someone or something approaching swiftly through the brush. The crackle of leaves and twigs, the sloshing of swamp water. Something this size: had to be a man. Or a bear. He wondered if there were bears in the swamp, hoped to God not.

Cosgrove kept still as the footsteps approached, halting and furtive. At last a man emerged from the brush, short and big-bellied with a hook arm and yacht cap. His eyes were wide and deranged in his filthy face.

"Hey, man," Cosgrove said amiably, showing his palms. "Hey. I don't mean any trouble."

The man blinked, his mouth a slack O.

Sunlight speared in coruscant shafts through the leaves. Cosgrove had to shade his eyes to see the man's face.

"Who're you?" the one-armed man asked, pondering him with an eye squinted.

"Lost."

"Who're you?" His voice harder, but playacting harder, with a high and trembling edge like bullied kid's.

"Nobody," Cosgrove said. "Just a guy lost."

The man stared. Insects buzzed in the boggy air, in the sun-shot leaves.

"I'm not looking for trouble," Cosgrove said.

Something in the man's posture eased and the wrinkles around his eyes softened as he looked about. "You seen those twins?" he said in a low voice.

"Hours ago."

"You with them?"

Cosgrove shook his head.

"They after you?"

Cosgrove hesitated. Nodded.

"Name's Lindquist."

"Cosgrove. Looking for my boat."

This news seemed to interest the man, who again made a gaping O with his mouth. "It close?"

"I don't know."

"No clue?"

"No."

The hope in the man's eyes was snuffed. He shook his head miserably. "Then you'll never find it," he said.

Together they slogged through the swamp, passing cypress knees and vine-strangled tree trunks and fallen logs teeming with pale larvae. They swatted at vines and branches that released showers of water, the cool drops wetting their shoulders and scalps.

"You got anything to eat?" Lindquist asked.

Cosgrove shook his head.

For a while they moved in silence, the mud slurping at their feet. Spiderwebs broke delicately across Cosgrove's face but he no longer paid them any mind. Bigger things to worry about now. His throat was silica-dry, sore with dehydration. His head hurt and his feet were numb. He worried about foot rot and gangrene.

"Hey, you look familiar," Lindquist said, looking at Cosgrove sideways.

"Thought the same thing."

"Saw you out there on a boat. With a little fella."

"How long you been out here?" Cosgrove asked.

"A week maybe?"

A week, Cosgrove thought. No wonder the man seemed bat-shit crazy.

Then Lindquist asked, "You out here looking for treasure?" He slapped a mosquito on his cheek, flicked the bug off his fingers.

Cosgrove thought he'd misheard him. Or maybe *treasure* was his euphemism for marijuana. "Say what?" he asked.

"Pirate treasure?"

"A buddy and me got into some trouble with those twins."

"Marijuana?"

Cosgrove glanced at Lindquist. "Yeah."

"The little fella?"

"Yeah."

"Where's he at?"

"They killed him," Cosgrove said.

Lindquist made a hoarse choking sound, almost a sob. He stared at Cosgrove loose-jawed.

"Blew his head off. Without even thinking."

"Blew his head off," Lindquist repeated. He took off his filthy yacht cap and raked his fingers through his hair, his eyes roving with panic. "Oh man," he said, "oh man."

"We're going the wrong way," Cosgrove said.

"This is the right way. Toward land. The only way."

"Away from my boat."

"You'll never find that boat."

"This looks familiar."

"It all looks familiar. It's swamp."

"No, I remember this place."

"You sure?"

"Real familiar."

Hope lit again in the man's eyes. "You find it, you'll take me?"

Cosgrove looked at him. The O of his mouth, his filthy hair, the dried spit curdled in the corners of his mouth.

"Make it worth your while," Lindquist said. "Rich man now. Just got to get out of here. Once I do? Very, very rich man."

They kept moving. Cosgrove took the end of his T-shirt and pulled it to his face and wiped the sweat. He paused at an elephant ear and stooped and funneled a trickle of water into his parched mouth. Then he caught up with Lindquist.

"You stole their dope?" Lindquist said.

"How you know?"

"They got an island full of it. Everybody knows. And everybody knows to stay away."

If only he'd spoken to this man before, Cosgrove thought. Then Hanson would be alive. Then he wouldn't be out here in the middle of nowhere, probably about to die. He found himself pining for his days of community service. For the days he roofed in Austin in the miserable bone-baking heat, the sun like an iron searing down on his neck.

What a paradise that now seemed.

Early afternoon the terrain turned completely unfamiliar to Cosgrove. What once seemed half recognizable was now alien, an endless stretch of hyacinths and water flowers and lily pads. Hundreds of jewel-bright dragonflies hovered and darted.

Lindquist was right: it all looked the same.

Cosgrove halted. "This isn't right," he said.

Lindquist hissed bitterly through his teeth.

"We gotta turn around," Cosgrove said.

Lindquist stopped, looked at him. For some reason he kept patting his pockets with his hand. "That boat's gone forever," he said.

"How far to land?"

"Fuck, three miles. Four."

"We'll never make that."

"Just come with me, mister. Better we stick together."

Cosgrove shook his head. "I'm turning. Finding my boat."

Determined, Lindquist waddled again through the muck. "Come on."

Cosgrove stayed put. "I can't."

"You're gonna die!" Lindquist called over his shoulder.

"Shut up," Cosgrove said. "They'll hear."

"You'll die," Lindquist said. "Don't be stupid."

Cosgrove turned and started back toward from where they came.

"We're gonna die!" he heard Lindquist shout, but he kept moving.

LINDQUIST

Nightfall Lindquist careered through sloughs of water and thickets of cane, flashlight held over his head in his hand. Most of the time he kept the flashlight off so the brothers wouldn't see. This far into the swamp, the dark was incredible. Unlike any other darkness he'd seen. Behind a kerchief of cloud, the moon was only bright enough to make shadows out of other shadows, the gnarled silhouettes of bushes and trees and cypress cisterns.

Sometimes the shapes looked human, as if his pursuers were suddenly in front of him. Like he'd taken a wrong turn in a fun-house maze. And sometimes the shapes were hulking and monstrous, gargoyle-faced figures loosed from the pages of a brothers Grimm book.

His boots were full of sludge and his socks were sopping. How long before he started to lose his fingers and toes?

Hours? Days? What then?

Don't think about that, he thought. Or said.

He hoped he wasn't losing his mind.

Every so often from a distance he saw their flashlights Morsing in the brush, one second there, one second not.

He wondered what would be worse: the Toup brothers catching him, or a wild animal attacking first. A cougar, a black bear, a wild dog. They were all out here.

And alligators. There had to be hundreds, thousands, of alligator nests within the square mile, some of the alligators rumored to be a hundred years old and as big as sedans, creatures that could swallow a deer whole.

And then there were coral snakes, copperheads, cottonmouths, rattlers, a few with venom so potent they could cripple you within seconds. What was it his father used to say? There were two kinds of snakes in the world: live ones and dead ones.

Who knew what else lurked in the swamp. Some guys collected rare reptiles from the Amazon, guys with too much spare time on their hands, and they released the snakes and lizards in the wild when they grew too big for captivity. Lindquist bet there were pythons and cobras out here. Some fucked-up seven-foot thing from Borneo with teeth like a Great White shark's.

As he moved, Lindquist fell face-forward and he shot out his hook arm to break his fall. He screamed in anguish when the rim of the prosthesis bit into his flesh and jammed into his shoulder bone. He righted himself, and then he tottered over to a tree stump and sat, nearly sobbing from the pain in his arm. He patted his pockets to make sure the coins were still there. He felt their comforting ballast, heavy and cool, against his legs.

What he wouldn't give for one of those pills right now. Yes, even some of this gold.

What he wouldn't give for another arm.

For a way out.

———————

It was a small swamp shack cobbled together of oddments and scraps: vinyl storm siding and piebald car tires and tangled chicken wire. Buoys—mint green, sherbet orange, pastel yellow—hung like fey ornaments on the sides. Otherwise, the shack looked so weather-warped and crooked with rot that Lindquist would have figured it abandoned if it weren't for the yellow-orange lantern light glowing inside and showing through the cracks.

Lindquist stood for a dumbfounded moment, half convinced he was hallucinating. He had only the faintest notion of where he was. He'd been using the moon and stars to guide him east through the swamp and he knew he still had a ways to go, far enough that he would have never expected to come across this place. Far enough that he hardly believed he was seeing it now.

He staggered forward in the shin-deep water, hello'd. Waved his arm, not knowing why. Hello'd again.

An old man in grimy overalls answered the door. Or, really, the pretense of a door: a piece of sheet metal hinged with rope. He opened it only wide enough to peer out, his eyes livid within his seamed face. "You government?" he asked.

"Government?" Lindquist said. He might have laughed if he weren't so scared and in so much pain. "No, sir," Lindquist said. "I ain't from the government."

The old man opened the door a little more. His hair stood awry, thin as corn silk. His eyes went to Lindquist's hook arm and stayed there. Usually Lindquist would have told him to mind his business, but such proprieties now seemed a thing of the past.

"You Lindquist?" asked the old man.

Lindquist jerked back his chin, unsure if he should answer.

"You Lindquist, ain't you? The one with no arm."

Lindquist gaped silently.

"Yeah, you Lindquist all right. Heard all kinds of stories about you over the years."

"Out here?" Lindquist asked, aware he sounded addled.

"Oh, I ain't always lived out here. Used to live in Jeanette. Before things went to shit."

Lindquist waited. Dirty and panting, face swollen with bug bites, hair caked with filth. He probably looked every bit as insane as this man did to him.

"So what you want?" the man asked.

"I'm lost."

"Figured that." The man cast an apprehensive glance over Lindquist's shoulder. "Anybody with you?"

"Naw."

"Well," he said. Then he gestured Lindquist forward.

Inside a sterno stove burned in the middle of the plywood floor. Above it hung a small cast-iron kettle bubbling with navy beans and a livery gruel. In the corner was a water-stained mattress with a blue blanket and a pillow. A transistor radio, a stack of ten or twelve paperback books with creased spines. Lindquist saw a few of the authors' names, Thoreau and Franklin.

They sat on the floor facing one another across the guttering fire. A ribbon of smoke rose from the kettle like a charmed snake. A draft caught it and sucked it through a crack outside.

"You pissed off a whole lot of folks over there in Jeanette," the man said. He stroked his stubbled chin, his look coy and punitive.

Lindquist barely had the strength to shrug. "I guess," he said.

He wondered if he could ask the man to let him stay the night. If he could just slouch over there in the other corner and get an hour or two of sleep. But he knew he couldn't do that even if the man agreed. The Toup brothers couldn't be far away. Maybe they were outside right now with their guns, their knives. Maybe this old man was in cahoots and would shiv him in the heart the second he shut his eyes.

"People say you dig through graveyards," the old man said, matter-of-factly.

"Graveyards? I never dug in any graveyard, me."

"Not what I heard."

"Well, hell. I didn't."

"They say you been digging up bodies."

"Well, hell. I never dug up any damn bodies either."

The man stared.

"Is that what people say? I dig up bodies?"

The old man swatted. "Never mind all that," he said.

"Well, I didn't. For the record."

The man reached for the ladle and stirred the pot.

"Say your name was?" Lindquist said.

"I never said."

Lindquist waited for the man to tell him but he didn't. Lindquist looked uneasily about the dim hovel. Behind the paperbacks he saw three plastic jugs of drinking water. "Get some water?" he asked.

The man flicked his hand, which Lindquist took to mean yes. He leaned over and hauled a jug by its handle. He flipped the cap with his thumb and tipped his head back. As soon as the liquid hit his mouth he gagged and spat. Stuff tasted like paint thinner, whatever it was. He wiped his lips with the back of his hand.

The old man slapped his overalled thigh and cackled, the few rotted stumps left in his lower jaw awry. "You got the wrong one," he said. "Get you the other one."

He did and this time it was water. He gulped it down, swallowing eight or nine good swallows until he was breathless. Then he put the jug aside. He hadn't realized how thirsty he was.

"Want something to eat?"

Lindquist leaned and craned his head forward and peered into the pot: small yellow pellets of fat, stringy clumps of gray meat. He nodded.

"Why you out here then?"

"Somebody's chasing me."

"Government?"

"Some guys. Just some guys is all."

"Sure they not government?"

"They're some guys who think I stole their drugs."

The old man seemed greatly interested by this. "You got any?" he asked.

"Drugs?"

"Yeah."

"No."

The man frowned. "That's too bad."

Lindquist was unsure how to respond so he said nothing.

The old man rose and rummaged through the scraps and junk behind him. He fetched up a blue plastic bowl into which he ladled five big scoops of stew, and then he handed the steaming bowl to Lindquist.

"Thank you," Lindquist said.

"No utensils," the man said.

Lindquist nodded and scooped some of the stringy gruel out of the bowl with his fingers. He tasted Zatarain's and sauce piquant. Cayenne pepper. He was surprised by how good it was. Just as fine as anything he tasted on those rare trips he'd taken with his ex-wife to New Orleans. Hell, better.

"Good," Lindquist said.

The old man nodded, firelight flickering in his rheumy eyes.

"You ever hear of the Toups?" Lindquist asked. "Twin brothers?"

"Naw."

"Well, that's who's after me."

"Yeah. So?"

This answer took Lindquist aback. "Well, I guess if anything happens to me. That's who it was."

The man said nothing. Lindquist kept looking at the old man and the old man kept looking at Lindquist.

"What you lookin' at?" the man said.

"Nothing."

"You think I look weird?"

"Naw."

"If you can answer then you were lookin'."

Lindquist shook his head. "Well."

The man narrowed his eyes at Lindquist. "What you got in them pockets? You keep on touchin' yourself."

"Nothing."

The man craned his neck forward. "Bullshit," he said. "What you got? Drugs?"

"I told you, I don't got any drugs."

"Then what is it?"

"I'd just as soon not say."

"Then you must be in trouble," the old man said.

Lindquist finished his stew and placed the empty bowl aside. "I need to get back to Jeanette," he said.

"Good luck with that."

"How far away you think that is?"

"Three miles exactly."

"Three miles?" Lindquist said. How in God's green fucking earth would he make it three more miles?

"Three miles exactly."

"How would you get there? What's the best way?"

"Boat's the only way." He anticipated Lindquist's next question and jerked his thumb over his shoulder. "Little motorboat in back."

"Would you take me back to Jeanette?"

"No," the old man said.

Lindquist waited.

"I can't see so good at night," he explained.

"How about I drive? You can spend the night and drive back in the morning."

"I'm not much for slumber parties."

"I got to get back to Jeanette, me."

"I don't know you."

"Well, hell. I can give you money."

"Shit."

"I can give you a lot of money, me."

The man peered steadily at Lindquist over the fire. "How much?"

"How much would it take?"

The man shook his head. "I'm eighty-three years old and don't need bullshit."

"I can give you gold."

The man let loose a wild yodeling laugh. "You really crazy, aren't you?" He shook his head and kept shaking it. Or maybe it just shook on its own. "They always said I was kinda crazy myself. Never gave a shit, me."

"Sir. I'm begging you."

"Get to sleep if you want. Draw you up a blanket over there. We'll talk about it in the morning."

"Sir."

"I already answered you," he said, his voice gone harder now.

"Well," Lindquist said. He got up and went to the door and waited for the man to change his mind. To show some mercy.

Silence, only the soft crackling of the fire.

"Well, I better get going I guess," Lindquist said.

"I guess you better be," said the man.

THE TOUP BROTHERS

After midnight and the black-green swamp was swollen and dripping, moonstruck jewels of dew trembling on the leaves. The Toup twins came across a fallen oak, its trunk worm-bored and teeming with larvae. The log was too large to leap so they climbed on top, boots crackling in the rotten wood, and then they hopped down to the other side.

For the better part of a day they'd been chasing after Cosgrove and Lindquist and every time they were about to turn back, figuring the men either lost or dead, they heard or saw a sign ahead. Something large crashing through the brush from a distance, a pinpoint twinkle of a roving light.

Now they came upon a spiderweb as big as a shrimping trawl, stretched between the tumorous trunks of two alders. A hand-sized spider like a blown-glass objet d'art lazed in the middle, motionless in the beams of their flashlights.

As they skirted the web a memory came to Reginald. At first he said nothing about it, only moved abstractedly along, his eyes someplace else. Or sometime else. Maybe the memory was a figment of his imagination, a neurological glitch caused by exhaustion and dehydration.

No, this was a memory. Reginald had no doubt. It had that quality, indelible as a dream, etched in acid. Realer than the moment he was living now.

"You remember being lost out here?" Reginald asked Victor. Even his whisper seemed loud in the dark.

They were wallowing along side by side, their pants muddy to the waist.

"We're lost now," Victor said.

"I mean when we were kids."

Victor looked at Reginald, breath rasping from his nose. "You finding God over there?" he said. "If so, I don't want to hear it."

"We were lost out here once. I swear it."

"Right here?"

"Not exactly here. But a place like it."

Victor shook his head.

"My God, I can't believe I'm remembering this."

"You probably dreamt it."

"I didn't either. You were beside me. Crying. I remember that now."

Victor swatted his hand. "Bullshit."

"We were young. Four or five. We were real little. I remember."

They treaded through the big slick-leaved plants, Reginald watching Victor for a reaction, some telltale flicker in his face, a subtle recalibration of the mouth or jaw. But his brother only scowled along.

"You have to remember," Reginald said.

"What we'd be doing out here?"

"Daddy dropped us off. Left us out here."

Victor forearmed the sweat from his brow. "You dreamt it."

"You can keep on saying that all you want but it's true. Daddy left us out here."

"All right."

"He left us out here and we had to find our way home."

"All right," Victor said.

"You remember how we wandered and wandered? We wandered all day. You kept on saying we had to keep in one direction. You'd seen that in some movie. Some cartoon. We stepped through a big spiderweb and you ran away all crazy, slapping yourself all over. Then you stepped on something and it went through your shoe. A piece of metal or something. A nail. I had to carry you piggyback for like a mile."

Victor grunted and shook his head.

"What?" Reginald said.

"None of that shit ever happened."

"You sure you're not just blocking it?"

Victor looked at his brother rancidly. "You a psychiatrist now?"

"Maybe he didn't want us to find our way back home," Reginald said.

Victor kept quiet and Reginald dropped the subject. Maybe he'd bring it up another time. A time when they weren't chasing a one-armed man through the swamp like assholes.

"We should turn back to the boat," Reginald said.

"We'll never make it back now."

"What're we doing when we catch up with them?"

"What you think?"

"This is crazy," Reginald said. "We need to get to the boat."

They moved along in silence. The electric stammer of insects.

After a minute, Victor said, "Nobody's dreams are interesting except to themselves."

COSGROVE

Cosgrove heard the twins before he saw them, one telling the other in the dark that something was crazy, damn-fool crazy. Then his brother told him to stop being such a pussy. The rest Cosgrove couldn't make out, the voices muffled by the jungly bracken, the susurrus of swamp life. It was several hours since Cosgrove parted ways with Lindquist. Now he could hear the popping of twigs as the twins came toward him through the brush. He looked around for a stick he could use as a weapon, for a hiding place. Anything.

A few yards away was a fallen tree trunk near a bright clump of swamp flowers. He went to it and dropped belly-down into the sludge and snake-shimmied into its hollow.

When he heard the twins stepping near he held his breath. He was slathered in mud and worm shit and God knew what else. Bugs scuttled across his arms and face, their eyelash legs tickling his skin.

The squelching of shoes ceased.

"See those holes?" said one.

"That's a snake nest. Get."

"Leg-sized. Somebody's been here."

A big daddy longlegs spider dropped onto Cosgrove's chin and scurried up his face. It dipped into his open mouth and crawled quickly out.

Then on string-like legs it climbed onto his nose and paused there. Cosgrove shot out a breath and the spider scurried across his forehead and dashed across his ear before it was gone.

"Look, that's a boot print. Right there."

Cosgrove's heart clenched. He held his breath and waited for the boot that would bust the log apart, for the barrel of the gun. What then? Oblivion.

But now he could hear the twins moving away, the slow diminuendo of their bickering voices.

He stayed motionless for a time. Then he popped his head out of the trunk and looked around. Faint moonlight, dark leaves and branches against the paler darkness of night.

He crawled out of the hollow trunk and stood.

Then he ran.

LINDQUIST

Sometime in the night Lindquist began to talk to himself for company. Random jabbering, mostly jokes.

"What's the difference between a lobster with breasts and a Greyhound bus stop?"

"How do you circumcise a hillbilly?"

"How did Joe the Camel quit smoking?"

He didn't bother with the punch lines. He already knew them. The setups were the best parts anyway.

Sometimes his laughter sounded strange, not like him at all. He stopped, swiveled his head, but he was alone in the dark. He caught sight of his moonlit reflection in the black mirror of the water. He resembled an insane mage: hair stuck out in greasy tufts, white curds of dried spittle in the corners of his mouth, clutching his stick like a staff.

It was some wee hour of morning, the swamp rustling with a million small sounds, when Lindquist smacked square into something hard. He yelped and clutched his throbbing nose. Then he stepped back and held up his hook arm to fend away whatever it was.

A hulking human-shaped silhouette, a full head taller, stood before him. It said something in a low gruff voice. "Got you, asshole," it sounded like.

Lindquist jerked his torso back as if dodging a blow. The twins. Surely one of the twins.

He crabbed another step back, letting out a sound that was part sob, part whimper. "What I ever do to you?" he asked.

Silence. Only his own rasping breath, the myriad swamp sounds—buzzings and chitterings and rustlings—around him.

"I ain't ever done a thing. Why you got to do this?"

The wide-shouldered figure stayed quiet. As if to intimidate him. As if to drive him mad.

Lindquist was electric with panic. "Just leave me alone," he begged.

Silence.

Lindquist snapped, slashing maniacally with his hook arm, gouging into the twin's hard torso. A few times the hook stuck and he had to rear back and yank it out tug-of-war style. He hacked away until he was dizzy and could lift his prosthetic no more. Then, swaying punch-drunk on his feet, he reached out with trembling fingers. Tree bark. A tree, that's all.

Shaking and feverish and drenched with sweat, Lindquist collapsed to the ground, his legs giving out like a marionette's. The earth was damp and gritty against his cheek. His stump was bleeding, hot stitches down the right side of his torso. He couldn't recall such pain, not since the day he'd lost his arm, the day the coast guard helicoptered him out of the Barataria to the Mercy General trauma ward. The pain then had been so obliterating he couldn't make sense of what happened. He'd lost an arm? How? How did somebody lose an arm? What kind of asshole? What kind of loser?

Then, after the paramedic applied the tourniquet, they shot him full of morphine. At once the red-hot agony vanished, replaced with a cool bliss that made him feel hollow, billowed full of glacial air. He felt kissed by God.

Now, lying on his side across the mucky ground, panting and sobbing, he'd give half the coins in his pockets to feel such relief.

-- -- -- -- -- --

The cypress knees in the three-quarter moonlight looked like a mob of hunkering imps, their elfin faces leering in the bark, their wood-bore eyes tracking his passage. When the wind rose it clacked through the tree branches and Lindquist could swear he heard the moan of imp voices. What language was it? Maybe Latin, maybe Gaelic. Maybe some long-forgotten tongue silenced by history. The language of witches or succubi.

Whatever language, Lindquist got the gist. The imps were saying he was as good as dead. That he was never going to make it out of the swamp. That he'd pissed his life away.

"What if a bat pisses in my eye?" Lindquist said. Was this a joke? He didn't know himself, but laughed anyway.

"What if a bat pisses in your eye?" someone said. Startled, Lindquist looked left. Several yards away a cypress-stump imp stared at him, the enormous wooden gash of its mouth downturned like a grim head-master's. Now it cocked its head, a movement so slight that Lindquist would have thought his eyes were playing a trick if the cypress stump didn't also smile.

"What?" Lindquist said.

"What if a bat pissed in your eye?" the stump said. Its voice was deep, patrician.

"Shut up," Lindquist said.

"You shut up," the stump said.

Lindquist took off running into the dark, the cypress stumps cackling around him. He leapt over deadfalls of cypress and pine, until his left leg got sucked down in mud. Lindquist cursed and wrenched his leg free, the bog belching as it let go of his boot.

"Whoa there, fruitcake," said another cypress stump.

The surrounding stumps erupted in wild laughter.

So this is withdrawal, Lindquist thought. He could deal with jeering cypress stumps. If other men went through war, famine, plagues, droughts, then he could deal with talking cypress stumps.

When Lindquist resumed walking he kept his pace casual, a little more strut in his style. *Go ahead and laugh, motherfuckers,* he tried to tell the stumps with his walk.

He reminded himself that he was forty-five years old but might as well have been a hundred, the way he'd treated himself. Well, no more putting his body through the wringer of ritual abuse. Once he got out of this swamp, if he ever did, he would put himself on a vigorous health regimen. Quality vitamins, a top-notch juicer. He would buy a new arm and he would move away from the bayou, maybe even from the country. He would settle down with a black-haired girl with blue eyes and a dramatic face, a French girl who'd listen raptly to his recollections of the story he was living right now.

He pictured vividly this waking dream.

The girl looked very much like his wife.

Exactly like his wife.

THE TOUP BROTHERS

It was just after dawn when the Toup brothers came upon the swamp shack. They stopped and listened for signs of human life. The only sounds came from the half-sleeping wilderness. The myriad rustlings of bush animals. The distant calls of birds. Otherwise, the world was hushed in cloistral quiet.

Victor scouted through the weeds and picked up a rock and hurled it. It whomped against the side of the shack as loud as a gunshot. A covey of mourning doves exploded out of a bush, scattering above the treetops.

The brothers waited.

Nothing.

Victor kicked again through the weeds and picked up a stick and hurled it like an Olympian. It twirled and whistled through the air and smacked the front door.

Faint rousing sounds came from inside the dwelling. Human. Then a man's voiced, cracked with age. "What the fuck?"

Victor ran full-bore across the clearing. When he reached the shack he raised his leg without slowing and kicked the front in a kind of flying karate move. The shack listed and then froze crookedly still for a moment before collapsing like a magician's house of cards. As if nothing more than illusion had held it together.

Someone stirred beneath the junk heap.

At the edge of the wood Reginald pocketed his hands and came warily across the clearing. Another pain in the ass to deal with, this.

"What the fuck," said an ireful voice at the bottom of the pile.

"Get out," Victor said.

"Out?" said the man. "There ain't no in anymore."

Victor kicked the pile.

There was stirring from within the mound. Pieces of wood scrap and corrugated metal tumbled. A bony hand shot out from the rubble and picked up a two-by-four and flung it aside. Another and another. Finally a figure rose like a junkyard Lazarus, pieces of scrap sloughing from his shoulders and back. The old man brushed off his filthy overalls with an oddly foppish show of propriety. In the dim purple daybreak he looked at Victor and then at Reginald. His babyish white hair was awry, his eyes beneath their wily brows still puffy with sleep.

"We're looking for somebody," Reginald said.

The man glared at Reginald. "Well, why the fuck didn't you just knock?"

"Guy come through?" Reginald asked.

The man pointed to the ground, the junk pile. "Here?"

"No time for your shit," Victor said.

"A man with one arm," Reginald said.

Something in Victor's face gave the man pause. His body swayed in panicked indecision, his hands squeezing in fists at his sides. As if part of him wanted to fight, as if the other part wanted to flee. At once his defiance vanished. "Yeah, a guy come," he said.

"When?" Victor asked.

The man stared at the ground in bewilderment. As if waiting for the mud to tell him what to say. What to do.

"When," Victor said.

"I'm trying to think," the man said. "You woke me up from a deep fuckin' sleep."

The swamp had fallen eerily quiet, even the birds and crickets silent.

Maybe watching from their boweries and nooks, waiting to see how this scene would transpire. Meanwhile as daybreak grew brighter the swamp was seeping back into place, like an old oil painting revealed tint by tint by restorative solvent. Mushroom browns and moss greens and lichen grays.

"I guess it was four hours ago," the old man said. "Five."

"Which way?" Victor asked.

The man pointed east with a palsied finger. "Said he was going back to Jeanette. That he had something you guys wanted."

"Let's go," Reginald said to his brother.

"Drugs," the old man said.

Reginald's shoulders sagged. He pinched the bridge of his nose and closed his eyes.

"You drug dealers, right?"

"What makes you think that?" Victor asked.

"Shit, I don't care."

"What makes you think we're drug dealers?"

"He told me so."

"And you believe everything you hear?"

"Come on," Reginald said.

Victor stayed in place. Arms folded over his chest, a professorial cant to his head. "What if I were to tell you your mother was a whore?" he said.

The man kept silent.

"Was your mother a whore?"

"Look. Just leave me alone. You already done destroyed my house."

"I heard your mother is a whore. Is that true?"

The old man worked his mouth pensively. "Yeah," he said. "It's true."

"Really?"

"Yeah."

"Your ma was a whore?"

"Yeah."

Reginald started to walk back toward the woods. At the edge of the clearing he stopped and looked around at his brother. "Come on," he said.

"She was a whore," the man went on. "Big ol' one. So if that's it."

"I heard she gave blowjobs to strangers in bathrooms," Victor said. "Is this true?"

"Come on, goddamn it," Reginald said. "No time for this shit."

"Probably," the old man answered Victor.

"Who would sell his mother out like that?" Victor asked.

The man sat heavily on the rotted pile of scrap, liver-spotted forearms resting on his thighs, hands loose-wristed between his knees.

"Even if she were?" Victor went on. "Who would sell their mother out like that?"

The man shook his head. It was a moment before he spoke and when he did his voice was soft. "I don't even remember my mother."

"When did she die?"

"Long ago."

"When?"

"I was eighteen, nineteen."

"You have trouble with numbers."

"I'm fuckin' eighty-five."

"Are you sure?"

"You the Toup brothers?" asked the old man.

The brothers exchanged a glance.

"How'd you know our name?" Victor asked.

"The guy told me."

Silence.

"As long as you ain't from the government I don't care."

Victor waited.

"You guys got any drugs?"

"You're crazier than shit, aren't you?" Victor asked, smiling a smile that looked sharpened on a whetstone.

The old man thought about this but didn't answer.

"What's your name?"

The man looked up at Victor. A woebegone supplicant. "You already destroyed my house."

"That was a house?"

"I'm going to die out here anyway. I got no house now. And I sure as shit ain't goin' to Jeanette. So why not just leave me. Let the wolves have me."

"Wolves. Stop being so fuckin' dramatic."

"You ruined my fuckin' house."

Victor stared down at the man and lifted his shirtfront and reached for the gun tucked in his waistband.

"Hey," Reginald said from the edge of the wood.

Victor ignored him.

"My mother wasn't a whore," the man told Victor.

"So?" Victor said.

"Just for the record."

Victor rested the muzzle of the Sig Sauer against the man's forehead, pushing hard enough to make a divot in the flesh.

"Yours was," the man said. "Your ma was a whore."

Victor cocked the gun.

"She must have fucked a real piece of shit to squeeze out a turd like you."

"Hey," Reginald called.

Victor finally looked at his brother.

"Cut the shit," Reginald said.

Victor uncocked the gun and tucked it back into his waistband and began to walk away. To his back the man spat quick French curses, his voice soft but full of fury. Without turning Victor called him a crazy son of a bitch. The old man reached into the pocket of his overalls and threw gray ash-like powder into the air. It silted softly down, sighing in the weeds and leaves.

COSGROVE

Twig by twig, leaf by leaf, the tangled wood around him gathered shape in the pale gray dawn. He could hear water sounds, splashing baitfish, and he could see the bay's smoky shimmer through the leaves. He stepped tentatively forward, eyes stinging with exhaustion, shoulder throbbing with every heartbeat.

There it was across the channel of foggy water. The island. A fucking miracle.

Cosgrove went running high-kneed in the water, a few times tripping in the mud. He rose and cast wild looks about because now he was out in the open and one of the twins could shoot him easily. When the water deepened and his shoes no longer touched bottom he paddled and kicked, a flailing swim. Then his shoes touched bottom again and he staggered dripping wet onto the island.

In the clearing what was left of Hanson lay belly-up in the mud. Cosgrove stared down at the body. There was blood, already drying dark, on the ground. Blood splattered on a cypress stump. Blood speckled on the leaves of a trumpet creeper.

Horseflies as big as grapes supped on the gore.

Cosgrove looked away from the mush of Hanson's head and doubled over with his hands on his knees and retched into the underbrush.

Then he squatted over Hanson, averting his face, reached into one of his pockets. Nothing. He rooted through the other and felt the keys and pulled them out. Then he scrabbled backward, half expecting Hanson's hand to shoot up and grab him. A crazy thought, he knew. He was half delirious.

It took him ten minutes to find the motorboat, moored in its bowery of bulrush and vine. Still convinced that a bullet might go through his head any second, he leapt into the boat. It rocked away from the shore, water splashing over the gunwale and puddling on the floor.

He pulled the choke and the engine grumbled and the boat shot into the water, the prow lifting and smacking back down. Cosgrove glanced back at the island, its shape blurred behind gray morning fog. His shoulder hurt, his chest, his heart.

He breathed deeply. The wind blowing off the bayou smelled like salt and crude and sun. *You're not out of it yet,* he thought.

He judged it almost ten by the time he reached the harbor, the day already hot enough that the sun was burning on his shoulders. Parked in the lot among the other pickups was Hanson's flatbed Dodge. No one else in sight. For this small mercy he was thankful. If anyone saw him, no doubt there would be suspicions. A man looking like he did, they'd make a point of remembering his face.

When he got to the motel he sat in the truck for several minutes with the engine idling and his hands gripped around the wheel. Trucks shunted by on the access road, slowing as they passed.

In his room he washed his face in the sink and cleaned his aching shoulder with a wet towel. Afterward he put on a new T-shirt and jeans and stuffed the dirty clothes in a plastic shopping bag and threw the bag in the garbage. Then he got his money out of the motel room safe. He thought about going into Hanson's room and taking his money too, but he didn't know the combination. Some maid was going to have the best week of her life.

After he shoved his clothes and sundries into his duffel bag he went to the window and pulled back the curtain and looked out. Across the way, the motel maid pushed a cart from one room door to the next. In the lot, a man in gray slacks and a polo shirt locked the door of his Town Car and strode toward his room.

No one else.

It was eleven when Cosgrove walked out of the motel room and got into the truck. With the duffel bag on the passenger seat holding the several thousand dollars and everything else in the world he owned, he put the truck in first and turned onto the access road toward the highway.

This is happening, he thought. *I'm getting away and I'm alive. Poor Hanson's dead but I'm alive. This is happening.*

He didn't know where he was headed except away. If a cop stopped him, he'd tell him the truck was a friend's.

LINDQUIST

Lindquist was only asleep an hour when he heard the voices. It was just after dawn, light shafting in rusty smoking columns through the leaves. He jerked upright in the makeshift hammock of the hollow log. Listened. The brothers? It had to be. Who else would be out here? From twenty or thirty yards away, he heard the drawl of their voices. Stirring leaves and snapping twigs.

Lindquist shot to his feet and plunged through the bulrushes, saw briers lashing his arms and face. After a while it occurred to him that maybe there were no voices at all. That maybe he was in the middle of some mad dream.

Every part of him ached. His eyelids, his fingertips, his teeth.

He ducked under a lichen-furred hickory branch, gave wide berth to a black olive tree hung with a mud-daub nest boiling with wasps. Fat leeches clung to his skin. He felt one puckering on a rib, another on his kneecap, another on his forearm. He let them be. He had bigger worries. His gold. He kept frisking his pockets, making sure it was all still there.

A statue-still heron stood one-legged on a cypress stump, watching him. A stone's throw away, where the bog deepened into a lagoon, an alligator sluiced through the water, the leathery bump of its head poking just above the surface. It changed its route and tailed away from Lindquist.

Further on he saw a brightly colored coral snake dangling from the low branch of a willow, its tongue flicking like an obscene party favor.

Lindquist jerked away and whimpered.

He sounded crazy. He knew he better keep his wits about him. Once you let one weird thought slide, then others quickly followed, an avalanche, and before you knew it you were stuck forever in the middle of the swamp, a ranting madman doomed to checking the gold in his pockets over and over again.

"A one-armed man staggers through the swamp," Lindquist said. Or thought.

"Fake it till you feel it," he said. Or thought.

He stopped and listened for sounds of pursuit. He could hear nothing now but buzzing locusts, the *wee-tee-tee* of a cowbird. It was full morning and white light blazed down on the bog. Cypress stumps and water lilies and purple-flowered hyacinths as far as he could see. Hundreds of hovering dragonflies. Halloween pennants and spangled pond hawks and roseate skimmers.

He felt feverish and dizzy. He'd had hardly any sleep for days, only rainwater from leaves to drink. Mosquito bites festered on his face and arm.

On the bright side—*bright side!* Lindquist let out a deranged titter—he had to be close to solid land. Jeanette might be just beyond that fringe of spicebush, that clump of loblollies. Surely he'd make it home by the end of the day. Take a long cold shower and make a lunch fit for a king. Count how many gold coins he had left. Then he'd drive to New Orleans and sell them. By the end of the day he'd be a rich man with a plane ticket to a new place, a new life.

He was passing a bush of swamp honeysuckle when he heard a sound in the water and looked down. A snake about two feet long sidewindered across the surface. Lindquist didn't know what kind of snake it was, but it was black-and-orange-scaled and coming straight toward him. He told the snake to shoo.

The snake kept coming. Five feet away, now two.

Lindquist yelled and took off running.

He plowed through the jungly vegetation until pain like molten buckshot seared his torso. In a patch of lady ferns and swamp grass he lay on his back. His heart raced and his tongue was scorched with fever. He would wait here until the kid came back. If the kid came back in the next hour, in the next two, he could boat him to shore and take him to the doctor. He would even give the kid a few pieces of the gold, enough that it would make a big difference in his life.

He shut his eyes and felt the deep strong suck of oblivion. In a panic he opened his eyes again. If he fell asleep, maybe he'd never wake.

He tried to get up but couldn't. He would lie here until the kid came along and took him to the doctor's. He wondered if the doctor would accept Spanish pirate gold for payment.

He reached for his pockets, felt their heaviness.

His eyes shut, opened, shut, opened. Above him, morning sun pierced through the swimming jade leaves. The pieces of light looked like a thousand shimmering coins of gold.

THE TOUP BROTHERS

Midmorning it dawned on the Toup brothers that it would be insane to venture further. They turned around and headed back toward the boat. Whatever they planned on doing to Lindquist and the man named Cosgrove once they caught up with them the swamp had probably already done for them. No way could they have made it through this kind of wilderness back to Jeanette. Not when they themselves were on the edge of delirium.

Reginald led and Victor plodded behind, the veins in his forehead popping, his face sheened with sweat. The vegetation, sweet bay magnolia and swamp cyrilla and black willows, enclosed around them like a dripping jade-green cave. Sometimes they had to stoop to make it through the tunnel of overarching branches and leaves. The ravenous swamp wanted to swallow them whole.

After a while they passed the ruined shack, the old man already gone.

They were skirting the edge of a reedy marsh when Victor tottered sideways and stumbled crazily through the muck. He clung to the trunk of a green ash tree. Reginald stopped and looked around. Victor's face was flushed the color of a blood orange, his eyes a sickly hepatitis-yellow.

It was around eleven and already the heat was stifling. Whenever the foliage thinned they could see the sky, hazy washed-out lavender.

"That old guy cursed me," Victor said.

"That's crazy."

"Motherfucker cursed me."

"You're dehydrated. Exhausted. We both are."

"I still hear him in my head."

"Just keep your shit together."

Reginald took a few tentative steps forward but stopped and turned around when he didn't hear his brother following.

"Victor," Reginald said.

"How much longer?"

"An hour. Two. I don't know."

"He cursed me, Reggie."

"You're having a panic attack."

"Bullshit."

They slogged through the bog for what Reginald judged about forty-five minutes and came again upon the collapsed swamp shack. The brothers looked around in confusion. Reginald slapped his cheek and wondered how they ended up here again when they'd been traveling straight in one direction.

Was he losing his mind? Were they both?

"Reggie," Victor said.

Reginald said nothing.

"Reggie," Victor said.

"What?"

"We're back where we started."

"There's no way."

"This is the shack. The same fuckin' one. We went in a circle."

Reginald raked his fingers through his filthy hair and looked around. The noon sunlight pierced through the leaves ceiled overhead. A fat green katydid thrashed in the middle of a web stretched between two saw palmettos. A golden silk spider watched from the edge of the trembling skein.

"We went in a circle, Reggie."

"Wiggin' out's not gonna help anything."

"Maybe a tick burrowed in my ear," Victor said. "Maybe I got that Rocky Mountain fever."

"Vic? Shut up."

They sloshed along. Gnats and horseflies and pond striders. A yellow-throated vireo bird in a winterberry holly. Baby alligators by the dozen skimming away like rubber toys.

Then Victor saw it. A nine-foot alligator, a behemoth, sunning atop a barge of floating logs and detritus. He pointed, his finger shaking. "Jesus Christ, look at that thing," he said.

"Keep moving," Reginald said.

"Fucker's just staring at us."

"Stop screaming. Keep moving."

"Now he's coming."

"More scared of us than we him."

Victor collapsed to his hands and knees, bright green water lapping to his chin. He struggled up, fell again. Reginald turned and went back and yanked his brother up by the arm. Leaning on his brother, Victor tottered forward a few steps before collapsing. This time he took Reginald down with him. Reginald rose and grabbed two fistfuls of his brother's shirt and pulled him up. He felt Victor's heart laboring beneath his hand. Felt his fever, palpable as heat wafting off a stove burner.

"Another big gator right there," Victor said.

"Just keep going."

"I gotta sit."

"Move."

"Give me a piggyback."

"There's no way."

"You go on then. I can't."

Something was coming quickly toward them through the palmettos and brush, the water churning. A chevron of sparrows sounded a shrill one-note call of alarm and winged out of a red maple.

Then Victor was ripped away from Reginald. He let loose a lunatic scream before he was pulled underwater. Reginald gaped in mute horror. He saw pink flesh. A flash, pebbly black, of alligator hide. Then Victor's raised arm, grappling for something that wasn't there.

His hands quaking wildly, Reginald unholstered his Bearcat Ruger and took aim. He couldn't get a bead on the alligator in the churning chaos, the water already a tumult of red and pink curd. When he saw another alligator swimming toward him he shouldered the rifle and turned, rushed for the nearest tree. He scrabbled monkey-like up the gnarled live oak, perched on a middle limb.

He looked down at the calming water. Smaller alligators were now hemming in. A dozen of them swam off with glistening pink hunks of meat. Reginald glimpsed a floating length of organ, like a piece of raw sausage. He felt hot bile rise in his throat. He couldn't believe what he saw. Refused to believe.

He vomited down into the water.

When the alligators scattered away, Reginald remained on the branch and wept. He waited to wake from the nightmare and when he didn't wake he wept for a long while more.

WES TRENCH

Lindquist was missing almost a week when Villanova finally marshaled a search and rescue team: a few local trawlers, Deputy Melloncamp, another deputy from a neighboring parish, a coast guard ensign, a Louisiana Department of Wildlife and Fisheries agent. Midmorning a throng of boats dispersed in the bay, each assigned a parcel of the Barataria to canvas. Among the deputation were Wes on the *Jean Lafitte* and Wes's father on the *Bayou Sweetheart*. It was his first time on the water since his heart attack. Wes told him to stay home and rest, but he said he was sick of sitting on his ass at home and joked there was nothing good on television anyway.

It was a desolate windswept day, the sky and water the same dreary slate, the bay riled and whitecapped. Wes circled around the same islands he'd already circled, glassing shore and bracken with binoculars. Every time the radio box squawked, every time there was a blare of static before someone spoke, Wes's heart kicked with dread. A body dredged up in a trawl, he was sure. A mangled corpse washed up on an islet shore.

But no, the news was only more of the same: nothing. Nothing here, nothing there. Headed here, headed there.

Come late afternoon the clouds busted open. The bay hissed and boiled and snakes of steam shimmied off the water. The wind kicked up and rattled the hundreds of little loose parts on Lindquist's boat. Anything beyond ten yards of the *Jean Lafitte* was swallowed in murk. Over the radio the trawlers and the coast guard ensign said they were turning back. An hour later Wes was thinking about doing the same when Deputy Melloncamp came on the radio. A shrimper had found an abandoned pirogue near where the bayou met the bay.

So Lindquist had wandered off course after all.

Wes piloted fast, nauseous with dread. Soon distant boat lights glimmered in the gray murk. As he drew closer he saw smaller lights, flashlights and spotlights, skimming over the water. Then, through the hazy downpour, he could make out the deputy's boat, then his father's, then the LDWF's, idling in a loose cluster. Wes drew up and joined the posse and cut the gas. He clambered down the wheelhouse ladder and peered over the gunwale, windy rain lashing his face.

A pirogue bucked and spun in the heaving water. The little boat was like any other most people owned in the Barataria, but Wes spotted something on its floor, the toy-like colors among the scraps of trash.

Lindquist's Pez dispenser.

- - - - - - - -

The state of Louisiana, Wes's father often remarked, would forever have egg on its face. Always had, always would. No place in the country crookeder, according to him. What else could you expect, an outpost improvised and jury-rigged by outlaws and gypsies out of the swamp? A place which, in its fledgling years, was tossed back and forth between countries like a bastard child? Look at the evidence. State representatives caught with federal money in their freezers and prostitutes in their beds. Gubernatorial candidates ending up in prison. Federal Emergency money spent on swimming pools and sports cars and palomino ponies.

And the oil companies: God, the fucking oil companies.

Sooner or later, said Wes's father, they were all caught with their dicks in the cookie jar.

So when Wes asked him if he should speak again to Sheriff Villanova about the Toup brothers and Lindquist's disappearance, his father hissed out a bitter laugh. "You might as well write Santa Claus," he said.

Wes asked him what he meant.

"Look, Villanova's not a bad guy. Not compared with most. But you're living in goddamn Lebanon, Wes."

Wes had no idea what his father meant by *Lebanon*. He waited for his father to explain. They were at the dinner table eating rice and beans for supper and outside it was already full dark. The black windows threw back only their own reflections, the dim amber light glowing throughout the house. As always the television droned in the background. *All in the Family*, one of the only sitcom shows his father could abide. Archie was calling Edith a dingbat.

"Louisiana cops have their own way of running things," Wes's father said. "Like cops anywhere. They got to pick their battles." He put down his fork and nudged his plate away with his thumb and patted his shirt pocket, about to pull out a cigarette, but he stopped himself and leaned back in his chair. "Villanova looks the other way when it suits his purposes. Marijuana? He's not going to waste his time with marijuana. Not when his coffer's full. He's a laissez-faire guy. That's the way it works around here."

Turned out his father was right. In the morning he drove to the sheriff's office and spoke with Villanova about Lindquist and the Toup brothers. Villanova, sitting behind his desk, listened to Wes with avuncular forbearance, but impatience showed in his snapping eyes, the way he kept leaning back and nodding. At one point he rummaged in a drawer and took out a sachet of Earl Grey tea and dangled it in his coffee mug. The mug had a picture of a galloping racehorse on the side and said CHURCHILL DOWNS underneath. As Wes spoke, Villanova got up and went to the water cooler in the corner and twisted the red spigot, filling the mug with hot water. Then he sat back down, dunking the teabag.

Finally, when Wes finished explaining why he thought the Toup brothers were involved with Lindquist's disappearance, Villanova hunched his shoulders and spread his hands. "An abandoned pirogue," he said. "A couple of threats."

Wes waited, picking at his eyebrow.

"A threat," Villanova said. "I can't arrest someone based on a threat. The whole parish would be in lockup."

Wes thought about mentioning the marijuana, but Villanova knew he knew. Everybody knew. The subject seemed verboten, moot. And the sheriff probably wouldn't brook kindly a teenage kid telling him his business. So all Wes said was, "But they're known to stir trouble, right? They got a reputation is what I mean."

Villanova cleared his throat. Lifted and dipped the teabag. "Son, everybody has a reputation in a town small as this. Whether they like it or not. Usually half based on rumor."

Wes was trying to be polite and respectful but his patience with Villanova's indifference was wearing thin. "Worth checking out though, sir. Maybe?"

He knew even this much might have been pressing his luck.

Villanova stretched his arms and leaned back in his chair with his hands stitched behind his head. His face was pink and tight-mouthed. "Son, I'm sorry about your friend, but he's got a lot more history than the Toup brothers. And you gotta let me do my job."

Wes waited.

"How about you walk your side of the street and I'll walk mine," Villanova added, but then seemed to regret it, because he huffed a little laugh through his nose as if it were a joke. He picked up his mug and sipped his tea.

Some street, Wes wanted to say, but he knew it would serve no purpose. And his parents had taught him not to smart-mouth his elders.

Wes stood and thanked the sheriff, who rose and shook Wes's hand.

His fingers were fat and cold. "I'll keep my eyes peeled," he said, but somehow Wes doubted it.

One cool late-October night Wes was at the mini-mart out near the highway when Reginald Toup hunched into the store. By now everyone including Wes assumed Lindquist was dead. The police and game warden and coast guard were now looking for a body, not a survivor. And not really looking, just telling shrimping captains and crews to watch what they caught in their nets.

Wes was paying for a candy bar at the counter and did a double-take when he saw Toup. He watched Toup, and Toup noticed him watching. He looked away and started heading down one of the aisles but when he glanced over his shoulder Wes's eyes were still on him.

He stopped. "Help you?"

Wes wondered if he should. Made himself before he chickened out. "You do it?" he asked.

Toup put his hand behind his ear and leaned toward Wes. "Say what?"

"Did you do it?"

An ionic change in the air, like white noise or electricity. The old black man behind the counter opened the till of the register and broke a roll of quarters on the counter edge. For something to do.

Toup stepped toward Wes, his ears reddening. His face looked like a spring-loaded trap ready to snap shut. "Do it? Do what?"

Wes said nothing.

"Trench's kid, right?"

The man stood a full head taller and Wes had to tip his head back to look him in the eye. "Yeah," Wes said quietly. So this Toup brother knew who he was. How, he didn't know. Wes's bravery, what little there was, deserted him at once.

"You on crack or what?" Toup asked him.

"Sorry, I thought you were someone else," Wes said and turned.

He had his hand on the door handle when Toup said, "Hey."

Wes halted, his heart beating hard. He turned and saw that Toup was holding out his candy bar. "Forgot this," he said.

Wes thanked him and took the candy and stepped out of the store into humid night air. Before he reached his truck he was damning himself for thanking the son of a bitch.

CODA

Time ticked along. At last summer showed signs of ending, days growing shorter, nights cooler. Goldenrod bloomed yellow by the roadsides. Acorns fell from the live oaks and pinged on car hoods and toolshed roofs. Hurricane season wouldn't end for another few weeks, but people were relaxed enough that talk in the barbershop and grocery store turned from tropical depressions to football. Whether LSU would beat Auburn, whether the Saints would make the playoffs, maybe the Super Bowl. Flags of purple and yellow and flags of black and gold hung over house garages. Halloween decorations began popping up throughout Jeanette, papier-mâché bats strung from front yard trees, jack-o'-lanterns grinning their jagged grins on porches.

And of course there was talk of oil. Oil-sodden turtles and pelicans and redfish. Many Baratarians swore that the water had a funny tint to it, that the bay was darker and greener than before. Others said the shrimp and redfish had a metallic aftertaste, but people were eating Jeanette's seafood again and the National Oceanic and Atmospheric Administration reopened the water to shrimping and fishing.

For a while Wes clung onto hope that he'd hear from Lindquist. That maybe he'd run off with the treasure he found—if he ever found it. Wes half hoped one day to see Lindquist's funky avocado-colored boat, the *Jean Lafitte,* sailing once more in the Barataria.

But the boat remained untouched and neglected in its harbor slip, nettles fallen on the wheelhouse roof, tea-colored puddles staining the deck. Wes made a halfhearted pass at cleaning it, hosing the deck and windows, scraping crud off the hull. He might have approached Lindquist's daughter about it, told her that she should take care of the only thing of her father's that remained in the world, but he heard she up and left for New York, for God knew what. And Lindquist's ex-wife, a bank teller whom he'd met to express his condolences, seemed to have moved on.

The last time Wes had been to the hospital was in the summer after his father's heart attack, and he hoped that he wouldn't have to return anytime soon. But after the first frost of late October when the leaves were just beginning to turn he received a call from Sheriff Villanova. A body had been discovered, swept up by a trawler's net in the Barataria, and it needed identification.

Wes knew what Villanova meant. He thought the corpse was Lindquist's. Lindquist's daughter was still in New York and his ex-wife at a banking convention in Captiva, Florida, and Villanova didn't want to leave the matter a mystery until one of them returned.

The possibility—the probability—of Lindquist's being dead had of course occurred to Wes. But there were times in the weeks after Lindquist's disappearance when Wes believed that Lindquist had somehow made it, run off somewhere faraway without telling anyone.

A silly fantasy, perhaps. Like something from the movies. But wasn't it possible?

Wes recalled his conversations with Lindquist—how long ago that seemed now, though it was just months past—and how Lindquist told him that there was nothing he desired more than to start his life over again. Lindquist knew he couldn't reclaim the time he'd lost. The time had never seemed his to begin with. He'd begun trawling with his father just as soon as he was old enough to lift a champagne basket. And, like Wes, when the time came to decide whether to stay in the Barataria or matriculate to college: well, there wasn't much of a choice to make. His family needed the money and extra help.

And now Wes was driving to the hospital on a tranquil October morning, fine-spun sugar crystals of frost in the grass and in the trees, wispy autumn clouds like horsetails high in the sky, on his way to see a dead body that might be Lindquist's.

In the hospital the familiar smell hit him right away, the mingled sickly odor of dirty linen and bandages and mopping wax. Wes's breath stuck in his throat like hair in a drain. A pretty black girl with sapphire earrings sat behind the reception desk and Wes checked in. A few minutes later the coroner, Dr. Woodrell, met him in the lobby. A man with thick liver-colored lips and muddy eyes.

The morgue was on the fourth floor of the hospital, and as they rode the elevator alone the doctor tendered a fatigued smile at Wes.

"I warn you," he said, "this is never pretty."

Wes nodded.

"It's not like the television shows. Even the worst ones."

"I know."

They got off the elevator and walked down the hall, their shoe heels ticking coolly on the linoleum floor. At the door of the mortuary the doctor paused.

"So how'd he die?" Wes said.

"He was shot. In the head."

"Was he missing an arm?"

"He's missing both."

Wes blinked at the doctor.

"I should tell you this right now. To prepare you. The body's been eaten. The arms and a leg."

Now Wes was dizzy and his breath seemed not to be reaching as deep into his lungs as it needed. "Eaten by what?" he asked.

Dr. Woodrell rested his hand lightly on Wes's shoulder. A gesture more bureaucratic than benevolent. "Alligators. Crabs. Snapping turtles. Just about everything that could get to him. After seventeen years of

doing this, I'm still not sure when to tell people. Or to even tell them period. That's something they don't tell you in medical school. I guess they
decide you'll figure it out yourself."

Wes nodded.

The doctor opened the door and flicked a switch and the room flooded
with antiseptic light. Several cot-like tables were lined up in a row, a few
empty, a few with shrouded bodies on top. Wes followed the doctor
across the room, noticing the declivities in the concrete floor, little crater-
like places with drains in them. Wes couldn't help it: he thought about
all the blood and bile and vital juices running down those drains and
wondered where it all went. Into the Barataria, he guessed. Where else?

At the table the doctor gave him a white eucalyptus-smelling cotton
cloth and Wes held it over his mouth and nose. Then Dr. Woodrell threw
back the sheet.

At first Wes looked at the body without seeing it. As if there was something in his brain that blocked the image from reaching where it needed
to reach. Then when it did reach nausea swept through his stomach. Even
with the cloth held over his face, the smell was incredible, life-defying.
The body was black and purple, pulpy like waterlogged newspaper, and
there were tattered places where the limbs had been torn away. The nose
was missing, and the eyes, and in their place were dark wells. But the
hair was still there, and it didn't look like Lindquist's. Lindquist didn't
have that much hair. Lindquist prayed he had this much hair. It was long
enough to put up in a ponytail.

And Wes saw the T-shirt, a little faded and shredded but otherwise
strangely intact despite the ruin of the body. Lindquist never wore a
T-shirt like that.

TOM PETTY AND THE HEARTBREAKERS, it said.

"No," Wes said through the cloth. He would have never believed such
a strange mixture of repulsion and relief possible if he wasn't feeling it
now. "No," he said again. "This isn't him."

- - - - - - - -

Come November, Wes realized that another year would likely pass without his making plans to leave Jeanette. Without his making plans to do anything but shrimp for the rest of his life. If people ever left the Barataria, ever did something else with their lives, they did it when they were his age, or never.

The only other states Wes had ever been were Mississippi, Alabama, Texas, and Florida. He'd never stepped foot on the East or West Coast and the only sea he'd ever swam was the Gulf of Mexico. It bothered him that he wasn't troubled by this, that no part of him longed to see the Blue Ridge Mountains or the Pacific Northwest, that no part of him yearned to step inside a Tibetan monastery or spelunk the Carlsbad Caverns or behold up-close the Krakatoa.

It wasn't that he felt destined to live the rest of his life in the Barataria. What eighteen-year-old kid knew something like that? But: where else would being a Trench mean what it did here? The Trenches had lived here since the first settlers in the bayou. Now there were fewer Trenches than ever. Fewer Lindquists, fewer Arcinaux, fewer Thibodaux. Driving through town, you saw the boarded storefronts, the slumping shanties ceding to the elements, the piers collapsing plank by plank into the bayou.

And you heard about it in the news and read about it in books: the Barataria was disappearing, crumbling into the Gulf. Old-timers in Jeanette were quick to point out the tip of an ancient power line that once stood fully aboveground. The top of a salt-blanched cypress tree that once sat on a hill. Before long, the town elders said, Jeanette would be an underwater ghost town. Your parents' graves, your grandparents' graves, maybe even your own grave, under ten feet of water. A thought that gave Wes the frissons, as his mother used to say.

Wes didn't believe in ghosts, but he did believe that some part of his mother would always remain here. Not a spirit, per se, but an everlasting ineffable part that had no human name. This is where she'd lived. She'd looked at this cypress every day, this weeping willow, this patch of sky, this bay of water, and Wes was convinced that meant something.

In other places besides Jeanette, Wes felt like an outsider, a passer-through. The way he talked, the words he used, the dark mud color of his skin. People told him he had the swamp in his mouth. Other people, less kind, said he sounded like a coon-ass. They didn't know what a fais do-do was, a sac-a-lait. They didn't know what it felt like to have Cajun blood.

For better or worse, the Barataria was his home. Whatever that meant. Home was the peaty odor of Spanish moss in the first spring rain. Home was the briny sweetness of fresh oysters thirty seconds out of the water. The termite swarms of early May. The cacophony of swamp frogs in the summer. The locusts in the day. The crickets at night. The lashing five-minute thunderstorms of late July. The sugarcane trucks rumbling through town in the autumn. The carnival giddiness of Mardi Gras. The blessing of the fleet. The petit bateaux clustered in the bay. The pinprick points of their pilot lamps like yuletide lights on the horizon. The strange green glow, supernaturally vivid, of cypress trees in spring gloaming. The earthy smell of crawfish boils. The pecan pralines and boudin and gumbo. The alligators and herons and redfish and shrimp. The Cajun voices, briny and gnarled. The old wrinkled faces as strange as thumbprints.

Wes felt the tug of his future here. Or maybe it was the gravity of the past. Maybe it was both. Whatever, more often than not the Barataria felt like the place he belonged.

- - - - - - - -

One day in early December, just after the Christmas decorations were put up in Jeanette's town square, Wes went to the harbor and found Lindquist's boat vandalized. Someone, kids or vagrants, had broken the cabin door and ransacked the cabinets and drawers. Beer cans and cigarette stubs littered the floor. Wes doubted that it was one of the trawlers that used to hold a grudge against Lindquist. Now that he was gone, their ill will toward Lindquist had vanished overnight.

Some of the trawlers were even filled with phony nostalgia. "I bet he's off metal detecting someplace," they would say. Or, "Son of a bitch is probably in Barbados, someplace. Looking for his next treasure."

Now and then Wes saw one of the Toup brothers around town.

According to the locals, the other had left the country. Thailand, was the rumor. Why, no one knew, and the brother who remained in the Barataria, Reginald, never provided an answer. He kept to himself and without his other half seemed far less formidable. Diminished somehow. His eyes were spooked and darting, a look Wes associated with wounded animals and terminally sick people.

- - - - - - - -

Over the coming months Wes kept busy with his own boat. Hard to believe, but shrimping season was only four months away. Wes wanted his Lafitte skiff, years in the making, ready to sail by then. An arbitrary deadline, but one that he was determined to meet. He knew he was one of those guys who needed a bottom line in order to get anything done.

By Christmas the cypress keelson and ribs were laid in the backyard. By February, the hull sat full-bellied and sleek on top of eight black oil drums. By March, Wes started blowtorching one-hundred-pound pieces of steel, section by section. Before long, what had begun as a framework of sticks was beginning to look like a seaworthy vessel.

Every day Wes looked forward to his work. The good clean smell of the morning air, of earth in the shadows, of grass still wet with dew. He rose at dawn and worked until nightfall, breaking only for lunch and water. There were hours when he was so lost in his work that he didn't think of his mother or his problems with his father or his future. He didn't think about the oil spill or the next shrimping season or all the bills he and his father had to pay. He worked purely in the moment. The world seemed more focused, the edges sharper, this time of year. There was a satisfaction in standing back and looking at something that had not existed several hours before. Something that he'd brought into being with his own hands. He liked the way the wood dust moted the air, how one tongue of wood fitted into the groove of another. Sandpapering, hammering, drilling, he found them mysteriously fulfilling.

One mellow cloudless day in early April, Wes was painting the hull gunmetal gray when he heard his father step up behind him. It was late afternoon, the sinking sun making golden fire in the house windows and trees.

"What a piece of shit," his father said.

Wes turned. His father was smirking and stepped up to the boat and ran his hand along the hull. The whisper of his skin against the smooth grain of the wood. "I can't feel a fuckin' seam in this thing."

Wes waited, expectation sparking in his chest.

"Some work, I gotta admit," his father said. His face still looked ashen and slightly lopsided and he moved around more stiffly than he did before the heart attack. But he was down to three cigarettes a day, one after each meal, and his doctor said that his heart sounded healthier.

"Come on," Wes's father said. "I got something for you."

"What?"

"A palomino pony."

Wes followed his father to his truck, where a used engine waited in the bed. Wes's father said he practically stole it, he found it for so cheap.

"It's sweet," Wes said.

"Right?"

They lifted the engine out of the truck and carried it through the side yard to the back, where they set it on the porch. Wes said he'd pay back the money as soon as he could but his father told him it was a gift.

Later it occurred to Wes that if he had opportunity to write again his short story for Mr. Banksey, he might choose this moment for a more truthful end. Knowing himself and knowing his father, it was probably as close to reconciliation as they would ever come. If his mother had been listening from her grave several yards away behind the pink-blooming mimosa tree, she probably would have considered it enough.

– – – – – – – –

In early April the weather warmed and the bayou came alive again: the rain beat away the last trace of winter and the days grew longer and warmer yet, and the cypress and oak trees looked like they were erupting in gray-green smoke. And the water too began to stir and burgeon, the alligators sunning on the muddy banks, the snakes whipsawing like ink across the shallows, the herons stalking on stilt-like legs through the bracken. Everywhere near the water was the muddy smell of humus, the electric calls of cicadas and frogs.

The township also came to life. In backyards skiffs were reared up on cinder blocks for repairs. Along dock pilings nets were stretched like colossal webs and shrimpers worked at mending them with spidery fingers. The talk in the Barataria buzzed about the imminent shrimping season: where the shrimp would be, how long the season would last, who would catch the biggest hauls. No matter what they said on television, no matter what crap BP said in their commercials, everyone knew the oil was still in the water and would be for a long time. But people were buying Louisiana shrimp and oysters again and it seemed that Jeanette had already weathered the worst.

Wes worked day and night to have the boat done by the end of April. Late one afternoon he'd just finished painting the boat's name on the stern—*Cajun Gem*—when his father stepped up beside him and looked over the boat.

"I'll trade you my boat for this one," he said. He drank from a sweating bottle of Abita beer.

"I bet you would."

"That cypress smells good."

"It does."

"What else you gotta do with it?"

Wes took a beat to respond. "I think it's done."

His father nodded, hands on his hips. "Then let's take her out."

"Now?"

"Sure."

"Paint's still drying."

His father laid his palm on the hull. "Feels pretty dry to me."

"I want to look it over."

"You've been looking this thing over for three fuckin' years."

Wes picked at his eyebrow. "I don't wanna rush."

"Three years ain't rushing."

"It's got no gas in it."

His father fought back a grin, enjoying Wes's unease. "I put gas in it last night."

Wes shook his head and eyed the boat doubtfully. "We don't even have a trailer big enough. How would we get it to the water?"

"Same way they used to back in the day."

Wes's father called Teddy Zeringue and Davey Morvant. Wes called his friends Archie and Donny. Soon there were twelve people in the backyard. Twenty. Forty. Faces Wes had known his whole life, friends and neighbors. Chuck Jones, George Ledet, Elmer Guidry. Several guys Wes knew from high school, and a few brought their brothers and sisters. Wes saw Lucy Arcinaux, the jolie blonde he'd dated for a few lucky weeks. Young mothers brought their screaming and giggling toddlers. Long-necked beers were passed around as the crowd gathered in the rusty light of the evening sun.

After a while Wes climbed the port ladder and everyone gathered under the boat and took its weight on their shoulders. Together they counted to three, their voices loud and roaring, one voice. With a mighty shove they heaved the *Cajun Gem* off the oil drums. Then the tide of people carried Wes and his boat. Across the yard, past the house, into the street and toward the bayou. They passed houses where people stared from their porches, and some of them crossed their yards and joined the crowd. The Thibodaux, the Joneses, the Theriots. Soon there were fifty people, then seventy-five, loud and laughing and joking, carrying the one-ton boat down the two-lane street.

It was almost gloaming when Wes standing on the bow could see the glowing mirror-gray water of the bayou. The crowd carried him across a field of bulrush and bright blue dayflowers. They crossed the narrow hem of shoreline and in their clothes waded into the water with the boat on their shoulders like venerators in a solemn rite. At first Wes was worried that the boat would sink as soon as they let it go. He was filled with relief when the *Cajun Gem* floated sure and free on the water.

Wes started the engine and it sounded with a loud purr. He geared the boat and eased into the bayou. It was growing dark, but there was still enough daylight to see the faces in the crowd watching him as he drifted away. He spotted his father, but Wes was already too far out to read his face. He knew him only by the wiry shape of his body, the hunched set of his shoulders. What did you call feeling nostalgic for a moment before it was over? He didn't know, but he felt that feeling now as he cast further out into the Barataria. As he drifted farther he couldn't tell one face from another, nor soon after that man from woman, then man from child, until finally he was so far away that who he was looking at could have been anyone. Anyone at all.

ACKNOWLEDGMENTS

Thank you to my brother Michael Cooper for your very early readings of this book, and for your indispensable advice. Thank you to my partner, Kathy Conner, for the same. Both of you made this novel what it is. I'm lucky to have such kindred spirits by my side. Thank you to my grandparents, rest in peace, for all those trips to the bookstore and for so many other things. Thank you to old friends Joe Capuano and Claudia Sanchez and Richard Pearlman for sticking around all these years. Thank you to new friends Joe Wall and Brigette Paladon and Tyler Shepard for always lending a willing ear. Thank you to Reggie Poche and Cass Cross for your perspicacious readings of my early drafts. Thank you to my mentors for your wisdom and encouragement. Thank you to my agent, Lorin Rees, for believing in this book from the beginning. Thank you to Nate Roberson for the same. Thank you to Danielle Crabtree, Rachel Rokicki, Jay Sones, Rebecca Welbourn, and the rest of the team at Crown for working so tirelessly on my behalf. Thank you, reader.

ABOUT THE AUTHOR

Tom Cooper was born in Ft. Lauderdale, Florida, and now lives in New Orleans, where he writes and teaches. His fiction has appeared in dozens of magazines and anthologies, including *Oxford American*, *Gulf Coast*, and *Mid-American Review*. *The Marauders* is his first novel.